DIAMOND ANGEL

ZAKHAROV BRATVA
BOOK 2

NAOMI WEST

MAILING LIST

BOOKS BY NAOMI WEST

Zaitsev Bratva

Ruby Malice

Ruby Mercy

Aminoff Bratva

Caged Rose

Caged Thorn

Tasarov Bratva

Midnight Oath

Midnight Lies

Nikolaev Bratva

Dmitry Nikolaev

Gavriil Nikolaev

Bastien Nikolaev

Sorokin Bratva

Ruined Prince

Ruined Bride

Box Sets

Devil's Outlaws: An MC Romance Box Set

Bad Boy Bikers Club: An MC Romance Box Set

The Dirty Dons Club: A Dark Mafia Romance Box Set

Dark Mafia Kingpins

Devil's Sins

Devil's Scar

Other MC Standalones

Read in any order!

Maddox

Stripped

Jace

Grinder

DIAMOND ANGEL
ZAKHAROV BRATVA BOOK 2

Five years ago, I ran from the devil who got me pregnant.

I have a son now. A boy I'd do anything to protect.

But I left behind the sister I loved more than life itself.

So when Ilarion Zakharov finds me again, I have an impossible choice to make:

Do I go back with him to the world I left behind?

Or do I leave my sister to drown in the mess I caused?

Ilarion doesn't make choosing easy.

With every touch, every kiss, every searing look from those blue eyes, he reminds me of the truth:

I love him. I'll always love him. I can't help but love him.

Even if loving him costs me everything.

DIAMOND ANGEL *is Book 2 of the Zakharov Bratva duet. The story begins in Book 1,* **DIAMOND DEVIL.**

NOTE: This is a light mafia contemporary romance. No cheating. Ends in HEA.

1

TAYLOR

FIVE YEARS LATER

It's funny how someone can look so familiar and still feel like a stranger.

The high society blonde beaming at me from the photograph in the news article isn't my sister. She's wearing too many jewels, smiling too perfectly, holding herself too gracefully.

And yet she is. She's Celine.

This is the sister who dutifully did my hair every morning when I obsessed over French braids. Who baked me cookies on the days I was too sick to go out and play. Who built blanket forts and read books with me by flashlight when Mom and Dad went out on their increasingly sporadic date nights.

I used to think I knew her better than I knew myself. How do decades get wiped away in five short years?

Not that they were short for me. The past five years have felt like a life sentence. I'm only twenty-seven, but in my bones, in my heart, I feel so, so much older.

"Good afternoon, Tater Tot," Dad chimes, ambling into the kitchen.

He's really committed to this whole suburban grandfather persona. Some might say he's slightly *over*committed. Sweater vest, brown corduroys, the works.

He makes a beeline straight to the coffee pot and pours himself a mug. "Why the long face?"

I swipe out of the news app on the tablet and lay it facedown away from me. "Nothing."

He frowns, clearly not buying my half-assed poker face. Taking the seat opposite, he drags the tablet toward him and flips it back over. I don't want to watch him stumble across the exact same picture I was just obsessing over, so I let my gaze wander elsewhere. To the steam spiraling up from his cup of coffee. To the afternoon sun peeking through the window blinds. To his pale hand tapping on the tabletop.

He still wears his wedding ring. It makes my heart hurt to see that.

I'm jittery as hell, so caffeine is the last thing I need, but when I see Dad pull open the news app, I get up to refill my own cup.

I chose this house purely because of the kitchen. The garden window sits in front of the sink, which is big enough to bathe a toddler in. I tested it with Adam when we first moved in. He loved splashing around, blowing raspberries at the window, giggling when his rubber duck bobbed in the suds.

I cried when he got too big for it a year or so ago. He caught me with tears in my eyes, hugged me, and told me he'd squeeze himself back in it if it would make me smile.

I told him he didn't need to. The image made me smile, and that was enough.

That's my son, though. Kind-hearted. Sweet to a fault.

I decide against a refill, so I pour out the dregs and leave my mug to soak. When I turn back around, Dad has the tablet tilted forward, and I catch sight of the photograph I'd been staring at for the last half-hour before he walked in.

I've practically got it memorized at this point. But I still walk up behind him and look again. I'm becoming more and more of a masochist these days.

Celine is a vision, in a teal dress with a skirt made of shimmery fringe that seems to move even in the still image. The strapless corset highlights how much weight she's lost since I last saw her. Not sad skinny, not scared skinny or sick skinny, but the toned contours of someone who's worked hard to carve out the figure they want for themselves.

Diamonds glitter from her ears and neck, and the rock on her finger is big enough to sink a warship. Her blonde hair is lighter than I remember. It's funny—we've got the same nose, the same chin, but on her, it looks glamorous and chic; on me, I just look ordinary.

Of course, as dazzling as this version of my sister is, it's hard not to be distracted by the man standing beside her. The suit clings to his body like a second skin, and his features look harsher under the unforgiving flash of the camera. But rather than take away from his appearance, he just looks fiercer, more hauntingly handsome than I remember.

Dad closes the tablet and sighs. "You need to stop Googling them."

I slide back into my seat. "It doesn't affect me as much as you think it does." I've taken years to home in on this tone of voice—something detached and uncaring, like, *Oh, that silly stuff? It's nothing.* "It helps, actually."

My father's eyes are watchful and sharp. "I know what you're thinking."

"What am I thinking?"

"That Celine is happy, so it's all worth it."

I can't see the picture on the screen anymore, but the memory of her restrained smile is burned into my mind's eye. I don't know if I'd call her happy. Satisfied, maybe. Contented. But not *happy.*

"That's not what I'm thinking."

Dad shakes his head. "Yes, it is. But pictures are never a good indication of happiness."

"And what if you're wrong?"

He looks at me with sympathy. "Then her happiness came at the expense of yours."

It takes a lot to keep my face from betraying me. That's taken practice, too. "You're implying that I'm not happy?"

"I'm not implying anything. I'm coming right out and saying it." He leans back with a sigh. "You are *not* happy, sweetheart. You haven't been in years."

I reach for an apple in the fruit bowl between us. "You read too much into things. I just don't like having to hide. I don't like living under an alias. And I don't like looking over our shoulder every single second of every single day."

Dad purses his lips and brings the mug up to his mouth. There's a sadness in his eyes that I've grown used to by now. Most days, that sadness is for Mom. But sometimes, I think it's for me.

"It's that time again, isn't it?" I ask quietly. "Time to leave."

He strokes his chin. "We could manage another year here," he muses. "Adam's just settled into kindergarten. It would be a shame to uproot him now."

"The alternative is what? Give him another year to form relationships he can't keep? Make friends he'll have to leave? What's the point of that?"

With every passing year, I sound more and more angry. But if I stop long enough to examine my choices, I might have a full-on nervous breakdown. So I fall back on denial and hope that everything works out in the end.

So far, so good.

Well, good enough, at least.

"Just think about it," Dad says calmly. "If you're ready, I can have new identities sent our way by the end of the month."

A little shiver runs down my spine. He references his old life a little more often now. Probably because I've slowly gone from fighting with him about it to just accepting it.

My dad was a bad person. The father I thought I knew did bad things and hid them from his family.

It used to be jarring. I'm numb to it now. I'm numb to everything, really.

"Priority customers, huh?" I say, rolling the apple in my palm without actually biting into it. "We're probably keeping this guy in business single-handedly."

"He's a friend."

"Can you even *have* friends in the underworld?"

"It's rare, but it happens."

"Have you thought about what might happen if your 'friend' decides to rat you out to Ilarion?"

He tilts his head to the side. "Is that something you're hoping for?"

I set the apple down hard and shove myself away from the table. "Excuse me. I've got to get ready to go pick up Adam from school."

"Taylor!" he calls after me, but I ignore him and make for my bedroom.

I lock the door as the sobs collect in my throat. I'm familiar with the taste of tears now. More familiar than I ever thought I'd be. I bang the back of my head against the door, trying to distract myself with pain. But just like all my other tricks, that stopped working a while ago.

I'm not sure what I'll do when I run out of coping mechanisms.

I turn, put my back to the door, and slide down to a seat on the floor. Clutching my knees to my chest, I let the sobs shudder through my body.

And through the prism of tears in my eyes, I see something on the corner of my bookshelf.

I try not to look at the snow globe. Most days, I make a studied effort to look anywhere else but at it. Today, though, I'm drawn to it like it's the only thing in the room.

It's easy to remember things when I watch those snowflakes meander through the painted gray sky. I can almost smell the mountains again. Fresh bark. Pine-scented moss.

I told myself when we fled the Diamond like two thieves in the night that I'd leave the past behind me. I'd shut the door on my old life and burn the memories to ashes. What good would they serve me in the future? The answer is none. Not at all. So let them die, right? Let them wither away and disappear.

But that's the thing about old memories.

They're awfully hard to kill.

2

ILARION

"Kill me if you have to, sir. But don't judge me for closing my eyes. I've never wanted to see death coming."

I look down at the sorry bastard at my feet. His face is turned up toward me, but true to his words, his eyes are squeezed closed.

"You should *want* to see death coming, Osip," I scold softly. "How else can you ever hope to avoid it?"

The man trembles as his eyelids flicker open. Fear has washed the murky blue into a mottled gray. "Some things can't be avoided, sir. Death comes for us all."

He's a poetic little fuck. I'm in no mood for it, though. "Get to your feet. You're not dying today."

The man's eyes widen. "S-Sir?"

"On your feet. Now."

He glances to my left and then to my right. But neither Mila nor Dima, standing at my sides, offer any indication of whether I'm actually sparing him or if I'm just playing with my prey before I slaughter it.

"B-but the warehouse," he stammers. "It burned down on my watch. Carelessness…It was my fault…"

I look behind him at the scorched skeleton of the warehouse. Black cinders coat every surface. The metal I-beams are twisted into grotesque shapes by the heat, though the fires have long since been put out. And in every corner, hundreds of thousands of dollars' worth of merchandise has been torched to a crisp. A total loss.

"You were careless. You were negligent," I agree. "But I'm not about to pin the entirety of the blame on you."

Osip gulps. "Sir…?"

"The fire wasn't an accident," I tell him. "It was arson. Benedict Bellasio may have only rats at his beck and call, but they do the job well enough. They can slip in and out without being heard or seen. Long enough to do damage. Enough damage to fuck with me."

I'm not really talking to Osip anymore. I'm more just thinking out loud, grappling with this shadow war that's never quite taken off. Benedict has spent five years nibbling at the edges of my empire. A theft here, a fire there, a corpse turning up in the wrong place at the wrong time.

It's maddening.

"Osip."

The man's eyes snap to mine, scared all over again.

"You get one more chance. Mostly because Celine likes you," I growl. "And she'd be annoyed if I killed you. But if you falter on the job again, I will kill you. And I'll make you welcome death with *open* eyes." He gulps and nods at the same time. I nod back. "I'm glad you understand. Now, get out of my sight."

He lunges to his feet and scurries away. When the door slams shut behind him, Mila and Dima walk around to face me. They've been doing that a lot lately—moving in perfect harmony, each a mirror image of the other. It's eerie. I don't like it at all.

"That was unusually romantic of you," Mila observes with a raised brow. "Ilarion the Merciful."

I nudge a burnt chunk of rock at my feet. It immediately crumbles to ashes as soon as I touch it.

Everything is a fucking metaphor these days.

I glance up to see Dima with that about-to-piss-his-pants look he gets when there's something he wants to share. "Spit it out, man," I bark at him.

He shuffles back and forth in place nervously. "We found a… a note, I guess you'd call it."

I freeze. "A what?"

"A note. Tacked onto a body around the corner. The fire burned the flesh right off the poor guy's face, so I couldn't tell who it was…but this was pinned to the front of his shirt." Dima pulls out a scrap of singed paper and hands it to me.

Two words, scrawled hastily on the blistered paper.

Missed me?

It's unsigned. But no points for guessing who wrote it.

"*Blyat',*" I snarl, crushing the note in my fist. "Five fucking years of this Hide & Seek, Whack-A-Mole bullshit, and now, Benedict thinks it's time to be cute?"

"He's just trying to goad you. Get in your head," Dima suggests. "Why else would he write notes like some lovestruck schoolgirl asking you to *"Check yes if you like her'?"*

"No." I throw the crumpled note into a pile of embers in the corner. "He's getting ready."

"Him and what army?" he scoffs. "In case you forgot, we burned everything he ever loved to the fucking ground."

I look around me again. "And now, he's returning the favor. In the last twelve months alone, how many times has he struck? Half a dozen warehouses sabotaged. A safehouse raided by the FBI. The devil only knows how many of our foot soldiers missing or tempted off-course or killed outright."

"Because that's all he *can* do."

I shake my head and turn my back on the carnage of my property. "It's not just that. He's trying to tell me something. *He's been preparing.*"

Stepping out into the open air, I pick my way to the jeep. This warehouse was a recent purchase, and a pricey one to boot. It'll take money to restore it, but I'm not concerned about the cost. Money is something I have in spades.

Patience, though? I'm running rather short on that.

"We need to find him." I gesture for Mila and Dima to get into the Wrangler.

Mila climbs in the passenger seat while Dima hops into the back. "It's not as though we haven't been trying," he pouts. "The rat bastard just disappeared into thin air."

He's not wrong. That's the problem. We've scoured the city, traced every footstep that Benedict and his brother Gregor ever laid down. And come up with a grand total of…

Jack shit.

No one has laid eyes on either Bellasio man since the night I reduced their empire to rubble.

The few of his followers we've managed to ensnare since then have all died without snitching during interrogations, or they genuinely had no clue where their dons had gone.

"If only you'd had that talk with Archie before he ran," Mila murmurs.

I clench my teeth. As if I needed more reminding of *that* particular mistake.

"There's no guarantee that Archie ever knew a damn thing," Dima argues back. "And even if he did, that information is probably null and void now. Benedict's a rat, but he's not stupid."

"I don't know about that."

The theory is sound; I just tend to avoid thinking about Archie and… all the shit that the man's name stirs up in me.

But that doesn't mean I've buried my head in the sand. For as many places as we've combed through in search of the Bellasio brothers, there are a few I've left untouched. Intentionally, of course.

I want Benedict to think I don't know everything. If he's been lulled into a false sense of security…if he thinks that maybe Archie took his secrets with him when he ran…then maybe he'll make an unforced error.

One crack. One mistake. That's all I need.

Then I'll have his head on a silver fucking platter, and I can pretend that my life is going according to plan.

Even if it's been five long years since that felt true.

3

ILARION

I speed up as we near the gates of Zakharov House. It looks the way it once did, as if nothing ever happened. The architects ensured that every single bullet hole was patched back to perfection.

Celine and I moved here immediately after Taylor and Archie disappeared, at my insistence. I wasn't about to continue to live in the Diamond, marooned in a house that haunted me with memories of a woman I'll never see again.

The guards hear me coming and open the gates. I drive through without so much as touching the brakes. We grind to a halt in the gravel driveway, kicking up a cloud of dust upon our arrival.

Inside, I find Semyon, my housekeeper, waiting for me with his hands clasped anxiously behind his back.

"What is it, Semyon?"

"There's a gentleman that's here to see you, sir," he says, looking distinctly uncomfortable. "He, um, declined to give his name. But Ms. Zakharov allowed him entry."

I grit my teeth. *Of course she did.* "Where is Ms. Zakharov now?"

"She said she had a meeting at the country club, sir. Something about a charity ball she's planning."

As always, mentions of Celine's philanthropy makes me roll my eyes. I spend more time gladhanding politicians on her behalf than I do bribing and killing them these days. All for the benefit of society pages that nobody reads in magazines and newspapers that nobody buys.

Why do I do it? That's a loaded question. Partly to keep her satisfied. After everything else was ripped from her, after she spent days loitering on death's door…it felt like the least I could do.

But a deeper part of me does it for Taylor's sake, too. It's what she'd want—to see Celine happy.

Then there's the deepest part of me at all, a part that lives in darkness and never raises its head above ground. That part does it with the hope that she'll be one of the few who picks up that magazine and sees me there.

And that she'll remember what we had, if only for the briefest of moments.

"Where is this 'gentleman'?"

"In the family room, sir."

In the corner of my eye, I see Dima and Mila exchange a look of concern. "Should we be armed?" he asks, reaching for his gun.

"No need. If Celine granted him access, then he's safe."

"Are you sure about that?"

"Celine knows enough to know who to let in and who to turn away," I remind them. There's another glance I sense being exchanged, but I stopped caring about their opinions in this department a long time ago. Celine and I have a unique relationship. Fuck knows it's not perfect, but it works.

"Wait a sec. Do *you* know who's in the living room right now?"

"I have a guess."

"How is it that Celine knows, and you know, and we don't?" Mila demands.

I ignore the question. If they can't handle it now, they won't handle it if I spell it all out for them.

"Fucking hell. She's your—"

I whirl around, forcing both Dima and Mila to come to a stop just outside the family room. "I've got a lot of moving parts at play," I tell them. "I can't be expected to share every bit with everyone. This is a Bratva, not a goddamn kindergarten classroom."

"We're your *right hands*," Mila hisses. "If you don't fill us in, what good are we?"

"Precisely—you're my right hands. And as a result, you're both busy. I decided not to burden you with this particular piece of information." I sigh and relent. "But since you're here now, you can meet him."

"Is this the part where you tell us who 'him' is?" drawls Dima.

I straighten my shirtsleeves. "Zane Krono."

Mila stiffens. "You hired a private detective?"

"I'm trying to find three different people who've scattered to fuck-knows-where," I point out. "And since we'd had no luck locating them ourselves, I thought it was time to bring in some extra help."

"Gee, how's that gone for you so far?"

I wrinkle my nose in distaste. "So far, he's come up blank. Just like you. Now, no further questions. Let's go see what the bastard has for me today."

I turn and march into the family room. The irony of the name isn't lost on me as I enter, but I brush those nagging thoughts aside and focus on the task at hand.

The P.I. is standing in the middle of the thrown-wide French doors, hands tucked awkwardly in his pockets like an alien imitating human posture. He pivots robotically toward us as we enter.

"Don Zakharov," he greets, his shrewd eyes passing over each of us in turn. "I'm sorry I've been *incommunicado* for the past ten months, but I didn't want to resurface until I had something worthwhile for you."

The air feels suddenly charged. Dima is wriggling with anticipation, but Mila stays mute and still. Optimism isn't one of her strengths. It's hard to blame her—Zane looks more likely to die of anemia than to uncover a trio of missing persons that not even the full might of the Zakharov Bratva can sniff out.

"Ten months?" she spits. "*Ten months* to find something?"

Zane cocks his head to the side. "If I may be so bold, it's been five years and you still haven't found anything, either, madam."

That shuts Mila up.

I told her I would have others handle the search missions. But she insisted on taking it upon herself. She claimed that she wanted to do her part to help me. But really, I think she committed herself to the job for other reasons.

It wasn't about helping me at all. For her, it was personal.

"You have a location?" I interject.

"Oh, yes," Zane proudly confirms. "I've verified it myself. It's definitely him."

Dima's eyes are glowing. "This is great! That slick rat is ours. All we need is a handful of men to gag Bellasio like a fucking turkey and bring him right to our—"

"Oh, no, sir," interrupts the detective. "Unfortunately, where Benedict Bellasio is concerned, I will need to keep looking. The man really has done a thorough disappearing act."

Dima stops short. "Then who have you…" He trails off when he realizes the only other possibility in play. "Archie. You found Archie." His gaze teeters to me. "God help us all."

Mila steps up to my side and grips my elbow. "Ilarion, you need to be prepared for the fact that Taylor might not be with him."

I shake my head. "She's with him," I say firmly. "I know it. Where Archie is, so is Taylor. And where Taylor is…so is my child."

4

TAYLOR

"…I'm telling ya, there's nothing like getting your pussy eaten out after a ten-hour shift. *That's* livin', baby."

"Mabel!" I groan, trying hard to drown her out while I refill the ketchup bottles. A diner throws us both an uncomfortable glance as he snatches up his receipt and heads out the door as fast as his legs will carry him.

My boss watches the man leave with her hands fisted on her hips. "That one has *definitely* never eaten pussy before," she remarks dryly. "No wonder he was so sour-faced. And he didn't finish the pecan pie I made this morning. Clearly has no taste whatsoever."

I remove his half-finished plate from the counter and push it into the kitchen through the old-school box window that connects the front of the diner to the back. "This is a small town, Mabel," I remind her in a hush so the other diners don't overhear us. "People here are conservative. They don't want to hear about your sexual exploits over a piece of pie."

"My pie tastes so good, though!" She winks at me and giggles at her double entendre.

For a seventy-one-year-old woman, she talks like a sailor.

I'm giggling, even though I'm also blushing the same color as the ketchup bottles I'm restocking. It's busy work, but that's fine by me. There's been a lull for the past hour, which is fairly normal for this time of late afternoon. Things will pick back up around five-thirty when folks start trickling in for dinner.

Here in Kent, dinner is 5:30 PM on the dot. That took some getting used to. But a lot of things in my new life have also taken some getting used to, so I've learned to just roll with it.

"Tell me, when was the last time you got your 'pie' eaten?" she asks.

"Mabel!" I cry again. Honestly, I think I use her name more often than I use Adam's. "Seriously."

"It's a serious question."

"Which I'm not answering."

"I'm your employer," she says, putting herself in front of me. "You're legally obligated to answer."

"Pretty sure I'm not. And in any case, that question qualifies as sexual harassment."

"Not if I mean well."

Laughing, I open up the cash register to check on our turnout for the day. The breakfast shift is always busy; the lunch shift tends to be less so, because people usually grab a meal wherever they work. Dinner is the most hectic, mostly because we're one of two restaurants in town and the

Chinese place is usually reserved for when people are feeling "exotic."

I love Mabel, but she's not much help when the evening rush hits. She usually just parks herself behind the counter, spouting unsolicited advice and scaring off some of the more reserved customers by talking about threesomes with truckers and skinny dipping in the local river.

I'd told her as much once, and she'd just giggled and told me that if some people couldn't take a good "your mama" joke, then she didn't want them eating in her establishment.

"Anyhow, a little saltiness makes the food taste better," she added with a wink and an elbow to the ribs.

It's not the only quote of hers that's stuck in my head. During my job interview, she told me in lurid sexual detail about the night she met her third husband. She'd convinced him to get married four hours into their first date.

"When you know, you know," she told me.

Our lives are very different, Mabel and me. But I found myself agreeing with that part.

"I'm still waiting on an answer," she interrupts, nearly closing the cash register on my fingers. "Pie eating or no pie eating?"

"Hey!" I protest, "Mabel, I need to empty the till."

"I'm your boss, and I say take a break. There's no one here anyways." She rolls her eyes. "You know, you are such a square, Sugar Tits. I thought you'd be more interesting, coming from the big city and all. But you haven't stolen from me once."

I laugh. "Sorry to disappoint."

"Is it the boyfriend?" she asks sympathetically. "He doesn't like eating you out, does he?"

I sigh. We've been down this road before; she's not going to let up until I give her an answer.

"First of all, he's not my boyfriend. And second of all, we haven't...gone that far yet."

"You really ain't fucked him yet?!"

I cringe at her choice of words. "I haven't slept with him, no."

"Why? I've seen the boy. He's cute."

"It has nothing to do with him. I'm just..."

"In love with someone else?"

I narrow my eyes at her. "No."

We've been down this road before, too.

"I wish you'd just tell me about *him*," she sighs. "Properly. I'm dyin' to know."

"It's not worth telling, trust me."

She smiles, a rare moment of seriousness amidst the never-ending stream of off-color teasing. "The fact that you refuse to say much about your past tells me that it's *definitely* worth telling."

"You know more than anyone else in this town already."

"Only because I got you drunk that one night."

I grit my teeth. "That was a mistake." But she caught me in the right moment. The anniversary of the day Dad and I left the Diamond always does a number on me. I've done four and counting of them, and it never gets easier.

Mabel laughs. "Playing hide-the-sausage with Callan might help put the past behind you!" she suggests. "Just a friendly idea."

"I…can't," I offer up lamely. "Or at least, I shouldn't. I'm a mess and Callan's a sweet guy. He deserves better."

"And yet here we are—six months later and you're still leading him on."

"Do you think that's what I'm doing?" I ask with a frown, leaning against the counter. "I mean, I told him I needed to take things slow. I told him I didn't want to label us. I even told him he could date other women if he wanted to."

"Oh, honey," Mabel says, patting my arm. "You and I both know that boy has been following you around town with his tongue hanging out like a damn mutt for over a year now. He ain't interested in dating anyone else."

I glance out the windows. It's hard to see far, though—the walls drip with pictures and mementos of Mabel's travels, and much of it obscures the view outside. I asked her once why she spent most of her life trekking to every corner of the earth, only to settle down in the most boring place of all.

After a life of Technicolor, I craved a little beige. That's how she explained her decision to move to Kent.

I can relate. Albeit probably for slightly different reasons.

"Callan's a sweet guy. I think it's time I—

"Fucked him."

I narrow my eyes. "I was going to say, 'Break up with him.'"

"Why would you do that?!" she cries out. "At least give him a ride once before you cut him loose! Then, if nothing else, you'll have made an informed choice."

"I don't need an informed choice," I tell her. "I've always known what I want."

"Ahhh. I see."

That all-knowing look in her eye makes me shrivel up. "I just want to focus on myself," I amend quickly. "And my son."

"Your son is beautiful," Mabel says, patting my hand with her many-ringed fingers. "Honestly, he's the only little runt I've ever actually liked, and that's saying something. But he doesn't need you to sacrifice your life for him. Trust me: he won't thank you for that later."

I glare at Mabel. "Can we please stop discussing my personal life?"

"Hell no. I believe I made that a condition of your hiring."

I roll my eyes. "I thought you were joking."

"That's kind of a 'you problem' then, ain't it?"

She pushes her bright blue hair away from her eyes. It's been this shade for a few months now, but half the town still rubbernecks at her every time she walks past. She loves that, of course. If there is one thing Mabel Lane likes doing, it's shocking people.

Sometimes, I wish I had her fire. Other times, I worry that if I had it, I would burn my life to the ground.

There are days when it feels like I already did.

"Seriously, kiddo," she says, "you can't mope around for your whole damn life. Gravity's not a woman's friend. At some point, it's gonna turn on you. The only question is when."

I roll my eyes and go back to the ketchup bottles. "You're just a fount of knowledge, aren't you?"

"And don't you ever forget it." She throws me a saucy wink. "How's that old man of yours doing?"

"Dad's okay," I say reluctantly. "He likes working at the library. And the hours are flexible, so he can take care of Adam in the evenings when I have a shift here."

"I've always wanted to have sex in that library," Mabel muses. "Do you think he'd be willing to help me out with that little fantasy?"

"Mabel!"

She laughs. "I'm only teasing. He's cute, but not my type. The two of you are a lot alike, you know."

"We are absolutely not," I snap defensively.

"Oh, you can gnash your teeth as much as you want, little kitten, but let's face it: just 'cause you run from something don't mean you're safe from it."

Her words land in my gut with that dull, aching thump that means they're way too true and way too accurate.

"I think I have some more work in the back." I carefully pivot on my heel and make my way to the kitchen where Bruce, the line cook, is massaging burger patties into shape.

"You stop gettin' laid and it starts to show on the face, Taylor! Remember that!" Mabel calls out after me. I'd like to think that she's loud because there's no diners around to hear, but I know from experience that that's not true. She doesn't give a rat's ass who's listening.

Bruce offers me a sympathetic smile when I round the corner. "Don't let her bully you."

"She's not bullying me. She just wants me to be happy. Apparently, everyone's under the impression that I'm miserable here."

"Oh, I disagree."

"Thank you, Bruce."

"I think you'd be miserable *anywhere*."

My face falls. "*Et tu, Brute?*"

He laughs and places the next patty on a tray lined with parchment paper. "You've lived in this town for two years, Taylor. And I can count on one finger the number of times I've seen you laugh."

I roll my eyes and lean against the counter. "You got anything for me?"

He pulls out a tray of jam pastries and holds it out for me to take one. "Go on. Gorge yourself."

I take one and pop a bite into my mouth. "See?" I say as I chew. "These little desserts make me happy. It's the simple things for me. And contrary to what Mabel thinks, I don't need a man. She's been married five times, and none of those worked out. So who is she to give me love life advice?"

"Mabel's talking about sex, not love."

"I'm one of those old-fashioned cranks who believe the two things go hand in hand."

Bruce nods solemnly. "I've always suspected there was someone."

I try not to choke on the pastry. "There's no one, okay? For God's sake, everyone's always pestering me about it. But I'm not running from anyone or anything."

Even to my own ears, that sounds pretty strident. Needless to say, Bruce is unconvinced. "That was defensive." He offers the tray again. "Eat more sugar. You're cranky."

I scowl, but I accept the peace offering. As I eat it, we hear Mabel's laugh from the diner. She's got her hooks into the first brave lemming leading the dinner rush.

"He must be good looking," I chuckle. "That's her 'turned-on' laugh."

A moment later, Mabel walks in through the swinging double doors. Her eyes are bright with excitement, and her cheeks are flushed. The new customer must be fresh meat.

Ping. I reach into my pocket and check my phone.

CALLAN: *Hey beautiful, what time does your shift end? I can pick you up and take you home, if you want?*

"First of all," Mabel declares, "you need to get out there and take that man's order. And second of all—keep your paws to yourself. I got dibs."

I chuckle at her as I type in a quick reply to Callan. *I finish at 8. See you then.*

"Taylor, did you hear me?" Mabel asks as she uses one of the meat cleavers to check her reflection.

"Yes, yes, I heard you. I'm going out now."

"Not that bit. The part where I got dibs."

I snort and raise my hands in surrender. "All yours. There's no way I stand a chance against you anyway."

She gives me a wink and I pull out my order pad from the front pocket of my white apron and head into the diner. I look up just past the double doors.

At first, I think my mind's playing tricks on me. Or maybe I'm just ensconced in a *very* realistic dream. I blink a few times, but his image doesn't resolve into anything that makes sense.

Ilarion Zakharov's icy blue eyes bore into mine. Feelings I've spent years burying out of sight come roaring back. I'm sure he can see it all on my face: the sorrow, the guilt. The hope. The death of that hope, all its ashes, its many crumbling remains.

But him? He's a mystery. Total stone. I can't tell what he's thinking.

Is he angry? Triumphant? Vengeful? Relieved?

How did he find me?

And, most importantly of all…*why?*

5

TAYLOR

Words lodge in my throat. So does all my oxygen. I'm pretty sure I'm about to faint.

When I do manage to croak a sentence out, I'm very aware my tongue is suddenly dry. "H-how did you find me?"

"I have a better question: how did you manage to hide for so long?"

He's calm. He's pleasant. But every syllable is drenched with accusation. Five long years of the stuff.

I shrug a shoulder. "I have my ways."

"You mean *Archie* has his ways. Incidentally, guess who he learned them from?" He reaches for a menu without ever taking his eyes off me. "Tell me, what's good here?"

When I finally find my courage again, I walk over to the counter and snatch the menu from his hands. "Don't bother with the mind games, Ilarion. You didn't come here to eat. And seeing as how this is a restaurant, if you're not eating, you should leave."

His cruel mouth tilts up in a smirk. "Or else what?"

I swallow. He's lean and chiseled, but the years have been good to him. When he shifts his hand, my eye immediately veers to the gold band around his ring finger. Seeing that sobers me right up. My knees buckle, but somehow, I manage to stay on my feet.

"How is she?"

"She was heartbroken when you disappeared," he answers sharply. "She spent months crying, begging me to track you both down. She felt betrayed and abandoned. And angry. Very angry."

I flinch, but what if this is just another mind game? I have no idea whether he's telling the truth or not. He might just be punishing me. Personally, I'm hoping for that.

Like I said—I've become a bit of a masochist in my old age.

"And now? Is she still angry?"

"You know Cee," he says with a carefree shrug. "She doesn't hold onto anger." Then his eyes dim again. "But she and I don't have that in common."

My whole body ripples with goosebumps. Even the hair at the back of my neck is standing on end. Seeing Ilarion again after all this time shouldn't be this much of a shock to the system. He shouldn't be able to get under my skin so damn easily.

But he's there. Where he's always been.

Maybe he never left in the first place.

"The waitress outfit suits you," he observes wryly.

"Fuck you," I snap, slamming my notepad down on the table. "We reserve the right to refuse service to anyone we choose. And I'm refusing you service right now."

"Taylor, dear, what's going on? Everything peachy out there?"

Shit. *Mabel.* It's the first time I've actually been genuinely annoyed with her inclination to stick her nose where she doesn't belong. She peeks her head out of the double doors and glances back and forth between Ilarion and me like we're in a tennis match.

"I'm kicking him out," I inform her curtly.

Mabel raises her eyebrows. "Why?"

"Because he's an asshole!"

"I'm not disagreeing with that," Ilarion chuckles. He's cranking the charm dial up to eleven out of ten, flashing Mabel that hotter-than-sin smile of his. "But if you refused every asshole who walked in, you'd be out of business."

Mabel licks her lips. "He has a point, darling."

"Are you siding with him?" I exclaim with no shortage of exasperation.

I'm completely losing my grip on the entire situation. My messy bun is falling apart, my cheeks are flushed to the point of burning, and my voice is just this side of a whiny, croaking wheeze.

I only have myself to blame.

I should've known this day was coming.

"Why are there sides at all, darling?" Mabel ponders before turning to Ilarion. "I'm guessing the two of you know each other."

"You could say that," he drawls. I feel my heartbeat start to race with panic. He wouldn't blow up my life. He wouldn't. Not like this. "I'm the father of her child."

On second thought…

Ka.

Fucking.

Boom.

6

TAYLOR

"You son of a bitch!" I cry out, reaching underneath the counter for something, anything, to hurl at him and that smug, life-ruining smirk. "How dare you waltz back into my life and—"

"Excuse me," he interrupts, so softly that I immediately fall silent. "If I remember correctly, you are the one who left. I'm not walking 'back' into anything."

"It was the only way—"

"Keep telling yourself that."

"Well, it worked out, didn't it?" I ask, feeling the blood drain from my face. "You and Cee are happy in your little corner of the world. And I'm happy in mine."

I can feel Mabel's gaze on me, and I'm just praying her loyalty to me outweighs her need to meddle. But I can't take my eyes off Ilarion long enough to get my point across.

"Are you happy here, Taylor?" Ilarion asks.

When it rains, it really does fucking pour. Why can't people just accept what I tell them? "Less happy than I was five minutes ago. Before you walked in here."

"Okay, let's start over!" Mabel announces, clapping her hands together. "I'm Mabel Lane, the proprietor of this charming little establishment. And you are Adam's father, whose name is…?"

"Ilarion Zakharov."

She whistles. "Well, isn't that a million-dollar name for a million-dollar man!"

I gawk at Mabel in disbelief. "Are you actually *flirting* with him?" I hiss under my breath.

"Honey, I'm old. Not dead. And *you're* the one who should be flirting with him. I mean, just look at this specimen."

I roll my eyes and turn back to Ilarion, who I'm pretty sure has heard the whole whispered conversation. The proud smirk on his face says as much. "Are you here alone?" I ask.

"Why? Trying to determine if I'm going to drag you back with my own two hands?"

"You can try. I'm not going back."

"What makes you think I give a flying fuck about *you*?" He delivers the line with so much calm that I have to repeat his words in my head just to make sure I heard correctly.

Normal people don't do this. They don't track you down five years after you ran from them and threaten you with a smile.

"Oh, dear," Mabel murmurs. Her own smile is fading fast. She must be realizing just what a formidable presence Ilarion

Zakharov is when he turns off the charm and turns up the deadliness.

"When you ran, you took my child with you. Until just a minute ago, I didn't even know if I had a son or a daughter."

A small part of me feels a twinge of guilt for that. "You have a son," I say coldly. "He's four years old and his name is Adam."

Something flickers across those impregnable blue eyes. "What have you told him about me?"

"Absolutely nothing." I stack the menus sharply on the counter. "When he's in need of a paternal presence, he has Dad."

"Ah, the two-time traitor. How nice it is for me to know that the man with fickle loyalty is the one responsible for raising my son."

I lean against the counter, meeting the fury in his eyes. "I'm not sure you have the right to get all bent out of shape about loyalty, Ilarion," I spit. "Considering you never breathed a word to me about who my father really was."

"If I did, you wouldn't have trusted me."

"And I would have been right!"

"Fucking hell, he's filled your head with nonsense."

"Don't do that." I jab a finger in his face. "Don't act as though I can't think for myself. Like I'm incapable of making my own judgments."

"Your inability to make sound judgments is exactly why we're here."

I grit my teeth. What I wouldn't give for a kitchen knife in my hand right now. "My father has his version of events," I continue. "Everyone has their own side of the story."

"Indeed. And yet I notice you haven't asked for mine."

I'm dangerously close to needing a paper bag to breathe into. Or to suffocate him with. If this conversation continues, I'm going to completely break down, and I don't want him seeing me like that. I don't need him making *his* judgements like he always has. Looking at me like I'm pathetic and weak.

That may have been me, once. A long time ago. It's amazing what motherhood does to a woman, though.

I'm stronger now.

I can handle Ilarion Zakharov.

"You had months to tell me your story, and you chose not to. You didn't trust me. So how can you expect me to trust you?"

His eyes cloud over. "Did you ever consider that maybe what I was doing was trying to protect you? You had just lost your mother. Archie's fate was unknown. I figured I'd spare you the pain of knowing that your father wasn't just a member of the Russian Bratva—he was a dishonorable, *disloyal* member of the Russian Bratva."

I feel a shiver coming on, but I push it back and try to maintain a brave face. "Whatever you may think, he's still my father."

"Are you bargaining now, *tigrionok*?"

So much for holding back the shiver. It surges through me, making every hair stand on end. How is it possible that hearing him use his old nickname can flood me with so many old feelings? How is it possible that he can still feel so familiar?

Like he's still mine?

"Does Celine know you're here?" Saying her name makes me feel instantly nauseous.

"I didn't want to get her hopes up."

"Where does she think you are?"

"Celine doesn't ask questions. She simply trusts that I will tell her what she needs to know, when she needs to know it."

"Right." I nod. "That's why you chose her."

"She has proved to be perfectly cooperative," he agrees in a deadpan snarl that leaves me feeling cold.

"Well, then, I suggest you go back to her," I snap. "And leave me alone."

"I have every intention of leaving you alone." He leans back in his seat. "I'm only here to see my son."

The fear that surges through me then is as hot as that shiver was cold. I have to grip the counter to keep from falling over. I feel Mabel at my back, ready to catch me if I fall.

"You're not—"

"I think emotions are running high!" Mabel quickly jumps between us. "I find that having a nice meal always calms me down. Ilarion, why don't you order something? On the house."

Ilarion just glares at me. I glare right back. "My shift doesn't finish for another hour and a half."

He barely nods. "I can wait."

"Take that booth by the window," Mabel suggests with a sunny smile. "I'll bring you a piece of pecan pie. Made it myself."

Ilarion doesn't acknowledge that, and he doesn't move to the booth by the window. I retreat into the kitchen. Mabel follows me there.

"What's going on out there?" Bruce asks, his brow furrowed.

"Rowdy customer," Mabel explains, giving him an unconcerned smile. "Brucie baby, take five. Taylor and I need a minute."

He raises his brows, but he doesn't ask questions. He just slips out of the kitchen and into the back entrance that leads to the alley with the dumpsters.

"Oh, God," I whisper, looking towards the swinging doors. "Oh, God…"

"I always suspected that you were interesting," Mabel gently teases. "I just had no idea you were *this* interesting."

"Mabel, what do I do? He's here for my son!"

"Oh, that's not all he's here for, girl. No matter what he says."

I try not to choke on my own spit. "You're wrong. I know him. The fact that I ran…he's never going to forgive that."

"I caught the words 'Russian mob'…?"

"Bratva," I correct automatically.

"Hot *and* dangerous," Mabel purrs. "This day couldn't possibly get any better."

"Mabel!"

Her eyes focus on me. "Is he capable of hurting you?"

"I think…no. Not physically, no," I hedge. "But I can't be sure that he won't hurt my father."

"I take it they have history?" I nod and Mabel's face scrunches up in concentration. "What do you want to do, honey? Just tell me, and I'll help you."

"I have to…I have to tell Dad. I need to get Adam and…" I trail off, realizing that I was right earlier—we *have* stayed in this town too long. "Oh, God, Mabel—he's found us."

"Sweetheart," she says softly, resting both her hands on my arms, "look at me for a moment." She waits until I'm still before she asks in a quiet, cigarette-stained rasp, "Tell me this: why did you run?"

"Because…my sister… They're married… We… I… Adam…" I'm a stuttering, stammering mess, but Mabel seems to grasp the big picture in an instant.

"You were in love with her husband and you decided to take yourself out of the equation?"

"He wasn't her husband then. When Adam was conceived, they hadn't even met yet."

"Complicated." Mabel purses her lips and nods. "One day, you'll have to tell me the whole story. But right now…if you need to go, I'll stall him." Her eyes are bright with determination. I have never loved her more.

"Are you sure?"

"Are you kidding? Did you see the man? I'm more than happy to keep him company for as long as he could possibly require. He did seem interested in the pie. And if he likes *that* flavor…"

I manage a weak smile. "Thank you," I say, giving Mabel a quick hug. It's the only goodbye we're going to get if I succeed in what I have planned next.

I head into the back room, snatch up my bag, and follow Bruce out through the service entrance.

I don't look back as I go.

I know from experience: looking back can get you killed.

7

ILARION

"Smoke?"

I shake my head. "Quit years ago."

The man nods sadly and puts the packet of cigarettes back in the pocket of his grease-stained chef's pants. "Same here, actually. Wifey made me do it. So if she asks, I did quit."

"You must have a penchant for self-sabotage." Under my breath, I add, "Apparently, so do I."

We turn in unison when we hear footsteps approaching from the alley behind us. Bruce looks surprised. I'm just quietly resigned to the next stage of this never-ending war.

Sure enough, a moment later, Taylor rounds the corner, bag in hand. She catches sight of me and her eyes bulge out of their sockets.

"Going somewhere?" I ask casually.

Her hair is mussed around her face and sweat slicks her forehead. She still looks like every fantasy I've had in the last five years. Not everything is exactly the same: she's lost some weight in her face, gained some fear in her eyes, and her jaw is clenched tighter than ever before.

Come to think of it, she looks like a car is about to run her down in the middle of the road and she's just accepted her fate.

So maybe not that much has changed after all.

"I…I finished early," she lies, brushing her flyaways out of her face and trying to collect herself. "Bruce, Mabel wants you in there."

The chef looks hesitantly between the two of us, starting to realize that he's caught smack in the middle of something he doesn't want to be caught in the middle of. "Uh, sure. You… you gonna be good out here?"

I can see the sigh work through her throat. "Good enough."

He shrugs and ambles inside the diner with one anxious backward glance. When we hear the door close, the forced smile evaporates from Taylor's face.

She storms right up to me, all fire and ferocity. My body instantly heats up when she's close enough to touch. "Isn't it enough to know that he's happy and healthy and safe?" she hisses in my face.

"You'd think," I agree. "You would certainly think."

She's as much of an open book as ever. I can practically read out the thoughts racing through her mind. *Run or fight? Fight or run?*

"There's no point in running anymore, Taylor," I inform her, nipping that route in the bud. "Wherever you go, I'll find you. And next time, I won't be so kind."

"Is this you being kind? It doesn't suit you."

I reach out and finger the thin silver chain draped around her neck. The pendant is a small oval with the letter "A" inscribed on the front.

"Why did you name him Adam?" I ask abruptly.

She blinks, jarred by the subject change. "I, um…" Sighing, she gives up whatever half-baked lie she was starting to spew and offers something more vulnerable instead. "I wanted him to be like the first person born into a new world. A fresh start. I thought…" She suddenly brushes it off with a slight shake of her head. "Never mind what I thought. Now, you know his name."

"How thoughtful of you." I sneer. "Considering you weren't planning on letting me be a part of his life at all."

"I'm still not planning on it."

I grind my teeth. It's been less than an hour and I'm being repeatedly slapped in the face with reminder after reminder of how easily she pushes all my buttons. The bad *and* the good ones. "Yet another terrible decision you have no reason to make."

"You know why I had to go," she spits. "You know why I have to do this."

"No, I don't. So why don't you explain it?"

She jerks her chin up haughtily. "Answer me honestly: you were planning on killing my father, weren't you?"

The question ignites a skewed sense of *déjà vu*. Except that Celine never asked me a question at all; she just stood in front of me and pleaded for his life.

Please, she'd begged. *Let him live. Stop looking for him. Let him go.*

"Your father's betrayal cost me several men," I tell her. "Are you trying to tell me his life is worth more than all theirs put together?"

Taylor hesitates. "I didn't know any of those men."

"What makes you think you know your father?"

She hesitates again. Her cheek dimples in as she gnaws at it uncertainly. She may be pleading his case now, but all is not right between Archie Theron and his younger daughter.

Strangely, it's not as satisfying as I expected it to be.

"What do you want, Ilarion?" she asks softly.

It's a question I've been asking myself since Zane materialized in my living room. What the fuck *do* I want?

I'm about to answer her when Taylor's eyes move past me.

"Tay? Everything okay?"

I turn. When I see who it is, my jaw clenches tighter.

You have got to be fucking kidding me.

8

ILARION

The man is tall, blonde, passably handsome. But the look in his eyes when he glances down at Taylor makes my blood boil.

So does the way she looks back at him.

"Callan!" she exclaims with forced cheer. "You're here early."

He ventures down the mouth of the alley, skirting the dumpster wide, before coming up to Taylor's shoulder. I don't like how close he stands to her. How he keeps trying to catch her eye, like they've got some nonverbal shorthand for him to ask, *Is this guy bothering you?*

"I figured I'd just hang out at the counter and wait for you." He peeks at me. "Is something going on?"

"No."

"Yes."

Taylor throws me a glare when I interrupt over her. I return fire. "Whatever plans you had with Taylor have just been canceled," I inform him. "Her evening has been spoken for."

His chest puffs up instantly, and honestly, if I weren't so pissed, I'd be laughing. This fucking *mudak* really might consider going to war with me.

It'd be the last mistake he ever makes.

"Taylor?" he says, glancing at her.

She's nervous, but she forces a smile onto her face. "This is Ilarion, an old…acquaintance." *Fucking ouch.* "He ended up in town unexpectedly and decided to, y'know, stop by."

"An old acquaintance, huh?" I ask, unable to let that one go. "I'd say our relationship runs much deeper than that, wouldn't you?"

Blondie doesn't like that anymore than I like him. But he's insulted on her behalf, not on his own. He must look in the mirror every morning and see a knight in shining armor.

"Listen, pal, I don't think Taylor wants to spend the evening with you."

"Have you asked her that?"

He stops short, his gaze veering to Taylor's for a moment. "Uh…"

"Don't bother." I adjust my watch. "Taylor, get rid of your preppy little friend so that we can talk."

She flinches, but her boy toy puffs himself up again like a parakeet on show. "I am her *boyfriend*," the man proclaims in a wobbly voice that says neither he nor she are quite sure the shoe fits. "And you need to leave."

"Boyfriend, hm?" I repeat, looking at Taylor with an expression that suggests I don't give a fuck.

But just like he's convincing himself that she belongs to him, I'm working hard to convince myself that I don't care what he thinks.

Given how fucking furious I feel, though, it seems to be a losing effort.

The best I can hope for is to feign indifference. Which would be way easier to do if I weren't feeling so goddamned possessive.

"I'm surprised," I comment with a shrug. "I expected you to pick someone with a little more…" I wave a hand over him. "I don't know. *More*."

Her unfortunate little Ken doll takes a half-hearted step towards me. "Okay, man, you need to go. Now."

I meet him halfway. "You are way out of your depth here," I snarl. "Friendly advice: walk away."

"My name is Callan."

"I didn't ask." I tighten my fist enough for every knuckle to crack. "I suggest you take my advice before you're spitting blood on the sidewalk."

"If you have to ask, you're even dumber than you look."

"Come on, Taylor," the moron says, grabbing her arm. "Let's go."

My palm shoots out and meets him in the solar plexus, forcing him to a stand-still. "Let. Her. Go."

He's a big enough man in his own right, but he doesn't stand a chance. His eyes go wide when he sees the hollow determination in mine.

A smarter man would have cut his losses and run. Even now, there's still time for that. But then this wannabe knight in shining armor decides this is his hill to die on.

"Listen, buddy—"

I turn to Taylor and sigh. "Can't say I didn't warn him."

I grab him by the scruff of his shirt and lift him into the air. His feet flail about helplessly and his hands scrabble at my wrists.

"Ilarion!" Taylor screams. "Let him go!"

My eyes snap to hers. "Make it worth my while."

She's a quivering, anxious mess. But I see it in her eyes: she's resigned to all this. She's known it was coming. Maybe even from the second she stepped foot through that gate in my gardens, she knew it would end up like this.

"Half an hour," she whispers. "We can talk for that long before I leave."

"One hour, and I might decide not to throw him into the dumpster."

She narrows her eyes. "Fine."

Satisfied, I release him. He crumbles to the ground in a wheezing puddle of pathetic.

Taylor rushes over and helps him to his feet. I'm sure his ass hurts, too, but his ego took the brunt of the fall.

"Taylor," he mumbles, "don't go with this guy—"

"Fucking hell, is he still talking?"

She places a protective hand on his chest. That's all it takes to tempt me to rip him away from her and make good on my earlier threat to fling him in the dumpster. Or worse.

"Ilarion and I just need to talk through a few things," she says urgently. "I'll be fine. Just go, okay? I'll call you tomorrow."

"I'm not leaving you."

I roll my eyes. "I'm losing patience here."

"Callan," Taylor says urgently. "Go."

"No, I can't just leave you with him—"

"You're not my boyfriend!" she snaps. "Stop pretending that you are."

Well, this suddenly got interesting.

Ken Doll's face falls. Taylor's cheeks flush red. "I…I'm sorry, but…I really need to handle this, Callan. And I can't do that if you're standing next to me like a guard dog."

"An ineffective one at that," I chime in.

Taylor skewers me with a glare before she turns back to him. "Please?"

He eyes me sidelong, but to his credit, he doesn't pick another round of this losing battle. "You'll call me?" he asks her.

"I will," she insists. "Tomorrow."

"Okay," he sighs. With a grimace, he turns and limps down the alleyway.

It's a fight to keep from smirking as Taylor turns on me. A losing battle in its own right.

"Did you have to be such an *asshole?*" she hisses.

"If you remember correctly, it's what I do best. Now —where to?"

She struggles with several choice curses before her shoulders slump. "Come on," she says, gesturing for me to follow her out of the alley.

I let her get in a head start, mostly so that I can stare at her ass as she walks. Still as pert and perfect as ever. Maybe even more so now.

She stops at the sidewalk and waits for me. We cross together, making our way toward the river slicing through the heart of the town.

"Your guard dog's still on duty," I point out.

Sure enough, Blondie is lingering by the front of the diner, watching us walk away with a morose scowl on his face. I get perhaps a little bit too much pleasure out of that.

"You didn't have to humiliate him like that," she says flatly. "He's a good man."

"Just not good enough to be your boyfriend?"

She glares.

I chuckle.

This is going to be *fun*.

9

TAYLOR

I'm expecting him to break the silence. But we've been walking for a while now and he still hasn't said a word. I look at my feet, in the distance, at the sky above, but there's nothing to see except grass and trees and cloudy gray skies.

I feel horrible about Callan, but not horrible enough to regret what I said to him. I've suspected it for a while, and now, the proof is in the pudding: my inexorable transformation from compassionate human to cold, hard bitch.

I glance at Ilarion. I have *him* to thank for that.

"Do you bring Adam here?" he asks suddenly.

"Almost every day. He likes open spaces. He likes running around."

I can't read his expression. Does that little morsel, as meager as it is, make him emotional? Happy? Sad?

"Who does he look like?"

"From the moment he was born, he's looked like you," I admit. "He's got your eyes and everything. He's not prone to violence, though, so at least his personality is all me."

"I seem to recall you stealing my sister's firearm and threatening her at gunpoint."

I wince. "Forgot about that."

"Chose to forget, you mean." He stops walking and turns to me. I don't meet his eyes, because as long as I don't look at him, those icy blues can't strip away the armor I've spent five long years building around myself.

"Yeah. I chose to forget. It's easier to bury things than to carry them around all the time. Sue me."

"No, *tigrionok*," he murmurs as he saunters closer. "I have other ways of making you pay."

My nostrils pick up his scent. That smell is a short-circuit to exactly the kinds of memories I've fought to abandon. It drags me kicking and screaming into a past I can't run from, no matter how hard I try.

His taunting, salacious smirk is the final hook in me. Suddenly, I'm not here in this park in this dusty, forgotten little town; I'm back in the mountains. I'm back in the cabin. I'm back amongst lazy, hazy pillow talk conversations and stolen kisses in the rain.

"It's surprisingly cruel of you to lead that poor sap along, you know."

My spine goes rigid. "That's not what I'm doing."

"No?" Ilarion asks. "He's not your boyfriend? You said it, but, oh, I don't know… It just didn't have the ring of truth, if you ask me."

I roll my eyes at him. "That's because your ego talks so loud that you can't hear anything else."

He chuckles and smooths his knuckles over my cheek. I don't know whether to flinch away or nuzzle into him like a needy cat, so in the end, I do neither. I just stay there and suffer under the sensation of a touch I've spent five years dreaming about.

"I see everything, Taylor. And you see it, too. I'd bet my life that you knew from the moment he first opened his mouth that he wouldn't be it for you. No matter how hard you tried to convince yourself otherwise."

I close my eyes so Ilarion doesn't see the tears welling up in them. "He's a good man."

"He was a good distraction, maybe. He was never going to be anything but that."

I squint out at him. "Are you *jealous*, Ilarion?"

"Are you *deflecting*, Taylor?"

"Maybe, but the question still stands. No—you know what? I don't need to ask the question. I can see it in your eyes. You *are* jealous." He wants to pick me apart and expose me? Then turnabout is fair play. I know him as well as he thinks he knows me. "And you have no right to be. I'm not the one who *married someone else*."

I didn't actually mean to say that last bit; it just slipped out in the heat of the moment. Which is why being around Ilarion is never a good thing. I'm always in the heat of the moment when he's near.

"You make a lot of assumptions."

"Pot, kettle." Way back when, I would have caved to his little mind games. Not now. Not today. And hopefully, not ever again. Still, I notice the way his eyes dim and it tugs at something gentler inside me. "It doesn't matter. I'm not...I'm not mad about it."

The light in his gaze flickers back on. He smirks coldly. "You need to work on that line. It's not nearly as convincing as it needs to be."

"Did you just reappear in my life to torment me?"

"Partly, yes," he concedes shamelessly. "But this is about so much more than that."

"I know you want me to take the bait, and I know you know that I'm going to." I take a deep breath and look him in the eye. "But before we get into anything else, I need your word on something."

He knows exactly what I'm about to say, but he's going to make me say it anyway. "Depends on what that 'something' is."

"My father."

"Ah."

Ilarion turns to face the river. It's still cold right now, but in the height of summer, it gets warm enough that the kids can swim in it. I can picture Adam giggling during his first swim, his chubby little fists hitting the water like he was trying to coax it into a fight. I can feel that warm sun on my face. I can remember how it felt to take that first breath and let myself believe we'd be safe here.

I should've known how wrong I was.

"He's my dad, Ilarion. He's all I have left. I know what he did, and I'm not asking you to forgive him. I just need you to promise me that you won't hurt him."

He pivots slowly in place until his eyes find mine again. "No traitor has ever received a pardon in my Bratva."

"If that were true, you would have killed Dad a long time ago."

"I needed him at the time. I don't anymore."

I swallow. My mouth is acidic and dry. The fear tastes like sawdust. "If you do, Cee will never forgive you."

His eyebrows knit together, but there's a cold sense of amusement lingering there. "You're still assuming a lot." I frown, but he doesn't explain. He just sighs and turns away from me once again. "Speaking for Celine, I mean. Pretending you know how she will feel."

"I know my sister."

"Correction: you *used* to know her. Time has passed. Things have changed."

He's filled with so much confidence, I'm losing my own. "You're just trying to scare me. Celine is still Celine."

His profile, what little I can see of it, is bleak and austere. His eyes are seeing things that aren't there. Memories. Threats in the shadow. "She was in a coma for a long time. When she woke up, her mother was dead. A few hours later, her father and sister vanished without a trace. She spent a year undergoing physical therapy, all alone. She had to re-learn how to walk and write. *Alone*. She suffered through intense depression and survived two separate assassination attempts. Again, *alone*, without her family to support her."

By the time he's done, my jaw is in the dirt. *"What?!"*

Ilarion barks out a laugh. There's no humor in his eyes. "Did you think Benedict Bellasio would just scamper off into the darkness and die there? I took down the man and his empire in the span of one night. And, as you know, he always has to have the last word."

"So he tried to kill Celine?"

"He tried," Ilarion echoes. "It didn't work. After that, he went silent."

"And you still haven't found him?"

He grits his teeth. "I'm working on it. My point is, Celine Theron is not the sister you grew up with."

"Zakharov…"

"What?"

I look at him, wondering why I'm even going down this road. "Celine Zakharov," I repeat, like he might have forgotten. *Fuck*, maybe I'm just trying to remind myself.

His forehead smooths out. "Ah" is all he says.

"Okay." I know I'm beating a dead horse, so I take a deep breath and focus on what matters. "Okay, I'll give you that. Cee may have changed a lot in the last five years. But I refuse to believe she's changed so much that she wouldn't care if her dad was killed."

"She understands that some things are necessary."

It's a terrifying thought. Even more so because I'm starting to believe that he's not making anything up. I think about the image of the beautiful, composed woman that stared back at me from the tablet this morning.

There was so much that was familiar about her.

There was more that was strange and alien.

"Fine. Maybe I don't know her anymore. But *I* still care. So if you ever cared about me at all…promise me."

There's nothing on his face that suggests surrender. I'm on tenterhooks, skin crawling with desperate, pleading hope. I'm ready for it to be snuffed out.

But then, his head inclines by an incremental amount.

"Very well."

I let out a breath I didn't even know I was holding. My heart pounds painfully against my rib cage. So apparently, he does care about me…or he did at one point, at least.

"Thank you, Ilarion."

"Don't thank me just yet," he growls under his breath. "I came here for a reason."

Out of nowhere, I think about my recurring dream. It's been the same one since the night we left.

In the dream, I wake up from a deep sleep and look over at Adam's crib. Something about it always strikes me as eerily wrong. I'll frown and get up, and when I walk over to it, it's empty. The windows are open, curtains fluttering softly against the wind. When I rush to the windowsill, I can see Dad's beaten-down little Honda driving fast through the night, headlights dwindling to flecks before they disappear into the horizon.

I know it's retribution. Someone will take my son, the same way I took Ilarion's. Karma is a wheel, and in my dream, it's rolling away from me faster than I could ever hope to catch up.

"I…I am sorry," I whisper. "For how I left. I didn't have a choice."

"Yes, you did." His voice twists harshly. "You had a choice. You chose to run."

I close my eyes for a second. "Okay, yes. I chose to run," I admit. "But I was trying not to hurt anyone."

"You were trying not to hurt *Celine*," he corrects softly.

I sacrificed so much to ensure Celine could have the life she wanted. It's only now that I'm beginning to see just how much it cost me. It's only now that I'm beginning to wonder if it was a mistake.

I clear my throat. "D-did it work?"

The twilight is fading slowly. Golden shadows dance across his face. His eyes are sadder than I've ever seen them as he sighs.

"The thing about the assassination attempts: I could do something about them, and I did." He takes a breath. "It was the time she tried to kill herself that left me powerless."

10

ILARION

There were days I understood what she did. Why she ran. Why she took my child away from me.

But there were also days where I didn't understand. And on those days, I was angry.

I was very, very angry.

It was on the angry days that I planned these words. I wasn't about to spare her feelings simply because her heart was in the right place.

She sure as hell didn't spare mine.

Her face pales the moment the words are out of my mouth. There's a twinge of guilt in my chest that I extinguish with memories of the months right after she left.

She bartered away her happiness and sacrificed mine for her sister's. Now, she needs to know what that sacrifice wrought. Actions have consequences. It's time she learned that.

"Suicide?" she gasps.

There's a slight breeze in the air. The sun's all but gone now, and the wind has turned cold. "Did you think you were leaving Celine to skip off into a happily-ever-after?" I scoff. "If so, that was horribly naïve, even by your standards."

"You're not joking?"

"Why would I joke about that?" I snap. "I have no desire to see someone I care about die."

Her eyes go wide. "W-why?" She trips over her words. "Why did she try to ki—to do that?"

I'm irritated that she even feels the need to ask. *Actions have consequences.* It's as simple as that. You don't get to just do what you want and get away with it scot-fucking-free.

I glance over at the river. Through the rushing water, I see stones in every shade of white and gray, their edges softened by the currents. I try to imagine my son sitting there and splashing, learning how to skip a rock.

But my imagination refuses to conjure up anything.

I sigh and turn back to Taylor. "The physical therapy was hard on her. She hated being helpless. She hated having to rely on other people for everything."

"She was always the one looking after me when we were younger," Taylor murmurs. She has the look of a woman losing herself down memory lane. "And just when I became more independent, Mom got sick and Celine started looking after her instead."

"She felt like she was a burden to me."

"Was she?"

I stop short. "You have no right to ask me what Celine was to me. Or what she is to me now."

Her mouth opens and closes without saying anything. "You made a promise to my mother," she says at last.

Ah, of course. The promise.

A promise I should never have made. It's not the type of thing that would usually bind me. But the woman was dying. And she loved her daughters in a way that my parents never loved Mila or me. How could I refuse? It felt unnecessarily cruel to deny an innocent woman some peace of mind right before she died.

But there were days over the last five years when I felt that promise weigh on me so heavily my shoulders ached from the pressure. From the responsibility of it.

So much so that I couldn't quite keep it from my eyes whenever I looked at Celine.

"What are you thinking of when you look at me like that?" she asked from her bed one day.

I'd come in to check on her before she began yet another session of physical therapy. "Like what?"

"I don't know how to describe it," she sighed. "There's just this... regret in your eyes. Resentment, maybe."

"That's ridiculous."

"He says defensively."

"Celine."

"Ilarion," she snapped right back. I preferred those days. The days when she was full of fire and fight and everything pissed her off, including me. The days when she got so quiet, she seemed to cave in on herself—that was when I knew I needed to worry.

"I don't know what you're talking about," I told her. "I don't look at you in any particular way."

"Don't you think that's a problem?"

"No."

"I can leave," she said quietly. "I have a house to go back to."

"This is your home," I snapped through gritted teeth. "If there are things you need, make a list and I'll have Mila or Dima pick them up for you."

Celine sighed. "Is that it, then?" she asked. "You're angry that my recovery is taking so long. You resent the fact that you have to take care of me."

I glared at her, trying to find my humanity underneath all the anger.

"It's okay for you to say so," she added quickly and quietly. "You're entitled to your feelings. I know I'm a burden. You wouldn't be out of line admitting it."

I could see the tears brimming beneath her lashes. She wanted to cry, but she was keeping it at bay for my benefit. She didn't want to manipulate me into giving her the answer she wanted to hear. Of course, if that were really the case, she would never have asked for it in the first place.

"I made your mother a promise just before she died," I told her, because that's the only thing I could think of to say. "I promised her I would look after you and keep you safe."

Celine frowned. "Is that the only reason you're doing this?"

"Fucking hell," I snarled, jerking up to my feet. "What the fuck do you want from me, Celine? I'm here, aren't I? I'm here."

I left the room so she could cry in peace. But years later, I'd look back and remember that conversation as the moment I stopped thinking of Celine as a pawn and started thinking of her as a person.

"You made a promise," Taylor reminds me, catapulting me back to the present. "Or have you forgotten?"

"I don't forget, Taylor. Even when I try, I don't forget." I rub the back of my neck. "I'll admit that Celine was just a piece in my chess game. Bratva business, and all that. But that was a long time ago. She's no longer a pawn. She matters."

I see something then: the little whirlwind of insecurity that spins through Taylor's eyes. Whatever doubt I have about her feelings for me dissipates in the face of it.

She can talk a big talk. She can make demands and remind me of old promises. She can run as far as her legs will take her.

But she hasn't been able to outrun her feelings for me.

Join the fucking club.

"It seems that way," Taylor softly agrees.

I cock my head to the side. "Does it?"

She shifts uncomfortably on her feet. The uniform she's wearing is a sad blue with a deep-v neckline that I'm sure has been responsible for bringing in a generous customer or two. But as good as she looks in it, she doesn't look comfortable.

"I…sometimes see Celine in the news bulletins online," she admits. "Some days, I barely recognize her."

I know exactly what she's talking about. The *Daily Star* ran a picture of us front and center, standing outside the arched doorway of Titan's Ballroom where Celine had hosted her annual charity gala to raise funds for Syrian refugees resettling in Chicago. I remember that photograph showing up in my daily briefing from Mila.

I remember imagining, just for a moment, that it was Taylor on my arm instead.

"Why? Because she looks happy?"

She hesitates before answering. "I can never really tell," she confesses. "The pictures are always beautiful. But they don't capture everything."

"It's hard to recognize happiness, isn't it?" I ask. "Hard to catch and even harder to pin down. The irony is, misery loves being caught."

It's a barb at her. Not a particularly subtle one, either.

Her lashes flutter against the wind. She looks uneasy.

I wonder how often she's allowed herself to be honest these last few years. I wonder if there's anyone she trusts enough to let them see her deepest, darkest thoughts. The places where she hides her feelings for me.

"I have Adam," she says, at last. "He's the light in my life."

"That's a lot of pressure to put on a child," I remark. "You love him; of course you do. But he can't be your only source of light, Taylor. Because when he leaves—and if you do your job right, he *will* leave—he'll take that light with him."

Her skin pales. "What are you suggesting, Ilarion? You can't possibly be saying what I think you're saying."

"Maybe that's part of your problem, Taylor," I snap. "You think entirely too much."

"And you don't think enough," she hisses, stepping in front of me.

I hesitate. There's so much I want to tell her. So much I want to clarify.

But my pride won't let me breathe a word of it.

"Oh trust me, *tigrionok*—I've had five long years to think. In fact, that's all I did. That's why I'm here now."

"To remind me of shit that would be better off left in the past?" she asks angrily.

"No. To prove what I already knew: that your sacrifice was meaningless. You deprived yourself of future and freedom, you deprived me of my son, you deprived Adam of his father…and all for what?"

Her eyes are glistening bright with unshed tears. "I had to make sure she would be happy."

"Her happiness was never yours to determine," I growl. "It was not yours to make."

"No, it was *yours* to make."

I shake my head and take another step forward. "Don't you put that on me. I made a promise to keep Celine safe. Happiness was never part of the deal."

Taylor freezes. "Still an asshole, I see."

"Still a martyr, I see." I straighten up tall, looming over her. "You did it your way, and it failed. Miserably. Now, it's time to put an end to this."

She fidgets with the hem of her uniform. "Y-you can see Adam—"

"'See' Adam?" I raise a brow. "I didn't come all this way just to 'see' my son, Taylor."

She backs away from me slowly. "What…what do you mean?"

"I came to bring him home."

Even in the patchy darkness, I can see the shock on her face. The woman really is delusional if she thought I was here to check in and then leave without upending her perfect little farce of a happy ending.

"You can't do that!" she blurts.

"I think you'll find that I can. You're welcome to come, too, but I'm taking Adam regardless."

"Ilarion—"

"Look at your life, Taylor!" I spread my arms out as if the gesture will finally highlight everything she's blind to. "You're miserable here. Time to admit it and come home."

"You're not taking my son."

I grab her arm and pull her into me. She hits my chest with a strangled gasp and I stare down into her beautiful green eyes. They're just as deep and haunting as I remember.

"Here's the thing, sweetheart: I'm not asking."

11

TAYLOR

I stand there, shaking like a leaf, for a long time after Ilarion disappears.

Then I start running. I run back to the diner just long enough to grab my bike. Then I ride it home, reckless in my mad dash to get to my child.

I don't bother locking my bike when I get home. I slide off, leave it sprawled across the grass, and sprint into the house. The moment I'm through the front door, I freeze.

The smell of freshly baked cookies hits my nostrils. I can hear the TV on in the next room. It's *Cocomelon*; that tune has been ingrained into my brain so deep that I hear it in my nightmares sometimes. I glance into the living room, and Dad spots me. He's sitting beside Adam, reading a book on his Kindle while Adam stares transfixed at the screen.

Dad takes one look at me, and his face twists with unease.

"I'll be right back, li'l man," he says, patting Adam on the head before he leaves the living room to follow me upstairs.

"Taylor? Is everything alright?"

I don't answer until I'm in my bedroom. It looks out over the street, so I walk over to the windows immediately and peek out through the closed blinds.

"That car down the road… Can you read the license plate number?"

Dad joins me at the window. "The Chevy? I'm not sure. Why? What's going on?"

"I'm pretty sure it's Ilarion's," I say, snapping the blinds shut. "Pretty sure he followed me here. Or put someone on me."

"What in the world gives you that idea?"

I pace to the opposite end of the room. "The fact that he showed up at the diner today."

Dad's face pales. "Fuck… He found us."

"Yes, he found us," I repeat, wiping my sweaty palms against my apron. I'd forgotten to take it off at the restaurant. Looks like it's coming with us wherever we go next. *Sorry, Mabel.* "My question is, *how* did he find us?"

"Relentlessness usually tends to bear fruit."

I stop short and close my eyes. "Okay. Okay. We have to think of a plan. We have to—"

"Taylor."

"We have to pack our bags and disappear. You'll need to call some of your contacts, get some help. We'll need to lie low for a few weeks, maybe a few months, until our trail goes cold. And he—"

Dad walks up to me and puts his hands on my shoulders. "Taylor, take a breath."

I twist away from his touch. "I hate when people say that. It doesn't help. Did you not just hear what I said? Ilarion has found us, Dad. He's here. I thought he just wanted to see Adam, but it's so much worse. He wants to take Adam back with him."

"Does Celine know?"

"If she doesn't already, she will soon enough. And when that happens, all hell will break loose. When Ilarion shows up at their house with a four-year-old who looks exactly like him, she's going to have plenty of questions. She'll know. Then all this will be for nothing. Every last fucking bit of it."

"Sweetheart, you need to calm—"

"*Don't tell me to calm down!*" I don't full-body scream it, but I so desperately want to.

Dad holds his hands up in surrender. "Listen. I've been expecting this day for years now. I guess I always knew that Ilarion finding us would be inevitable."

"And you have a plan, right?" I plead. "Tell me you have a plan. You always have a plan."

"Taylor." He slowly shakes his head. "I'm not sure a plan is going to help us now. We won't be able to make a move without him knowing."

My legs suddenly feel too weak to support my weight. I lower myself onto the bed, trembling everywhere. "We've been running for five years. And for what?"

"I ask myself that all the time, to be honest."

Frowning deeper, I look up at my father. He's shrunk in the time we've spent in exile. I never noticed quite how much until right now. Probably because he always seems so larger than life when he's with Adam, and I tend to see things through Adam's eyes.

It's easier than using my own.

"There must be something we can do. Someone we can call."

"I wouldn't trust anyone we've used before, Taylor. Something went wrong there; otherwise, Ilarion wouldn't be at our doorstep."

I take a deep breath, but it doesn't help. The walls are closing in, and I need to make sure they don't crush us. "It sounds like you're telling me there's no way out of this."

"There may not be, Little Bird." He hasn't used that nickname for me in a long time. Not since I was a little girl.

"I don't remember why you started calling me that," I murmur. "But I remember I loved it when you did."

Dad moves to my side and sits down next to me. "The bronchitis years were hard on you," he says gently. "All the other kids were out running and swimming and playing, and you were stuck indoors, wheezing and coughing."

I snort bitterly. "That part, I don't need any help remembering."

He pats my knee. "I used to tell you to imagine that you were a little bird, and you could fly anywhere you wanted."

The way he says it makes me realize the feeling I'd carried around as a child, that feeling of being trapped in my room, unable to participate in the outside world... I've been carrying the same feeling around with me for the past several years.

Deeper down, something in me whispers that Ilarion saw it long before I did. I just didn't want to listen to him.

"If we run, Taylor, you won't be free. Ever."

"If I go back, I won't be free, either."

"You won't be in hiding," Dad argues. "I think that'll make a difference."

"You really think I should go back?"

"Well, I'm not sure you have a choice," he says bluntly. "Which means *deciding* to go will at least put you in charge of your own choices."

"That's a fake autonomy," I snap. "That's pretending I have a steering wheel, when in reality, the brakes are cut and we're going faster and faster down a collision course with something that won't yield."

He chews his nail. "Acceptance of what's beyond our control is sometimes a necessary evil, Little Bird."

"It's quitting. That's all it is. It's giving up."

"Not everything is worth a fight."

I can feel the fatigue in his words as he says them. I think about how hard he tried to keep us safe. What he'd ended up with was one daughter married to the most dangerous man he knew. And another daughter pregnant by the same man. All that fighting and scheming and hoping…all for nothing.

There are days when I resent my father for all his bad choices.

But not today.

Today, I pity him.

"It helps a little," I say. "To know why you were so protective of Celine and me."

"Does it?"

"Some days, it does," I answer honestly. "Other days, it feels like you were lying to us about everything for no reason at all."

He glances at me warily. Any time we've really talked about the past, it's ended up in a fight. Then he says something he regrets, and I say something I regret, and it ends with several days of tense silence, before the minutia of the day-to-day makes us forget that we're angry with one another.

"It felt right that I should carry the burden of knowing. It didn't seem fair to bring the three of you in with me. In any case, you girls were too young. But your mother…I came close to telling her so many times."

"What stopped you?"

It feels silly that I'm only asking these questions now. But it's not that I haven't asked them before; the difference is that I genuinely want to know this time.

"The first time, I chickened out," he says with a heavy sigh. "I lost my nerve at the last minute and decided it was okay to be a coward because we were going out for ice cream and no one tells his wife that he's a low-level *vor* in a Russian Bratva over a pint of rocky road."

"Fair." I can't argue that. "You were low level?"

"At the time, yes. It was Ludwig who brought me on board. You girls were tiny then."

"Ludwig?"

"Ilarion's father."

"Fuck," I breathe, wishing there was a bottle of liquor lying around. I'm not a big drinker, but some days, and some conversations, just require a stiff drink. "It's so weird to think that you knew Ilarion's father. That you *worked* for him."

"He was not a good man."

"The organized crime thing tipped you off, huh?" I ask sarcastically.

"You have every right to be mad at me. I apologize if I've ever made you feel otherwise. I know that my actions had consequences. It's just hard for me to take your anger. It's the coward in me, I suppose."

"Dad. You're not a coward."

He shakes his head mournfully. "Yes, I am. And one day, I'll tell you the exact moment I knew that for sure." He exhales deeply, his eyebrows dip down, and I know he's thinking about Mom. He gets a specific look on his face when he thinks of her. Like a man who's drifting in outer space and has no idea if he'll ever find gravity again. "The second time I tried to tell her… Well, your nana passed away, and that took up a few months of our lives. And the third time, she was diagnosed with cancer."

"I'm sorry you weren't there to bury her," I suddenly say, taking his hand. "You should have been."

"I should have been." He nods. "But in some ways, I'm actually relieved I wasn't." He must see the surprise on my face, because he chuckles bitterly, points at his own chest, and says, "I told you: coward."

"Well, if you're a coward, then so am I. The only reason I came with you the night we left is because I didn't want to have to tell Cee that I was pregnant."

"At least you had noble intentions. You were trying to protect your sister."

"And you were trying to protect us," I emphatically remind him. "I may not always believe that, but today, I do."

He gives me a tired smile. "So I suppose what we can agree on is that we're both cowards with good intentions." I know he's joking, and despite everything that's happening, it almost makes me laugh.

"We should talk more, Dad." I gently nudge him. "Like this, I mean."

"The irony is, without Ilarion, I doubt it would have been possible."

I glance at him. "I made him promise me that he wouldn't hurt you, you know."

His eyebrows lift for a moment, but he doesn't seem as relieved by that assurance as I would have thought. "He promised you that?"

"Well, I mean, we didn't pinky swear or anything, but he did tell me he wouldn't. And I believe him."

Dad gazes at me for a second before he stands and walks over to the window. "I guess that answers that question," he says, peeking out into the street through the blinds.

"What question?"

"If he still cares for you."

I stiffen. "If he does, it's only by association. I'm his son's mother. A means to an end."

He side-eyes me but lets the topic fade into the tense silence. The air conditioning clicks on and blusters sadly for a few moments before sighing away once again.

I'm just starting to breathe and calm down when Dad speaks up. "Did he mention anything about Celine?"

Then I clench right back up again. How do I tell him that for his eldest daughter, the last five years were filled with depression, near-assassinations, heartache, physical therapy, and a suicide attempt?

"He said she was doing okay."

Dad sighs, and in that rise and fall of his chest, I swear that for the briefest of seconds, I can actually see the weight he's carried with him all these years. Like chains drooped over his shoulders.

"Well. I suppose that's something, then."

12

ILARION

I expected to feel something when I saw him.

I just didn't expect the feeling to be so *intense*.

He is my son. I think I would have known it in my soul, whether he looked like me or not. Of course, the fact that he does look like me helps a lot.

His hair, a shade lighter than mine, flops over his forehead as he scampers around the garden. His fingers are dark with dirt, as are his mother's, but both of them are laughing.

She is wearing shorts that show an expanse of smooth skin and a thin white cotton blouse that glows translucent when the sunlight hits her. I can see the pale outline of her pink bra and the slim lines of her torso.

As I watch, she hoists him into the rope swing hanging from a tree in the yard. His laugh grows louder as she pushes him back and forth.

It's easy to notice things as I watch. It was only after she left that I kept reminding myself of all the things I never paid enough attention to. The crease in her forehead when she is deep in thought. The way her cheeks dimple when she smiles. The little tremble in her fingers when she is resisting the urge to bite her nails.

Suddenly, Adam's laughter cuts off. I blink out of my daze and realize that they're both looking at me.

"Mama, who's that?" the boy asks.

Even from here, I can see Taylor's throat bob as she swallows. "Go inside, sweetheart."

"But I wanna know—"

"Go inside!" she yells too harshly. Then she softens her voice. "You can have a cookie if you go get it right now."

He doesn't bother asking any more follow-up questions. He just darts off into the house and Taylor focuses her gaze on me. Slowly, she pulls herself up to her feet and I ease my way into her garden.

"I haven't prepared him for this, you know," she warns me.

"I don't expect you to tell him who I am. Not right away."

She takes a deep breath and looks toward the house. "I thought about running," she quietly admits, her expression somber and thoughtful.

"What changed?"

She sighs and turns her back on the house. "I decided that I didn't want to run anymore."

"Smart decision." I venture a little closer to her. "He's..." I work my jaw from side to side, but I can't think of anything to say besides the obvious. "Perfect."

The moment I say it, her whole face softens. The uncertainty drains out and all that's left behind is a love so deep that I start to feel it chip away at my emotional wall.

That's less than ideal. I need to be strong. Stoic. Unmoving.

But damn it all—there's something in the way this woman embodies motherhood so effortlessly that makes me feel like crumbling to my knees.

"He is, isn't he?" she murmurs.

"He does look like me. But there's a lot of you in him, too. You've done well with him, Taylor."

She's obviously not expecting that, because her eyes immediately glisten. She turns away just long enough to blink the tears from her eyes. "He's a special kid," she whispers. "I'd like to take the credit, but he's always been kind, sweet, imaginative. I didn't teach him any of those things."

Then she peeks at me tentatively out of the corner of her eye and closes right back up. The wariness creeps back into her features and I can feel her silently pushing me away already.

"I'm gonna introduce you as an old friend, okay?"

I loft a brow. "Is that what I am, Taylor? A friend?"

"No," she says decidedly, taking a step back. "You're my brother-in-law. We both need to remember that."

"Mama?"

We turn as one to face the kitchen door. Adam is standing at the threshold with a cookie in hand. His eyes are fixed on me with awe.

"Adam, come down here and say hello. This is a friend of mine. His name is Ilarion."

He lingers anxiously by the door. Instead of waiting for him to come to me, I take a few steps in his direction.

"Hey, Adam." I smile, hoping it's as bright as his. I'll be the first to admit I haven't smiled like that since…ever. "It's very nice to meet you."

He glances at his mother and then towards me. "You're tall."

I laugh. "I'm pretty sure you will be, too. What are you, eight? Nine?"

His face cracks into a brilliant smile. "I'm only four and three quarters!"

"No way! Seriously? You're so tall; I thought you were older."

He ventures one step down towards me, and all I can think is, *Progress.* "Your name's funny."

Taylor starts to scold him, but I flash her a smile so she knows it's okay. "Yeah, you're right. It kinda is. I guess I'm used to it now."

He giggles, then he glances at his mother. "Are you really Mama's friend? 'Cause Mama doesn't have any friends."

"Adam!" Taylor exclaims, flushing an even brighter shade of pink. "I have friends."

"Only Grandpa, and he doesn't count because he's your dad."

"What about Mabel?"

"She doesn't count because she's your boss."

"What about Miss Maisel?"

"She doesn't count because she's my teacher, and you only meet her at school."

"You're my friend," Taylor insists.

Adam giggles. "I'm your son. I don't count."

The boy makes no mention of Callan, which is quietly satisfying. Motion at the periphery draws my attention. I glance toward the house in time to catch sight of a shadow at the window.

Of course. *He's* watching.

"Adam, sweetheart," Taylor says. "Remember how I tell you stories sometimes about your aunt Celine?"

So she talks about Celine. Interesting.

Adam bobs his head up and down. "Yeah?"

"This is her husband. They're married."

He frowns. I want to frown along with him and set a few things straight, but I also want to avoid scaring him. "Oh," he says, turning to me. "Did you bring Auntie Cee with you?"

"Not this time."

He seems confused by that. "Where is she?"

"At home. We don't live in this state."

"Oh. Why hasn't she come to see us?" Adam asks.

"Because she's very busy," Taylor says, jumping in before I can answer. "And who knows? Maybe you'll meet her soon."

"Does she bake cookies, too?" he asks, a smile growing on his sweet face.

Taylor nods. "Grandma taught us, so yes, she does. Or at least…she did."

Adam looks between us. "I hope I get to be as tall as you one day," he announces. Then he turns to his mother. "I knew he wasn't your friend. He's my uncle."

I pretend as if that doesn't land like a sucker punch.

Taylor glances at me. "Yeah, I suppose you're right."

"Hey," Adam says, jumping off the last step and tugging on my hand. His fingers are gritty with cookie crumbs. "Wanna see my tire swing?"

"I would love to," I say. "But first, I think I'm gonna go get a glass of water. Is that okay?"

Adam shrugs. "Sure." He scampers off to the swing without waiting for either of us to follow.

"Ilarion…" Taylor warns, her forehead taut with worry when she sees me glance to the window again. "You promised me he was off-limits."

I made no such promise. I promised I wouldn't *hurt* him.

I meet her gaze. "I just want a glass of water, Taylor."

She swallows hard. "Just so you know," she says softly, "he means the world to Adam."

13

ILARION

When I enter the kitchen, Archie is leaning against the counter, waiting for me.

"*Pakhan*," he says with a respectful nod.

"Archie."

Even that two-word exchange is a departure from how things used to be. For years, we met in shadows, didn't use names. Things have changed now. There are no more shadows to hide in. There are no more innocents to protect.

Through the window, Taylor is watching Adam play on the swing, but the calm from earlier is gone. Her back is too straight, her shoulders too tight.

"Can I offer you something to drink?" Archie asks. "Coffee? Tea? Juice?"

"I'm good."

"We also have brandy, if it's gonna be *that* kind of conversation," he adds.

"What kind of conversation do you imagine it will be?"

Archie shifts to the side so that the kitchen table is directly between us. He's fidgety, but trying to hide it. As if I don't notice every fucking thing.

"An honest one," he says after a small pause.

I can't help but laugh. "I think we left that in the past, my friend."

His throat bobs with the force of his swallow. "I'm not the man you think I am," he says bluntly. "I made bad decisions. That doesn't make me a bad person."

"Forgive me if I find that hard to believe."

He's aged considerably in the last few years. His face is paler, gaunter, but his potbelly looms over his belt and his patchy beard is streaked through with gray.

"I would like a chance to explain, though," he adds. "If you're willing to hear me out."

I'm quiet for a moment. There's no need to rush this. We've waited five years to have this conversation—an extra few minutes won't kill anyone.

At least, probably not.

"You know, I think I will take a cup of coffee." I pull out a chair and sit down at the round table.

Archie pours two mugs and joins me. I watch as the black liquid sloshes over the edge of the rim when his hands tremble.

"I suppose you're going to tell me why you did what you did," I say, taking the cup from him. "And I'm hoping to God you won't say it was something as petty as 'more money.'"

The guilty shimmy of his eyes tells me everything I need to know.

"For fuck's sake, man," I spit. "I was expecting more from you."

He flushes pink and abandons his mug of coffee to one side. "I know it sounds bad. Betraying the brotherhood, betraying you...for something so pedestrian." His eyes fall to his hands. "But sometimes, money is the difference between life and death."

I sigh. I can guess exactly what he needed the money for. If I begrudge him that, I'm just as much of an asshole as he is. Maybe even worse.

"Are you going to tell me why you didn't just come to me for money if you needed it so badly?"

It's not just impatience laced in my words. The part of me that recognizes Celine, Taylor, and now Adam as family is stinging from the insult that Archie didn't trust me to care.

But, to be fair, I *didn't* care—until I met Taylor.

Fate is a double-edged sword.

"First, will you permit me one question?"

I want to say no, mostly because I know what his question is going to be. Some derivative of the same, at least. I want to remind him that his life sits in the palm of my hand. All I have to do is bring my fingers together and crush him.

I look out the window again. I can only see half of Taylor's profile. The breeze toys with the ends of her hair.

"One question," I sigh, turning back to Archie.

He nods gratefully. "Celine...has she forgiven me?"

That's not the question I'm expecting, but I don't betray my surprise. "Has Taylor?"

He leans back heavily in this chair, his finger stroking the handle of his mug as though he's forgotten why it's there. "She says she has. I don't really believe her."

I nod. The coffee tang on my tongue is bitter. That feels fitting.

"Celine told me about the last conversation the two of you had," I remark. "When you tried to convince her to leave with you."

Archie snorts. "I underestimated her feelings for you. I suppose that was my first miscalculation. She didn't want to hear me speak after that."

"Nobody likes being lied to."

"Considering we're having quite a civil conversation, I'm going to refrain from pointing out that you've been lying to Celine for the last five years." He pauses, then looks at me again. "And Taylor, too, in a way."

I grit my teeth. "Taylor made her decisions. Just like the rest of us."

"You don't strike me as the type of man who defers to anyone against his own judgment. In fact, I know you're not."

"I'm getting impatient with this detour we've taken," I snap. "You never were one to get to the point, were you?"

"You'll have to forgive an old man. The pondering gets worse with age."

"If you're looking for sympathy, I don't have any left to give. Traitors don't just walk away unscathed, no matter how old they are."

Archie nods, unsurprised. "Yes, I know. Your father had the same rule."

I flinch at the mention of my father. Then I curse myself for the tic.

One moment, I'm so sure I've put him and his shadow behind me. The next, he's right there, reminding me that his DNA will always be a part of my own.

A part of Adam's, too, I realize with horror.

"He was ruthless with traitors. But then, he was ruthless with everyone. His enemies, his colleagues, his *vors*… And his children. It took a brave man to approach him about anything."

I clench my jaw and swallow back bitterness that has nothing to do with the coffee. Archie mentioning my father wasn't a mistake; it was canny. More cunning than I expected, in fact. I guess I shouldn't be so surprised. The man hasn't survived this long by coasting on luck alone.

Then it clicks. "You asked him for money."

Archie nods, confirming my theory. "A loan, a raise, an advance—weighted against a salary cut if that's what it took. I only wanted twenty-five thousand at the time. Twenty-five thousand meant nothing to a man like Ludwig Zakharov."

"A penny meant everything to my father. He'd bleed you dry for the change in your pocket."

"I thought he would make an exception for me," Archie whispers. "I had always been one of his most loyal *vors*."

I smile darkly. "You thought he would be grateful."

"When you say it out loud, it sounds foolish," Archie mumbles. "But as I said, I was desperate at the time. Fiona had just been diagnosed. I was still paying off her student loans, taking care of her parents' nursing home bills. I had the girls to provide for."

"So he turned you down, and you went running to the other side."

"I didn't make the decision lightly. I knew the risk I was taking."

"And it seemed worth it to you?"

He meets my eyes. "The question was not whether or not it was worth it; the question was whether or not *she* was worth it."

I want to fault him for thinking that way. I can't.

And I hate that I can't.

"You may think I'm a fool. And a traitor. And I very well may be all those things. But first and foremost, I was Fiona Theron's husband, and I will never apologize for that. She was my entire world."

The grief paints his face dark. The downturned corners of his mouth look weighed down by something heavier than time, heavier than gravity.

Losing his wife killed most of him.

Losing his daughters will kill anything that's left.

"I was in too deep by the time you took over. I had thrown my lot into the Bellasio clan's fire and there was no turning back. I had to continue playing the mole in order to protect myself and my family. But, I want you to know: there were secrets I never betrayed, deals I feigned ignorance on."

"And Benedict believed you?"

"I told him I was a low-level *vor*. That I didn't have access to all the secrets. Just enough to be worth his while. Just enough to wet his tongue and keep you safe." He clears his throat. "If it helps, I'm not proud of it. I never was."

"Of course it doesn't help, Archie," I snarl. "Because for all your good intentions, for all your remorse and regret, you couldn't protect your family. Your wife is dead, killed by the same men you betrayed me for. Your daughters turned against you, and your days are very numbered."

He nods again, already resigned to whatever fate has in store for him. "No, I never expected to get away with it. So... what's it going to be? Will I be the victim of a hit-and-run? A random shooting? A sudden heart attack?"

I have to give it to the man—he doesn't look afraid of death. He just seems nervous over what he's leaving behind.

I've only been a father for all of five minutes.

I fucking hate with every fiber of my being how much it makes me actually understand him.

"You choose."

He shrugs. "Death is death. I don't care about how I get there. So long as it doesn't hurt my daughters. Or my grandson."

"Your death *is* going to hurt them. That's unavoidable. No one can do anything about that. Not even me."

Archie only shrugs. "The moment I realized Fiona was gone, I died with her. The only thing that keeps me going is that boy out there." His eyes flicker over the window where Adam has abandoned the swing and is now climbing the tree. "Funny, really...that you of all people should be the father of my grandson."

"For what it's worth..." I sigh heavily. This is about as close as I'm ever going to get to confiding in him as if we were family. "Nothing went the way I wanted it to. Not by a long shot."

His eyes harden, but a second later, the door opens and Taylor slinks in, looking nervous. "Everything alright in here?"

Her voice is bright with hope. She wants this to end amicably. She doesn't see that it can only end the way it started: with pain.

14

TAYLOR

I drop a kiss on Adam's head before Dad ferries him off to bed. The moment they disappear into Adam's bedroom down the hall, the atmosphere in the living room shifts.

It's not the first time that Ilarion and I have been alone since he showed up. But it's the first time that he's *here*, in my living room, consuming space that I've always considered to be sacred. Intimate. Protected.

Mine.

It's a small room, which is probably why Ilarion looks so out of place in it. He's still standing by the messy bookshelf in the corner, but he could be on top of me in three steps if he chose. Maybe that's why I'm so on edge.

Or maybe it's because his fingertips are running along the edge of a framed photograph of a baby Adam. He was nine months or so when the picture was taken. His eyes are a pre-dawn bluish gray and his cheeks are cherub red. I know what Ilarion is thinking, because it's the same thing I thought when I took that picture.

They look identical.

I've put that picture up everywhere we go. No matter how many times we've run or moved houses in the middle of the night, that photograph gets hung on the wall first. I still haven't decided whether it's because I just like it, or because I'm using it to torture myself with thoughts of what might've been.

"Nice house," he says.

I roll my eyes. "Don't be condescending."

"I was trying to pay you a compliment."

"Try again."

"You've done a great job with the boy," he says. "He's polite, sweet, curious. He says 'please' and 'thank you' without thinking about it, and he loves to read."

The smile lasts maybe three seconds on my face before it dries up. I'm caught between the conversation we have to have and the one I want to have. Neither one is going to leave me feeling anything but dissatisfied.

"You have nosy neighbors, though," he says abruptly.

"Excuse me?"

"Half a dozen people have walked past the house, and all of them tried to catch a glimpse of what was going on in here. They weren't subtle about it."

"That's life in a small town for you."

"I don't know how the fuck you live like this."

I cast a quick look toward Adam's room, and for a fleeting moment, Ilarion actually looks sheepish. Being a parent can do that where language is concerned. You start to second-guess yourself. Start to see yourself through their eyes. It changes things.

"Because I had to," I whisper.

"You didn't have to do anything," he snaps, his eyes turning to flint fast. "You could have stayed where you belonged and made your life more than...*this*."

"Excuse me?" I suck in a sharp breath.

"Look at you." He gestures toward the side of the room where my waitress uniform is hanging up next to my tattered coat. "A diner waitress in this hick town. You could have been anything."

I flush, but it's equal parts indignation and embarrassment. "You have no right to just waltz into my life and criticize me. I did the best I could!"

"If you had stayed, you could have finished college. Become someone important. Done something important."

My face twists into a scowl. "It's lucky that you ended up with Cee then. I would have been nothing but an embarrassment to you."

He walks over to me slowly. "This has nothing to do with Celine."

"When will you realize? Everything has to do with Celine!"

He shakes his head, but the flexing of his hands at his sides says he wants to shake *me* instead. "The two of you are more alike than you think," he mutters. "Each of you pointing at the other and saying, She's *the good one!* I'm *the fraud!*"

I frown. "She doesn't think that."

"Of course she does." He groans with frustration. "She always has."

I grit my teeth. "If only she could see me now, huh?"

Those blue eyes of his narrow, and I feel my stomach tighten in response. "I'm taking him back with me, Taylor," he says quietly. "The only question is, are you coming, too?"

I laugh right in his smug face. "Do you really think I would just let you take my son and leave me in the fucking dust?" I demand. "You're not really giving me a choice."

"Just speaking your language."

I freeze. I want to snap back, but his point lands. I never gave him a choice. I never even asked him to come with me—not that he would have, of course. But after watching him with Adam, I have a sinking feeling I should have at least tried.

"I don't want to fight," I murmur, my gaze falling to the floor.

"Neither do I," he says. "But I will if I have to."

I sigh. "You won't have to. I'm not about to start a battle with you that I can't win."

He lofts a brow. "So…you're going to come back with me?"

"Yes. But—I have one condition."

He nods. "Let's hear it."

"Cee can't know that you're Adam's father."

Ilarion does an incredulous double-take. "That's ridiculous."

"It's not. You go back, you tell her that you managed to find us, and you were just as shocked as she will undoubtedly be when you tell her that I have a son. You don't know who the father is, just that the baby was conceived sometime after I left. That way, I get to preserve my relationship with my sister, and so do you. It's a win-win."

Ilarion laughs brutally. "Have you *seen* him? How blind do you think she is?"

"Does it matter?" I retort. "People see what they want to see. And eventually, he'll think of you as a father figure over time. What does it matter if he calls you 'Uncle' instead of 'Dad'? If you love him and he loves you, that should be all that matters. And most importantly, Cee won't be suspicious."

"She might be when I name him my heir."

My eyes go wide. "You wouldn't."

"Why the hell wouldn't I? He's my firstborn child and my son. It's his birthright."

I'm doing everything I can not to splutter incoherently. "What if he doesn't want it?"

"He will have to be the one to decide that."

"Ilarion—"

"I *will* claim him as my son," he snarls, cutting me off. "I won't pretend otherwise. Fuck, Taylor, I've spent the last five damned years pretending. I'm still pretending."

The crack and tremble of his voice catches me by surprise. There's emotion there. Real emotion. The kind I didn't think he really was capable of feeling. Is it possible that there's more going on beneath the surface than I thought? No happy person has to pretend *that* much.

"You don't want to hurt Cee, do you?" I ask softly.

His jaw thrums with tension. "I don't want to keep lying to her."

"Some lies are meant to protect."

"Like the ones you tell yourself?" Ilarion fires back, moving closer to me.

That's the thing about him: he doesn't give me room to wriggle out of a tough spot. To pretend as though there aren't cracks in the foundation. Sometimes, denial is an act of self-preservation, too.

He won't stand for it.

"You and Celine are married, Ilarion. And in our family, marriage is for life."

He rolls his eyes. "For the love of God—"

"Have some respect for us, for once!" I keep my voice low, so it comes out in a whispered shriek. "We actually value things, things you obviously don't understand."

"Oh, believe me, I understand." He glowers at me. "The only thing I don't understand is your inability to see past your own stupidity."

I grind my teeth, then point to the door. "Get out."

"Make me." He knows I can't. When he sees me hesitate, he rolls his eyes again. "She'll be mad for a time. But she'll get over it."

"And then what? We all live together like one big, miserable, dysfunctional family?"

His eyes cloud for a moment before it clears again. I get the feeling he's not telling me something. Actually, he's probably not telling me a lot of things.

"The trick is not to think too far into the future. Just think about now."

"If only my brain was wired that way."

He's standing right in front of me now, radiating the same intoxicating musk he had when we first met. I feel the same way I did then—confused, overwhelmed, more asleep than awake.

"Did you ever even consider staying?" he asks softly.

I can't look him in the eyes. "Of course."

"But…?"

"But I was scared." It comes out in a shaky whisper. Fuck, I wish I could last longer before he wrung the tears from me. "I was fucking terrified."

"Of your sister?"

"And you," I mumble.

His eyes are bright and piercing. "I'd never hurt you, Taylor. And you know it."

Do I? I know he'd never raise a hand to me—but what about my heart? He's already smashed it to pieces and ground those pieces to dust. What's stopping him from doing it again?

"Why go there?" I ask desperately. "It's done, Ilarion. It's over. We made a huge mistake, and it's never gonna happen again. So why bring it up?"

He grabs my arm and pulls me towards him so that our noses are nearly touching. "Because it's not over," he growls. "It's nowhere near over."

Heat spreads through my arm like wildfire. I've never experienced anything remotely similar to this since I left. The desire that rises inside me is so definitive, and so visceral, that there's no way I can deny it. I couldn't lie to pretend it's not there.

Even if that lie would save me.

"All the more reason you should just leave us here," I rasp. "Forget that you ever found us. Let it end."

"You know me well enough to know that will never happen." His eyes flicker between mine. "And I know you well enough to know you don't really want that."

"Ilarion…"

"You've been waiting for me, Taylor. You might not admit that to yourself, but I saw your face in the diner. You've been waiting for me to find you for five endless years."

"Th-that's not true…"

He shakes his head, his breath tickling my nose. "I know you, Taylor Theron. Better than every single person in this town. Better than your own father. He looks at you and sees a little girl who was manipulated into wanting me. But I see the truth. I see the woman who made her own choices a long time ago."

"No."

"*Yes.*" His grip tightens. "The night you met me was the first time you made a decision that was purely for yourself. You *chose* me."

A sob escapes through my lips. "And that choice has destroyed everything that ever meant anything to me."

"Because you refused to own it!" he yells. "And now, you've made a mockery out of my life as well as yours. You keep saying you don't want to hurt anyone, but that's all you ever do. You're hurting everyone around you by burying your head in the sand, and even still, you don't. Fucking. Care."

I shudder back from his dark gaze. He releases me at last, but I don't stumble back the way I expected to. I stand there, pinned to the spot, and drown in the full force of his fury. Maybe I deserve it; maybe I don't. It's hard for me to think when his words keep swirling in my head like a tidal wave.

I swallow hard and try to find my bearings. "You've heard my condition," I say, sticking to my guns, because they're all I have keeping me upright. "And I'm not compromising on it."

His face passes through half a dozen emotions. Most of them don't have names. I see them in the patterns of tension across his lips, the storms in his eyes, the way he swallows and breathes and consumes every spare bit of oxygen in the room.

Then, at last, he sighs. "For the moment, I will accept that." It might be a short-lived victory, but I take it anyway. "We'll leave tomorrow morning."

"No."

"No?"

"I have goodbyes to say in this town before I leave. I need more time."

He doesn't look happy. "You don't have friends here, Taylor."

"I have Mabel," I snap. "And Callan."

His eyes narrow, but he doesn't say anything. "Fine," he huffs, heading for the door. "You have two more nights. Then we're leaving."

I let loose a sigh of relief, but it's not even halfway through my lips before he stops and whirls back around.

"By the way," he says, looming huge in the threshold, "if your goodbye with Callan involves any physical contact, I'm going to tear his tongue out through his throat. That's *my* condition."

Hearing the jealous threat shouldn't be so satisfying. And yet…

Fuck.

Me.

15

TAYLOR

Mabel is sprawled out across my bed, eating a slice of homemade pizza from the open box I'm ignoring while I pack.

She's supposed to be helping me get ready to leave. But she seems more content to just "supervise." Which, in Mabel's world, means talking smack.

"I wish you'd told me all of this before," she remarks, slurping up a strand of cheese. "I mean, really, you're way more interesting than I thought."

"Gee, thanks." I roll up an old sweater that I decide is too nostalgic to donate.

"I'm just saying, I could have provided you with insight. Advice. Encouragement."

"You would have told me to go back home, tell my sister the truth, and face my fears head-on."

Mabel considers that for a moment. "Hm. That does sound like the kind of advice I would give."

In another world, to anyone not me, so would I.

"That's because you are honest to a fault. And you'd never *dream* of hiding something, no matter how painful it was." I sigh. "Unfortunately, I'm not that brave."

Mabel licks her fingers clean and moves the pizza box to my bedside table. Then she dusts off the front of her silky blouse before fixing me with a pointed look.

"You realize I wasn't always that way, right? It took me a few decades before I perfected the art of honesty. I lost friendships because of it, family members, even a couple of husbands. But in the end, I get to live my most authentic life, on my own terms. You can't put a price on that, darlin'."

"You don't have siblings you're close to," I point out, turning back to my wardrobe. "You don't understand."

"You're overcomplicating everything, as usual," Mabel insists. "There's only one question you need to ask yourself."

"And what's that?" I finally abandon my packing altogether and sit cross-legged on the floor in front of her. She's distracting me so I might as well take a break.

"Do you love him?"

"Mabel."

"I'm a straight shooter, honey. You know that. Do you love him?"

"He's my brother-in-law." Cue the nausea.

"Doesn't answer my question."

"I have…complicated feelings for him."

"Sounds a lot like love from where I'm standin'." She grins at me. "Not that I can blame you! The man is sin personified. Reminds me of a better-looking version of my third husband. The man was boring as hell, but he could fuck like a stallion."

I roll my eyes. "I'm shocked it didn't work out."

She laughs. "Point is, sweetheart, you just gotta do what feels right in the moment. And I wanted to be Mrs. Alexander Hershwig more than anything else at that point in my life."

"So you don't regret the marriage?"

"Not even when I walked in on him with the next-door neighbor."

I sigh. "You really have lived."

"Sure have. You should try it sometime."

I smile and ignore the all-too-familiar jab. "I'm gonna miss you, Mabel."

"Don't say that like we're never gonna see each other again. You own a phone, don't you?"

I frown. "You never answer your phone."

"Only because I'm scared it's gonna be an ex. I'll text you."

I laugh. "You better."

Mabel sits up straighter and takes my hands in hers. "Listen, Taylor: I've felt maternal exactly two times in my life. The day of my twelfth birthday, when I was gifted a baby turtle. And the day you walked into my diner and asked me for a job. As I recall, you told me you'd be the best damn waitress I could ever want."

"Did I live up to the hype?"

"Not even a bit. You're a shit waitress. But," she adds with a grin, "you're a kind soul."

I'm torn between wanting to laugh and wanting to cry. In the end, I do neither. I just smile and squeeze her fingers. "I think I'm supposed to say thank you here. Not totally sure, to be honest."

Her bracelets jangle as she strokes a loose lock of hair from my face with tender fingers. "The point I'm trying to make is, I don't make a habit of telling folks what to do. But that's because, with most people, I don't usually care enough about them to worry about how their lives will turn out. But you... I want you to be happy. And sometimes, that means being a little selfish."

I close my eyes. "Ilarion told me not to think too far ahead. He says we need to take one day at a time."

"Smart *and* sexy. If only I were twenty years younger."

I smile. "He's married."

She tilts her head and peers at me. "Is he, though?" The way she says it sounds like she actually doubts the fact. But then she shrugs. "Well, never stopped me before."

I shake my head and get to my feet. "You realize you're supposed to be helping me, right?"

"I just did." She wipes her hands together and gives me another shrug paired with a rather maternal sigh. "Not my fault you're probably not gonna take my advice." She walks over to the shelf adjacent to my bed and picks up the snow globe that I've carried with me like a memory capsule all these years. It's not an accident that it's one of the last things left to pack. Along with Adam's photograph in the living room, it's the first item out of my bags and the final one in. "This thing is gorgeous. Where'd you get it?"

"Oh, um…at this shop…somewhere…"

Mabel turns to me pointedly. "Is it from him?"

I curse myself internally. "No. I mean, sort of. He never actually gave it to me."

"You nicked it? My girl! You're more like me than you're willing to admit."

"I wasn't really thinking straight," I admit. "We'd just got word that Cee was awake and Dad was back. And I'd spent most of the day sleeping with my sister's fiancé. I guess I knew that we'd never have that again. So…I took it."

"See?"

"See what?"

"No woman takes a keepsake like this unless it's love."

"Or maybe I'm just an undiagnosed kleptomaniac."

"Also possible." Mabel laughs as she examines the snow globe carefully. Then she passes it to me. "Safe to say, this isn't going to charity. Unless you wanna leave it with me…?"

She's testing me. But I can't bring myself to pretend like that snow globe doesn't mean the world to me. In any case, I'm okay with exposing myself to Mabel. She's the one person in the world I know won't judge me.

I take the snow globe from her with a delicate grasp and nestle it carefully between sweaters in my suitcase. Then I sink to a seat on the floor.

Muffled through the wall, we can hear the sounds of Adam and Dad negotiating which books he can bring with him.

"Does he know what's happening?" Mabel asks.

I shake my head and shrug at the same time. "It's hard to say. I mean, I've talked to him about it, but it's a lot to ask him to grasp the concept that we're not coming back here. It was easier when he was a baby."

"I'm gonna miss that little rugrat," she sighs.

Her words hit me harder than both of us expect. My bottom lip starts to tremble, and suddenly, before I know it, I'm crying.

"Oh, honey." Mabel gathers me up in her arms and leads me to the bed. "Honey, c'mon now."

I mean to say, "I'm just overwhelmed," but what I actually say is, "I miss my mom."

Mabel nods and presses my head to her chest as she holds me close. I close my eyes and try to think of Mom. It's shocking how hard it is to remember some days. Toward the end, she smelled like sickness and sanitizer. But before then, long before then, it was caramel. I used to put my head down in her lap and she would run her fingers through my hair. She'd kiss my forehead and tell me everything was going to be okay. It was impossible not to believe her.

When I finally pull back, my vision is foggy and my cheeks are wet. "I'm sorry. It's been a long time since I cried about her."

"Never apologize for your tears." Mabel squeezes my hand. "I remember when I lost my mother. She was a mean old snake, but still. It feels a bit like you've lost your training wheels, and suddenly, you're expected to ride on your own without any help. And the handlebars are falling off. And also, the whole bike is on fire."

I snort a snotty laugh. "That's pretty spot-on."

"'Course it is. I've never been wrong yet." Mabel smiles. "You know what helps?" She waits a beat, then finishes, "Talking about her."

"I tried. I *do* try. But Dad gets really upset whenever she comes up. So I mostly just stopped trying. I guess it took too much out of me to try to get him to open up. And if he won't talk about it…there's only one person left who loved her like I did."

"Your sister," Mabel supplies.

I nod. "She was there. She's always been there. That's what family does. That's why I'm doing this."

She sighs and rubs her eyes with the heel of her hand. "It's your bed, honey," is all she says. "You're the one who's got to lie in it."

16

TAYLOR

I hoist Adam onto my hip and spin around the room with him. He walked in on me halfway in the middle of getting dressed, so I'm managing this in just my shorts and bra.

"Blech," I groan. "Adam, baby, I'm getting dizzy."

"One more time, Mama!" he squeals.

"Fine, fine, you little monster," I tease breathlessly, adjusting my hold on him and circling on the spot. "Three, two, one… blast off!"

I spin faster and faster until we collapse back onto the bed. Adam laughs hysterically, his little hands clinging to my neck. I catch my breath and stare up at the ceiling while he wriggles his way under my arm.

"Will you still spin me when I'm all grown up?" he asks.

I laugh. "Oh, boy. You'll be much taller then. *You* might have to spin *me*."

"Will I get to be as tall as Uncle Illy?" Adam asks.

It's alarming how easily and often Ilarion's name flies out of his lips. It's been two days since Ilarion crash-landed in Adam's life, but you'd think they've known each other for years.

"I don't know, sweetheart," I mumble. "Maybe."

"I hope so. Then I'll be able to touch the sky."

I poke him in the side until he giggles. "We just took a rocket ship into space. We're way past the sky."

With a wince, I push myself back to my feet. "Where are you going, Mama?" Adam protests.

"To see a friend."

"But you don't have any friends!" He shoots me a shit-eating grin, but when I lunge for him, he cackles and races out of the room, leaving a trail of gleeful shrieks in his wake.

My smile fades as soon as he's gone. That's par for the course these days. Adam's grin is as bright as ever. It's the world around it that seems increasingly bleak.

I strip off the shorts and replace them with baggy high-waisted pants and a crop top from my college days. Then I comb my hair out and grab my bag on the way downstairs.

I find Dad and Adam in the living room, sorting through the last of our boxes. Well, Dad is; Adam is mostly just bouncing between the chair and the sofa.

"I won't be more than a few hours, okay? You boys be good for me."

Dad glances over, his thinning hair plastered with sweat to his scalp. "I'm surprised you wanted to give him a special goodbye. I didn't think he was very important to you."

Was it that obvious?

I don't meet his eyes. "I'll be back soon." I throw Adam a flying kiss and then I leave the house.

On my way out of the door, I check around to see if anyone is following me, but I don't notice any suspicious cars or strangers on my tail. Of course, that doesn't mean Ilarion hasn't assigned someone to shadow me; it just means I can't see them.

Alec was technically my first relationship, but since it was so short-lived, I never really count him. It feels unbalanced, though, given how much of an impact that whole ordeal made on my psyche. To be fair, that has more to do with Celine than the relationship. If I don't count him as a boyfriend, maybe I can erase the fact that he ever was anything to us. And then I can forget the pain Cee endured.

For most of my brief foray into college, I didn't have boyfriends; I had flings, sporadic and uneventful. It was easier that way. Safer. There was just a small stream—not even a stream, really; more like a trickle—of forgettable men.

Then, of course, there was Ilarion, who was anything but forgettable.

And after Ilarion came Callan. Who is...well, forgettable might be his best quality. Come to think of it, it might be why I chose him in the first place.

He's sitting at a booth by the window when I walk into the café, wearing a button-down shirt and a nervous wince. He stands when he sees me, forcing a smile that doesn't quite reach his eyes. "Hey."

We hug, but it's awkward. I know right away there's not going to be any small talk.

"You're here to break up with me, aren't you?" he blurts.

Bingo.

He's ordered something that looks like an iced tea, but it smells strong. He's two-thirds of the way finished with it. Might explain the subtle slur in his words.

"No," he says before I can respond. "Actually, you can't really break up with me, can you? We were never really together."

I sigh and drop into the open chair. "I'm sorry, Callan."

"It's because of him, isn't it?"

"It is," I acknowledge. "But not in the way that you think."

He frowns. "What do you mean?"

"He's Adam's father."

He nearly chokes on his own tongue. "You're screwing with me now."

"I'm not."

"Taylor." That's it. He just says my name as though that covers all his bases. He stares at me for a moment and then barks out a bubble of dark laughter. "Shit. You're serious."

"Why would I lie?"

"You never talked about him."

"I did my best to avoid it." I peek out the window, aware of how harsh that sounded. A few dusty cars sit parked outside the café on the opposite end of the street, but I can't spot Ilarion in any of them. "I've spent a lot of time burying the past."

Callan plummets down into his seat so hard that the wood squeals in protest. "So you're back together with him. Just like that." His voice is dead and flat.

This time, I'm the one who almost chokes on my tongue. "Excuse me?"

He just raises his brows. "Oh, come on, Taylor. You don't expect me to believe that your relationship with him is platonic, right? Because any idiot can see through that. I hope you don't actually think I'm *that* stupid."

Goosebumps erupt on my forearms. First, Mabel; now, Callan. Everybody seems to want the exact thing I'm trying to run from.

"It's…complicated."

"I hate when people say that," he grumbles. "It just means that they don't want to tell you the story."

"In this case, it's true."

He waves his hand in a silent *whatever.* "He seems like an asshole, by the way."

I chuckle miserably. "Oh, he is."

"And you love him because…?"

I grab the salt and pepper shaker set in the middle of the table and start playing with them. They're ceramic figurines, designed to look like two people hugging. I start pulling them apart and then clicking them back together just so I can do something with my hands. In my head, I sing-song in a childish little voice, *He loves me... He loves me not... You love him... You love him not...* as the figures click and clack, running toward each other and away from each other again and again.

"Let me guess," Callan says when I don't answer his question right away. "'It's complicated'?"

I look up at him. The hurt in his eyes is obvious. I can't say that I blame him. He put in the time and effort. He was more patient with me than any other man would have been.

I owe him something more than this.

"I met him at a time in my life when I was trying to find myself," I explain haltingly. "Purely by chance. I was trying to find a little independence, a little bravery. I felt like I was screaming, and no one could hear me. But…he did."

"He did."

I nod. "Then, a few months later, I discovered he was engaged to my sister."

His eyes widen. "Fuck."

"Yeah," I say with a grim nod. "My words exactly."

"And your sister…?"

"Had no clue—*has* no clue—that he and I, you know… What happened between us happened before she and Ilarion got together. And he didn't even know she was my sister, or vice versa. So I thought that telling her would be cruel."

"Except that you still love him, and clearly, he feels the same." Callan leans back in his seat and blows out a shocked breath. "Honestly, Taylor, it seems to me that, given those circumstances, *not* telling her is crueler."

Guilt chips at the knot in my gut. *What is it today with people and honesty?* Better question: *What's with me and lying?*

"Haven't you ever kept a secret to protect someone?" I protest.

"Never one this big," he says with a slow shake of his head. "In my experience, those secrets are never worth keeping, no matter what." He must see the angst on my face, because he leans forward sympathetically. "Sorry. I know it's not for me to try to tell you how to live your life. I just…I care about you, Taylor."

My stomach twists with guilt. "I know. And I'm so sorry about…shit, about everything."

He shrugs and leans back against his seat. "The truth is, I knew from the beginning that your heart wasn't really in it. I mean, it took you months to say yes to a date with me. You ducked the first time I tried to kiss you. The second time, you acted like you were forced to take a bullet."

"That's not true!"

He smiles patiently at me. "Come on. We've been seeing each other for over six months now, and we haven't even slept together. Not that that's required, but…we haven't even come remotely close."

I close my eyes. "So why did you stick around for as long as you did?"

"Because I was hoping to break through your walls. I was hoping you'd fall in love with me, eventually. " His smile softens. "You're worth the wait."

Did he just use the 'L' word? Fuck. "I'm sorry, Callan. I haven't treated you very well."

He chuckles. "I'm a big boy. I'll survive." And then he cocks his head to one side. "Besides—I get it. What brought him back to you. It's not easy to lose you, and I barely had you to begin with. I can only imagine what that guy's been through all these years."

I reach out and take his hand. Callan is a good guy. He's handsome, thoughtful, and sweet. But he's right: he never stood a chance. It makes me question whether my decision to go back is the right one. It's been hard enough getting through the day when I didn't see Ilarion all the time. But now…?

Now, not only will I have to see him a lot—I'll have to pretend that seeing him isn't my own personal hell.

"You don't have to stay," Callan offers. "I'm just gonna get something to eat and go home myself."

"Right. Yeah. Okay. I do have a lot of packing to do."

"Packing?"

"We're moving," I explain. "Tomorrow."

He pulls his hand from mine. "What, are you serious?

I nod. "Time for me to go back. Face my sister."

"Did he convince you to do that?"

"It was a team effort, to be honest. Him and Mabel and you and everyone else kinda shoving me out of the door."

That way lies happiness, they all seem to be screaming, jabbing insistent fingers in the direction of Zakharov House. *That way lies your future.*

Personally, I doubt it.

He walks me out of the café, then turns to me on the street. "One last request. Can I give you a hug goodbye?"

It's such a simple request and still, I want to say no. Maybe that's the reason my face drops, and Callan nods with resignation. "You really fell hard, huh?"

"Callan…"

"You don't have to say anything," he assures me with a smile. "Never mind. It's okay."

"No, I just—You're—Yes. I can give you a hug goodbye."

He opens up his arms and I step in. But before I can even make contact, a harsh voice drops between us like a guillotine.

"Back away from her. Now."

Callan drops his hands immediately and turns to face Ilarion. The man towers over both of us on the street, his hooded eyes boring holes through Callan's skull.

Where did he even come from?

17

ILARION

I'm watching Callan await Taylor's arrival in the café when my phone vibrates. A three-way call from my sister and second-in-command.

Dima doesn't bother with hellos. "Zane is dead," he informs me.

I freeze. "The detective?"

"The creepy little fuck you hired to sniff out Archie, yes," Mila confirms. "We found him dumped a few miles from our northern safehouse with a bullet in the back of his head. We're pretty sure the Bellasios know about that location."

"Fuck," I snarl. "That means Zane had him. He found the fucker."

"We have reason to believe that he might have found Gregor, not Benedict, but still. Same thing. You find one, you find the other."

That deepens my frown. "Explain."

Mila clears her throat and launches into it. "A Zakharov scout in the territory reported a sighting of Gregor last night at a local strip club. Dima and I spoke to the girls who worked the shift, and two of them confirmed seeing him there. It lines up with the timing of us finding Zane's body. Seems like he showed up around midnight, paid two dancers for the night in a private room, then dipped out around four in the morning. He must've run across Zane sometime after that."

"Fuck," I growl, pacing in circles around the small clearing where I'm waiting while I shoot glances over at the café. Callan hasn't moved. "Fuck! That means we were close. And now, we're back to where we started."

"These Bellasio fucks can't stay ghosts forever."

"We've been saying that for years, Dima!" I peel my phone away from my face to see another call coming through. I decline it immediately.

"Well, you've found the old man now," Mila points out. "Has he coughed up any information?"

"Not yet, but I haven't really broached the subject. I can't afford to spook him now. Once he's in my territory, on my property, it'll be easier to get information out of him."

"You'll also be under the watchful eye of both his daughters," Mila observes dryly. "Surely that will make things easier."

"I can handle the Theron women."

"Right. Famous last words." Mila cackles. "Have you called Celine, by the way? She told me that she's been trying to get through to you since yesterday."

Speak of the devil. I wince as another call comes in. I decline it a second time. "She's calling me now. I'll talk to her later."

"Not sure that's the smartest plan, but you do you, brother."

I grind my teeth. "We need to resolve the Bellasio threat fast," I growl. "Especially with Taylor and Adam coming home."

"Shit. Forgot about the little runt. I can't believe it's actually happening," Dima breathes. "What's he like?"

"You'll see. He's a great kid."

"Despite half his genes coming from a fuckhead," Mila mutters. "How's your baby mama?"

There's a certain terseness in her sarcasm when she mentions Taylor. I never expected Mila to take Taylor's departure so personally, but apparently, I'd underestimated the connection the two of them made. Mila has always been one to hold onto a grudge.

"She's...fine." When I glance up again, I see she's arrived and is seated across from Callan. He's leaning toward her desperately. Even from here, I can see the puppy-dog earnestness in his eyes.

Every time it looks like he might reach out, I have to swallow angry bile to keep myself from walking over to the café and breaking every finger he's daring to touch her with.

"When are you coming home?" Mila asks.

"Tomorrow."

"Good, because we really need to sort this—"

"I got it, Mila," I snap. "I'll see you tomorrow. And when we get back, take it easy on Taylor, okay?"

There's silence on the other line for a moment. "I don't think it's fair for you to ask me that."

"I wasn't asking anything; I was ordering. I'll see you tomorrow." Scowling, I hang up and check to see I've now missed a grand total of four calls from Celine.

I peek again towards the café, but Callan and Taylor are still talking. So I bite the bullet and call her back.

"Where have you been?" Celine asks the moment the line connects. "I asked Mila and Dima, but neither one of them told me anything. Just that you were off chasing a lead."

"I was. I mean, I am."

"For God's sake, Ilarion, I was worried."

My eyes are fixed on Taylor. She's wearing her hair down today, exactly the way I like it. But if her hair was up, I'd find something to like about that, too.

Focus, asshole.

"I've been…caught up over here."

"Where is 'here', exactly? I hate that I'm never kept in the loop."

"We've discussed this, Celine. You said you preferred it that way."

"I thought I did," she admits. "Sometimes, I still do. Ugh…I don't know what I want." She's silent for a moment. "There's a gala coming up that I need you to be there for."

"Fine. I'll be there. Anything else?"

She sighs. "I hate this. Every time I call you, I feel like you're distracted or trying to get me off the phone as fast as you can. Don't think I don't notice. I'm not stupid, Ilarion."

"It's just been a rough couple of weeks with work."

"It can't be *that* rough. Benedict has been quiet, hasn't he?"

"Doesn't mean he's not out there, plotting his revenge." She pauses, and I can feel the unease seeping through the phone. I curse myself internally. "That was stupid of me to say."

"It's okay."

"No, it's not. You're safe, Celine. You know that, right? I'm not going to let anything happen to you."

"Too much has happened already."

For the millionth time, I berate myself for the choices I made. Things would have been so much easier if I hadn't let my dick make the decisions. This could have remained simply business, the way it should have been.

Instead, it's all a fucking disaster.

"Can we…can we please talk when you get back home?" she asks. "I feel like we haven't actually talked in a while."

Fuck me. I know what she wants to talk about, and the thought makes me want to postpone returning home indefinitely. "Yeah. We can talk."

I say my goodbyes and hang up.

When the line is dead, I rest my forehead against the trunk of the tree. "Fuck me," I mutter under my breath.

I stay there, breathing softly for a moment, before the chime of the café door draws my attention. When I look up, I see Taylor and Callan emerging.

I'm happy that their meeting didn't last long, but my happiness is cut short the moment I see him going in for a hug.

A huge part of me realizes how irrational I'm being. I have no right to crash her goodbye. I have even less right to tell her whom she can and can't be near. But the rational part of my brain feels like it's on hiatus at the moment. The only thing that's working is the primal side of me.

The side that's saying another man has his hands on what is mine.

I cross the street in a few quick strides. Neither of them notices me coming.

"Back away from her. Now."

He drops his hands immediately and they both turn to me. He looks bewildered. She shifts from surprised to suspicious. I can't blame her.

"Time to say goodbye, Callan. A distant wave will do."

Of course, her claws come right out. She steps in front of Callan as though she's protecting him and puffs herself up. "What the hell do you think you're doing?"

I give her a condescending sigh. "Shouldn't you be at home packing?"

"Don't you have someone else to micromanage?" She throws her hands in the air with a huff and then crosses her arms over her chest. I do my damned hardest to ignore how that pushes her breasts together above the low cut of her blouse. "Get lost, Ilarion."

I shake my head. "Can't do that. What I *can* do is stand right here and wait until you're done with him." I lean in. "Though something tells me you were done with him a while ago."

"You—"

"It's okay!" Callan cuts in. "It's okay. I don't want to make trouble. We've said our goodbyes; it's all good. I'm just gonna head home."

She looks like she wants to stop him, to soothe his bruised ego...but she also looks like she's relieved he's finally leaving. "This isn't how I wanted it to end," she mutters quietly.

His expression sours. "Come on, Tay. He's right. Things between us ended before they even started. I'm not about to stick around just so you can use me to make him jealous. At least let me leave with my pride intact. You owe me that much."

I feel the urge to point out to him that she doesn't owe him a fucking iota of consideration, but I bite my tongue. I'll bite it until it bleeds if that means allowing Taylor to start making better decisions—like ditching this Nice Guy who clearly doesn't respect her boundaries as much as he claims to. He doesn't offer me a glance as he turns and walks away, his shoulders slumping as he rounds the corner.

A more sensitive man might have just kept his mouth shut. But not me. "Aww. Poor fella."

She whirls around, her green eyes shining with renewed fury. "Fuck right the hell off, you...you pompous ass!"

And all I can think is—*I've missed this.*

18

TAYLOR

"I had things handled."

Ilarion rolls his eyes. "He was about to ask you for some panties to sniff and a lock of your hair to wear around his neck. I saved you from becoming the newest pet locked up in his basement."

"You're jealous."

"And you're welcome."

My palms itch with the desire to slap him. "Every time you open your mouth, I'm reminded of why I left. You didn't have to step in. After the way I treated him, I could handle—"

"How did you treat him?"

I frown. "Mind your own business."

He smiles that wolfish grin that never touches his eyes. "I think we both know that's never going to happen."

I pivot on my heel and start marching away. "I'm going home."

"My car is parked right down the street. I'll drive you."

"I prefer to walk."

"It's a thirty-minute walk to your house."

"That's thirty minutes without you hovering over me. Sounds like a dream."

It's annoying how easily he keeps pace with me. My breath is already coming in drags, and he just looks like he's strolling along casually.

"Someone's very defensive about Mr. Nice Guy—"

"His name is *Callan*. You know that."

He ignores my correction. "Might that be because you led him on, and you're just taking out your anger on me?"

I come to a screeching halt. "I'm taking my anger out on you because you deserve it. What do you want from me, Ilarion? This is already exhausting."

"What I want is to know, why *did* you lead him on? As much as I despise saying this, you're free to make your own decisions. I want to know why you made *this* one."

"It w-wasn't like I planned to lead him on," I stutter. "It just sorta…happened. I was lonely. I needed adult company outside of work and home, and…I don't know. I was hoping my feelings would catch up with his. I wanted to try my hand at a relationship. Someone without strings attached. But I just couldn't bring myself to take the next step. All I could think about was—"

I stop short, teetering on the cusp of saying something I won't be able to take back. It's his eyes that do it to me. Five years since they first tore me open and they still have the same scalpel's edge effect whenever he deigns to use it.

"About what?" he presses.

Just to be safe, I quit looking directly at him and start walking again.

I can hear him chuckling behind me. "I'm impressed at your willingness to keep this up, Taylor."

"There's nothing to keep up," I snap back over my shoulder. "I left you and I built something here. You're the one who's decided to drag me back to a life I never wanted in the first place."

"Don't you ever get tired of your own bullshit?"

"Stop talking to me!"

I yell so loud that two people turn to me in shock as they pass by me on the street. "Sorry, Mrs. Melman," I say, realizing belatedly that it's my next-door neighbor. "Fuck," I hiss. "Look at what you've reduced me to. I'm becoming the neighborhood crazy lady."

"Oh, dear, what ever will the neighbors think?" he drawls with exaggerated sarcasm. He stops next to a sleek black sedan and taps the hood. "This is me."

I stay rooted in place. "I'm not going home with you."

"Fucking hell, Taylor. This is not that big of a deal. Get in the damn car. God knows it's not the first time you've climbed in."

I swallow back the flush that sparks in me and scowl at him. "Make me."

Then I put my back on him once again and resume my march home.

He trails along next to me at a mile or two an hour, trawling me without giving a damn about the traffic piling up in his wake.

"You're blocking people," I scold when his passenger window rolls down.

"You could solve it. Get in."

I flip him the bird and walk a little faster. Now that I've taken a stand, I can't back down without looking like I'm surrendering. And if I surrender to him now, I will spend the rest of my life surrendering to Ilarion Zakharov again and again.

No. Fuck that.

Fuck him, too.

I hold my chin high and keep putting one foot in front of the other.

Once we're out of the town center, I relax a little. Other cars are few and far between and there's no honking adding to my already-frayed nerves.

Just Ilarion in his stupid car.

"You're really going to follow me like this the whole way back?"

"I just want to see how long you'll keep this up."

"Bet."

"Fucking hell," he snarls again, and the vehicle comes to a not-so-abrupt stop. I hear a door slam and the next thing I know, he's right there, in my face, in my space, working his way beneath my skin.

"I forgot how infuriating you are." His breath is minty sweet in my nostrils. "I should have disciplined you better when you were with me."

My eyes almost pop out of their sockets. "I'm not a dog that you can train to come to heel," I growl, stabbing my finger into his chest. "You're not my master!"

I go to bypass him, but he slides over and I collide with his rock-solid chest. He's so unyielding that I'd go tumbling off the curb if he didn't catch me by the elbow. He lets go as soon as I'm steady again, but the afterburn of his fingers on my bare skin linger.

"Maybe that needs to change. Because even now, when it's so fucking obvious I've lived in your head and your heart for the last five years, you're trying to lie and lie and lie until you're blue in the face. Wake the hell up, Taylor."

My whole body is tingling. It's been a long time since I've experienced this sensation. This curious sense of breathlessness, of weightlessness. Of terrifying elation. "Or maybe that's just what you want to believe."

He grabs me around the waist and shoves me backwards, coming along with me. My ass lands on the hood of his car and I find myself gazing up into those stormy eyes, feeling as though I—we—are on the edge of a precipice.

Dreading the fall.

But dying for it, too.

Maybe even literally.

"Look at me, Taylor," he orders in a low voice that reverberates through my body. "Do I look like that dumbass you were kinda-sorta pretending to date? Do I look like the kind of man who tells himself lies and half-truths to get through the day?"

"I don't know what you tell yourself. I don't know you anymore."

"Yes, *tigrionok,* you do."

I flinch. Considering he's pressed up against me, I know he can feel it. A car zooms by, and I can hear catcalls and wolf whistles as the back windows are rolled down.

"Get it, girl!"

"Awooooga!"

My cheeks flush with heat. With my current position on the hood of his car, and his position between my legs...well, it doesn't exactly look innocent.

"Get off me." It comes out as weak as it feels.

"Not until you tell me one honest thing."

"What makes you think you deserve my honesty?"

He glowers at me, no doubt loading another scathing insult into the chamber, when his phone starts to vibrate in his pocket. When he plucks it out, I catch a glimpse of the name on the screen.

Celine.

My blood runs cold. *Celine.* It's a reminder of how much I'm risking going back. How much I'm risking every time I let him inside my orbit.

How much I'm risking *right the fuck now.*

Instead of answering, he turns his phone off. It dies mid-buzz. I place my hands on his chest—his impossibly hard, unfairly-sculpted chest—and push him away. I'm still holding out hope of finding the last of my dignity somewhere between here and home.

But before I go…

"Why didn't you answer?" I ask.

His jaw twitches dangerously. "We're in the middle of something."

"No," I retort, "we're not in the middle of anything. She's your wife. You should pick up her calls."

"Are you telling me what to do?"

"That's the pot calling the kettle black if I've ever heard it. Telling me what to do is your favorite hobby."

"Only to save you from yourself!"

"I was doing perfectly fine before I met you! You…you ruined me. You ruined *everything.*"

A shadow flickers across his eyes and he turns away from me. "I didn't do anything you didn't ask me to do," he rasps, so softly I almost miss it.

I can only shake my head in disgust. "I wouldn't expect you to understand," I say. "You've never done anything for anyone else. You destroy people's lives and call it altruism. You aren't God, Ilarion. We aren't little insects in your ant farm."

When he turns back to me, his eyes are simmering with a deep anger that fails to hide the pain beneath them. "You don't know a goddamn thing about me. You don't even know how I became what I am. Or how I happily let my father die."

I take a step back, shocked by the force of his words. He's mentioned his father a handful of times, but nothing specific. I knew that he didn't have the best childhood, I knew his father wasn't exactly warm and loving, but I always thought that there was a certain amount of respect there. A begrudging sense of responsibility.

Maybe I was wrong.

"W-what do you mean?" I ask.

He bitterly scoffs. "Forget it."

He looks like he regrets what he's said. In fact, he looks like he wants to get the hell away from me as fast as possible. He walks over to the car and slides inside.

"I'll meet you back at the house," he says in a hard voice. "I'll get Adam packed."

He doesn't ask me to get in again. He just revs the engine and, seconds later, he's disappeared down the road. I stand there for a minute, staring after him, wondering how he managed to hide those demons from me for so long. I never even suspected that his relationship with his father hid something so dark.

And yet I remember Mila's story and the little she told me about what happened to him.

I should have paid closer attention. Not everyone offers up their pain like you deserve to hear it. I've been so wrapped up in my own nightmares that I haven't asked the right questions.

But I am going to pay attention this time.

For *all* our sakes.

19

ILARION

I don't know why I brought up that son of a bitch. I've buried him so deep at this point. He ought to stay buried.

But then again, the nightmares have been popping a little more frequently lately. The last time this happened, we'd only just put his coffin in the earth. Mila had become a hermit. She stayed locked up in her room at all hours with the blinds drawn, and it wasn't like I could talk to just anyone about the things clawing at my mind every night when I closed my eyes.

Well, maybe I could've talked to Dima, but I wanted to protect him from what had happened. From what we'd done. If I told him the truth of it all, he'd have to carry the weight of it around with him for the rest of his life.

He would have never looked at Mila the same way again.

It just seemed unnecessarily cruel.

The nightmares are always the same. Not even really a nightmare—just a memory that plays on an endless loop, and every time it starts over again, the details are more grotesque. Eyes bigger. Voices wilder. Emotions heightened.

"You handled the deal well," Dad told me after my first solo effort at closing an important arms deal. "I spoke to Don Hernandez afterward and he was very satisfied." Very satisfied. *I remember those words only because of how he said them, like it was the absolute bare minimum. "You impressed him."*

"I wasn't trying to."

"Good. That's precisely why you did. I may have been wrong about you."

I raised my brows, refusing to take the bait. Any answer he'd give would just hurt. But he answered the unasked question anyway. "I worried that you were too soft to take over for me. I thought you'd be too weak."

I cringed. "I've been watching you for a long time. I've been a part of the Bratva for a long time."

He blinked languidly. I remember that specifically, because his eyes were the same blue hue as mine, and I'd always hated that. I wanted to rip those parts out and replace them with new ones that wouldn't always remind me that his blood ran in my veins. That he was part of me and I couldn't get rid of him if I tried.

"The way you used to be, the way you sometimes still are with your sister...it had me worried."

"What do you mean?"

"I used to find her in your room at night."

I frowned. "That was when we were kids. When she was scared."

"You should have kicked her the fuck out."

I gritted my teeth. "As I remember correctly, you would wake us both up and drag her back to her room and lock the door. Seems like you did the job for me."

"It had to be done."

"Why? She didn't have a mother to go to. And she knew better than to run to you."

"My children shouldn't need anyone," he snarled ferally. "Needing others is a weakness that must be eliminated. True strength is being an island that exists on its own."

"No Bratva can function that way. You need men."

"No." He pounded a fist on his desk and pointed at me. "They need me. Every man is expendable. I can replace them with others."

"Some fucking philosophy," I'd growled, gnashing my teeth. "You're every child's dream father."

He fixed me with those blue eyes that looked too much like mine and smiled in a way that made my skin crawl. "That 'philosophy' made you a man. It made Mila strong, too. What you see as kindness will only hold you back. To be pakhan*, you must be ruthless. You must take what you want, no matter what it is."*

I always wake up with those words ringing in my head and my hand tightening around an invisible gun.

You must take what you want.

It got worse after I found out what he'd really been up to. What he did to Mila. They were a reminder of my failure, of my weakness. The son of a bitch was wrong.

Kindness is not weakness.

Ignorance is.

I pull up outside the little white bungalow housing my son. White picket fence, patchy yard, sunflowers on the windowsill—it looks too quaint and quiet to be real. I know better than anyone that this is not real life.

Real life *bleeds*.

Out front, Archie and Adam are tossing a ball around. A rush of resentment blinds me for a moment.

How is it possible that the man who betrayed me and my Bratva is the one to experience all the moments that I missed out on with my son?

I park and step out of my car. The moment I shut the door, Adam looks up and sees me. "Uncle Illy!"

The name is both a gut punch and a tug on my heart. I want so badly for him to call me something, anything, that tells me he knows who I really am to him. I want to rip the veil from his eyes, to pick him up and shake him and bellow, "I am your father!" again and again until the whole fucking world hears it.

The boy hugs me around the waist. I pat him on the back a few times before he relinquishes me and goes chasing after the ball again.

Over his shoulder, Archie offers up a smile, but it's for Adam's benefit, not mine. His eyes flick toward my car and then down the street. "Taylor's not here."

"I know. She insisted on walking."

The ball rolls to my feet. I stoop down and pick it up, then toss it to the old man. He catches it with a start, looking up at me wide-eyed like I just threw a bomb in his lap.

"Grandpa! Pass it here!" Adam takes up a stance. Archie swallows, then reluctantly underhands the ball over to the boy.

We end up in a skewed triangle, circulating the ball between us. I wonder if the kid is picking up on anything. If he senses the tensions rippling between us. I wonder if Archie feels as weird about this as I do—a Russian mob boss playing catch with a traitor.

The game lasts maybe two more minutes before Adam grows bored. "Can I go get my truck? I wanna play in the sandbox."

"Sure," Archie says. "I'll drag the sandbox out."

Adam ducks inside and Archie ambles over to the corner of the yard where a large rectangular trough sits. He bends over and tries to drag it out from the sideyard, but it barely budges. I watch for a moment as he strains. He looks frail. With a sigh, I bite back my resentment and stride forward to help him.

My father's voice echoes in the back of my head. *Soft. Weak. Fucking pathetic.*

If he knew that I was breaking bread with a traitor, he'd be rolling in his grave. The man never even asked questions when someone was accused of betrayal. He always punished first and asked questions later, or never.

It strikes me, very suddenly, that showing Archie mercy would be a giant middle finger to the bastard.

Tempting.

Very. Fucking. Tempting.

"Let me." I grab the edges of the trough and haul it out into the center of the grass for him.

"Thanks," Archie mumbles. When I glance over at him, his face is red with embarrassment, his eyes hooded with something that looks a lot like shame.

"It shocks me, sometimes," he explains sheepishly. "The body just won't do what it's supposed to."

"Age comes for all of us."

He shrugs and drops to a seat on the concrete steps. Adam brushes past him through the front door a moment later. He runs over to the sandbox and dumps an armful of trucks into the trough.

"Uncle Illy, I'm gonna build a city. Watch me, okay?"

"I'm watching."

He climbs into the sand pit and his little face scrunches up with concentration. Mila and I never had sand pits or tire swings growing up. We had martial arts classes and gun training instead. For a long time, we thought we were lucky to be taught those kinds of skills. It made us different. It made us special.

But that was before we realized it was because we were being *groomed*.

I turn my back to Adam and face Archie again. "Are you all packed?"

"Should I be?"

My silent glare is all the answer he needs.

He smiles sadly. "I figured as much; I just had to ask. I suppose you need me close for that inevitable accident, huh?"

I stiffen. He's seeing visions of car crashes and pianos falling off roofs right when he happens to be walking beneath them. Death around every corner.

"It would be easier on them," Archie continues softly. "If I wasn't around, I mean. If there was distance between us before I…disappeared on them."

"You're not staying behind, Archie."

"I wouldn't run."

"Forgive me for not believing you."

He goes silent for a while, his eyes glistening with old regrets. "You want me to come back with you for a reason, don't you?" All I do is look at him, and he nods. "I don't have any information, Ilarion."

"Yes, you do. You have something."

"It's been five years."

"Exactly. Five years and Benedict Bellasio has become a virtual ghost. But I know he's still out there. He still targets my men when we least expect it."

"How many have you lost?"

"Enough to be irritating. Mostly low-level *vors* who were caught on their own." I crack my neck, grimacing as the faces of dead Bratva men float through my mind's eye. "But it's enough to get the message across loud and clear. He didn't disappear with the intention of staying that way; he left in order to come up with a plan, a way to hit back at me."

"And you think I'll be able to help you?" Archie asks uncomfortably.

"You were his rat," I remind him. "The man trusted you—"

"Benedict Bellasio doesn't trust anyone," Archie insists. He almost laughs at the suggestion. "It took me a long time to learn anything significant."

"But eventually, you learned. Someone had to teach you," I point out. "You will know secrets, and those secrets are going to help me zero in on where he's been hiding all this time."

Archie sighs. "I disappeared, too, Ilarion. He must have changed the locks and the passwords that I knew about, just to cover his bases."

"Benedict doesn't have many options left. But neither do I. So you're coming with me."

"You're asking me to dip my toes in again, Ilarion. That's a death sentence."

"Grandpa!" Adam calls. "Look what I made!"

The terror on Archie's face artificially clears away as he smiles at the misshapen sandcastle. He claps his hands. "Well done, kiddo. Amazing."

Adam beams from ear to ear and goes back to his creation.

"You're lucky that kid loves you," I add. Even as I say it, I shake my head in disgust.

Fucking hell. I'm beholden to a kid. Every move I make from this point onward as the leader of the Zakharov Bratva is solely dependent upon this child. *My* child.

Soft. Weak. Fucking pathetic.

Screw it. My father and his advice can get fucked.

Archie nods. "It was my job to protect them," he says softly. "My girls, my grandson. But in the end, they're the ones who always end up saving me. Time and time again."

He's not wrong. Both Celine and Taylor begged for his life, and even though Adam doesn't know it, he has, too. With his innocent love for the only grandfather he's ever known.

At least for that, I can be grateful. The grandfather Adam would have gotten from my side of the family tree would have killed the little boy inside him.

Godfuckingdammit. Yet another thing I owe Archie for.

He shakes his head and pushes himself upright with a groan. "I'll go finish up my packing. Will you watch him?"

I meet his eyes and nod. I'm not sure if it's a gesture of trust or an olive branch or completely meaningless. But either way, it's too little, too late.

And we both know it.

20

TAYLOR

I'm winded by the time I get back to the house. But what really knocks me sideways is the image that awaits me there: Ilarion and Adam, sitting at the sandbox, their heads put together like they're hatching some sort of plan.

Adam doesn't even notice me until my shadow falls over his lopsided sandcastle. "Mama!" he greets happily. "Are we having pizza for dinner?"

I frown in confusion. "Why would we have pizza?"

"Grandpa says it's a special night because we won't be here tomorrow. He says we're leaving the house and we're not coming back."

I crouch down so that I'm at eye level with Adam. "What do you think about that?"

Adam considers it for a moment, then shrugs. I glance at Ilarion, wondering if he's feeling guilty at all for ripping Adam from yet another home. It's what I felt every time we moved towns, and that was before Adam was even aware of things.

"Will you and Grandpa be there?" he asks.

"Of course I'll be there, honey," I say with a surprised laugh. "But you'll have to ask Uncle Illy if Grandpa will be."

The pause that follows is damn near deadly. It's like the invisible drawstrings of the tension between us got pulled to maximum tightness. I can feel my pulse in my throat.

Then: "Of course he will." Ilarion says it lightly enough to be convincing, even to me.

Adam smiles, unaware of the drama roaring all around him. "Does this mean we're going to see Auntie Cee?"

I nod. "Yes, we are."

I try not to glance at Ilarion, but it always feels as if I'm seconds away from looking at him anyway. Like we're two magnets with opposite poles. Like it's inevitable.

And that's what terrifies me.

That, even when I'm mad at him, even when I want to slap him and walk away, I don't *really* want to walk away. I want to walk away just far enough that he runs after me, stops me, and kisses me so hard that I forget how to put one foot in front of the other.

Shivering, I get to my feet and step inside. I don't see Dad in the living room, but he materializes at my door a moment later. "All set?" he asks.

"Not really," I admit. "But I don't have much of a choice."

He walks over and sits down on my bed. He's developed a limp over the last year. Neither one of us knows where it's coming from. I've suggested some physical therapy, but money has been tight and my father is as stubborn as they come.

"It'll be strange, going back."

I'm not sure if he's come to comfort me or if he's come to me for comfort. A little bit like the blind leading the blind here. "I know," I say. "It's going to be weirder seeing Cee again."

"You're going to have to see them together."

I throw him a sharp look. "I'm aware."

"I'm just saying—"

"Dad!" I say firmly, cutting him off.

"I can't just pretend I don't know."

"That conversation happened a long time ago," I remind him. "And I don't… How I felt back then is not how I feel now."

"Oh, honey."

The way he says it, the sympathy in his tone, the pity in his eyes—it all makes me want to cry. It makes me want to turn back the clock and not say all those things I'd told him back when I was still pregnant with Adam and I was terrified of doing it on my own.

Dad found me sobbing on the floor of our new kitchen. My tears fell into the cracks between the tiles and disappeared into the grout like they'd never fallen at all.

"Taylor! What's wrong? Is it the baby?" He sank to his knees in front of me and took my hands. "Do I need to take you to the

hospital?"

"No, it's not the baby..."

"Then what is it?"

Things had been hard for us since we left. The first year of our self-imposed exile was filled with passive-aggressive tension. He was angry with my choices and I was angry with his.

"I...I just miss him."

I hadn't meant to say it out loud, but after the words slipped out, I felt relieved. It felt nice not to have to hold that in anymore.

"Taylor..."

I pulled my hands out from under his. "I don't expect you to care. You hate him."

"I just know the kind of man he is."

"No, you don't," I argued. "He was your boss; you don't actually know anything about him. But he was different with me. He opened up. He could be sweet...kind..."

Dad grimaced. "How could you, Taylor?"

"How could I what?"

"Fall in love with a man like him?" he explained. "Didn't I teach you anything?"

"The only thing you taught me was to be afraid of everyone and everything!" I pulled myself up to my feet. "If you could have locked Cee and I away in a tower, you would have."

"Maybe I should have."

I shook my head and walked around him. "This is your fault."

"Excuse me?"

"He chose her because of you. *But he and I... There was no ulterior motive. When he met me, he didn't know who I was. What we have —what we* had*—it's real."*

"A man like Ilarion can't truly love, Taylor. He would have gotten bored with you eventually. He'll get bored with Celine, too. I tried to make her see that, but—

"She's in love with him, too!" I laughed crazily. The sound was unhinged, even to my own ears. "Isn't it ironic that the man you betrayed is the same man that both your daughters fell for?"

"You're tired," Dad said. "You need to sleep."

"I'm never going to stop loving him, Dad. Does that burn you up inside? Does it make you hate me?"

He looked at me then away, his eyes clouding with sadness. "It just makes me sad. You deserve to love a man who can give you the same love in return. For Ilarion Zakharov, his Bratva, his empire, his legacy will always come first. He will throw you to the wolves before he sacrifices a single iota of what he's built."

"I'm serious." I lean against the pane of my window as I face Dad on the bed. "I *have* moved on from him. You don't have anything to worry about."

He sighs. "I have so many things to worry about that I can't possibly keep them all straight. But at least I get to see Celine again. That's something."

"What do you think she'll be like now?" I ask.

"Different in some ways," he says vaguely. "The same in others."

"Gee, that's helpful. Thanks."

"Has he...talked about her much?"

I think about that phone call from her that he declined. I might have been able to discern something of their relationship if he had just picked up the call. But as it stands, I'm just as in the dark as Dad seems to be.

"He's great with Adam," he says absentmindedly, but he doesn't seem angry about it. "That's a good thing. You should encourage that."

"What are you talking about? Cee can't suspect anything."

"It's more than that." Dad rubs the bridge of his nose. "If Ilarion genuinely loves his son...you have no idea how much power that holds over him. How much power Adam holds over him." He clears his throat and stands up straighter. "You need to allow Ilarion to name him heir."

I scoff. "We are not having this discussion. I said no, and I'm not changing my decision."

He slowly nods. "You've always been stubborn like that."

"I wonder where I get that from."

He laughs sadly. "That's exactly what frightens me the most. It scares me to watch you make the same mistakes I made, Little Bird. You're more like me than either one of us realized."

I pause. Damn it all, he's right.

I've become my father.

And I'm suddenly realizing that, like Dad, going back with Ilarion just might be my death sentence.

21

ILARION

Zakharov House is asleep when we arrive.

I planned it that way on purpose. I wanted to make sure that Adam and Taylor were settled in and I prepared Celine properly before I told her that they were here.

Dima is standing out front with Semyon as we pull up, anxiously plucking at his nails. I park and walk around to pick Adam up. He doesn't so much as stir, apart from a little sigh now and again.

"Hiya, Taylor," Dima says, walking forward to assist Taylor in stepping down from the car. "You look good."

She ignores his outstretched hand. "Hi, Dima. Thanks. You look the same."

I snort without turning around to intervene in their conversation.

"The house looks the same, too," Taylor adds. "Weird. A few things stay the same. Everything else changes."

"I'd say so." Dima inclines his head toward the sleeping Adam. "That your boy?"

"Yeah," Taylor says softly. She reaches over to stroke hair from his forehead. "This is my boy."

Dima opens his mouth to say something else, but then Archie emerges from the car, so he stops mid-sentence and his face flushes. "Well, well. Look what the cat dragged in. You are one lucky son of a bitch, Archie. If it were me, you would've been cold in the dirt already."

"He's off-limits," Taylor asserts, putting herself in Dima's line of sight. "Ilarion promised me that himself."

Dima raises his brows infinitesimally, but his gaze veers to me. "Well, then. I guess all is forgotten and forgiven." His sarcasm is impossible to miss.

"Come on," I growl. "It's late and I want to get Adam into bed." I glance toward Archie. "Semyon will take you to your room. It's been prepared especially for you."

I see Taylor freeze like a fawn in the headlights. She looks up at me and I stare impassively down at her. Then she sighs and her shoulders slump. "Goodnight, Dad. See you tomorrow."

"Goodnight, Little Bird." Archie turns toward me and gazes longingly at Adam. He settles for running his hand down the boy's back. Then he gives us a parting nod and follows the housekeeper down the hall.

Dima fidgets where he stands. "Wait for me in the den," I tell him.

"Got it," Dima mutters. He looks over at Taylor. "It's good to see you again, Tay. We were beginning to lose hope."

"How's Mila?" she asks, as though she can't wait for the morning to find out.

"You know her. Stoic as ever. Pissed at you, though." Then, without further explanation, Dima is gone, disappearing down the corridor.

Taylor doesn't get it yet. She doesn't know the full extent of what Mila has been through, of how precious a friend is to her. Taylor spit on that friendship. It's not the kind of thing Mila is likely to forget.

"Come on," I say, leading her upstairs to another of the guest wings. "Adam's room will be ready soon. Until then, he'll bunk with you."

She doesn't say anything. Not even after I've walked them into their room and set Adam down on the bed.

"The bathroom is fully stocked," I say, turning to her. "But if you need anything, just…"

I trail off when I realize she's not actually listening. She's standing by the bay windows, gazing down at the moonlit lawn. "It's weird," she whispers so softly that I nearly miss the words. "It's so weird to be back here."

"You'll get used to it."

"This is the house where my mother died. That doesn't feel like the kind of thing you just 'get used to.'"

"Taylor…" I reach out and gently touch her arm.

She flinches back as though I've burned her. "I…I'm sorry," she says, her chest rising and falling hard. "I just didn't expect this to be so overwhelming."

This time, I don't give her the chance to flinch away from me. I gather her into my arms and hold her tight. Tight enough that her breaths even out and her shoulders go limp against my chest.

"Ilarion, you need to let me go." But she isn't anywhere close to convincing, and she makes no attempt to push me away. Her body language is saying the opposite. It's calling to me, begging me to hold her harder, telling me to *never* let go.

Her tears soak into my shirt, and still, I hold her. I breathe in her scent, reeling when I realize that it's changed. Now, she smells like baby powder and honey.

"I hate this," she whispers when she finally pushes her face off my chest. "That I still need you." She blinks and a fat tear slips down her cheek. "Tell me I had no choice. Tell me you made me. Tell me I had to come back."

"You had no choice," I murmur. "I would have dragged you back, kicking and screaming. Or just thrown you over my shoulder and carried you the whole way."

She almost smiles. But instead, she drops her hands and steps out of my arms. "This won't happen again."

"What won't?"

"This," she says, gesturing between us. "Me, coming to you for comfort. You, feeling like you need to play the hero and actually give it."

I snort. "I think we both know I'm no hero."

"Isn't that the truth." She smiles sadly. "Goodnight, Ilarion."

"Goodnight, *tigrionok*. Sweet dreams."

22

ILARION

In the den, Dima has worn a deep furrow into the rug with his pacing. He'd rip through it straight to the concrete below if I'd spent any longer upstairs with Taylor.

"Took you long enough. What happened?"

I pause in the doorway and frown. "I don't think you want to ask me that question, *sobrat.*"

And I don't think I want to answer it.

Dima takes a deep breath. "Are you sure you've thought this through? I mean, bringing Taylor back, it's a ticking time bomb waiting to go off. And when it does, it'll blow up your entire life."

I look him in the eye. "Do you promise?"

I turn to the window, picturing myself back in the cabin—just Taylor and me. I'd never had a happy place before that trip. I go back there often. But only in my head.

"What about Celine?"

"I'll tell her tomorrow."

"*What*, precisely, will you tell her tomorrow?"

I continue to stare out my window. I had damn near every blade of grass ripped out and replanted after the Bellasio attack. But in the end, it's still the same garden, still overgrown with the same stubborn memories.

"That I've found her sister and father. Convinced them to come back," I say, turning towards Dima. "I agreed not to tell Celine about Adam's true parentage."

Dima raises his eyebrows. "Fuck. She got to you. Never thought I'd see the day."

I don't like the way he says it. Like it was inevitable. "She didn't convince me of anything. The truth will come out sooner or later. I don't see the harm in giving her a temporary victory now."

To be honest, that quiet drive gave me plenty of time to see the harm in throwing that information in Adam's face while he's still adjusting to his new home. His new life.

His new world in the Bratva.

Dima strokes his beard. "The boy looks exactly like you, you know."

I can't help but be proud of that. It's a stupid thing to be proud of. It's genetics, for fuck's sake, but still—something primal in me growls appreciatively.

"Hm. Hadn't noticed."

Dima snorts in disbelief, but he doesn't press the issue. Instead, he strolls over and slaps me on the back. "Well, congratulations, man! You're a father."

"Shit," I breathe.

Dima laughs. "Terrifying, huh?"

"You have no clue."

"You're gonna crush it."

I shake my head. "I'm more likely to royally fuck it up. But I have Taylor. She'll keep me on my toes. Make sure I'm the kind of father that Adam deserves."

"You're already the kind of father he deserves." He claps me on the back again. "You brought them home. You didn't give up hope."

"I was never going to give up."

"Tell me something I don't know. You're the most stubborn man alive." Chuckling, he saunters away to leave me with my thoughts.

Long after Dima leaves, I sit by my desk listening to the rain hit the roof in a melancholy staccato rhythm. I close my eyes and, just like that, I'm back in the cabin. Back swimming in her intoxicating scent. Back luxuriating in all the possibilities that stretched out before us.

Every time it rains, I think of her. And when the clouds are clear and the skies are dry…

…I find myself praying for a storm.

23

ILARION

I wait until 8:30 AM before I knock on her door. She opens it almost immediately, mouth parted in eager surprise, before her gaze dips down to the mug of coffee I'm holding.

"You've come bearing gifts," Celine observes, smiling shyly.

"I've come to say good morning." I hand her the mug.

It's her favorite one. A white one with gold rimming that says "Boss Babe" in big bold pink letters. It was a gift from one of the maids when we threw a small party celebrating her full recovery. She laughed when she first opened it, as though it was too silly to use, then she promptly started using it and never stopped.

"Come on in," she says, her eyes scanning down to the crumpled front of the t-shirt I'm wearing. "Did you sleep at your desk again?"

"I didn't mean to."

She laughs. "We need to talk about work-life balance."

"Says the boss babe."

She snorts and ushers me inside the room. All the little touches in here are Celine's. The ivory curtains, the blush rugs with the deep piling, the ornate ironwork bed frame. Taking a seat on the jade green sofa, she pats a spot next to her.

"Come," she says. "Sit with me."

I sit, taking care not to be so close that our legs are touching.

"Not that I'm complaining, but I don't usually get early morning visits from you. Are we about to have the conversation you promised me we would have?" she asks, setting her coffee mug aside without even pretending to take a sip.

"We will," I assure her. "But first, there's something important I need to tell you."

Her brows fly up her forehead, but she nods. "Okay." She takes a deep breath. "I'm all ears."

"I didn't say anything before because I wasn't sure what I would find. But now… I found them, Celine." I look her in the eye so she knows I'm serious. "I found them."

She freezes, then closes her eyes and shudders. "Say that again."

"I found your sister. I found your father."

Her eyes flutter open, but they're clouded and incredulous. "Where are they now?"

"Here."

Her gaze snaps to me. "Here? As in—"

"In the house. We got in late last night. I had the staff show them straight to their rooms."

She's moving in stuttering start-and-stop slow motion. She keeps looking toward the windows, though I don't have the faintest idea what she expects to find there. "I…what…how did you even…?"

"Just walked into the diner where Taylor worked," I explain. "She was surprised."

"I'll say. And Dad?"

"Less surprised. I think he always knew I would find them. Eventually."

She jumps to her feet suddenly as a flush spreads from her cheeks to her chest. "You promised me, Ilarion," she says. "You promised me that you wouldn't hurt him. He's my father."

"I remember. I'm aware."

"And—"

"Celine!" I snap, raising my voice just loud enough to get through to her. "You don't have to worry. I'm not going to touch your father."

"Then why is he here?" she pleads. "You can't tell me he wanted to move back and stay in your house."

I rake a hand through my hair. "It's not about me. You're his daughter. Is it so hard to imagine he'd want to see you again?"

Sadness creeps into her eyes. "We…we didn't leave things well," she mumbles. "When he said he was going to disappear that night…I guess I didn't believe him. I thought I could talk him out of it. I was groggy and—"

"What happened is what happened. But he's back here, so whatever you wished you had said to him then, you can say now."

The flush on her cheeks and chest slowly recedes. She takes a deep breath. "I can't believe they're here."

"They'll be sleeping now. We came in late, but you'll see them at brunch."

She nods absentmindedly as she slowly rotates in place. She looks like she doesn't know what to do with her body. Her hands keep fluttering at her sides, grasping at nothing. "H-how are they? How do they look? And how did you manage to convince them to come back? *Why* did you convince them to come back?"

"That's a lot of questions."

"Ilarion," she says softly. Realization spreads across her face. "I didn't even know you were looking for them."

"I handed it over to a private detective. It wasn't like the search was taking up any of my time." The lie is pathetic and huge. The search absorbed every waking—and sometimes sleeping—moment of my existence. But she buys it, and that's the important part.

"But why?"

"Because…" Celine doesn't deserve to be lied to. But in this case, the truth would only hurt her way more. "You've missed them, haven't you?"

"I lost my entire family in the span of one night," she says quietly. "Of course I missed them."

I nod. "Well, now, you don't have to anymore."

She stares at me for a split-second before walking into my arms. She holds me tight and I hug her back. "I can't believe you found them."

I'm uncomfortable, but I know better than to pull away as she tightens her grip on me. Eventually, though, it's too much. I drop my arms from around her and break the embrace.

"Celine, there's one more thing. You're…" *Fuck.* I didn't expect this to be the hardest part. "You're an aunt."

She blinks slowly. "Huh?"

"An aunt," I say. "Taylor has a little boy."

Her face screws up in a confused frown. "Taylor…has a *child?*" Sucking in a breath, she stumbles a step backward. "Taylor. My Taylor…is a mom?"

"His name is Adam. He's four. He's a sweet kid."

Her eyes connect with mine. "A nephew…and he's four? Then—shit—that means she would have gotten pregnant pretty soon after she left that night with Dad. Is she—*shit!*—is she married? Where's his father?"

I'm tempted. I'm so tempted that the words are on the tip of my tongue. It feels wrong, completely unnatural to stand there and not claim him as my own.

Sad. Weak. Fucking pathetic.

But I promised Taylor. I don't need to give her any more reasons to alienate me.

"That's your sister's story to tell," is the best response I can think of. It'll have to do.

Celine frowns, her eyes darting from side to side. "This is…a lot."

"I'm sorry," I say, turning away from her.

I feel her fidgeting behind me. The pregnant silence of someone who's about to broach a topic I'd rather leave for later—or, better yet, for never.

"Have you thought about it?" Her voice goes cold to hide the hurt underneath. "The request I made?"

"Celine, I—"

"Five years, Ilarion," she snaps. "Five years and I've only ever asked you for one thing."

"Other than giving your father immunity," I point out.

She stops short and her eyes go wide. "Are you saying it's either-or? It's one or the other?"

I grit my teeth. "I'm saying there's only so far I can bend before I break."

"Funny," she says. "I could say the same thing myself." She takes a step forward and her eyes blaze with the kind of fight that she's acquired over the years. Living among a Bratva can do that to a person. "My little sister is a mother, Ilarion. She's experienced more of life than I have. At this point, what do I have to show for myself? A handful of charities, endless parties and galas…"

"You love what you do."

"I had to learn to love it; it wasn't like I had much of a choice. It's not like you let me in, the way you do with Mila and Dima. I'm still an outsider, kept on the fringe of things. Included, but not really."

"Celine—"

"Yes, I do love what I do. But it's not enough, Ilarion. You know that. I want more."

"Now's not the time."

"When is?" she presses. "Just tell me when. If I have a timeline, then at least I have some hope. Something to look forward to. But every time I bring it up, you avoid the subject. You treat me like I'm some sort of pariah. It would help if I knew why. It would make me feel better if I understood. But I don't because you refuse to fucking talk to me!"

She's crossed the threshold from talking to screaming. She's so worked up that she's not even aware that her words are bouncing off the walls and filtering out into the hallway.

To unsuspecting ears, maybe.

"You need to calm down."

"You like saying that to me, don't you?" she snaps. "I'm not some hysterical woman, Ilarion. I have a right to be angry. I have a *goddamn right* to be frustrated."

There are moments when I look at Celine and I hate myself. It's the same thing I used to feel when I saw Mila. That feeling that, despite my best efforts, I've fucked up so bad that I can never repair the damage I've done.

I walk over to her and cup her face in my hands. She goes still, surprised by the sudden proximity. By the sudden intimacy.

I love her like this, early in the morning when she hasn't put her face on yet. Her eyes are clear and bright, her face free of foundation and blush. She looks so much younger, so much less haunted by what she's seen.

She looks like Taylor.

"You have every right to hate me, Celine."

Her eyes soften instantly. "I don't hate you," she whispers. "That's the problem. It would be so much easier if I did."

I sigh and drop my hands. She has no idea how right she is. Or how much like her sister she is, either. "Right now, your father and Taylor are here. Let's just focus on that for the moment, shall we?"

Her eyes fall to the ground and she sighs wearily like a woman twice her age. Then she walks over to her bed. "What will they make of me, I wonder?"

"You're the same woman you were when they left."

She scoffs at that, looking at me with irony spilling out of her eyes. "Come on, Ilarion. Let's be honest with each other at least. I'm not the same woman I was when they left."

"Maybe not on the surface, but you're still there. You're still strong and kind and caring."

She lofts a brow. "You know, it hurts when we fight," she says. "I hate when we're at odds with one another. But sometimes, it hurts worse when you're nice to me."

I can see the tears in her eyes, but all I can do is nod.

"I know."

24

TAYLOR

I wake up to the strangest feeling. Like someone snuck in during the night and painted the walls a different color. Everything is as it should be, but it's all just *wrong.*

Adam's still sleeping soundly, so I pop a kiss on his cheek and walk over to the windows. I don't open the blinds; I just peek out from between them. The garden looks less threatening in the morning, but I don't know if I will ever scrub the horrible memories from my brain. I swear I can see the patch of blood my mother left behind, like it's permanently stained into the grass.

But I can't trust my memories anymore. The more I revisit it, the more it shapeshifts. Did Mom make eye contact with me before she was shot? Did she scream? Was there as much blood as I think I remember, or is my mind exaggerating the details?

Shuddering, I step away and twist the blinds fully shut.

I want to rinse this creeping feeling of wrongness away, so I go take a long, languid shower. But even when my skin is raw and rosy from the heat, I'm still feeling scatter-brained. I keep thinking about the moment when I'll turn and see Cee for the first time. Will she be happy? Angry? Annoyed?

Will she be suspicious?

Will she know what I've done?

Grimacing, I slip on a pair of denim shorts and a tank top and step back into the bedroom.

Adam is slowly stirring. "Mama?"

"Hey, buddy," I coo, slipping into bed beside him. "Did you sleep well?"

"Where are we?" He uses his entire fist to rub the sleep from his eyes. I know he's going to outgrow that habit one day; I just hope it takes a while.

"We're at Uncle Illy's house," I explain. "You were sleeping when we got here."

"Oh." He yawns and sidles a little closer to me. "Where's Grandpa?"

"In his own room. We'll see him soon."

I hope.

I cajole him up to come brush his teeth and get ready for the day, then we go downstairs to the garden.

"Does Auntie Cee live here?" Adam asks as we meander down the halls in search of the kitchen.

"Yes, she does." My eyes dart from corner to corner as if I expect her to jump out at us at any moment like a horror movie monster. "I'm sure we'll see her soon."

A few wrong turns later, we end up pushing through a door and out into the gardens. It's not the kitchen, but even though my stomach is rumbling, Adam's gasp of delight is too sweet to ignore.

I let him rush out onto the lush grass. The sun is perched high in the sky, but it's mostly covered by clouds. He does half-baked cartwheels and falls into a giggling puddle in the middle of the lawn.

"I wish we could stay here forever," he murmurs, just loud enough for me to hear it.

It's an innocent statement, but I find myself cringing on the inside. Living here forever would be hell on earth for me.

Taking his hand, I help him up and we keep wandering through the topiary. Rounding a rose bush, we come face-to-face with a dark-haired woman on a yoga mat.

Did Celine change her hair color?

And then I realize—it's not Celine at all.

She eases out of her pose and fixes me with a look that I'm extremely glad Ilarion prepared me for. It's sharp enough to hurt.

"Hi, Mila," I say awkwardly. "It's been a long time."

She looks good. Her hair's shorter, but it suits her. Her eyes veer toward Adam, and just like that, the coldness melts.

"You must be Adam," she infers with a soft smile.

He blushes and hides behind me. "He's shy," I explain to her. "Just give him time to warm up to you."

Mila ignores me and walks forward. She squats down on the grass and smiles brighter at him. "I love those pajamas. I mean, they are seriously cool."

"What do you say, Adam?"

"Thank you," he mumbles. Raising his head, he asks, "Are you my Auntie Cee?"

She chuckles. "No. My name's Mila. I'm Ilarion's sister."

"Oh." Adam furrows his brow. "Do you live here?"

"As a matter of fact, I do." She grins and holds out her hand to him. "Wanna see the birdbath?"

I stand awkwardly off to the side. She still hasn't looked me in the eye, and when Adam takes her hand, she puts her back to me as the two of them go skipping down the crushed gravel path. I trail in their wake, skin crawling with unease.

"Look, Mama!" Adam says when we pass through a circle of hedges to find a huge stone birdbath in the dead center of the garden. "Birds!"

"I see them, honey."

He rushes over to the fountain. A pair of sparrows flits off immediately, but the larger crows perch studiously on the rim and ignore him.

Mila stands a few yards off. Watching him. Ignoring me. I can't decide if I should wait for her to break the silence or if I should just say something.

Her profile is mildly terrifying. She reminds me of her brother more than usual. Latent violence pent-up in a beautiful frame.

She's got that chiseled, granite stubbornness, too. Like her whole body is reminding me that you can't outwait a mountain. You'll crumble long before it does.

"Mila…you know why I left. Why I had to leave."

She doesn't so much as glance at me. Doesn't even acknowledge that I've spoken. But now that I've started, I figure I need to keep going.

"It would have been too complicated to stay," I try to explain. "I knew Celine wanted him. If I stayed, she would have seen. She would have figured out the truth, and—"

"And you think all these years will make a difference?" Mila demands, snapping to me so fast I recoil instinctively.

"I…well…"

"Well?" she asks, with one arched eyebrow.

"I…I don't have feelings for…him…anymore."

She scoffs right in my face as though I've just said the most ridiculous thing she's ever heard. "You don't have feelings for him anymore," she repeats, her eyes rolling dramatically. "You've had five years to practice that line, and it isn't even remotely convincing."

"It's true."

She sighs and shrugs. "Maybe it is. Time will tell." *Great.* Now, I have another person who's going to be watching me like a hawk. "Your son looks just like my brother. You realize that, right?"

"Weird coincidence."

She scrunches up her nose. "You better hope your sister shares your delusional denial."

I squirm in place, feeling completely put on the spot. "If you're trying to make me feel bad, don't bother. I already feel horrible. About all of this."

"Which part, exactly?" Mila asks. "Lying to your sister? To your son? Forcing a good man to forgo raising his own child? Kidnapping my nephew? Or the part where you just up and left so you wouldn't have to face the consequences of what you'd done?"

No one has ever said it quite like *that* before. My cheeks are burning hot enough to burst into flame.

"All of it," I finally croak. Rhetorical or not, her questions deserve an answer. "But I never intended to avoid the consequences. Only hurting my sister."

"You keep saying that like it's never going to happen." She rolls her eyes again. "You keep acting like your sister's a blind idiot. You and I both know she's far from it."

She's brutal right now, and a weird, masochistic part of me actually likes it. I never had a best friend to verbally slap me with harsh truths; truth be told, I never let anyone get close enough to try.

"All I'm asking for," I say carefully, "is some time. Please…just don't tell her." The stone in my gut says I have no right to ask her for anything. The fool in my heart says I have to try.

She glares at me. "Fucking hell, Taylor. How little do you think of me? Of course I'm not going to tell her. It'll be way more painful to make you do it yourself."

I'm torn between a laugh and a tear. I smile, but it fades away at the sight of the ferocious look in her eyes. "I'm sorry I left without saying goodbye. I just thought—"

"I'd tell my brother and stop you from leaving?" she asks.

"Well…yes."

She sighs. "I can see why you might have thought that, but if you'd made up your mind…I would have tried to help you."

"No way. You worship your brother."

She throws me a glare. "I love my brother," she corrects. "I look up to him, but I don't worship him. I get it, though—you thought my loyalty to him would trump our friendship. Wait —Sorry. That's silly of me, assuming we even had a friendship. Clearly, I was wrong."

I frown. "Mila, that's not—"

"I've been trapped before in a situation that I wanted to escape from." She folds her arms and sighs. "I was desperate for a way out and nobody could see that. Not until I finally asked for help. My point is, I would have helped you if you told me that you wanted to leave. That you were determined to leave. And yeah, I would have appreciated a goodbye."

"I'm sorry." I smile sadly. "I understand if you're mad at me, and I understand if you want to stay that way forever. But if you do want to forgive me… well, I'll be here."

"I may never get to that point."

I nod. "I suppose I'll just have to deal."

Adam slaps the surface of the water, splashing it everywhere. Fed up, the crows flap away and squawk in irritation.

Mila turns her gaze to him and she softens almost instantaneously. "He's beautiful," she breathes.

"Yeah," I murmur. "He is."

"What's it like?" she suddenly asks. She looks over at me. "Being a mother?"

Nobody's ever asked me that question before, so it takes me a moment to answer. "It's…everything. It's horrible and wonderful and satisfying and terrifying and incredible all at the same time." I sigh, that one breath brimming full with every wild emotion I've had since I first saw him in the ultrasound. "It's not for everyone, but as it turns out, it's for me. I'm not sure I'd survive without him."

"Why?" Mila asks.

"Why?"

She nods. "What's so hard? You escaped, you're free… That's what you wanted, right?"

I bite my lip. "Yeah. That doesn't mean it's been easy."

She scoffs. "No shit."

I choose not to respond to that. "How's Cee?" I ask. "Are the two of you friends?"

Mila's eyebrows knit together. "We get along," she says, but that answer alone tells me everything.

"How are things with Dima?" I try to ask the question as innocently as possible, but it still earns me a glare from her.

"The same."

"Really?" I let her see my disappointment. "But—"

"Stop right there," she snaps. "You can't just pick up where we left off, okay? We are not there yet."

I raise my eyebrows. "'Yet.' Promising word."

She suppresses a smile and shakes her head. "I'm walking away now," she informs me, floating over to the fountain where Adam is standing.

"I'll be here!" I call after her.

"It'd be great if you weren't," she throws back over her shoulder.

I laugh, and I catch the shadow of a smile on her face before she turns her back on me and focuses on Adam.

I take a look at the gardens around me. The morning air is fresh and crisp. Everything is green, fragrant, and beautiful. And then—

I see a silhouette in the distance. She's blurred in the shadow from a looming tree, but I don't have to see a single scrap of detail to know who it is. To know what's coming.

Celine.

25

TAYLOR

"Come on, Taylor," I tell myself under my breath. "Don't be a wuss."

I repeat the mantra to myself silently as I swallow and go to meet my sister under the shadow of the weeping willow tree. Celine stands in the pool of shade, watching me approach. She keeps her hands clasped in front of her, unmoving.

The old Celine would have run to me with open arms. But this Celine seems more reserved, more composed. Far too cultured and elegant to be caught running across the garden with her arms outstretched.

"Hey, you," I say, stopping at the foot of the hill.

She looms above me on the steep embankment. She's smiling, but it's a mysterious smile that shifts with every passing second. "Well," she says at last, "come up here and give me a hug."

I bound up the slope and wrap my arms around her. The moment I do, I forget about the new woman who stands in front of me. She feels like my sister again.

"You smell different." The words slip out of my mouth before I can think them through.

"You've been gone a long time." Again, I'm not quite sure what to make of that. Is she mad? Aloof? Or just neutral? She's not wrong, obviously. So many things have changed since I ran out of this garden in the dead of the night. "Come on. Walk with me."

She turns and meanders down the path without waiting to see if I'm following. I linger under the willow tree for a moment, taking the chance to watch her without her watching me in return.

She's lost more weight than the pictures showed. Her arms are slim and the peaks of her spine poke through her linen dress. She moves slower, too, as though she's thinking about every movement before she makes it. I suppose coming back from the brink of death will do that to a person.

She leads me to a table in a far corner of the garden. The birds don't chirp here. The table is laid out with tea, coffee, juices, a spread of breakfast pastries. But I'm much more focused on Celine.

"Have you seen Dad yet?"

"Not yet. I'm told he's still sleeping." She pours herself a mug. Tea, not coffee. That's new, too. She used to hate tea. "Would you care for something to drink?"

The whole ritual feels strange, like she's playing hostess to avoid a real conversation. "Uh, coffee, please. Black."

She hums like that interests her, but she doesn't actually say anything. She just pours a cup of black coffee, plates it on a saucer, and passes it to me. Then she sighs and leans back in her chair, one manicured finger stroking the edge of the wrought iron table again and again. She doesn't take a single sip of her drink.

"It's so good to see you, Cee," I blurt into the weirdly taut silence. "There were times I thought I'd never get to sit next to you again."

"Oh?" She tilts her head to one side. "I knew we'd see each other again, at some point. I was sure of it."

I arch a brow. "You were sure of it?"

"Ilarion was so determined," she explains with a nonchalant twirl of her hand. "I knew he wouldn't just let the two of you disappear into the night."

Determined. I get what she's saying, and it's not that the word is *wrong.* It just doesn't seem to fit. It's too dry. Too unemotional. The Ilarion who found me in that tiny, dusty town was rippling with rage, sorrow, fear, a thousand different things.

Celine, though… She *does* seem dry. She does seem unemotional. And maybe that's exactly what worries me the most—it sounds too perfectly calm. Rehearsed, maybe.

It's the word of someone who's hiding what she really feels.

Old Cee would have talked to me immediately if she had a problem about something. But New Cee seems like she'd lure me into a corner and then toy with me before going in for the kill.

"He…he could have," I say nervously. "We could have stayed in our little corner. Dad wasn't going to do anything else."

"He couldn't be sure of that, Tay," Celine remarks, finally picking up her teacup and taking the tiniest taste. "Dad's betrayed him once before."

That surprises me—the judgment in her tone. The slight accusation in her eyes. She blames Dad. Or maybe it's more that she's taken Ilarion's side in all this. I shouldn't be surprised, really. She chose Ilarion over her family when she decided to stay with him.

"That was before, Cee," I point out. "Before we… Before you were involved."

She doesn't frown, but her eyebrows pucker just slightly. "Trust is a hard thing to win back once it's broken."

My palms are starting to sweat. I feel like she's driving towards a point. I'm getting increasingly concerned that the point is to expose me and my lies. My betrayals.

Does she know?

Everyone in my life has told me that I wouldn't be able to keep the façade up for long. I've steadfastly refused to believe them, but now, faced with her steady gaze and her glacier-like composure, I feel like I'm unraveling.

"Yeah. I know."

She takes another prim sip of her tea. "Croissant?" she offers, pushing the basket toward me. "They're homemade."

"Did you make them?"

She laughs. "Me? No, of course not. No, Maurice, our chef, did. Go on. You look like you could use one; you've lost so much weight."

"You're one to talk," I gently tease, taking a croissant just so I have something to do with my hands.

She smiles and waves away my comment. "I work so much that I forget to eat."

"I've been following you," I tell her. "Your charity work, your philanthropic causes. It's all so amazing."

"Ilarion is the one that suggested I try it out. I did it to make him happy, but I never expected to fall in love with it the way I did. Turned out to be the saving grace of my life."

Her face lights up when she talks about her work. "I'm happy for you, Cee. Really."

She gives me that polite, curated smile of hers. "We have a lot to talk about, don't we?"

I nod. "So much."

She sets down her mug with a subtly haunting *clink* of ceramic on porcelain. "Maybe we should start with the fact that, as I'm told, you're a mother now."

Something shivers through her eyes when she brings it up. It passes too fast for me to catch what it might be.

My gut churns. I knew this was coming, of course, but it's so much worse than I expected. Maybe because Celine seems so set on staying distant. Her face is perfectly composed. Her hands are neatly folded on the table. She's the picture of calm.

I'm the one who's falling to pieces.

"Ilarion told you."

"Yes. But he didn't say much."

I feel relief, but it's fast and fleeting. "I…I was pregnant when I left with Dad that night. I was actually going to tell you at your engagement party. But…"

"Shit hit the fan."

I manage a soft laugh. Not because anything is funny; I'm just uncomfortable. "Exactly. And afterwards, there was never really an opportunity to tell you."

"Of course. Makes sense."

I swallow and it hurts. She's watching me, waiting for me to tell her the rest of the story. "Um…there's nothing else, really." Now that I'm knee-deep in it, it's surprisingly difficult to lie. "It was a one-night-stand. I didn't get the guy's name. Never gave him mine. It happened, we went our separate ways, and a few weeks later, I found out I was pregnant."

"Remarkable," she breathes. "You didn't ask for his name? Before you…you know."

"I guess I was rebelling a little."

She raps a nail on the edge of her saucer. "I do wish you'd told me."

"By the time I knew I was pregnant, you announced your engagement. I didn't want to steal your thunder."

"Oh, please," she says with a wave of her hand and a slight roll of her eyes. "Surely we can share the spotlight, no? There's always room for the two of us. I've never understood why you've always felt like you need to make space for me."

"Well, you made space for me when we were growing up," I remind her. "You were always there for me. You missed parties and stuff just to stay home and hang out with me when I was sick."

"I wanted to," she says simply. "It wasn't a sacrifice. I loved doing it. You're my baby sister."

For a moment, that steely mask cracks and I see *Celine* again. My Cee. She may be different now—more cultured, more controlled, more confident—but deep down, she's still my sister. And that gives me hope.

"That's why I didn't tell you. Because you're my big sister, and for once, I wanted to return the favor."

She purses her lips, then reaches out to place her hand over mine. For a second, the gesture transports me back a few decades, back to when we were young girls and we used to hoard our secrets like treasures and share the bounty after bedtime.

"To be perfectly honest, I would have preferred to be told," she says. "I could have shared the experience with you."

Why does she sounds so damn sad when she says that? Almost as though I've denied her something she's been craving.

But then she shakes her head and the melancholy passes. "So Dad's a grandfather, huh?"

"He's good at it," I say with a happy sigh. "Adam loves him to death."

"Adam," she says, laughing softly. "That's funny."

"What?"

"You don't remember? You went through a phase where you named everything Adam. Our pet hamster, the potted plant in our bedroom, the cloth doll that Aunt Marianne gave you for your third birthday."

My eyes go wide. "I don't remember that at all."

"You grew out of it," Celine says with a shrug. I stare at her, realizing how many memories she has of me that I don't share. "Sometimes, I'm not sure I remember things because I genuinely recall them, or because Mom told me certain stories so often that I made them my own memories to match hers."

I didn't want to bring Mom up, but here we are. And some things do need to be spoken of. Processed.

"It's still weird, isn't it? Not having her around."

Celine closes her eyes. In the slanting sun, I can see the brushstrokes of her makeup, contoured perfectly along those too-gaunt cheekbones.

"It's weirder not having been at her funeral," she whispers, eyes still closed. "In some ways, I've never been able to truly accept her death because of it. I never got the closure."

"Have you been to her grave?"

"Ilarion takes me every year." My chest tightens at the thought of them standing hand-in-hand at the gravesite. "I see her headstone, I see the engraving, and…I just don't feel a connection to it. I don't actually believe she's under there, listening to me."

"She's not," I assure her. "She's somewhere better. Somewhere warmer, sunnier, cancer-free, sipping cocktails and smiling down at us."

To my surprise, Celine frowns. "Oh, God, I hope not. She'd be so sad if she saw what's happened to us. The one thing she wanted for us was to be there for each other, to have each other's backs. But we haven't seen each other in years, Tay."

My heart thuds hard against my chest. For a moment, it's so tempting to tell her that the reason I left was for her. So she could have what she deserved.

"I didn't mean to abandon you—"

"Then why did you?" She snaps it so fast, I feel the whiplash. "You could have stayed. You could have convinced Dad to stay. I get that he doesn't like Ilarion, but you never even gave him a chance."

Oh, God…

If she only knew.

"Celine—"

"You didn't even give us a chance to have a conversation. You know everything by now, I'm sure?"

"Of course."

I think.

She nods. "Ilarion promised me a long time ago that he wouldn't retaliate against Dad for what he did. He doesn't break his promises. He may seem like a hard man on the surface, but he's a good one beneath it."

"Well, I'm here now," I say apologetically. "I want to get to know you again. I want to know your life. I want to be a part of it."

It sits there between us, all the secrets we're not telling each other. I don't want to bring up the suicide attempt until she mentions it, but it's there on the tip of my tongue. The questions…the fear…the reasons behind it all.

Her smile turns careful, almost secretive, and it strikes me that I've never seen Celine smile like that before. She's never been a calculated person. She used to be an open book.

But maybe I don't know her as well as I thought I did.

Maybe I *never* knew her as well as I thought I did.

Or maybe…I chose to believe what I wanted to.

26

TAYLOR

"Where is he?"

"With Mila, by the birdbath," I say. "Would you like to meet him?"

Celine tenses instantly, as though I've suggested something far more controversial than simply saying hi to her nephew for the first time. Her eyes cloud over and she glances over towards the fountain.

"I'd love to," she says, although her tone strikes me as strange. "But how about we take a walk around the gardens first?"

Puzzled, I nod. She abandons her still-full cup of tea and glides back into the heart of the garden. I follow her as she veers right onto a winding pathway set in broken tile pieced together like a mosaic.

"I spent a lot of my time in these gardens that first year," she explains softly. "I used to take my physical therapy out here because it was better than staring at blank walls all day. I had enough of that during my bed rest."

"That must have been a horrible time for you."

She glances at me. "It was hard not to feel abandoned."

I wince. "I'm sorry."

She comes to an abrupt stop, and her dress billows around her in the gentle breeze. She looks like a ghost floating among the flowers. Something ethereal. Not quite real.

Compared to her, I feel clumsy, earthen, gravity-bound. All-too real and human and dumb.

"I don't think you *are* sorry, Taylor," she says. "You were off living your life. Being a mother." Her eyes flash with anger, her body tensing. "I was left behind, alone, trying to navigate through a whole new life without my family by my side."

I swallow the acrid taste of anger. "Cee, can I ask you something?"

"It doesn't sound like I'm going to like the question."

I sigh. "You might not. But just so you know, I'm asking because I'm curious. Not because I plan on judging you."

She nods. "Go ahead."

I purse my lips to think the words over, then blow out a puff of air. "Why *did* you stay? I understand you thought you were in love with Ilarion, but...you'd known him for such a short time. And you saw what he—what his life, his world, did to Mom."

Her forehead creases. "'You thought you were in love with him...'"

"Excuse me?"

"That's what you just said." She takes an aggressive step forward, her voice icing over. "Do you doubt that I love him? Even now?"

"No, of course not! I just—"

"People assume that love is something that comes with time. But it's not always the case. Sometimes, love can smack you in the face. No warning, no punches pulled."

She draws in a shuddering breath and turns to face out over the rolling hills of the property. The wind flirts with the hem of her dress, toying it around her legs in low, lazy waves. I stand still, silent, and stupid, with not the faintest idea of what the hell I'm supposed to do next.

Celine pushes her hair away from her eyes and sighs. "It took me a long time to recover from the coma. I had severe bed sores, urinary infections, blood clots in my legs. But what it did to my body was nothing compared to what it did to my mind." She glances at me. "I felt horrible back then. Ashamed of myself. I didn't want to be seen. But he never made me feel bad. He looked after me like I was the most precious thing in the world."

Everything she's saying makes me want to weep with both gratitude and heartbreak. I never knew it was possible to feel two contradictory things at once, when both are still valid. That is the very nature of this sick, twisted love triangle we're in—a love triangle that Celine isn't even aware she's a part of.

"Cee…" She hasn't looked me in the eye for a while now. "Is there something you're not telling me?"

She glances at me with a brow raised. "I don't know, Taylor. Maybe. We've grown apart. It's not as natural as it used to be between us."

"But it can be," I insist, stepping forward and taking her hand. "It can be. Just talk to me."

"What would you like me to talk about?"

"Whatever it is that's making you look so sad."

I regret it the moment the word slips out of my mouth. Mostly because of the way Celine looks at me when I say it. Like she's somehow let herself down by revealing too much to me. Of course, I'm only guessing. I have no idea what she's thinking right now. She's become a mystery over the years.

I only have myself to blame for that.

"I'm not sad, Taylor," she demurs. "I'm content. I made my choices and even though they haven't turned out exactly as I'd envisioned, I still have hope."

I nod. "I'm glad to hear that."

I hear Adam's shrill giggle from across the garden. The scampering of his feet. The birds are chirping over here, I notice. The corner of the garden where we were just sitting was a cone of silence in comparison.

"Who'd have thought?" Celine softly laughs. "Mila's good with kids." She turns to me. "I *am* looking forward to meeting Adam. Please don't interpret my reaction as disinterest. It's just…I've wanted a baby for a long, long time now. I suppose it felt a little jarring to find that you had a child without even trying. All I've done is try."

"Oh, Cee—"

I reach out to her, but she flinches back out of my reach. "Ilarion will give me what I want, though," she says. "Eventually."

Her words are vague, but there's only one thing that she can possibly mean.

They're trying to have a baby.

They've been *trying to have a baby.*

On the face of it, it doesn't seem like a betrayal. But somehow, that's exactly how it feels.

I gulp and force a smile on my face. "You'll be an amazing mother, Cee. I've always known that."

She smiles sadly. "I saw what a good mother looked like. I experienced it firsthand."

My eyes wander. To the sky, to the hedges, back to Celine. Then I look down and I see it: the paper-thin scars across her wrists.

I suck in a sharp breath. Her eyes follow my gaze and she covers her wrist with her hand self-consciously.

"Celine…"

"It's nothing."

"Nothing?" I repeat incredulously. "That doesn't look like nothing."

"It's nothing. It was a long time ago."

"When?" I croak, still too afraid to even voice the actual words. "Why?"

Her eyes cloud and she turns her face away from me again. She keeps it rooted in the distance when she finally speaks.

"Six or seven months after you and Dad left," she murmurs. "As for why…that's more complicated." She pivots back towards the path and gestures for me to follow. "And I'm not willing to talk about it now."

"Was it Ilarion?" I ask. "Was it something he said? Something he did?"

She glances at me from over her shoulder. "Ilarion has never done anything but be honest with me," she says. "I was the one who couldn't handle that honesty."

I frown. If he didn't tell her about us, about Adam, how honest exactly was he for her to feel like suicide was the only way out? And whatever it was, if death had been her go-to, if that had been her only solution…

It makes me think that keeping the truth from her was the best decision I've made in a long time.

27

TAYLOR

When we emerge from the maze, I spy Mila and Adam on the other side of the lawn. The two of them are kicking a ball back and forth across the grass.

"Adam!" I call, even though my head is reeling with new doubt. "Come over here. There's someone I want you to meet."

He runs over to me and promptly hides behind my back when he notices Celine standing there. "Guess what, kiddo?" I say in the calmest voice I can muster. "This is your Auntie Cee."

Her eyes go wide. "You've told him about me?"

"Of course," I say. "I've told him a bunch of stories about you and Mom. Isn't that right, buddy?"

He peers around me and looks at her. She watches him tentatively, but I can see her smile brighten. She hikes her dress and kneels down in the grass in front of him.

"Hi, Adam. I'm so happy to meet you."

"I like your garden," he mumbles shyly. "And the fountain."

She smiles. "I'm glad. I had it installed years ago when I realized that the birds didn't have a place to come and relax."

"I like birds."

"So do I," she says. "But I don't like cages. Which is why I keep them outside."

She doesn't talk to him like he's a kid. She talks to him like an adult, and bit by bit, he sidles out from behind me.

"Do you want to see the rest of the gardens?" she asks. He nods and she holds out her hand. "Maybe we can take a walk, and I can show you?"

He nods again, head bouncing like a bobblehead, and Celine laughs. I realize it's the first time I've heard her laugh since I've been back. It sounds different. A little softer, a little heavier, a little more self-conscious.

Then Adam looks past her and his face lights up. "Grandpa!" he yells. "You're awake! You have to see the birdbath!"

He takes off at a run and jumps from the grass to the veranda to Dad's arms in a matter of seconds. Celine straightens up and watches the two of them. I wonder what she's feeling right now, because for the life of me, I can't tell.

I don't know what I'm feeling, either.

"Grandpa," Adam says, pointing towards us. "Look! It's Auntie Cee, from my bedtime stories."

I smile. It must feel a little bit like a fairytale coming to life for him. Celine has always been just a character in a story and nothing more.

Celine walks forward as Dad steps off the deck to meet her. I glance off to the side where Mila is standing with the ball. She gives me a small nod and vanishes into the house to give us some privacy.

"Hi, Dad," Celine says coolly. "I've missed you."

Tears well in Dad's eyes. "Oh, honey…" It's all he says before he gathers her up in his arms and hugs her tight.

I blink back my tears and try to figure out how Celine can stand there and keep her emotions in check. She used to cry at the drop of a hat. And now…nothing.

I wonder if life and the reality of it has made her cold. If the nature of what I left her to suffer through alone has forced her to be tougher.

Or if maybe it's all just smoke and mirrors, hiding secrets I have yet to find out.

I'm not sure what I say to excuse myself; I just mumble something dumb and slip away. No one is really paying attention to me, anyway. Adam is back to running around the garden. Cee and Dad are sitting by the deck and talking.

Me? *I'm freaking the fuck out.*

I don't know what I was expecting. I thought I'd prepared myself for coming back. But apparently, I'd just avoided thinking about what it would be like. Which, I'm now learning, leads to nervous hyperventilation in an empty room of a house that's too big and too fancy and too full of Ilarion Zakharov to be safe for me.

"Ma'am?"

I jump and scream.

The maid who spoke backs away in alarm. "Oh, I'm so sorry, ma'am. I didn't mean to startle you. I just came to clean."

"No, no, it's okay. I'm sorry. I…I was just…going upstairs. Pardon me."

I rush past her as fast as I can without actually running. The moment I clear the room, I feel my mind go blank again. It's a defense mechanism—you can't think about bad things if instead you just think about nothing at all.

But that doesn't last forever.

As soon as the adrenaline ebbs, the terror creeps back up in my throat like a red tide. The plan is to get to my room, but my knees give way somewhere between the landing and the door. I end up sitting on the floor of the corridor with my arms wrapped around my knees, rocking back and forth. I take in big breaths, but that isn't helping.

Oh God…oh God…why did I come back? This was all a huge mistake. I wandered into a vipers' nest with my throat bared and my hands spread wide. They're lunging now and taking chunks out of me—all the mistakes I've made come back home to roost.

By the time I register footsteps, it's too late for me to scramble away. I have just enough time to turn to the side before I spot him.

Ilarion looks so much taller from where I'm curled up on the floor. Those piercing blue eyes of his land on me with menacing curiosity.

"Go away," I croak.

He lofts a brow. "This is my house."

"Don't care," I grumble. "Go away."

He does the opposite of what I asked, instead dropping to a squat in front of me. "What's going on?"

"'What's going on'?" I snort. "What kind of question is that?"

"The obvious kind," he replies with a tilt of his head. "You're lying on my floor in the fetal position."

"There's enough room for you to pass."

"Not until you tell me what's going on. Did Mila say something?"

"This has nothing to do with Mila." I keep my gaze averted. *Why the hell couldn't I have just dragged myself the rest of the way to my room?* My cheeks flame with color, but I have no choice but to ignore that and pretend like I'm not making a complete fool of myself right now.

"Celine, then?" I flinch, giving myself away, and he nods. "Ah. The two of you have been catching up."

"Can you please go? Tell the maid to clean around me if I'm still here when she comes."

"Do you need help getting back to your room?"

"I need you to walk away."

I hear him sigh wearily and feel the warm brush of his exhale on my skin. "Asking for help doesn't make you weak, Taylor."

"I don't mind asking for help. I just don't want any help from *you*."

He bristles for a moment, his eyes boiling with those thousand-and-one emotions he refuses to uncage. Then he nods, rocks back, and sits on the opposite side of the hall, facing me.

Wonderful.

"I'm going to sit here until you start talking."

The sun beams down through a skylight overhead. It picks up my foot and Ilarion's where they linger near each other on the hallway runner. The rest of each of us is bathed in sharp shadows.

"She slit her wrists." I meant for it to come out far more accusingly, but I'm emotionally drained. It just sounds as sad as it makes me feel.

He slowly nods. "I'm surprised she told you."

"She didn't tell me." I sigh and close my eyes against that image I can't quite scrub from my mind. "I saw the scars."

"Ah."

His lack of emotional response at all, per usual, is grating against me. "She tried. To slit. Her wrists. My sister tried to fucking kill herself, Ilarion! That deserves more than an 'Ah.'"

He frowns. "I told you about it. It's not as though you were unprepared."

"I just assumed she swallowed a bunch of pills," I admit.

"What's the difference?"

"The difference?" I gasp, shoving myself more upright. "The difference is that she took something sharp and she literally tried to slice open her flesh. That kind of thing is desperate. That's rock bottom."

"Whereas pills are a nice, mellow option? Death is death, Taylor, no matter how we choose to meet it."

I cringe. He's making sense, but sense is the last damn thing I want right now. "It's not as violent."

"No, it's not," he agrees. "But you're acting as though this happened yesterday, *tigrionok*. This was years ago. It's faded from everyone's minds. Including hers."

I shake my head. "Why?" I rasp. "Why did she do it?"

"Did you ask her?" When I nod, he nods right back. "That's what I thought. And if she didn't tell you, I'm not about to do it for her."

"Ilarion—"

"You've asked me to keep secrets from her," he reminds me. "What makes you think she hasn't extracted the same promise from me?"

That stops me in my tracks. Like a trickle of cold water running down my back. A stark stab of realization. "She's so…different."

"Yes, she is. That's not a bad thing."

"Yes, it is," I retort. "She used to be so much more open, and carefree and… and…just *herself*. She used to wear her heart on her sleeve. Now, it's as though everything she says and does is rehearsed. She's like a marionette, and I don't have any fucking idea who's pulling the strings."

"Maybe that's just for your benefit."

I flinch. "You were supposed to keep her safe."

"And I did." He all but rolls his eyes. "She's alive today because I stopped two assassins from putting a bullet in her head. She's alive today because I found her in that bathtub before too much blood ran out of her veins. There was a lot you missed when you ran, Taylor. I'm not about to sit here and fill in the blanks for you just to make you feel all warm and fuzzy inside about your choices. I doubt Celine is, either. We moved on."

I can't figure out the way they talk about each other. It doesn't sound like love, but maybe this is how two sharks love each other. It doesn't sound like marriage, but maybe this is how a *pakhan* and his wife are married.

"She wants a baby," I blurt out before I can really think about what I'm saying.

The only sign of his surprise is a slight arch of one brow. "She told you that?"

I nod. "She also told me that you're…trying."

I stumble over the last word, like an idiot, betraying all the shame and jealousy roiling in my chest. Ilarion's eyes bore into mine. He sees it all, I'm sure. He always does.

I shake my head and clench my jaw until the desire to cry passes. "It's none of my business, but—"

"You're right," he snarls. "It isn't."

I grit my teeth, defensiveness rising to my throat like bile. "Why did you bring me back here, Ilarion?" I finally ask. "There's no place for me here. You have everything. You have a beautiful home, a beautiful wife…and soon, you'll have a beautiful family. Why couldn't you just leave Adam to me?"

"Because he's not just yours. And I'm not the kind of man who's okay with replacing one child with another."

"You brought us here hoping the truth would come out. Didn't you?"

He shrugs, neither confirming nor denying. "In my experience, the truth always comes out. Benedict Bellasio is a prime example. He may have been able to hide for all these years. But he can't hide forever."

I force myself up to my feet. Ilarion follows suit. "I don't give a flying fuck about Benedict Bellasio. The only thing I care about is my sister, and she's clearly not in the right frame of mind to be able to handle the truth."

"You're underestimating her."

"No, you're *hoping* that I am. Because that means you can blow up her life without feeling guilty about it. She tried to take her own life! I refuse to be the reason she ever tries again."

"What's the alternative, Taylor?" he asks, stepping towards me. Even when I'm standing, he towers over me and blocks out all the light—literally and figuratively. I'm ready to stand my ground, though. I'm ready to claw his eyes out if I have to.

I'm just not ready for him to challenge my truth.

"Are you going to spend the rest of your life lying? Hiding? Pretending you don't have feelings for me?"

28

ILARION

Her face screws up tight and her cheeks tremble with indignation.

But I knew from the moment I laid eyes on her in that diner: this was going to be an uphill battle. The woman has the kind of stubbornness that could rival… well, mine.

"I don't have feelings for you," she snaps.

"Very convincing." I could almost laugh, if I weren't so irritated. "Do you practice that in the mirror? Or is it just a constant echo in your head?"

"Fuck you." She tries to move past me with a shove to my chest.

I grab her arm and step into her space, forcing her against the wall and pinning her there with my hips. "Running away again, Taylor?"

"Let. Me. Go." Her green eyes dance with fury. She's never looked more alive. It's a relief to see that fire in her soul reignite—for a while, I wondered if her new life had snuffed it out. But here it is, blazing right back to its former glory, and seeing it makes me breathe a sigh of relief. I'm proud to be the match.

I'm just not going to tell her any of that.

"What makes you think I'm going to make this easy on you, Taylor?" I murmur. "You took my son and you ran. I didn't bring you back to just forget that anything ever happened."

"Cee—"

"Is a grown woman who can make her own grown decisions. Same as you. Stop acting like she's a fucking child."

Her eyes flare with panic. "You promised me—"

"I'm allowed to change my mind."

"She seems to think you're a man of your word. I'd hate to think she's wrong." Taylor shudders and lets her eyelids close. "Telling her was never the plan. I don't know what exactly is going on between the two of you, but I know that you care about each other."

"I do care about Celine," I admit. "I never said I didn't."

It's true. It was unexpected, but Celine did grow on me. She's family, and that means protecting her from—even her own kin.

"It was to me. Honestly, I can't read either one of you. Are you hopelessly in love and just denying it? Or strangers who share a bed? Do you have some sort of weird arrangement that no one knows about?"

"Maybe we do."

It's childish to toy with her emotions this way—I'm well fucking aware. But for five years, I've laid awake at night wishing I could make Taylor feel a fraction of what I felt in her absence. I wanted her to know how it felt to punch holes in every wall that I passed. To burn down one Bellasio depot after the next because the only way I could vent my anger and sorrow was to destroy things and watch them crumble to ashes.

I wanted her to know that I loved her and that I fucking missed her. I imagined finding her and telling her those things, just like that.

But now that she's here…I just want her to agonize right along with me.

"Celine would never agree to an 'arrangement,'" she says confidently.

I shake my head. "You said it yourself, Taylor: Celine has changed. You don't know her as well as you want to."

"No one changes *that* much."

I can't help but smirk. I'm stubborn enough to make Taylor suffer with me. But she's stubborn enough to keep pretending like she doesn't want to ask the question that's burning up inside of her.

What does she mean to you?

"You keep telling yourself that. It's not like you became a mother or anything. You're exactly the same person you were years ago, right?"

My biting sarcasm forces her to freeze in her tracks. She's so close that I can smell the apple cinnamon spice in her hair. I can even smell Adam on her.

"The assassination attempts," she whispers out of nowhere. It feels like she wants to keep talking just to keep herself from feeling what is obviously between us. "Was it Benedict?"

"No, it was another deranged Italian I pissed off." If I roll my eyes anymore, I'm going to go blind. "Yes, of course it was Benedict."

"Don't be an asshole. You're not exactly Mr. Warm and Cuddly," she hisses. "Any number of people could want revenge against you. Or they could just want your money. Your houses. Your wife."

"No one else would dare. Benedict, however—he's got nothing to lose anymore."

"But why Cee?"

"Are you kidding? She was my fiancée! And she was the most vulnerable. Mostly because she insisted on going back to her apartment." I slap a hand on the wall so I don't make a fist; fuck, these women know how to crawl under my skin and itch. "You two definitely have that in common, you know? Fucking stubborn as hell, even when it's stupid."

Taylor frowns. "Wait—why did she go back to her apartment?"

I turn away from her. "She moved back for a short time right after her suicide attempt." I start walking down the corridor, knowing that she's going to follow me.

"Ilarion!" she calls, rushing after me. "Why did she move out?"

I don't look back. "Ask her."

"I'm asking *you*," she insists through gritted teeth.

When I don't respond, she reaches out and grabs my arm. I let her twist me around, but even when we're face to face, she doesn't drop my hand.

"What aren't you telling me?" she demands.

"The better question is, what isn't Celine telling you?"

I hear footsteps, and Taylor's head snaps up along with mine. She drops my arm as though it's on fire and a second later, one of the maids rounds the corner with a vacuum in hand.

"Excuse me, sir," she says. "Ma'am. I'll come back later."

She disappears down the adjoining corridor. Taylor's cheeks are flush with color; even her chest is pink.

"Why do you look so guilty?" I can't help but tease her. It's a bit of vengeance for the torment she put me through.

She tries to look indignant when she glares at me, but she mostly just looks frustrated. "I just… I don't want it getting back to Cee that we're…we're—"

"Having clandestine meetings in empty hallways?"

"No!" she cries out. "That we're more…*familiar* with one another than we should be."

"Fucking hell, Taylor. She knows that you stayed at the Diamond for weeks while she and Archie were hostages. She knows that we have a history. She knows we grew close."

"How close, though?"

"Well, I omitted the part where I fucked your brains out."

She cringes back. "Don't say that so loud. And so…vulgar."

"Is this what it's going to be like from now on?" I press. "You jumping at your own shadow because you're terrified your sister might get wind of the fact that your feelings for me aren't strictly familial?"

"They aren't even remotely familial," she hisses. "I *loathe* you."

I back her against the wall again. "Is denial really so addictive? I know you have to lie to Celine, but what's the point in lying to me? To yourself?"

"What do you want?" There's a catch in her voice that tugs something attached to my heart. *Irritating.* "What do you want from me?"

"For starters, I want you to be honest with yourself. Maybe then you can be honest with me."

"And then what?" she asks. "If I say I don't have feelings for you, you'll refuse to believe me. If I say I do, it changes nothing. You'll still be my brother-in-law. And I refuse to betray my sister."

"How is what you're doing now any different?"

"Excuse me?"

"You're lying to her now, keeping secrets from her, gaslighting her—isn't that a different kind of betrayal? Honestly, it's fucking manipulative. If you think you're being a hero, I have some bad news for you."

Taylor looks like I just slapped her across the face. Someone really needs to; it just won't be me. I'm an asshole, not a villain.

"Don't make me out to be the bad guy here," she whimpers. "I didn't come back here because I wanted to."

"Do you enjoy going around in circles, Taylor?" I ask, pushing my chest against hers. "Or do you just enjoy making me dizzy?"

"Please, Ilarion…"

"What are you pleading for, *tigrionok?*"

God help me, I like this kind of teasing. I *prefer* this kind of teasing. It's the way her breath catches, her lashes flutter, and her bottom lip puckers. I stare at that lip, resisting the urge to bite it.

I hate being denied what I want. I'm more in the habit of just taking.

Taylor blinks again, looking away for a moment. "For… for…"

Her eyes meet mine, and even though her mouth opens, nothing comes out. She clamps her mouth shut, and I raise my fingers to her lips.

Her lips tremble beneath my touch. Her chest rises and falls with heavy breaths. We're trapped within the present and the past, trying to find solid ground where there is none.

"Since you seem incapable of telling the truth, let me do it for you," I murmur. "I didn't just bring you here so that I could have my son back. This was about more than just Adam. I brought you back here as punishment. You left; you ran from me; you betrayed me. And I vowed that I would find you and bring you home. I vowed that I would punish you for what you did."

She's so quick to assume every wrong thing, so I know for a fact she's instantly thinking about her father. About what I do to traitors.

And she's right, at least a little bit. I do love playing with my food.

She swallows hard. "What are you going to do to me?"

I stare into her soft green eyes. They're filled with uncertainty now. Nervous tension that doesn't know where to go. *Good.*

That's why I turn on my heel and leave her in my wake. All I offer her is a single sentence, tossed casually over my shoulder on the way out.

"I guess we'll just have to see."

29

ILARION

I'm on the way to the den when Celine walks out of the day room that looks over the swimming pool. She's wearing her favorite ivory silk slip, the one that I used to imagine Taylor in.

She takes me by surprise by throwing her arms around me. It takes me a second to return the hug.

"What's going on?" I ask. It's not like Celine to give in to sudden bursts of emotion. Not anymore, anyway.

"I just wanted to say thank you," she says with a small smile. "For bringing them back." She releases me, but takes my hand instead. "You should have told me you were still looking."

I shrug stiffly. "I didn't want to get your hopes up."

Her smile gets a little wider. "Sometimes, I think I don't deserve you."

Before I can figure out how the fuck to respond to that, we hear Adam giggle from the pool, and her head swivels in the direction of the sound.

"I'm an aunt," she says longingly.

"He's a sweet kid."

"He's wonderful." Her voice is soft with love. I'm not a sap, but I get it. Adam has that effect on people. I'm no exception. "A real little heartbreaker. And he and Mila are already thick as thieves. I didn't see *that* coming."

"Where's the old man?" I ask.

Her smile curdles into a frown. "My *father* is sitting by the deck, watching Adam in the pool." I don't miss the light scolding in her voice, a subtle reminder to show respect for her family. I guess it's only fair, at least for her sake. "And I hope that the fact that he's here means that you've decided to let bygones be bygones?"

When I hesitate, she squeezes my hand and pulls me into the adjoining room. It's still open to the garden, but the pool is hidden from view.

"You made me a promise," she reminds me in a lowered voice.

Fucking hell, what is with these women? "He's here, isn't he?" I snap. "Unhurt and all limbs accounted for. Walking around my home freely without any consequences for his betrayal."

"That was the deal."

"There was no 'deal,' Celine," I remind her. "You begged, and I agreed. That was all."

She arches a delicate brow. "Sure sounds like a deal to me."

"Then you can go ahead and explain to my men why a fucking traitor is having tea and cookies in my goddamn garden."

I don't usually snarl at Celine; she's too gentle for that. But this is really grating on my nerves.

She frowns. "Are the men unhappy about it?"

"Wouldn't you be?" I ask. I have to admit—at least to myself—that she deserves some credit. She cares about my men, my brotherhood, with the same dedication as if they were her own. In a way, they kind of are.

She shuffles on her feet, her eyes darting toward the garden. "I know I asked a lot of you. I know I'm *still* asking a lot from you. But—"

"He's your father." I nod. "I get it. As I said, I made you a promise and I intend to keep it. I just assumed that you trusted me."

She drops her gaze. "I do trust you." She clears her throat and shuffles her feet before she speaks again. "I know it sounds ridiculous. I know you're not one for emotion. But you've been so wonderful to me. You're always wonderful to me."

She takes my hand again. But this time, there's a new softness in her touch. An intimacy that makes me want to redraw the boundary between us and remind her that this is crossing it.

"Anyone ever tell you that you shouldn't settle?" I ask, only half-joking.

She smiles shyly. "I'm not in the habit of giving up on people. You might think that's naïve—

"I don't," I say. "I think it's foolish."

She cringes for a moment before composing herself. "Maybe I am," she admits. "But I believe there's hope, Ilarion. I look at our future and—"

I pull my hand out from under hers. "I have to go," I interrupt. "I've got work to do."

She doesn't bother to hide her disappointment. She used to in the beginning, but I think she's figured out that I'm actually affected by her sadness. It's so much harder to ignore than indifference.

"Is it Benedict again?" She hasn't asked about him in a while now. "You still believe he's a threat?"

"I will never stop believing that. Not until I've seen his dead body splayed out in front of me. It's not in the *mudak's* nature to give up. You should know that better than anyone."

She sighs. "Is this why you've been so reluctant to move forward?" she asks. "You're worried that if we start a family, then we'll become an even bigger target?"

"That's part of it," I admit.

Or at least, it *would* be a reason—if I were interested in having a family at all. But I've never been interested in marriage, or kids, or any of that heartwarming bullshit that can bring a Bratva to its knees.

Until I met Adam.

Or really…until I thought I'd lost him.

Fucking hell. I might need to lay off Taylor a bit. She's not the only one keeping secrets around here.

"You've protected me all these years," Celine murmurs. "You'll protect our family, too."

"Celine…"

"I know, I know," she wards off uneasily. "We've had this conversation before. But you always seem to table it the moment it starts and nothing ever really changes. I'm tired of waiting, Ilarion. I've been waiting for years. I want more than the charity galas and the fundraisers. As much as it's filled my life, it's stopped fulfilling me."

Neither one of us says it, but it's there between us—her work is no longer compensating for the emptiness in our fraudulent relationship. It's no longer making up for lost time, or keeping her too busy to ignore the wait. She's trying to fill the gap by coaxing us forward, and I don't have the heart to tell her there's nowhere to go.

"Go spend some time with your family," I encourage her. "You have a nephew that I'm sure you'll want to get to know."

Her mouth twists to the side. "Is that why you found them and brought them back here?" she asks. "You thought it would distract me?"

Again, it's part of the reason. A solid one, too. Just not the *whole* reason.

Sometimes, I feel as though my life with Celine has been a series of broken parts. Nothing we've shared has ever been whole, or true, or real. Just fractured pieces that we've learned to avoid slicing ourselves open on.

"Celine, please. I have work to do."

"I let you brush me off all the time, Ilarion," she groans. "At some point, I'm going to stop letting you change the subject."

I say nothing. She looks at me and shivers like a cold draft just blew through. But then she glances away, and I wonder if she feels that ominous sense of foreboding in the air like I do.

"Oh, one more thing before you go?" She's shifted into something more direct, more professional.

I pause at the doorway. "Yes?"

"I want them to stay here with us," she says. "Taylor and Adam, and Dad…I want this to be their home."

"Okay."

She raises her brows. "Okay? Just like that?"

"I figured you'd want that," I say with a shrug. "And I already decided to allow it if you asked."

Sure. Let's go with that. It sounds better than the truth.

Which is that I want them here, too.

I clear my throat and add, "Anyway—if Archie has to be around, I'd rather keep him close."

Celine frowns. "He's not going to try to get in touch with Benedict, Ilarion. He's got everything to lose if he so much as attempts it. He loves his family too much to risk us again."

I want to challenge that, but I remember what Archie said about why he betrayed me. And despite the way it makes me grind my teeth with frustration, I know she's right.

"I guess we're just one big, happy family, then."

"Thank you," she says as I'm walking out the door. "For allowing this."

I'd tell her she's welcome, but why bother?

I never had a fucking choice to begin with.

30

ILARION

I finally make my way to the den. Most nights, I ignore my bedroom in favor of this room. It's quieter in here. The walls are thick enough to keep out all the unwelcome reminders of the life I'd rather be living.

But when I walk in, it becomes immediately obvious that there's no peace to be found anywhere today.

"Mila."

She's sitting in my chair with her legs propped up on my desk. She pivots the chair to face my direction and gives me a pointed smile. "Hey there, big brother. Kept your seat warm for you."

I walk over to the sofa and throw myself down on it. "Lucky for you, I need to lie the fuck down."

She doesn't respond. When I look up again, she's standing over me, gazing down with a curious gleam in her eyes. "Well, what the hell did you expect, bringing them back?"

"You see why I did, though."

"Adam's worth it," she agrees. "He's an angel. He's going to be your spitting image when he gets older."

"Don't remind me."

"But let's be honest," she says bluntly. "This was never just about him."

"I can't go on like this," I admit. Because if I can't admit it to her, who can I be honest with? "The first few years, the promise I made to her mother pushed me forward. But now...I fucked up."

"You fucked up by making the promise?" Mila clarifies.

"No, I fucked up by letting that promise take over my life. Celine and I...living here in this house...it's wrong."

"You did that for a reason. Benedict was acting under the misguided assumption that Celine was going to be your wife. That she *is* your wife. He would have come after her regardless."

"I was there, Mila," I snarl angrily. "I fucking remember. I just can't, for the life of me, remember why I thought it was a good idea."

"Jaded, are we?"

"You're one to talk."

She smirks and perches on the coffee table opposite me. "The men are unhappy," she informs me, changing the subject to yet another one I'm loathe to discuss.

"Don't remind me of that, either."

"Having Archie here is an insult to the rules that bind this brotherhood together. We lost a lot of men because of what Archie did. I've heard rumblings."

"What kind of rumblings?"

"The kind that suggest, if you don't punish the man, they will."

I sit up and drop my feet off the sofa. "They wouldn't dare."

"They feel that your hands are tied. They figure going rogue in this case might not earn them a severe punishment." She cocks a brow. "And Archie is a good example of why they're pretty sure you'll go easy."

"Then they'd be wrong," I say darkly. "You make sure every Zakharov man knows that Archie Theron is off-limits. No one touches him. Not until I give an explicit command."

"That won't go over well," she argues. "And things are fragile enough as it is after the rumor that Benedict started circulating."

"Are we calling it a rumor, then? It's just you and me here, Mila."

Her eyes darken. "*I* was the one he hurt, Ilarion," she whispers. "Not you. I was the one Father tried to break. I was the one who deserved to pull the trigger."

"I know," I agree. "Which is why I let you do it. But that doesn't make it any easier for the men to swallow."

"Then we do what we've been doing for the past few years: deny it."

I snort. "Not you, too?" At her curious stare, I shake my head. "This whole fucking house is full of denial."

She grits her teeth. "Sometimes, I think it would be a fuck-ton easier if I just came out and said it. Admitted it to everyone once and for all. I did it. I killed our father and I don't regret it."

"No one likes an honest woman, Mila. They'll crucify you for it."

She waves a dismissive hand. "I'm not afraid of death. It's not as though I've done a very good job with my life."

I'm tense now, given the topic we're skirting around. But she has to know that I would never just forfeit her like that. No matter what, she is my sister. And I will protect her until my last breath—even against herself.

"You can change that."

"No," she says firmly. "I've tried. It's not gonna happen."

"Talk to Dima."

She abruptly jumps to her feet and walks to the door. "I'm going to speak to our tracking team, see if there are any new leads that we can follow."

"Mila—"

"And then I'll go check on Taylor. She looked a little pale when I last saw her."

"Mila—"

"If there's something to report, I'll let you know."

She slams the door on me. I lie back against the sofa, staring at the textured ceiling, hoping that the answers to my problems are etched somewhere in the plaster.

But I've been doing this for too long to believe that things will just magically sort themselves out. There's no such thing as fate; there's no such thing as luck. Luck and fate are what I make of them.

And if I can't make them better…

I'm going to make everything else worse.

31

TAYLOR

I'm back to square one.

Five years since I left and nothing at all is different. I knew that if I stayed, I wouldn't be able to keep up the pretense for long. My feelings for Ilarion would cloud my judgment, and eventually, we would end up doing something stupid. We'd end up hurting Celine. We'd end up blowing up our lives.

And yet I still tried fooling myself into believing otherwise. *This will be different,* I told myself when he reappeared in our lives. *This will work.*

Yeah fucking right.

After what had just happened in the corridor, I can't keep lying to myself anymore.

That's why I'm lying in the fetal position on my bedroom floor, clutching the snow globe I stole from a place I never should have been, and trying to remember how to breathe.

"Oh God," I gasp. "Oh, God…"

It's all too much. Just way, way too damn much. Celine. Ilarion. Dad. I looked at him today and saw something like resignation on his face. As though he knows his days are numbered and he is just biding time until the end arrives.

I stare at the snow globe, shaking the base every now and then to start up the spiraling snowflakes once again. My breathing slowly settles.

Then I hear a knock on the door. I shove the snow globe under the dressing table so fast that I take a chunk out of the floorboards.

A second later, Mila walks in. This whole family has never been great at waiting patiently. She stops short when she sees me. "What are you doing on the floor?"

"Um…resting?"

"There's a bed over there," she says, pointing at it just in case I hadn't noticed. "A couch over in that corner and even more chairs in the other one. And you chose…the floor?"

"I like the floor, okay?"

"Riiiight," Mila drawls with a knowing nod. "Or perhaps you were having a little meltdown."

I glower at her. "Sometimes, it's polite to pretend like you don't know what's going on when people are in distress."

"Never been my forte. I call it like I see it."

"But can you take what you dish out?"

I'm being catty, but then again, I'm not really feeling in the mood to play nice. This family has never been great at sparing feelings, either.

Mila walks over to the bed I've ignored and sits down on it, facing me. "Good question. Why don't you hit me with something? Then maybe we'll find out."

"Have you told Dima about your feelings for him?" I ask bluntly.

Her face doesn't change, not really. It just tightens. Solidifies. "I have no idea what you're talking about."

"Then I guess we have our answer. You can dish it out, but you can't take it."

She grinds her teeth. "I forgot how annoying you are."

"Is that why you were so offended when I left without saying goodbye?" She growls at me, and I laugh. "We're friends, Mila. Whether you like it or not. It comes with the territory. Now, you wanna keep denying it, or you wanna tell me the truth?"

"I can't have sex," she blurts out.

I pause. I was not expecting…that.

"Sorry…what?"

Mila nods, looking more uncomfortable than I've ever seen her. "Every time I think about sex, I think about…things I shouldn't be thinking about. Things that make me turn into the worst version of myself. I do have feelings for Dima. Always have. But if I tell him about how I feel, I'll also be asking him to commit to a sexless life with me, and that's not fair."

"So you'd rather just watch him go off with other women?"

"How is that any different than what you're doing?"

I cringe and close my eyes. When I talk, though, I'm not sure if I'm talking about Mila's situation or my own. "Maybe he wants you more than he wants sex," I suggest. "Maybe he wants to be able to make the choice for himself."

She scoffs. "This is not fantasy-land, Taylor. This is real life. Men want sex. You won't believe the lengths they'll go to just to get it."

I push myself off the ground and walk over to the bed to sit beside her. I don't touch her because I know she'll reject it, but I stay close enough to let her know I'm there.

"I've thought a lot about you over the years, Mila," I say. "I haven't been through what you've been through, but I know intimacy can't possibly be easy after you've been…taken advantage of that way. After you've been…"

Her eyes snap to mine. "So you figured it out, then."

I nod and swallow. "How old were you when it happened?"

Mila stares at the floor for the longest time. I'm pretty sure she isn't going to answer me, when she finally speaks up. "It started when I was eleven." She's steeled herself, but I can still hear the hint of tremor in her voice.

I close my eyes at the horror she must have gone through. "I'm so sorry. But did you ever think to go to your father? Tell him what was happening?"

Mila laughs bitterly and shakes her head. "Ah. So you didn't figure it out after all."

Maybe not.

But *now*, I have.

My blood runs cold for the little girl peeking out through Mila's eyes.

"No one challenges the *pakhan*, Taylor. Not even when he climbs into his daughter's bed."

A hiss escapes between my teeth. I hate myself for making her say it out loud. The possibility crossed my mind once, but I pushed it away, disregarding it as too awful, too cruel, too terrible to be true.

I knew that Ilarion and Mila didn't have the best relationship with their father. But that didn't necessarily mean he was *that* kind of monster.

And I've answered my own question before I even ask it: the whole Bratva probably thought the same thing.

"Mila…"

She smiles sadly at me. "Sex has never been anything but pain and horror for me. Every time I think of it, I see *him*. A cruel world would've closed up my heart along with the rest of it. Taken away my ability to love. But that remained. It's everything else that died."

I almost reach out and touch her, but I hold myself back at the last minute. "I'm so sorry."

"Don't be. I did what I had to do to sleep at night," she says. "And since then, I have slept better. Don't ever feel sorry for me, Taylor. I'm no victim."

I let my hands linger in my lap, hating myself for how useless I am to do anything to help someone who's hurting so badly.

She gets to her feet. "Ilarion isn't going to make this easy for you," she remarks. "You know that, right?"

"Yeah. I know."

She nods. "But maybe you can make it easier on yourself. By being honest with your sister, coming clean, admitting to yourself that you love my brother."

"I *used* to love your brother," I mumble. "But those feelings are gone now."

Mila smiles. "Look at that. She can dish it out, but she can't take it." She moves towards the door, but she stops at the threshold to look back at me. "If you need anything, I'm here."

Then the door clicks shut. The floor looks mighty comforting again. I want to curl up and disappear from the world, for a few hours at least.

But if Mila refuses to be a victim, maybe I can do the same. I can look out the window at the world instead of cowering on the carpets.

I do exactly that, going to the window seat and tucking my feet beneath me while I peer out at the gardens. But the world doesn't look any different than it does when I admit I'm afraid. The gardens are still the gardens. The sky is still the sky. My past is still my past.

My future is still a nightmare.

32

TAYLOR

I'm still trying to figure it all out when I happen to catch sight of my father pacing through the garden. His face is hidden, but his shoulders are tense. He rounds every corner quickly, like he wants to catch anyone who might be waiting for him.

He's Scared Archie again. I know those signs, those twitches, those tremors. The constant worry and panic. The helicopter father who considered going out in the rain to be a dangerous pastime.

Then he turns as though someone called his name.

I see Ilarion walk into view. I push myself to the very corner of the pane so that if either one of them happens to look up, neither will be able to see me.

I can't hear a word they're saying, but it looks like a serious conversation.

Ilarion's gestures are measured. His composure never wavers. That's where Celine must've gotten it from: that glacial calm that makes me shiver.

Dad seems much less put together. He's waving his hands around a lot, but then, he was always a hand-talker. Still, I can see it in his body language. More panic. More fear.

Should I go down there? I don't want to miss what's about to happen. But I also don't want to risk watching something happen that I could have prevented.

Before I can make up my mind, Ilarion's composure cracks. He reaches out suddenly and grabs Dad by the collar of his shirt. I gasp so loud that I'm worried they'll be able to hear me from the garden.

What the hell is going on? What are they talking about?

Why would Ilarion do this after he promised both Celine and me that our father was off-limits?

Their noses are practically touching as Ilarion growls something to Dad. But then, mere seconds later, he lets him go. And both men play it off as though nothing had happened.

Why...?

A second later, I see exactly why. Adam runs past the pane and into my line of sight. Both men turn to him with fake smiles on their faces. Both men pretend like everything's alright.

They put on an act for Adam's sake.

And it's pretty clear to me now: they've been putting on an act for my sake, too.

33

TAYLOR

I splash cold water on my face before I go back downstairs. My first instinct would have been to go straight to Cee and confide in my sister. But I'm no longer certain of her loyalties.

Which is a sobering thought in and of itself.

When I emerge downstairs, Adam is sitting at the picnic table, stuffing a chocolate croissant into his mouth. He's got chocolate smeared all over his face and fingers. Cee is sitting beside him, dabbing his mouth pointlessly after every bite. She looks almost as delighted as he does.

"Wow, what's going on here?" I ask, trying to sound normal.

I scan the surroundings. Dad is standing on the steps of the deck, looking out over the garden. Ilarion is nowhere in sight.

"Auntie Cee got us yummy treats, Mama!" Adam sprays the table with bits of pastry and chocolate. He shoves the last of it in his mouth, consents to let Celine wipe what she can of the mess off of him, then goes scampering off in pursuit of a huge lizard capering over the porch railing.

She gestures for me to sit down and then pulls out a small notepad with a leatherbound hardcover. "If I'd known you guys would magically appear in my life again, I'd have moved some appointments around. Unfortunately, I have an appointment in half an hour that I can't back out of now."

"Oh, don't worry about it," I say. "You go ahead. Don't let us keep you."

Celine marks off something in her notepad and gets to her feet. "I'd love it if you would come with me, actually," she says. "It'd give us a chance to catch up a little more."

She seems so earnest about it that I'm having a hard time turning her down. But I also don't want to leave Dad and Adam alone here with Ilarion in whatever mood I just saw..

"Oh. Uh, yeah, sure," I stammer. "Can we bring Dad and Adam along, too?"

She raises her brow. "If they're interested. I'll go get changed and we can leave in ten."

She disappears into the house and I beeline straight towards Dad. "What the hell just happened?" I quietly hiss.

He peers over at me with a flustered frown. "What do you mean?"

"Don't play dumb, Dad. I was in my room looking out over the garden. I saw you and Ilarion talking. Fighting, more like."

He blinks at me. "I don't know what you're talking about."

"Dad, I saw you and Ilarion in the garden, like, ten freaking minutes ago! I saw him grab you. It looked like he was threatening you."

"You clearly misunderstood. We were just having a conversation."

"You're seriously gonna stand there and lie to my face?" I demand. "I thought we were past the bullshit."

He sighs. "Taylor, we're here now. We've finally been reunited with your sister. Let's just enjoy the moment, shall we?"

"What did Ilarion say to you?"

"I don't remember."

"Fucking hell!" Adam wanders closer to us, so I lower my voice into a hoarse whisper. "I can't believe this. We come here and you're back to being Ilarion's little puppet. The one who lied and spied and did God knows what else."

"Nothing is wrong, Taylor. You have nothing to be concerned about."

"I know what I saw."

"And I'm telling you: you saw wrong."

I stare at him, open-mouthed and flabbergasted. He's gaslighting me, and he's doing it with a straight face. It pulls me back a few years, when things between us were still so choppy that the slightest bit of honesty erupted into a fight.

It was easier to fight back then. Adam was young enough that whispered conversations and passive-aggressive replies just went right over his head. Nowadays, though, he can pick up on the slightest inkling of tension between us.

"Mama, are you angry with Grandpa?" he asks, materializing out of nowhere.

I bite back my anger. "No, sweetheart," I sigh. "We're just talking."

Dad glances between us for a moment, and I swallow the accusations buzzing on the tip of my tongue. "Auntie Cee and I are going for a drive," I say. "Why don't the two of you join us?"

"I'm happy just staying in today," Dad says immediately.

"If Grandpa's staying, I wanna stay, too," Adam proclaims. "Mila said I can go in the pool later."

I nod reluctantly. "Dad, I really think you should come with us."

"Maybe another time," he says. "But I do think it's a good idea that you join Cee. Quality time together will do you both some good." Before I can say anything else, he turns to Adam. "How about we go explore the rest of the gardens?"

"Dad!" I cry out, but he only throws me a goodbye wave.

I stand there, seething, left with no choice but to watch them walk away. The only thing that makes me feel slightly better is the knowledge that Ilarion won't hurt Dad with Adam around.

At least, I hope I'm right about that.

"Tay?"

I turn around and catch Celine by the open French doors. She's changed into a gorgeous suit made of a thick, buttery-white silk. The jacket is fashionably oversized and tailored at the arms to look as though they've been cuffed in. Beneath the blazer is a strappy red blouse and black, open-toed pumps. Her blonde hair is tied tight at the back of her head and clipped in place with thin hair clips studded with pinhead crystals.

She looks impeccable. There's not a hair out of place, and suddenly, I feel very much like the ugly duckling next to her.

"Wow," I say. "You look amazing."

She smiles and waves away the compliment. "It's just a lunch meeting, but I have to keep up appearances."

"Right," I say. "Should I change? I don't want to be underdressed."

"You look fine. And anyway, we should get going."

Reluctantly, I follow her to the driveway, where a tinted black sedan is waiting for us, complete with a uniformed chauffeur who opens the doors for us and bows.

"Ms. Zakharov," he greets, his head dipping low.

"Thank you, Giovanni," she says. "The Oval Room, please."

The chauffeur's gaze skims over me with disinterest. The moment I follow Celine inside the sedan, the door closes on me. Celine presses a button to her side, and the partition between the driver's compartment and ours rolls up before Giovanni has even climbed into the vehicle.

"I have to say: this life suits you." She arches a brow, so I rush to add, "I mean that as a compliment, by the way."

"Good to know."

"Was it easy?" I ask. "Adjusting to all this, I mean."

Celine looks me dead in the eye. "Nothing was easy, Taylor. Everything was a struggle. Everything was a fight. I went from having a mother, a father, a sister, and my health, to losing them all in one swoop."

"You could have come with us," I blurt before I can think better of it. I don't want to trigger a fight, but I also don't want to have to bite my tongue all the time with her.

There's too much we're leaving unsaid.

She raps her nails on the clutch in her lap. "There were days when I wished I had." Her gaze drifts to me and then out of the tinted window. "Like I said: it wasn't easy."

"If you don't want to talk about it…"

"No." She suddenly looks at me. "Let's talk about it. We might as well. You want to know why I chose to stay even after it was obvious that Ilarion's only interest in me was as a pawn in his game?"

It's a blunt and unforgiving way of framing the question, but I appreciate her transparency. Somehow, I wasn't expecting it from this new Celine. She seemed to have turned into the kind of woman who pretends everything is always perfect.

"Yes."

She nods. "I guess when it comes down to it, I chose to stay for myself. Because I loved him. And I suppose I thought that if I loved him hard enough, he would eventually love me in return."

"I…I admire your confidence…" I mumble, mostly because I don't know what else to say.

Celine sighs. "You think I'm dumb?"

"No! No."

"Yes, you do. I can see it in your eyes. It's okay. I was an idiot. I was never confident, just naïve and in love. I had the chance to be with him, regardless of his feelings for me. I thought that being with him was enough."

"And was it?"

She shrugs. "It's the choice I made. There's no turning back now. Of course, if I'd known then what I know now…I might have chosen differently."

I frown. My heart rate kicks up. "What do you know now?"

She stretches her silk-sheathed legs out across the seat. She looks like she belongs on the cover of magazines. Too bored for this world.

"That I never stood a chance," she murmurs. "He could never fall in love with me. Because he was already in love with someone else."

She glances at me, and for a moment, I wonder if she's lured me into this vehicle to confront me about the truth of my relationship with Ilarion. She's finally going to ask me point-blank, and I know that if she does, I will answer her honestly.

So I wait.

I wait for her to ask me the question that will sever our sisterhood forever.

"The worst part…"

I close my eyes. Brace for impact. In three, two, one…

"… Is not even knowing who the other woman is."

I don't know whether to breathe, laugh, cry, scream, run, pray, or just find the nearest hardwood floor and curl up into a little ball again.

The world inside my snow globe makes sense.

The world outside of it is a complete and utter mystery.

34

TAYLOR

The Oval Room turns out to be a lavish lakefront resort, with an invite-only membership that includes heads of state, minor royalty, rock stars, and a border collie who is somehow a YouTube influencer.

Of course, as a Zakharov, Celine sails in without lifting a finger. Doors are held open for her, heads bowed in reverence; the staff wait on her hand and foot.

She introduces me to the coordinators for her upcoming event, a pair of immaculately dressed, stunning blond Swedes whose names I immediately forget. The three of them embark on a dizzying conversation about canapes and seating arrangements that makes my head spin.

I just watch Celine. It's strange to watch the sister who used to consider pizza rolls a delicacy talk about shrimp ceviche hors d'oeuvres and her preferred vintages of champagne. She throws out sums of money with a shocking number of commas like it's nothing. Fifty grand for this, three hundred for that.

I want to shake these Swedes and scream in their faces, *Who is this woman? What have you done with my sister?*

"Sorry, Tay," Celine says suddenly. "I'll only be another minute or so."

"Oh, don't worry about me. I'll just go look around."

I leave them to it and go wandering through the ballroom doors. They open out onto a patio with white iron tables and chairs carved from a dense white stone. The flower arrangements are exquisite.

This is the world Celine has spent half a decade in.

It couldn't be any more different from mine.

My world has been filled with sleepless nights and colic. With soiled diapers and temper tantrums. With endless tears and constant regrets.

Although I'm starting to wonder if Celine and I didn't have that last part in common. One thing's for sure: I've seen enough of her life to know that it's not perfect.

Sometime later, she finds me leaning against the balcony looking over at the lake. "Sorry that took so long," she says, taking up a position next to me.

"Nothing to apologize for. I liked watching you. You're impressive."

Celine laughs. "I've had years of practice. Throwing myself into the work has kept me from thinking too much."

I glance at her, wondering if I'm being selfish by asking the question that's burning in my head.

Just when I've decided not to let sleeping dogs lie, though, Celine calls me out. "Go ahead and ask."

"Ask what?"

"Don't play coy, Tay. I can see the question on your face."

I grimace. "I don't want to make you uncomfortable."

"It takes a lot more than a mere question to upset me these days."

"Well…fine. I guess I was thinking about what you said in the car. I was just wondering why you assume that Ilarion is in love with someone else?"

She's quiet for a while, looking out as ducks slice across the mirrored surface of the lake below us.

"A woman knows when a man is thinking of another woman," she says vaguely. "I've confronted him about it, and he hasn't exactly denied it. But the thing is, I've never actually found evidence of another woman. And trust me—I tried."

I raise my brows. "Oh?"

Celine nods. "I'll deny it if you ever repeat this, but I had him followed our first year of marriage. He goes to clubs, bars, places where temptation runs rampant, and all he does is exactly what he tells me he'd do. Attend meetings, schmooze clients, make business deals, drink a little, and that's about it. Of course, that doesn't mean much in the end. Just because I haven't caught him in bed with another woman doesn't mean there isn't one."

I frown. "So…how is he with you?"

"He's good to me," she says without hesitation. "He can be standoffish at times, but more often than not, he's kind, thoughtful and attentive."

See what I mean? Something's not adding up.

"If he treats you well, and if you've found no evidence of an affair, then what makes you think there is one?" I ask. "Maybe he's loyal to you and you're refusing to believe that."

She shakes her head, certainty etched all over her face. "He's not loyal to me, Taylor," she insists softly. "He's loyal to *her*."

Her.

The word leaves a bitter taste on my tongue, and I'm not the one who's spoken. "I don't understand. What makes you say that?"

Her eyes cloud over and she turns away from me. She breathes in the air and exhales quietly. "I've always loved this place," she murmurs. "It's so peaceful."

She's avoiding the question, and I don't have the heart to push her to answer it. It's not like I have the right to push her.

"Ilarion mentioned that you moved out at one point," I say, shifting gears. "That you moved back into your old apartment?"

The only sign of her curiosity is a slight arch of one brow. "What else did he tell you?"

"Just that. He didn't say why." I decide to save my own skin with some truth. "We were arguing and he just…threw it at me."

"I suppose that was our version of a break-up," she admits. "I ended things with him. Well, I say that, but it's not like he was exactly fighting for me to stay."

"Was it because you suspected that he had someone else?"

"More or less," she says. "He was offering me less of a life and more of an 'arrangement.' I decided that I didn't want that, so I moved out, back to my old apartment. I was lucky that Vanessa hadn't sublet my room."

"Vanessa," I repeat, remembering Celine's old roommate as though she belonged to another lifetime. I suppose, in a way, she did. "How is she?"

"Dead."

I nearly choke on my own spit. "Excuse me? Vanessa died?" I repeat. "How?"

"It was meant to be me."

"I'm not following."

But I am. I just don't want to.

"Benedict Bellasio had eyes on me," she explains. "The moment he realized that I wasn't under Ilarion's protection anymore, he made a move. My new life wasn't even a week old when the apartment went up in flames. His timing was off, though. Ilarion suspects that he mistook Vanessa for me. I came home from a jog to find two firetrucks and a news team outside the building. Everything else was rubble and ash."

As calm as she is while telling me this story, there are goosebumps all over her exposed skin. Hell, there are goosebumps on *my* skin and I wasn't even there.

"So Vanessa…"

"The forensics team claimed the bathroom door was jammed and that was why she couldn't get out in time. She had inhaled so much smoke that by the time they pulled her out, there was very little they could do. Asphyxiation through smoke

inhalation. That was what they wrote as the cause of death."
Celine's eyes shimmer, but there's no trace of a tear in them.
"That was how I ended up back at Zakharov House. It was the
first assassination attempt and the first inclination I had that
Ilarion actually cared about me. I guess that's why I convinced
myself that staying with him might not be such a bad thing after
all. I mean, if he cared enough about me to want me alive, then
there had to be some feelings there. Like I said: it was naïve."

I'm silent. What the hell do you say to something like that? I
want to give her something, anything, but the words just
won't come.

She sighs. "I still have dreams about Vanessa. It should have
been me."

"Don't say that." I rest my hand on her arm. She flinches
away from me, but I don't take it back. "I am sorry for what
you had to go through, Cee. It can't have been easy, looking
over your shoulder all the time."

"You get used to it." She shrugs. "Of course, the first few days
after the fire were hard. I used to wake up screaming."

"I can't imagine going through that alone."

"I wasn't alone," she says. "Ilarion was with me. Every time I
woke up screaming, he was there. He held me together. So
much so that I was able to forgive him."

"Forgive him?"

She doesn't seem keen to answer that question, either. "You
know what I learned in those days? I realized that no
relationship is perfect. No marriage is perfect. Look at Mom
and Dad. I thought they were the perfect couple, but Dad
spent their entire married life lying to her."

"He was trying to protect her," I say, amazed that I find myself defending Dad in this. "He was trying to protect all of us."

"Didn't really work out that way, did it? That's the thing about fire, Taylor—if you play with it, sooner or later, you're going to get burned." She pauses to twist her rings around her fingers. "The difference is that, with Dad, we didn't know that we were living inside the fire. But with Ilarion, I was aware. I made a conscious decision to stay with him, despite our imperfect relationship. Maybe he was—is—in love with someone else. But she's not a part of his life. I am. That's enough for me."

"Is it, Celine?" I ask. "You don't feel dissatisfied with how things are?"

"I want a family," she says bluntly. "That's my only source of dissatisfaction right now. But like I said, I'm working on it. Ilarion will… We're trying."

Again, I get the feeling that she's telling me a version of the truth, just not the whole thing.

"Ilarion mentioned that there were two attempts made on your life," I say. I want to add, *Three, if you count your own,* but I'm still too chickenshit to ask directly about the suicide attempt again.

Her forehead wrinkles. "He's told you a lot more than I thought he had."

I shrug. "It was a long drive here."

"The second was a few weeks before we announced our engagement publicly," she tells me. "The announcement was meant to be a statement to Benedict. Fuck with me again, and he'd be dealing with the might of the Zakharov Bratva. After the engagement, there were no more attempts."

I frown. "All that means is he wasn't strong enough to try for a third time."

"Oh, I know," she agrees. "He's been rallying in the last few years, trying to build enough strength to hit back at us. I have no doubt that he will. But I'm not going to sit around and be scared. I'm going to continue living my life; I'm going to continue working towards my goals; I'm going to do whatever it takes to have my family. Fuck Benedict Bellasio. He's just a little cockroach. The moment he crawls out of his hole, Ilarion will stamp him out."

I feel the unease spread across my chest. I admire Celine's fight, her determination, but something tells me that the extremes of her life have desensitized her to the threats pointed at the Bratva—and by association, at her.

"Cee…"

This time, she's the one who puts her hand on my arm. "You're worried for me?"

"Of course," I admit. "Not just because of Benedict, though. It just feels like you've compromised on so much. You've just accepted how things are instead of working to change them."

"I'm in the Bratva's world now, Taylor," she says evenly. "I've learned to roll with the punches."

I frown. "I'd much rather you punch back."

"I fight when I have to," she assures me with a smile. "And if I ever find out who his woman is…well, she'll envy Benedict's fate."

35

ILARION

"Where are you?" Dima's voice echoes against the walls of my Ferrari. I reduce the volume on the car phone, but it doesn't fix the annoying echo.

"Corner of Oak and La Salle. What's up?"

"We got hit," he explains. "The southside warehouse. Three fuckers with Molotov cocktails. One managed to get away, the second blew himself up, and I've got the third rat right here. Squealing like a fucking bitch, I might add."

"What about the warehouse?" I ask as I punch the gas pedal through the floorboards and spin the wheel in that direction.

"Two walls down and a portion of the last shipment has been damaged, but we'll survive. Nothing too extensive."

"I'll be there in two minutes."

I race through the streets, blaring on my horn to get a couple of slow drivers out of my lane. I can see Dima's truck parked haphazardly across the entrance when I arrive. I screech to a stop right behind him and charge into the warehouse.

A handful of my men are scattered in front of the doors. They step aside quickly to let me pass. "Dima's in the back, sir," one of them informs me. "With the rat."

The damage becomes obvious when I walk inside. Smoke and ash fills my lungs along with the metallic odor of scorched metal. There's a chaotic energy in the air that crackles like static.

I'm on my way to the other side, where I can just about make out Dima nestled amongst the shadows, when I notice a forlorn foot sticking out from between two shipping pallets. I walk over and crouch down for a closer look.

This must be the *mudak* who lit himself on fire with his own weapon. Burns ripple down the sides of his face and his arm is melted like a candle, but I'd wager that it was the gunshot to the temple that ended him. His dark blue eyes stare lifelessly at the cracked ceiling above us.

He can't have been more than nineteen or twenty years old.

"Motherfucker," I growl under my breath. Only a soulless snake would send a boy to do a man's job.

I leave the body and stride grimly over to the end of the warehouse where Dima is surrounded by a few of my more senior *vors*.

There's another boy tied to a chair in front of them. His watery eyes dart around the space with obvious panic. There's no gag in his mouth, but he's biting on his bottom lip as though to keep his tongue from falling out.

"Does he have a mark on him?" I ask as Dima turns to me.

"Nope. None of 'em do. Plausible deniability for our old friend Benedict."

"Of course not." I grab one of the rickety chairs from the corner, drag it in front of the kid, and take a seat on it backwards. "You. Start talking."

The boy's eyes bulge with terror. "I…I don't know… I don't know anything! This…just…this is all a mis…m-mistake…"

Fucking hell. I stand corrected: don't send an *idiot* boy to do a man's job. I glance toward Dima, who saunters forward with a half-broken bottle from one of the Molotovs dangling in his fingers. "You're telling me that you and your friends made these yourself?"

The boy licks his chapped lips and nods.

Dima and I exchange glances. "Okay." I keep it conversational. Calm. "Tell me how you made these."

The kid is sweating buckets now. The ammonia stench in the air tells me that he's pissed himself, too.

"I…I… M-my friend did… He's the expert."

"Are you talking about your dead friend?" I ask. "Or your soon-to-be dead friend?"

"P-please," he begs. His voice cracks with the whine. "Let me go."

"Let's start over." I clap a hand on his shoulder. He flinches, but I don't do anything else to scare him. "I'm going to ask you a couple of questions. If you answer honestly, then we won't have a problem. If you choose not to answer, or if you choose to lie to me…well, then—problem. Understood?"

"Y-y-yes, sir," he stammers.

I nod. "Smart boy. We'll start with an easy question. What's your name?"

The boy just blinks at me. Dima clears his throat impatiently and that seems to snap him out of it. "Petyr Dobrev," he croaks.

"How old are you?"

"Twenty-two."

"Bullshit. But I'll let it pass." I point over my shoulder at the corpse I left behind. "Your friend, the one with the bullet in his head—how do you know him?"

"H-h-h-he's m-my…b-b-brother." He's sobbing so hard, he can barely get the words out.

"And the kid who got away?"

"Our cousin," he hiccups. "P-please…he's only seventeen."

"Old enough to know better," I snarl. "Who made the cocktails, Petyr?"

The kid's eyes flare, but he's smart enough to know when not to lie. "Th-they gave 'em to us. Told to bring them to this location and 'have fun.'" The words come a little easier now that he believes his cooperation will save him.

"Who is 'they'?"

He sobs again before he answers. "I…I honestly don't know!" he insists. "The man didn't give us a name. He just said that if we did it, he would pay us."

I arch a brow. "How much?"

"A thousand up front. And he promised another grand after the job was done."

Blyat! I'm going to be sick. "You bartered your lives away for two thousand dollars?" I rub a hand over my face and blow out a heavy breath. "First life lesson: know your fucking worth. When you're about to sell your soul to the devil, get a better price."

He gulps and sweats.

"See, here's the thing." I straighten up a bit and drum my fingers on the back of the chair. "You and your friends…your brother…" I nod toward the body across the room. "You took a very low price for a very big job. And you attacked *my* brothers, in my warehouse. I don't tolerate threats against the Zakharov Bratva."

The moment I say the name, the boy's face blanches. "Zakharov…? He…he didn't—"

"He didn't tell you who you were attacking," I finish for him. "Second life lesson, kid: always know what you're getting yourself into. You might have been able to walk away from him. But no one walks away from me."

His skin is deathly pale now. As pale as his dead, bloodless brother's.

"I didn't know!"

"You should have done your research."

"I…I can find him! Try and get you a…a name."

"Why bother?" I scoff. "I know who sent you even if you don't. Benedict Bellasio, although it's more likely the person who approached you and your friends was Gregor, his brother."

The kid starts crying. Snot and tears smear his face. "Please," he begs. "M-my mother…my mother is old. She needs me. I have a sister, too; she's only in high school. My father left us…please…"

Dima glances at me. Sighing, I slide off the chair and walk toward the back entrance of the warehouse, Dima close behind. The door has been singed, but it's still functional.

"What are you gonna do with the snot-nosed toddler in there?" Dima asks, pulling out a cigarette. Not a good sign— he never smokes unless he's stressed.

"You don't want me to kill him, do you?"

He shrugs, but I know him better than to take that at face value. "It's ultimately your call," he defers. "But for what it's worth, I believe the kid. He and his idiot friends were just trying to earn some cash. Wreak some havoc. Have some fun while they did it. They didn't know who they were fucking with."

"Since when is ignorance an excuse?"

Dima sparks his lighter. "You forgave Archie, didn't you?"

My eyes snap to his. "I haven't forgiven him," I growl. "I'm forced to keep him alive for now. That's all. He may still serve a purpose."

"The kid might, too."

"You want to recruit him?"

"Why not?" Dima shrugs. "He's strapped for cash, he's got dependents, and if he was bold enough to set fire to our shit, he stands to make something of himself in this Bratva. We could mold him. He'd be loyal, I guarantee it."

"Loyalty is never assured," I mutter. "Archie taught me that."

"Like I said, it's your call." Dima takes a long drag of his cigarette.

I glance back towards the boy. I'm starting to think that maybe it wouldn't be such a bad idea to bring in some new blood.

Especially if I'm planning on weeding out the old.

"Bellasio is getting bolder," I muse. "It's likely that he's gained in strength and numbers in the last few years. But he wants me to think that he has nothing to fall back on than green boys with no clue about whom they're facing. Double the watch on our properties and warehouses. We need to be ready for more attacks. No one can afford to be distracted."

"Least of all you," Dima says pointedly.

I narrow my eyes at him. "I know what I'm doing, Dima."

"Adam is a gem, " he says. "And so is the girl. I don't blame you for being distracted. But maybe for now, not claiming them might be safer for them. If Benedict finds out—"

"I know," I snap, annoyed by his logic. I turn back into the warehouse and walk over to the boy. His head is bowed in defeat, but he forces his eyes up to mine when my shadow falls over him.

"A-are you going to kill me?" he mumbles weakly.

"Should I?"

He shakes his head. "What do I have to do to live?"

I squat down in front of him. "As of this moment, your life is mine. I have not saved you from death. What I'm doing is giving you a way to pay me back for all the damage here. And maybe make a lot more than a measly fucking two grand." I hold his gaze. "Do you understand?"

He gulps and nods slowly. "I understand."

"First, you will give me the names of your mother and sister," I tell him. "You will give me their address and any other information I ask for. You will not be allowed to see or speak to them. You will disappear from their lives for the next year, and you will not be allowed any explanations or goodbyes. And *if* you see them again, it will be because you passed your initial training."

His eyes go wide. "Are…are you saying…I'm joining your Bratva?"

I smirk. "Don't fuck it up."

His eyes brighten with determination. There's hunger there. Hunger for life, of course, but it's more than that. There's hunger for glory and adventure and violence. The thirst to prove himself. I've seen that look on the face of every young boy who's been disappointed, hurt, and betrayed by their fathers.

Including my own.

And I realize something as I watch him…I don't ever want to see that look in Adam.

36

ILARION

"How bad was the damage?" Mila asks the moment I walk into the den.

"For fuck's sake—how long have you been here?"

"Walked in a few minutes ago," she explains. "Tidied up your desk, too. You're welcome. Answer the question."

I shoot her a glare. "Sometimes, I need peace and quiet, Mila."

"Then you shouldn't have brought Taylor and her kid back here," she retorts as she plops herself down on the sofa. "Dima told me you decided to spare the boy at the warehouse, by the way. Very merciful of you. Very uncharacteristic, too. I do wonder what could be fueling the change of heart. I've got some guesses."

My temples pulse. "He filled you in already?"

I don't want to sit down and give her the impression that I'd like for her to stay, but my legs are fucking aching and there's a sharp pain shooting up and down my spine.

"Sure did. Can I make you a drink?" Mila asks.

"Fine. But don't feel the need to join me."

She smirks and pointedly ignores my implied *get-the-fuck-out* as she pours two glasses of scotch. She hands one to me and gestures to the armchair opposite the sofa. "You gonna sit down?"

"Are you gonna leave soon?"

"Nope," she says, giving me a grin that says I'm fucking trapped.

"Fuck me," I mutter under my breath. I throw in the towel and sit down. The scotch does help. One sip in and the edge of the pain softens. "I thought you'd be in the garden with Adam."

"I was. But then Taylor left with Celine and I wasn't interested in making small talk with the ol' traitor."

"Mila…"

"What?" she asks innocently. "I'm not about to pretend like he didn't stick a knife in all our backs."

"He's off-limits."

She scowls. "Don't condescend to me, Ilarion. I can listen to an order when it's handed down, whether I like it or not." She takes a sip of her scotch and smacks her lips like our father used to. I make a mental note to never, ever tell her that. "Just curious: why did you spare the kid?"

"Because Dima asked me to. And because it didn't seem fair to kill him for being a stupid teenager."

"That, or you're just getting soft in your old age."

I give her the middle finger and take another sip.

"No?" she says, arching an eyebrow. "Well then, here's my other theory."

"Don't—"

"Seeing Taylor again has made you more sentimental."

"Stay in your lane," I snarl at her. "This is above your paygrade." Sighing, I slump back in my seat and run a finger around the rim of my glass. "Have you ever thought that maybe you spend a little too much time analyzing my life only because you have none of your own?"

The words whip through the air, harsher than I intended, but I refuse to take them back. Even after her mouth curves downward.

"I have a life," she says quietly.

"Other than following my orders and following Dima around? Where is it?" She says nothing in return, although a ripple of unease passes over her face. I lean forward. "It's about time you bite the bullet and tell him how you feel."

Her jaw tightens instantly. "Sure, I'll tell him—just as soon as you tell Celine that you're in love with her sister."

Here we go. It was only a matter of time.

"Celine knows where I stand."

"Sure, but she doesn't know who you're standing with. Should I just rip the Band-Aid for you?"

"Do that and you'll have hell to pay." I manage a smirk, though the thought alone makes me nauseous. "And not just from me."

She shrugs. "That doesn't really scare me anymore. I've lived through hell. Everything else after that is cake."

"Except when it comes to actually confronting your demons and being honest with yourself."

"Oh, you're one to talk!" She turns her dark gaze on me. "Let's face it: every single person under this roof right now is lying to themselves. Celine. Taylor. Archie. You. Me. It's fucking chaos in this godforsaken house."

"Honesty will set you free," I remind her, wondering if she'll shy away from this topic like she has every other time I've brought it up.

She shifts in her seat. "It did. But at a cost." She swallows and drops her head back against the sofa. "You had a hard time looking at me for a long time after that, Ilarion."

I don't bother denying it. It was difficult for me, coming to terms with the truth that I'd refused to see all those years. But it had nothing to do with her.

It had everything to do with my own failures.

I watched her fade. I watched the light leave her eyes, bit by bit. I didn't ask any of the right questions. I didn't push for answers the way I should have.

Until the day I walked into her room and found her sobbing on the bed.

Her tears had soaked through the top sheet and her eyes were so swollen she could barely open them.

"Fucking hell, Mila," I growled, rushing to her side. *"What's going on?"*

She didn't even hear me at first. I had to grab her shoulders, but the moment I touched her, she ripped herself away, her eyes wide with panic.

"Don't touch me!" she screamed.

She froze when she realized that it was me. Then she just stared, her expression distant and distracted. Like she was seeing me, but she was having a hard time remembering who I was.

"Mila," I said softly, trying not to make any sudden movements. *"It's me. Ilarion."* When she didn't respond, I tried again. *"It's your brother."*

She blinked. Twin tears rolled down her cheeks. "I-Ilarion..."

"Talk to me. What the fuck is going on? I haven't seen you in days and then I come up here and you're in bed, bawling your eyes out. Did something happen?"

"S-something happened," she stuttered. *"Something's been happening for years."*

She shook her head and sat up a little. She was wearing a loose tank top that revealed most of her neck and arms. I noticed the blotchiness on her skin. It looked like she had tried to peel the first layer right off.

When I reached out to examine her, she flinched back and let out a muted yelp. "Mila, did someone hurt you?"

She nodded silently.

"Who was it?"

She shook her head. "I can't tell you. You won't believe me."

"Of course I'll believe you. You're my sister."

"But he's your father."

There are some moments I will never forget. That is one of them. The gnawing in my gut, the ice down my spine. The way my legs went wobbly for the first time in my life.

I looked her in the eye. "What did he do?"

She shook her head. "I can't tell you," she said. "He'll kill me if I do."

"Mila—"

"There is something you can do for me, though," she says, grabbing my hand. Her palms were sweaty and hot. "Kill me, Ilarion. Kill me before he does. He's taken so much from me already. I don't want to die at his hands, too."

"Mila..." I said quietly, just to make sure she really heard me. "That will never happen."

Her face crumbled. She released my hand and wilted where she sat. I kneeled on the bed with her and grabbed her shoulders. This time, when she cringed away from me, I ignored it.

"I need you to hear me now," I told her. "Are you listening? Good. Yes, he is my father. He has taught me everything I know. But if it comes down to a choice, I will choose you over him in a heartbeat. Every. Single. Fucking. Time."

She stared at me, her mouth falling open.

"Do you believe me?"

It felt like an eternity before she finally nodded.

"Good," I said. "Now, tell me what he's done."

I'm not sure what I was expecting her to say. An arranged marriage? An argument turned violent? But when she opened her mouth to speak, I saw the shivers in her words, the horrible truth she was choosing to trust me with.

I sure as fuck did not expect what she told me.

"H-he... comes to my room at night," she said, her voice cracking weakly over the words. "He... he..."

I jerked away from her so fast that she broke off mid-sentence, her eyes flaring with alarm. "Ilarion!" she sobbed. "I'm not lying." Another tear cascaded down her cheek. "He made me promise never to tell a single soul. He made me promise never to tell you. He said that if I did, he would kill me."

I jumped off her bed and headed toward the door.

"Where are you going?" she cried out, her breathing growing heavy again..

I turned to her, just so that she could see the intent in my eyes. "To kill the bastard."

"No!"

I froze. "No?"

"No." She stood up, swallowed, and used the heel of her hand to wipe the tears from her eyes. "I want to do it myself."

"Hey." I blink once. Mila's face floats into focus in front of me. She's left the sofa, and she's crouched on the ottoman in front of my armchair. Her hand is on my arm and her eyelashes flicker with concern. "Where'd you go?"

"Where else?"

"Ah," she says, her voice dipping. "I figured. It wasn't your fault, you know. I've told you that before. It bears repeating."

I shake my head in disgust. "I was supposed to protect you."

"But not from him," she presses. "It was not your job to protect me from him. It was his job to protect the both of us. We were his children."

"And he died for it."

She nods solemnly. "I thought I would feel awful after it was done. I thought I would spend my nights plagued by nightmares. But the truth is, that night, I never slept better."

"Well, then, it was fucking worth it."

Her bottom lip quivers. She blinks fast and grabs my hand. She squeezes hard. "Have I ever thanked you?"

"Please don't." I shake my head. "Don't thank me, not for that."

"Because you feel guilty?" she asks softly, her forehead wrinkling.

"No. Because I should have noticed a lot sooner."

"I never cared about that. I cared that you listened when I finally decided to talk. I cared that you believed me. You have no idea how much that meant. How much it still means to me. That's why I stuck around all these years and devoted myself to this Bratva. It was because, if I was going to spend my life on anything at all, it was going to be you."

I bite down on my tongue. "Careful now. You just might make me cry."

She laughs softly, but she doesn't release her grip on my arm. "You deserve to be happy, too, Ilarion. It's not your job to save the whole world."

"I'm not interested in saving the whole world. Just a few people in it."

"Is one of those people yourself?"

I pat her knee and push her away gently. "Go and find Dima," I chide. "Tell him that we're going to tighten the noose around Benedict's neck. It's time to end him."

She nods with a cryptic smile. "Whatever you say, boss."

37

TAYLOR

"Where's Grandpa?" I ask the moment Adam runs up to me. It's no surprise my son is still in the garden, but he's with Mila and Dima. Not Dad.

"Grandpa said he was tired," Adam explains. "He went up to take a nap."

"When?"

"What's the matter, Taylor?" Mila butts in. "You sound worried."

I put Adam down and kiss the top of his head. "Why don't we head inside? Maybe get you something to eat?"

"I already ate. Mila made me sandwiches. They tasted bad, but then Uncle Illy came in and made me some pasta," he says, beaming the entire time. "He cooks even better than you, Mama."

"Does he?" I ask distractedly, looking back over my shoulder toward the house.

When we arrived back at Zakharov House, Cee went straight to her room to change. I came out here hoping to corner our father again. He is proving to be annoyingly slippery, though.

"Yeah! Can you ask him to teach you how to make pasta, Mama?"

"Later, baby. Wanna go inside and read a little?"

"I wanna stay outside with Dima!" he says, darting toward the grass. I'm left standing there, wondering when I lost my top rank in his Favorite People poll.

"You okay, Taylor?" Mila asks.

"No," I retort. "Where is my father?"

"Probably in his room. Unless, of course, he's snooping around and spying on us again. That's also a possibility." I can't quite tell if she's kidding or not.

"He's not doing that anymore, Mila."

"Can you guarantee that?"

"I can, but apparently, that doesn't matter."

She gives me a sheepish smile. "In order to believe someone, you need to trust them. No offense, but I'm not about to trust your father simply because he's your father."

She's very calm, but her movements are tense. There's a rigidity in her posture that suggests she's holding back.

"He's an old man."

"Old men are capable of doing horrible things," she says. "I know from personal experience."

I take a deep breath and try to keep my calm. "Mila, listen—"

"No, *you* listen." She takes three long strides toward me, then pulls out a chair, scraping the deck as she drags it away from the table. "Sit down."

"I'd rather stand."

"Suit yourself," she says with an unconcerned shrug. "The night that my father died, your father was in the house. He was on-duty," she says. "He was the only one who knew the truth of what happened. And then, shortly afterwards, Benedict Bellasio started spreading a 'rumor' that, in this case, happened to be true. Of course, at the time, it felt like a lucky guess. But when we found out about Archie's betrayal, I realized that it wasn't a lucky guess at all. Your father sold my secret to Benedict Bellasio."

I can feel shooting jolts of energy rushing up my spine. "He— You—Fuck, Mila. I am so sorry."

"For what? You didn't sell me out to our worst enemy," Mila says pleasantly. "You're only a runner. Not a talker."

I take a step back, feeling my throat constrict. It feels like someone has their hands wrapped around my neck.

"Okay." I pull out a chair and sit down next to Mila. "Okay. He was a traitor. He betrayed you and Ilarion. The entire Zakharov Bratva. And I'm aware that if he had been anyone else, he'd be six feet under by now." I meet Mila's gaze. "But he is my father, and as unfair as it is to ask, as deserving as he may be of retaliation, I'm asking you as a friend: forgive him. Forget what he's done. Let him live. Let him watch his grandson grow up. Let him be a part of my life, of Cee's life. Please, Mila. Please."

The calm in Mila's eyes has been replaced with shadow. She grinds her teeth so hard that I can hear the grating. "He must have been a good father, for you to speak up for him like this."

"We've had our issues," I admit. "We still do. I feel betrayed by him a lot of the time, too. But the thing is, I know that his intentions have always been good. His only goal was to support and protect his family. He went about it the wrong way, but his heart was always in the right place."

Mila regards me with a stoic expression. Then she sighs. "Fine," she mutters. "Fine."

I let out a breath I didn't even realize I was holding in. "Thank you."

She gets to her feet, but her eyes move toward the French doors. I get a whiff of lavender and honeysuckle and the citrusy notes of Cee's expensive perfume.

"Just so you know," Mila says, lowering her voice so that only I can hear her, "I think you're going about protecting Celine the wrong way, too. You and your father have that in common." Then she looks up and raises her voice again. "Hey, Cee, how'd the meeting go?"

"Smoothly," Cee replies as she walks over to us. "Where's my nephew?"

"Somewhere in the gardens with Dima. I think I'll go join them, actually. Excuse me."

Celine turns to me with a smile. She's changed into a silk beige romper. "Come with me; I want to show you something."

"I was actually gonna go check on Dad," I say as I get to my feet.

She waves away my plans. "He's resting, apparently. Just leave him to it. This is more important." Her bright smile betrays her excitement.

She grabs my arm and pulls me into the house, then takes me all the way up to a room on the second floor. It's huge and airy and the wallpaper is a soft, warm blue that reminds me of a baby nursery.

Oh my god, is she pregnant?

"So," she says, twirling on the spot, and pointing to the left and hand side corner of the room. "I'm thinking the bed goes over there. We can make it a bunk bed and add a slide if he's into that sort of thing. And over there, wall-to-wall shelves for his books and toys."

"Um, who is all this for, Celine?"

She rolls her eyes. "Adam, of course! He can't room with you forever. He needs a space of his own."

I'm hoping that she can't hear how loud my heart is thudding against my chest. "Cee, this is all very unnecessary. I'm happy to share with Adam, and he's not gonna care about having his own space."

"He will when he's older."

"We won't be here that long."

Her face falls and her shoulders hunch. "Oh, right. I'm sorry. I shouldn't have—I'm sorry."

"That's okay. I mean, this is your house. I don't want to impose—"

She grabs my hands. "But it's not an imposition; that's what I want you to know. It would be so lovely if you stayed. All of you. We've lost so much time together—it just makes sense for you guys to live here. I've already asked Ilarion and he's fine with it."

"You've already asked Ilarion?"

"Mhm." She nods. "So, what do you say?"

"I say…I'll have to think about it."

Her brows knit for a moment. "Well, in the meantime, Adam can use this room. And in the evening, I'll introduce you to his nanny."

"I'm sorry, his *what?*"

"Her name's Edna. She comes highly recommended."

"Celine, Adam doesn't need a nanny."

"Of course he does. We can't be with him all the time. And eventually, you'll find a job, and maybe even a boyfriend. I've spoken to Edna over the phone and she sounds wonderful."

"Celine, I really appreciate all of this, but—"

"You don't have to thank me, Tay. I want to help. It makes me feel good to know that I can make your life a little easier. It couldn't have been very pleasant living out of a suitcase all these years."

I have to bite my tongue from turning down her offerings. As sweet as the gestures are, neither one sits well with me.

"It honestly wasn't that bad," I tell her. "And as for Adam, I enjoy doing everything myself. If I needed extra help, Dad was always around. I never wanted a nanny."

Cee's gaze snaps to mine and her smile wavers. "I'm being pushy, aren't I?"

"That's not it at all," I say quickly. "I just don't need that specific type of help. We're just very different people now, Cee. And I think that maybe you're trying to live vicariously, and—"

I stop short when I see the way Celine's mouth falls open. *Fuck.* I spoke wrong.

"You think I'm trying to live vicariously through you?"

"No, that's not—I mean, it's what I said, but it's not what I meant."

Her smile has disappeared entirely. She shifts from one leg to the other. She still wrings her hands together when she's agitated. At least that hasn't changed.

"Cee, I'm sorry. That's not what I meant at all. I'm just not good at putting this stuff into words."

"No, you're right." She sighs and smooths her hands over her sides. "Adam is your son, not mine. I have no right to plan nurseries for him or hire nannies on his behalf."

Yup. I'm a bitch.

"It was a wonderful, thoughtful gesture."

"It was pushy and rude and obnoxious," she counters, her voice soft and self-conscious.

"I was just taken aback." Shit, I really have put my foot in my mouth. "I wasn't expecting it. But now that I think about it, he would love this room. And a nanny might even be helpful."

She glances at me out of the corner of her eyes. "You're backtracking."

"Yes, I am. Please let me."

That almost gets a smile out of her. "You're not wrong. Maybe I was trying to live vicariously through you. I just…" She sighs heavily. "I've wanted to have a family for so long." Her shoulders rise and fall heavily as her nose screws up tightly. "And now, I'm crying. Wonderful. Fucking perfect."

It's the first time since being reunited that I've seen her composure crack.

It makes me love her even more.

"Come here," I say as I gather her up into my arms.

She doesn't hug me back very convincingly, but she lets me embrace her anyway. When I pull back, she looks at me for a split second before she cringes. "That was awkward, wasn't it?"

"Could've been worse. Not much worse, but worse."

She laughs, but it doesn't dispel any of the nervous energy that surrounds her. "I don't have a lot of practice," she explains. "The people I hug are colleagues and society friends. I can't remember the last time I've had a real hug from someone I'm close to."

A lump rises in my throat and a million follow-up questions spiral through my head, but I keep my mouth shut.

"You ever need a real hug, just come to me. I've got you."

She looks away quickly. But before she turns away completely, I swear I glimpse a tear sparkling in the corner of her eye.

38

TAYLOR

Okay, so talking to Dad is a no-go.

I'm just going to have to go right into the lion's den.

But the lion isn't expecting me, that's for sure. Ilarion looks up from his desk and does a double-take. "What are you doing here?"

I shut the door and twist the lock to make sure we're not disturbed. Then I stomp over to his desk and slam both my palms down on either side of his table like I've seen people do in the movies. I figure, bring on the drama, right? I have nothing to lose. "What is going on between you and my father?"

"You worried I'm cheating on Celine with your father?" he asks with a straight face.

"Don't be cute."

"Oh, so you think I'm cute?"

I grit my teeth and try to exhale out all the nervous tension I've brought into the room with me. It goes about as well as you'd expect. "I think you're playing a game. And I think you think I'm too stupid to see it."

He leans back in his chair and sighs exasperatedly. "This might go a little smoother if you told me what the hell you're talking about."

He's wearing a t-shirt, which I've rarely seen him wear before. It's a crew cut in a soft gray that brings out the moody hues in his blue eyes. It's very annoying how thrown I am by that detail.

So what, he's wearing a t-shirt? Who cares? Big freaking whoop. I should not be so affected by what he chooses to wear. Or how he wears it. Which in this case…is well.

Really…freaking…well.

"You threatened my father."

He raises both brows and rotates around in his black swivel chair. "Did I?"

"I saw you. I saw you from the window of my room. The two of you were in the garden and you grabbed him by the collar. You only let him go because Adam came by."

He frowns. "Hm. I don't recall."

"Do *not* gaslight me."

"Had enough of that from your father, have you?"

I rear back as though he's tried to hit me.

He just nods. "Come on, Taylor. You wouldn't be here, demanding answers from me, if Archie had chosen to be honest with you. I'm guessing you already went to him and he told you that nothing happened. So why do you expect me to say anything different?"

I swallow hard. "Silly of me, really," I say as the hurt clogs my throat. "To expect honesty from either one of you."

"I think it's best you forget about whatever it is you think you saw," he suggests as he scans the documents littered across his desk. "Concentrate on getting to know your sister again."

I bristle at the insinuation. "I don't have to 'get to know' Cee. I already know her. I've known her my entire damn life."

"And yet she still hasn't told you about her suicide attempt, has she?"

It's the confidence that gets me. The arrogance. I'm way out of my depth here, and he knows it, and he's rubbing my face in it. Because the truth is, Ilarion doesn't just know my sister better than I do right now; he knows my father better than I do, too.

How the hell did that happen?

"I think I have a pretty good idea why she tried to hurt herself."

"Oh, let me guess," he muses. "I'm the bad guy in this story."

"She's not used to being *hugged*, Ilarion!" I'm pretty sure spittle flies out of my mouth when I yell that at him. "She acted like a hug was the greatest thing on Earth! Why is that? Why is she so starved for touch?"

He blinks placidly. "I'm not much of a hugger. And you've met Mila."

"You've hugged me." The moment the words are out of my mouth, I regret them. "Pretend I didn't say that."

"I'm not as good at pretending as you seem to be."

"The fuck you aren't." My god, he's infuriating. "Give me a break here, Ilarion. I'm trying to do the right thing."

"For who? Yourself?"

"This is not about protecting myself!" I furiously insist. "I can handle Cee being mad at me. What I can't handle is breaking her heart because she had the misfortune of bad timing."

"Fucking hell, woman." His eyes flash like thunderbolts. "You really think that's all it was? *Timing*?"

"Well—"

"It wouldn't have mattered when I met you or Celine. Before, after, it wouldn't have made the slightest fucking bit of difference. It was always, always going to be you."

Oh...God.

My legs have turned to jelly in the two seconds it takes for Ilarion to get to his feet. His blue eyes are sapphire bright. He's turning me to putty where I stand and there's not a damn thing I can do about it.

Truth be told, I was putty from the start.

"Y…you shouldn't say things like that."

He shrugs like what he just said wasn't absolutely life-changing, life-ruining—take your pick. "I'll say it because it's the truth."

"Then lie. Lie to me, to her, to yourself if you have to." I swallow the traitorous parts of myself that want to hear the truth. "Do whatever it takes to stick to the damn narrative."

"I didn't write this narrative for us. *You* did."

"And I would do it again!" I exclaim. "I'm not exactly sure why, but she still loves you."

"How are you so fucking blind, Taylor?"

I stop short, taking in the furrows in his brows. I glance down at his hands and I notice his knuckles are white. He's not even close to as calm as I first thought he was. Like me, he's burning up with wanting something that's so close and yet so very fucking far away.

"She suspects that you're in love with another woman," I say softly.

"Is there a question in that?"

"Have you been having affairs?"

"Are you asking for Celine, or yourself?"

"Fuck you."

The corner of his mouth twitches upwards, but it looks more like a grimace than a smile. He walks around the desk, his footsteps landing heavily against the wooden floorboards.

"I don't know why, but despite the fact that she thinks you're cheating on her, she's still decided to stay."

Now, he smirks at me, like he finds this whole thing hilarious. "Both of you have a habit of jumping to conclusions, you know that? Besides, she's living pretty comfortably with my wallet in her hand."

I snarl at him. "How *dare* you! Cee would never stay for something as superficial as money. She's staying because she's hoping that you'll fall in love with her."

"It's been five years, Taylor. If I haven't fallen in love with her by now, it's not going to happen."

"Not true."

"No?" he asks, though he seems only barely interested in my answer. "You think that I'm going to wake up one day and I'll just suddenly, magically be head over heels for her?"

"No, but I do think if you try, if you make an effort, you'll be able to develop feelings for her."

He narrows his eyes at me. "You want me to woo Celine?"

I flinch, though I try to pass it off as a nervous tic. I'm just not entirely sure which one of us I'm hoping to convince. "Why not? It's clear you only ever tried when you wanted to use her to get back at our father. Why not now?"

"The point was to get *her* to fall for *me*. Not the other way around."

"So change the point."

He takes another step towards me. My heartbeat rises and my cheeks flush with heat as he looks down into my eyes. Why the hell can't I look away? And why the hell did I shut the door and lock it?

"Ilarion, please."

"Please *what*?" His eyes bore into mine. We're so close now that I can see flecks of gold and amber. How have I never noticed that before? Or maybe I've just forgotten?

"Why are you trying to get in my head?"

"I'm not trying to do anything, *tigrionok*. Don't you get it? I'm already in your head. I have been since the moment you ran in front of my car. Just like you've lived in mine."

I blink to try to break our connection, but it does nothing. It just reminds me that our connection couldn't even be broken with time or distance. Not with a rainstorm or a violent mafia or a car speeding out of control.

This was fate.

There was never any hope of stopping it.

He's right, I know he's right, and it's breaking my heart. It's the only memory I can look back on without any guilt, because it's the only memory that's free of Celine. Her entanglement with Ilarion came after—so that night in the rain, in the car…that was just for me.

For us.

"Go ahead and deny it." His voice is chipped and curt, daring me to lie to him.

I want to, but I can't.

I used to think life was simple. That relationships weren't so complicated. Now, standing on the other side of motherhood and love, heartbreak and loss, and grief—*so much fucking grief* —I can taste each one of those emotions and I'm coming away confused and lost. I'm coming away understanding that I will never reach a point when everything feels clean or simple or easy.

"The night we met…" I stammer through the words. "It meant a lot to me, Ilarion. It still does. But that was our moment together. And it's over."

"No, it's not."

I shake my head. "Why didn't you ask for my number?" I hear myself demand. Where have I managed to bury this fury, this sorrow, for all these years? "Why didn't you want to see me again? You drove off like all we had was a meaningless one-night stand."

His blue eyes turn a shade darker. I wouldn't have thought it was possible unless I saw it myself. "You seem to forget that you were the one who refused to tell me your name. You just jumped out of my car and tried to run back home to your father."

"I—"

"Don't blame me for something that was equally your fault. Why didn't you ask for *my* name? *My* number?"

"Would you have given it to me?"

"I tried to. You stopped me."

I study his face, looking for signs of a lie. But then the memory fades into my mind, and I realize with a sinking sadness that he's right. "But you would have gone after Cee anyway."

"Not a chance. I would have taken you instead. And this time, I would have actually meant it."

My heart throbs inside my chest. Or maybe it just stops beating altogether. All I know is I'm floundering in a sea of hopelessness and disbelief.

He *can't* mean that. He can't.

"Well, here we are." I can't think of anything better to say. "You powered through before. Why not do it again?"

He turns away from me, his features ironing out in that way they do when he doesn't want me reading the expressions on his face. "Because this time is not about revenge, or the Bratva, or Benedict Bellasio," he says. "This time, I want what I want."

He glances back at me. His gaze is direct and burning. I can't look away, even though I know I should.

"And what I want is *you.*"

The air in the room grows hot and oppressive so fast that my skin feels like it's blistering. He waits for my response, but I have no idea how to respond to that.

If I answer him honestly, I'll be betraying my sister.

If I lie to him, he'll see right through me.

So I do the only thing I can do under the circumstances. I do what I did the first time when I couldn't see a way through the mess.

I turn and run.

39

ILARION

Once the urge to chase after her and drag her back has passed, I escape the den and venture out into the garden in search of Adam.

My son calms me down like nothing else. More than either of his daughters, Archie has Adam to thank for his life. Because when I laid eyes on the traitor again after so long, the urge to kill him wasn't quite as overwhelming as it once was. It was still there, of course, but tempered. Sated —for now.

Adam is equal parts storm and sunshine. I can see all the parts he's inherited from his mother, and I can see the potential he has in him to become like me. I can see the strength that's pure Mila and the kindness that's all Celine's. And even though I had no part in his upbringing, it makes me proud.

It makes me want to be a part of the rest of his life.

"Looking for someone?" Mila asks from the side of the pool when I walk out onto the deck.

"Adam."

She smiles. "He's in his nursery with Edna."

"Who the fuck is Edna?"

Mila smirks. "The new nanny, of course."

"Taylor hired a nanny?" I ask just before the realization hits. "No, *Celine* hired the nanny."

"Yeah. I believe she discussed it with Taylor."

"She should have fucking discussed it with *me*."

"Why?" Mila asks. "You're not his father."

I glare at her. "You really know how to push my buttons, don't you?"

She gives me a noncommittal shrug. "Don't kill the messenger."

"Upstairs in the nursery, you said?"

She nods. "Second floor. Third room on your right. If it's any consolation, the nanny seems nice. She knows what she's doing."

"I couldn't possibly care less," I mutter under my breath as I make my way upstairs.

The whole way there, I wonder if Taylor willingly agreed to a nanny or if Celine cajoled her into one. Somehow, I find the latter more likely.

Adam is sitting cross-legged on the carpet, surrounded by toy blocks, trying to fit two pieces together with his face screwed up in fierce concentration.

His nanny is sitting a few feet away from him, watching carefully as he toils. She's younger than I expected, probably late thirties or early forties, with blond hair swept back in a neat braid.

"Uncle Illy!" Adam calls when he spots me. "You came to see my new room?"

The nanny jumps to her feet. "Hello, sir."

I survey her. She's wearing white linen overalls, wrinkled from where she was kneeling on the floor. She looks perfectly nice. Perfectly normal. "You must be Edna?"

The woman nods. "And you must be Adam's father?"

A "yes" is on the tip of my tongue,—and then Adam beats me to the punch. "Ilarion's not my papa," he interrupts. "He's my uncle."

I grit my teeth and pretend like that didn't just rip my heart from my chest. I give the nanny a tight smile. "That's me."

"Ah. Miss Celine's husband."

I nod. "Something like that. Why don't you go take a break?" I tell her, desperate to be rid of the woman. "I can take it from here."

She looks a little uncertain. "Well…"

"I'm sure," I say dismissively. "Go on."

She hesitates. Her eyes flicker to Adam as though she expects him to ask her to stay, but when he ignores her and continues playing with his blocks, she gives me an awkward nod and slips out of the nursery.

I join Adam on the carpet. "What are you building?"

"A big tower," he says. "The kind that Rapunzel lives in."

"Great idea. I'll help."

We get to work. I watch him as we go. He has a habit of sticking out his tongue to the side when he's concentrating. His eyebrows scrunch together like mine do and his eyes squint into thin blue slits.

When the door whooshes open, I'm the only one who notices. I'm about to tell the nanny to fuck off for a while longer when I notice a sheath of dark hair swish into view.

I catch her eyes and she freezes, already halfway back out the door. That's when Adam notices her, too.

"Mama! Come and help me build my tower!"

"Oh, that's okay, baby. You're playing with Uncle Illy."

"But I want you to help!" he says. "Please, Mama?"

I can see her face fold. Like me, this kid has her in the palm of his hand. She bites back her reluctance and plasters a smile on her face. "Of course, sweetheart. I'll help you."

She steps cautiously into the room and finds a spot on Adam's free side, skirting as far away from me as possible. Of course, that puts us directly in front of each other. She glances up at me, notices that, and her lips curve down.

"Mama, make this part," Adam says, pushing a bunch of red blocks her way. "Uncle Illy, you can do this side."

We work in silence for a while. Adam's concentration never wavers as he presses pieces together and the tower begins to rise up from the carpet. I laugh when he starts humming under his breath as he works. I don't think he even realizes he's doing it.

Taylor laughs, too. I look up at her, and it's somewhere in this bizarre moment when our smiles collide that I realize that Adam might be the one thing we can actually compromise on. I may not have known the boy for long, but I would die for him. A part of me knew that truth from the moment I knew of his existence, back when he was nothing but a tiny little peanut in Taylor's stomach.

"Uncle Illy?" Adam says, suddenly breaking the silence out of the blue. "Why don't you have any kids?"

Taylor's eyes fly to mine. "Adam, you wanna help me with this part?" she asks, trying to poke her half-made tower in his face to distract him.

He gives me a confused frown. "No, Mama, that's your job." Then he looks pointedly at me as though to let me know he's still waiting for an answer.

"I…" I don't want to lie. Not more than I already am. *I had you, son,* is right there on the tip of my tongue. But I can't say the words, and I'm struggling to find others. "I don't know."

His nose wrinkles up a little. "They don't have storks in this part of the country?"

"Storks?"

He nods and glances at Taylor, who is full-on blushing now. "Mama says that storks come bringing babies. That's how she got me."

I force myself to suppress my smile. "A stork, huh?"

She licks her lips self-consciously. "It's, um, complicated, sweetheart. Some places have a shortage of storks."

"That's sad. Maybe you should go to the place Mama lived when she got me," Adam suggests. "Then you and Auntie Cee can get a baby, too."

"Actually, I might be allergic to storks."

He looks severely disappointed by that. "But don't you want a baby?"

"Honey," Taylor interrupts before I can speak, "we really need to concentrate on building this tower. Where's Rapunzel gonna live if we don't finish?"

"But I wanna know, Mama. Then I will have a friend to play with."

"You'll be in school soon, and then you'll make lots of friends."

His bottom lip juts out. "But then I come home and I don't have anyone to play with here. I wanted to call the stork again, but you said no."

"You want a baby brother or sister, huh?" I glance at Taylor again, wondering if she can see the heat flare in my gaze. Just the thought of making another baby with this infuriating hellcat...

Focus, Ilarion. Your son is watching.

"Yeah. For a long time. Mama keeps saying no. She says that she has me and that's enough. But I want a baby brother or sister."

I chuckle. "Maybe one day, huh?" *Maybe even one day soon.*

I'd have no issue with making a baby brother or sister for him. None at all.

He shrugs and goes back to his tower. When I look at Taylor, her eyes are on me. "There are great fertility experts in this state," she says softly. "Just saying."

I arch a playful brow. "I think you know damn well I don't need a fertility expert."

She goes bright red. "It's none of my business."

"It could be your business."

If she turns any redder, she'll catch on fire. "You can't be serious."

"I'll let you take a guess."

She rolls her eyes and walks over to the window seat that overlooks the garden. Adam doesn't seem to notice her absence, so I follow her. I lean against the supporting wall, giving her the space she clearly needs from me. But apparently, it's still too close, because she stiffens the moment I get there.

"You don't think she'll get suspicious?" Taylor murmurs. "If you keep showing interest in Adam?"

"She isn't here to see anything."

She sighs. "No, I guess not."

"So…storks?"

She drops her head into her open palms. "That kid. I swear. He asked when he was four and I just…panicked. I didn't want to have to get into the whole just-mommy-no-daddy dynamic. He'd have too many questions."

"How long do you think you can avoid those questions? One, two more years?"

She bites her lip and looks out towards the garden just so she can avoid my gaze. "He's too young to understand how messed up our lives are. And way too young for the birds and the bees talk. Hell, *I* need a refresher course on the birds and the bees."

"Do you, now?"

Her eyes widen for a split second and her skin goes blotchy with embarrassment. "I didn't mean it the way it sounded."

"It sounded like you haven't been laid in a while."

She flushes and rubs a hand over her face. "Can we not?"

"That small town hick didn't Nice-Guy his way into your pants, huh?"

"Stop that. Stop acting as though you know everything," she snaps. "I didn't sleep with Callan because I knew we had no future. I only sleep with men I have genuine feelings for."

I grin. I can't help it. "So just me, then?"

She narrows her eyes. "That rule happened post-you."

"Makes sense." My grin widens.

Taylor huffs out a frustrated breath. "You're impossible."

"Funny, I was about to say the same thing about you."

"Me?" she repeats incredulously. "Please—you're the one who's gone ages without hugging his own wife."

I catch her gaze, mostly because I want to see her reaction when I say what I'm about to say.

"If I *had* a real wife, intimacy would not be an issue."

He did that on purpose. He's just playing with words to get a rise out of me. To confuse me.

He definitely did not actually mean *"if."*

"Mama, look!" Adam cries, holding up part of his finished tower and waving it around in the air.

"Wow," I say without even really looking at the tower. "Well done, sweetheart."

"I'm gonna make the second tower, Mama. For Rapunzel's sister."

"Sounds great, baby." I can feel Ilarion's eyes on me, taking in my reaction, reading into every little pucker and cringe on my body.

"Red or yellow blocks, Mama?"

"Why don't you go with yellow, honey?"

"I like red better."

I have to grit my teeth to keep from screaming. "Whatever you want."

The smile stays on my face for as long as it takes to steer my gaze from Adam to Ilarion. Then it withers immediately.

"Is that supposed to be some sort of joke?" I hiss.

He folds his arms and puts his weight on the wall. "Another thing your sister hasn't shared with you, huh?"

"You're married."

"Are we?"

"Um, yes. I've seen the pictures."

"Well, there you go then, I suppose. Pictures always tell you everything you need to know about every situation."

"Are you going to actually tell me what the hell you're talking about, or are you just enjoying this game too much?"

"You want to know? You really want to know?"

"Yes!" I cry out. "For God's sake, yes!"

He shrugs. "Then ask your sister."

I swear I could strangle him right now. "I'm asking *you*."

"You want something from me now, *tigrionok*? It will only come at a cost."

"What cost?"

Ilarion's scowl deepens. "The fucking *truth*."

I push myself off the window seat and stand opposite him, chest-to-chest. "You didn't bring me here to get to know your son," I snarl under my breath. "You brought me here because you want to blow my world up."

He smirks, but there's darkness in his eyes. He still hasn't forgiven me for leaving. Maybe he never will. "Perhaps you do know me after all."

I brush past him, and even though our skin doesn't actually make contact, I can feel the kind of heat that only comes from touching him. I force the fury out of my face for Adam's sake before I turn to him. "Sweetheart, I'm gonna go get some water, okay?"

"Okay, Mama," he says without so much as glancing toward me.

I get the hell out of that room and out of his stifling presence. Why did I let my father convince me that coming back with Ilarion was a good freaking idea? I should have fucking run.

With adrenaline coursing through my body, I find myself stomping over to his room. I pound on his door until he throws it open. His room is dark, like he's been asleep, but his eyes are wide and alert.

I push past him, walk to the windows, and throw open the curtains to let the light stream in. That's what we need— light. Truth. There's been too much damn darkness in this family for too damn long.

"Taylor? What on earth are—"

I whirl around to face him. "Don't like the light, do you, Dad?" I demand. "It's probably easier to see all your mistakes with this sunshine coming through, I bet, hm?"

"Taylor, what is this tantrum about?"

"Tantrum?" I repeat furiously. "*Tantrum?* I don't throw *tantrums*, Dad."

"How about the night that you moved out of the house in the middle of the night without so much as an explanation or a warning? Isn't that the same night that you crawled into Ilarion's car?"

I'm not expecting the bite in his tone or the anger in his eyes. He's in fighting form today and I don't mind one bit. It's much harder to wage war when one person is waving around a white flag.

"What exactly are you trying to say?"

"Maybe if you had listened to me, if you had *trusted* me, you wouldn't be stuck in this position."

I stare at him for a moment in pure, stunned disbelief. "Wow," I say at last. "Just…wow."

"You're being dramatic."

"Me? You just blamed me for everything. Where's the accountability, Dad? Where's the fucking honesty?"

He draws himself up to his full height. "I am still your father, and you still owe me respect. I'm not saying I haven't made mistakes, but I have only ever done what I thought was best for you. You *and* Celine."

"Oh yeah, and that turned out real well, didn't it?"

"Watch your tone, young lady!"

I shake my head, squaring my shoulders with determination. We've done this song and dance before, but not for a while. It had been so long that I actually believed we'd put some of this baggage past us. Then again, you can't put anything behind you if it's never truly been resolved.

I scrub my hands over my face for a moment and take a deep breath. "Okay," I say. "Let's try and have a real damn conversation for once, shall we?"

"That never ends well."

"I'm not about to stop trying."

"Maybe you should."

I shake my head and squeeze my fists. "You don't get to be angry, Dad. You're right—you are my father and it was your responsibility to keep us safe. You might have stood a better chance of that if you'd just been honest with us from the beginning. Or, gee, I don't know, if you hadn't gotten involved with *literal fucking killers.*"

His face is blotchy with heat and his cheeks look swollen. It reminds me of the first time Mom was diagnosed with cancer. He kept his heartbreak so close that it turned physical. It was like his emotion went inward and puffed him up from the inside out.

On another day, the reminder might have been enough to convince me to back down. But I feel as though I've spent my entire life backing down.

The time has come to stand up instead.

"Have you ever considered that if we'd known what to look for, we'd have known what to avoid? Or *who* to avoid?" I yell. "You tried to warn us of the outside world, but you never explained why the outside world was dangerous. If you had told us the truth, I would have known who Ilarion was. I would have known to stay away from him. Shit…*you* should have known to stay away from him and his father."

"Is that what you would have done?" he asks. "Or would you just find a reason to be with him?"

"Ex-*cuse* me?"

His eyes widen and his nostrils flare. He looks angry and frustrated at the same time. He also looks like he's losing control. "Let's face it, Taylor: you wanted to punish me. That's why you jumped into his car."

"That's not true!"

"You were just trying to get back at me."

"No!"

"You couldn't stop yourself, even after you knew that he was Celine's fiancé."

I freeze on those words. It feels like he's slapped me across the face all over again. I adjust my feet, and for a moment, I feel dizzy. So dizzy that I think I might tip over. My vision blurs and by the time I blink away the haze, Dad's features come into focus, and his expression has changed.

He looks sad now.

He looks old.

He looks sorry.

"Tay… God. I'm sorry."

I should leave, but I'm pretty sure that if I move, I'll fall. I can see Dad reaching out to me, but I hold up my hand to keep him at bay. "Don't."

"I didn't mean it the way it came out."

I blink hard until my vision clears.

"I'm just a broken old man who can't reconcile his life choices with the consequences they made. I've taken that out on you, and that's not fair."

I exhale slowly and lean back against the wall, letting my eyes flutter closed. "Tell me about the time you met Mom," I say in a desperate attempt to retreat to a topic that doesn't make me want to tear my heart out of my chest. "I haven't heard that story in a long time."

"Now's not the time for that story."

"I hate that you refuse to talk about her," I hiss under my breath. "It's not fair. We've lost her presence. Do we have to lose her memory, too?"

"That's not—"

"Tell me the story, Dad."

He sighs so heavily, I feel it where I stand. "I ran into her when I was walking home from school one day. She had a pile of books that she was carrying and she dropped a couple. I stopped to help her pick them up. Then I offered to carry her books back to her place. We went out on our first date that same night, and the rest…"

He trails off, his voice hitching over the last few words.

"How long did it take you to fall for her?"

"Taylor—"

"Answer me, please."

"I knew she was the one when I picked up the first book."

"How?"

"Excuse me?"

"How did you know she was the one?"

He hesitates, his eyebrows hitching together. "I don't know. It was just…a feeling."

"What did it feel like?

He sighs again. "A feeling of being recognized, of something snapping into place. It was this sense of connecting with a complete stranger. And then just…being understood."

I nod. "*That*," I say softly. "That is what happened the night I met Ilarion. Yeah, he was this big intimidating guy. He was out to settle a score with someone I didn't know or know about. But we connected. And it happened before I knew about him or you or any of the politics that came to follow. I loved him freely, this nameless, powerless stranger, and I don't regret it. *I don't fucking regret it.* Maybe I should. But I don't." I meet my father's gaze. "I used to think the same thing, you know. If I'd never met him that night, it would have been okay. We could have avoided all this. But now, I realize, it wouldn't have mattered. I would have loved him regardless. Before or after. Because he recognized me the same way I recognized him. We were strangers, but we understood each other."

The silence that follows is long and deep.

"That's how you feel?" Dad asks. "Still?"

I hesitate. But only because I realize I don't need to lie to Dad. "Yes."

"Then you need to tell Celine."

41

TAYLOR

You need to tell Celine. I shake my head. "I can't," I whisper, unlatching the sob that's hiding in my throat. "And I can't be the only one who starts telling the truth. I can't…I can't be alone in this."

He sighs with resignation. "I know what this is about. You want to know what Ilarion spoke to me about in the garden."

"Apparently, neither one of you want to tell me what happened, so I'll let that one go. But maybe you can answer another question for me?"

He tenses instantly, his spine going ramrod straight. "What question?"

"Were you there the night that Mila and Ilarion's father died?"

His eye twitches. I've seen it a million times, but it never stood out to me as significant before. Eye twitches meant Dad's stressed, Dad's tired, Dad's blah. It wasn't exactly a smoking gun.

But now? I'm seeing it differently. Maybe it's a tell I never caught on to. A giveaway I ignored because I thought I could trust my father.

Apart from the twitch, however, his face remains stoically nonchalant. A little *too* stoic, actually. A little too nonchalant.

"Who's been whispering in your ear, Little Bird?"

My stomach twists and I drop my gaze, if only to collect my thoughts. "Dad…" I clear my throat and meet his eyes. "Things are never going to get better between us until you start being honest with me. You were there, weren't you?"

I expect him to ignore me, like he has so often whenever I've asked him an uncomfortable question. I remember the days after Mom's diagnosis. Celine and I were so confused, but neither one of us wanted to talk to her about the cancer. So we went to Dad.

What kind of cancer?

What stage?

Will she survive?

Will she need chemo?

Is there hope?

He would listen to the questions with dead eyes and then walk away as though the conversation was over. We didn't hold it against him; he was reeling from the news, too.

But that was personal.

This is different.

"Yes, I was there."

My eyes grow wide. More because he answered me, rather than the answer itself. "And…what did you see? What did you hear?"

He hesitates, his eyes flitting all over the room. "I saw the man die," he admits. "I saw the bullet pierce his flesh. I saw the knife cut through his skin."

"Knife?"

"She used a bullet to take him down. And then she slit his throat."

"She…" I breathe slowly. And then I remember what *she* said. "You told Benedict Bellasio, didn't you?"

This time, he doesn't hesitate. His lips are turned down, and his eyes are cast in darkness when he replies. "Yes, I told Benedict. I was an informant, Taylor. So I informed. At the time, I thought it was the least damaging intel to give him."

"Dad…"

"Ilarion protected Mila well."

"He's the *pakhan*," I say. "And his men respect him. They took his word rather than the word of a petty rival. But if they didn't, do you know how badly it could have gone? The danger you could have put Mila in?" I suck in a breath before I lose my temper on her behalf. "Were you really so willing to gamble with her life?"

"I had my own girls to think of," he argues. "I had no time to think of anyone else's daughter. Ludwig Zakharov was a fucking bastard, but he was still her father. And he kept her safe. What could he have possibly done to warrant being murdered by his own flesh and blood? Yes, Mila killed him.

But Ilarion stood there and watched. In the end, is it really such a difference?"

I try to imagine the scene unfolding. Mila's shaking hands, Ilarion's clenched jaw. But maybe it was the other way around? Maybe Mila was the one who was determined? Maybe Ilarion was the one coursing with fear?

"So, the informant doesn't know everything."

His eyebrows knit together. "What do you mean?"

"You wondered what could Ludwig have possibly done to deserve being murdered by his own flesh and blood? But you wrote off the answer before you ever found out why. Just so you know, if I'd have been in Mila's position, I'd have done the same fucking thing."

His eyes go wide and his nostrils flare. "What did he—"

"He *raped* her," I hiss. "He raped his little girl when she was only eleven. He didn't fucking stop until she killed him."

He pales instantly. His pinkish complexion sobers down into a chalky white. I'm glad to see the regret on his face. The horror at the part he played in making Mila's life more of a nightmare than it already was.

"Can I trust you with *that* information?"

He doesn't answer me. He's staring off into a corner, lost in his own thoughts.

But I'm not done twisting the knife. "Can I trust you? Can I rely on you not to go run off and sell it to the next mob boss who offers you the loose change in his sofa?"

I'm being cruel, I know. But Mila's as close to a best friend as I'll probably ever get. And my heart is breaking for her.

He nods slowly. Still horrified, still distracted. But I believe that nod. "Yes," he says resolutely. "You can."

"Good. Now, if you'll excuse me, I need some air."

42

TAYLOR

I leave Dad's room, hoping to find some refuge in mine. But I'm only halfway down the corridor when Celine turns the corner. She's changed outfits again, and now, she's wearing a strapless fuchsia corset with a white A-line skirt that reveals the outline of her slim legs.

"You look amazing," I mumble robotically.

She waves away the compliment like a woman who gets far too many of them to truly be flattered by one. "I'm glad I ran into you. I've just received word that we're to be hosting a charity gala a few weeks from now. We're on a tight deadline and a lot needs to be sorted. I'm going to need your help."

"My help?"

"Yes," she says insistently. "I have Ashton, of course, but it would be great if you could lend a hand? You might even find you have an affinity for it. And if you do, I can always find you work in society circles."

"Are you trying to help me again, Cee?" I cock an eyebrow.

She smiles. "Don't be so suspicious. Now, come on; Ashton is already here."

"Who?"

"Ashton St. James," she answers me over her shoulder. "He helps me organize big events like these. He's one of the state's top event coordinators. He has a jam-packed schedule, but he always makes the time for me."

"Why are you so dressed up?" I ask as I follow Celine down the stairs. Pear-shaped diamonds hang from her ears and a choker gleams on her neck.

Her back is to me so I can't exactly read her reaction, but I wish I could, because her answer comes too slow to be the whole story. "I'm a Zakharov," she says simply. "I have to keep certain standards."

The answer falls more than a little flat, but I'm not about to push her. Not now.

We enter the grand foyer. A huge white piano looms in the corner, set in front of a glass wall looking out over the southern gardens. A potted tree just on the other side of the glass drizzles pink petals down the windowpanes. As Celine turns in the space, I wonder if she's chosen her outfit to match the room.

No, it can't be...right?

"That's a great outfit," I compliment again.

"You can borrow it if you want."

As I move a little closer to her, I realize that the amazing smell I've been catching for the last few seconds is coming from her. Not her usual expensive perfume. Something far more exclusive, far more...well, *more*.

"Celine."

Then Ashton St. James walks into the grand foyer, and I'm immediately struck by two things.

One, the man is extremely good-looking.

And two, he's definitely drinking my sister in.

For some reason—maybe his name, maybe the fact that he's an event coordinator—I'd just assumed that he might be some bland, uninteresting background drone like every other person I've seen mill about any given room Cee's in. But the way he saunters in with this sort of Big Dick Energy, gaze honed on her...

Interesting.

He's wearing a gray suit that fits snugly on his large arms. His shirt is a blue button down, left open just enough for me to notice the muscular ripples on his chest. His beard is a shadowy scruff, his thick hair similarly disheveled but in a very attractive, still-professional way.

"Ashton," Celine murmurs, and I can't help notice that her tone downshifts into something purrier.

Very interesting.

"Cici!" He wraps his arms around her and places a kiss on her cheek. The hug lasts a good few seconds longer than a polite, professional hug ought to, and for a weird moment, I feel like some sort of voyeur.

He pulls away from her and she glances over to me. "I want to introduce you to my sister, Taylor."

"I'm so sorry!" he exclaims, doing a double-take upon catching sight of me. "I didn't see you there."

"No hard feelings. It's hard to notice me when Cee's in the room."

He smiles and he most certainly doesn't disagree. Instead, he extends his hand out to me. "It's a pleasure, Taylor."

We shake. "Likewise, Ashton."

"Taylor moved back into town recently," Celine explains vaguely. "She's going to be helping us coordinate the charity gala for The Metropolitan."

"Is she?" Ashton asks. I detect a note of disappointment in his tone, if not his eyes.

I'm aware that I might be reading too much into this, but I'm fairly certain that I'm intruding on something that used to be a two-person gig.

"But I really don't have much experience coordinating," I interject. "If I get in the way, feel free to kick me out."

"Nonsense," Celine replies immediately. "You're smart and capable. You'll learn fast, and if not, we'll teach you. Isn't that right, Ashton?"

"Of course."

He's being polite, though. His smile is tight and his mannerisms are stiff. He and Cee are standing close together with the casual comfort of intimate familiarity.

Which begs the question: why did Cee ask me to be here when I'm clearly the third wheel?

43

TAYLOR

"Celine."

She doesn't answer.

There's a chill out in the garden. The bent cherry blossom tree is offering its tissue paper pink flowers in our direction, but the romance of the scene is lost on me. I've got too many questions to ooh and ahh over the foliage.

"Celine."

My sister casts a glance towards the glass doors. Ashton excused himself a second ago to use the bathroom, so the coast is clear, but she's obviously nervous. Her eyes keep darting to the foyer like she's waiting for a ghost to lunge out from behind the piano.

"Celine!"

Finally, she blinks and remembers that I'm here with her. "Yes? What?"

I lean forward and plant my elbows on the table. "Why did you ask me to be here?"

Celine lofts a brow. "I thought it would be nice for you to get involved, have a project. A potential job, even. Waitressing was all well and good, but you're home now. You need a real profession."

"When did you become such a snob?"

One eyebrow comes down, but the other goes up. "Maybe I was always a snob."

"Bullshit."

She scrunches up her nose, the same way that I used to when Adam was in the terrible twos stage and threw tantrums over his banana breaking in half or having the wrong pajamas on for bedtime. "I thought it would be fun for us to do something together."

"Nope. Try again."

Her nostrils flare. "Why are you being so difficult?"

"Maybe I was always difficult."

Celine rolls her eyes. "No, but you were always annoying when you wanted to be. Apparently, that hasn't changed."

"Oh, *touché*," I drawl sarcastically. "Nice burn."

Her eyebrows flatten. "Will you stop acting like a brat?"

"I will, just as soon as you stop lying to me about why I'm here," I retort. "Or, better yet, why *he's* here."

"I have no idea what you're talking about."

"Shall I take a guess, then?" My mouth curves into a mischievous smile. "Because I think I'm here to serve as a buffer between you and Hottie Saint Handsome in there."

Celine's cheeks flush a delicate shade of pink, but she manages to keep her cool. "A buffer?" she repeats prettily. *Too* prettily, in my opinion. "Ashton and I get along fine. We don't need a buffer."

"Not that kind of buffer," I explain with a slow shake of my head. Oh yeah, I'm onto her. "Not the kind of buffer between two people who hate each other. I'm talking about the kind of buffer that you need to keep from ripping each other's clothes off."

The delicate shade of pink turns into an aggressive red. It spreads right over her chest, too, which is a dead giveaway that I've hit the nail on the head.

"Ding, ding, ding!" I proclaim with teasing triumph. "I think we have a winner!"

"For God's sake," she snaps, turning toward the foyer. "Stop talking so damn loud!"

"Scared Ashton will hear?"

"No, I'm scared the *staff* will hear. Not to mention Ilarion. Or have you forgotten about him?"

"Meaning what—you'd never cheat on him?"

"No, I would not." She's coiling up as though she's getting ready to throw a punch. I would have had nothing to worry about with the old Celine. But this one? Yeah, she has the potential to go Bratva on my ass.

I lean back. "Maybe you should."

She blinks at me a few times, her mouth half-parted, her eyes murky and hard to read. I see Ashton's silhouette materialize on the inside of the glass wall. She follows my eyes and sees it, too. When she does, she takes a deep breath and shakes her head like a frustrated horse.

"Get rid of him," she mumbles at me. "I can't deal with this today."

She stands from the patio table and walks away. Not back into the house, but further into the garden.

"Where are you going?" I call out to her.

"Away from you!" she yells back. "Just do this for me. Tell him something unexpected came up. Tell him that Ilarion needs me. Just…get rid of him."

I watch, but to my surprise, at the very end of the path, she steps off into the grass instead of following the winding gravel. She kicks off her shoes, leaves them behind, and carries on without them. When she disappears down the stone staircase, I turn to the foyer—only to discover that Ashton is standing in the doorway, watching her leave, too.

"I'm guessing the meeting is over?" he asks with resignation written all over his face.

I walk toward him, imagining for a moment what they'd look like together. *Fucking beautiful*; that's what they'd look like together.

I look him in the eye. They're a deep, dark brown, flecked with pinpricks of brilliant hazel. "Are you in love with my sister?"

His face doesn't so much as twitch. "If I were, would you tell anyone?"

"No."

He nods. "Then yes, I'm in love with your sister."

I run a hand through my hair. "Well, shit. That was…easier than I expected."

Ashton laughs bitterly. "It was the farthest thing from it, in my opinion."

I offer him a tender smile. I know a lot about forbidden love. "Does she know?"

"Yeah, she knows."

"As in, she's guessed?" I press. "Or you've told her?"

"I kissed her on a night a lot like tonight, almost two years ago." He sighs as his gaze slides over to the garden staircase that she disappeared down. "I guess that was my big declaration."

Good Lord, he marked it on his calendar and everything. "How did she react?"

"She slapped me, actually."

I bite back a surprised laugh. So much. There is *so fucking much* she hasn't told me.

Not that I can afford to be pissed. There's more that I'm not telling her. I have no right to be hurt by her secrecy.

"But she still works with you," I remind him. "Which tells me that she has feelings for you."

"Oh, I know she has feelings for me," Ashton says confidently. It doesn't come off as cocky or arrogant, though. More like…earnest. Hopeful. "She's just bound by her commitments. So instead of being honest with herself, she's choosing to lie to keep the status quo."

My legs feel like they've turned to jelly. He sounds exactly like Ilarion when Ilarion is talking about me.

What have I done?

"What happened after you kissed her? After the slap, I mean."

He rubs the side of his face wearily, like it's been paining him ever since. "She walked out on me. I left, expecting never to see or hear from her again. But then, three days later, I got a call. She kept it professional, we stayed on topic, she never mentioned the kiss or the slap, and I didn't, either. We just acted like it never happened."

"And you accepted that?"

"I tried to bring it up a few times," he admits. "She always changed the subject or deflected. Then, finally, she told me to stop. She said that if I continued to bring it up, she would have to stop working with me and she didn't want to do that. It was the first inclination I got that maybe it wasn't as hopeless as I thought."

Well...fuck.

"She claims to love Ilarion," Ashton says, his eyebrows pinching when he says Ilarion's name. "She says she wants to be faithful to him. But I know her heart belongs to me. She's just scared to admit it. She's scared to blow up her life. And I think she's scared of him."

I frown. "What do you mean?"

"Oh, come on, Taylor." It's a playful scold, but still a scold. I barely know this guy, but I feel like I deserve the judgment. "You must know what Ilarion is. Men like him don't tolerate their women screwing around behind their backs. Doesn't matter if they fuck a hundred different women; they expect theirs to be faithful."

"Ilarion is...different."

He does a double-take. "And you know this...how?" he questions. "According to Celine, you haven't been around for years."

"I just do, okay?" I say defensively. "Ilarion may be a mob boss, but he's not the kind of man who would hurt Celine just because she fell for someone else."

Ashton's frown is undeniably pitying. "You're underestimating his brutality."

"You don't know him like I do. I understand you need to hate him, but—"

"There is no 'but,' Taylor." Ashton's right hand balls into a fist. "It is what it is. And as much as I hate to admit it, the truth is, I can't protect her the way that he can. The proof is in the pudding, as they say."

"What are you talking about?"

"The attempts on Celine's life stopped right after she moved back in with Ilarion. At least that's what she told me. I met her about two years after it all happened."

"It sounds like he's just looking out for her."

What am I doing?

What am I saying?

Who am I defending, and why?

He shrugs. "I wouldn't know. She refuses to discuss her marriage with me. Anyway, I should go. Probably best you forget everything I just told you."

"Forgotten," I say at once.

Ashton nods gratefully. "I'm glad you're here, Taylor," he remarks just before he turns back into the foyer. "She's always seemed so lonely. It'll be good for her to have someone she can talk to."

There's only one problem with that: she doesn't talk to me. And it's looking a lot like she doesn't talk to anyone else, either.

It's almost like everything I did to make sure she would be happy has backfired. *Badly.*

It's almost as if Ilarion was right.

44

ILARION

I'm barely listening to Dima's briefing when I happen to look out my window.

Outside, Taylor is pacing back and forth with the savage gait of a caged animal. She's got a whole expanse of garden laid before her, but she keeps crossing the same four feet of space.

Back and forth.

Back and forth.

She's wearing denim shorts that put her slender legs on display and a soft white blouse with loose sleeves billowing around her arms. Every time she turns, I see a tantalizing inch of her taut, flat belly.

Fuck, does that do something to me. Considering how long it's been since I've been inside a woman, I'm surprised that I don't come in my fucking pants just watching her.

"Yo, man, are you even listening to me?"

Her hair is loose, flying wildly around her head, veiling her features from view. At one point, her arm rises as though she's having a passionate conversation with someone. Except there's no one around, as far as I can see.

"Ilarion!"

It's only when Dima's hand slices through my field of vision that I wrench my gaze back to him. But now, he's examining the view outside my window. "Ah," he says the moment he sees Taylor pacing. "Well, that makes sense. What's going on out there?"

"Your guess is as good as mine."

He frowns. "So you had nothing to do with it? I find that hard to believe."

"I've been up here with you for the last two hours," I remind him.

"I've seen you do more with less."

"I think we're done for now," I announce, knowing that he'll see right through my spontaneous break.

He doesn't crack a joke like I expected, though. "Brother... going down there might not be the best idea."

"I don't remember asking for your opinion on this. Or on anything, actually."

"Yeah, don't I know it," he grumbles.

"Take a break, okay? We'll resume in five minutes."

"I'm guessing that if you go down there, it's gonna take a lot longer than five."

"Fine, take an hour, then. Go hang out with Mila."

His brow hikes up and his lips turn down. "She's been avoiding me lately. You wouldn't happen to know why, would you?"

"Best you speak to her directly."

His frown deepens. "So you do know?"

"Fuck, Dima, we're not in high school. If you've got something to say to Mila, tell her yourself. I'm not passing notes between the two of you like we're fucking fifteen."

"I would talk to her, but like I said, she's avoiding me."

"Then make yourself unavoidable. Which is what I intend to do right now."

"You have it easy. Taylor's all bark. Half the time, I feel like Mila's ready to cut off my balls."

Chuckling, I get up and make for the door. I'm leaving the room when he calls out to me. "We're on a timeline here, Ilarion. That was your idea. We can't move forward unless you get the information we need."

I wave away his concern and head down into the gardens. I pass a maid on my way there, the shy blonde one who always cringes from me as though I'm going to take a bite out of her if she doesn't pay attention.

I pause. "Molly, am I right? Have you seen Celine?"

"Ms. Zakharov? She just went upstairs, sir," she says. "And if I may…she looked like she was crying. Her eyes were all red and swollen."

Ah. Well, that explains Taylor's furious pacing. "She was crying?"

The girl's eyes go wide with horror. "I, uh, I didn't mean…it just looked like it to me, sir. I don't know, maybe I saw wrong. I, um—"

"Calm down, Molly. It's alright. Thank you for letting me know. Just go about your work, okay?"

She nods timidly and scurries off into the next room. It doesn't even cross my mind that maybe I should be checking on Celine first. When I step out into the garden, Taylor is still there, still pacing back and forth over the same stretch of grass.

She doesn't catch sight of me until she turns. When she does, she freezes on the spot.

The wind flaps around her, sending her blouse flying up and her hair whips across her face. She's everything I ever wanted. It physically hurts me how beautiful she is.

"What are you doing here?" she blurts out.

"I'm coming to protect my grass." I saunter closer. "How long have you been pacing on that spot?"

She looks down and notices the grass she's flattened under her feet. "I'll pace somewhere else," she mumbles. "Do *not* follow me." She spins on her heel and strides away before I can respond.

"I'm just walking here," I say as I do exactly what she just requested I not do. "I can't help it if you chose the same route I did."

She pauses on the spot and I nearly plow right into her. Gritting her teeth, turning those furious, burning green eyes on me, she snaps, "I can't be around you right now, Ilarion."

I raise my eyebrows. "Why not?"

"Because…just…just because."

"Does it have something to do with why Celine is upstairs crying right now?"

Her face drops instantly. I can see the threat of tears in her eyes to go along with the anger. "Cee's crying?"

"What happened?"

"What happened…" she repeats softly as though she's talking to herself. "What happened is that I fucked up. I fucked up so badly that I don't have any goddamn clue how to fix it."

"Well, it's about time you realized that."

Her eyes dart to mine. They're shining with unshed tears, but I can still see the ever-present fight behind them. It's there in the set of her mouth, the square of her jaw. "Giving up" is not in this woman's vocabulary. Which is great sometimes, and horrible in others.

"Did she even *want* to marry you?"

"At one point, she did, yes."

"Really? Because from everything I've gathered so far, it feels like the marriage was about nothing but convenience."

"You keep talking about marriage."

"And you keep talking in riddles."

"I don't, Taylor. You just don't pay attention."

Her nostrils flare. I wonder if she knows that her father and sister have the exact same tells. Makes it so much harder to forget the fact that they're all related.

"I'm missing some piece of the puzzle. Something went wrong between the two of you."

"That implies that, at some point, anything was right between us."

"Something *was* right between the two of you," she insists, as though saying it often enough will make it true.

"Were you always this slow? Or is this a consequence of moving back home?"

"This isn't my home," she snaps. "And all I want from you is a straight answer."

"Fine." I'm losing patience. "Ask me the question then."

"Were you the reason she wanted to kill herself?"

I don't blink.

I don't hesitate.

I don't pause for effect.

"Yes."

That's all I give her. A single word that packs the kind of punch that you feel in your gut long before and long after the fist ever makes contact.

She releases a slow breath. When she blinks, a tiny tear squeezes out of her eye. She turns to the side so that all I can see is her profile. Then her eyelids close and she tilts her face up towards the sky as though she's calling on a higher power for help.

"Okay," she says at last, though her eyes are still closed. "What happened?"

"I told her I couldn't marry her."

"Why on earth would you tell her that?"

I stare at the woman as though she's lost her mind. She probably has. That would explain why she had put us through this hell. At least that would make sense. Make it easier to forgive her.

"I couldn't justify marrying her when I was—*am*—in love with her sister."

45

ILARION

It's not quite the way I'd imagined this conversation going. But at least it's finally out there. Not that I'd been very subtle about how I felt before now. Who fucking knows?

Then again, Taylor can be laughably obtuse when she decides to be.

Her eyes are wide and her face drains of color the moment the words are out of my mouth. "I...I didn't just hear you say that. I'm going to pretend that I didn't ever hear that."

"No, you heard it," I snarl angrily, desperately, hopelessly. "Worse, you already knew it. You've just refused to accept it."

"What did you tell her?" she demands. "Did you tell her you were in love with me specifically?"

"Of course not."

I'd come so fucking close, though.

It was the day she'd finally been returned to a proper room of her own after a seven-month stint in the hospital wing.

She was sitting by the window in the evening, watching the sunset. Everything was looking brighter in those days, both inside and out. She was starting to make progress. She could walk on her own, could feed herself.

Mila and Dima advised me not to speak to her just yet, but it had been almost seven months and I felt she was owed an explanation. She had to know that the world she woke up in was not the same as it was when she fell into the darkness.

"Are you okay?" Celine asked when I'd lingered at her doorway. "You seem preoccupied."

I glanced down at her hand, at the engagement ring sitting prettily on her finger. She never took it off.

"Is it wedding stress? Because I was thinking, we could—"

"There isn't going to be a wedding, Celine."

Fuck. The words ripped themselves out of my throat, but even when I saw the horror on her face as she processed them, I couldn't regret saying it. I'd been waiting so long. It felt good to speak the truth.

And I think, deep down, she knew even before I said it. In more than half a year of her recovery, I'd made zero attempts to touch her intimately. I avoided it whenever I could, doing little more than handing her her walking cane or helping her back to her feet if she fell.

I might as well have been her physical therapist.

In that moment, I had a coward's thought: *Please let her not ask any questions.* It was already so hard to see so much of Taylor in Celine's face. The same shade of green in her eyes. The same resolute twist of her lips. It's like I was being haunted by the ghost of the woman I wanted but could never have, as she possessed the body of the woman I could have but would never want.

She stared at me for a moment, a pained smile stuck on her face. "What do you mean? Dr. Baranov told me I was doing great, that I would be able to resume normal activity soon. So why…?"

"You know why."

She shook her head. "You were keeping your distance to help my recovery. You were just trying to…to be sensitive to my…"

Another sob, a fully realized one, escaped her lips.

"Oh my god…something's changed."

"Nothing's changed. Your father told you the truth before he left. I approached you, I wooed you, I asked you to marry me, all because I wanted collateral. I wanted to keep control over your father."

"And I stayed with you anyway," she pleaded. "Doesn't that mean something?"

"You didn't have a choice."

"Yes," she said adamantly. "Yes, I did have a choice. And I chose to stay with a man I knew didn't love me, in the hopes that one day, he *would* love me."

I stood there for a long time before I summoned the courage to shake my head. "I'm sorry, Celine," was the last thing I said to her before the walls between us built up forever. "I really am sorry that it had to happen like this."

I left her room with her eyes on my back.

I never looked back once.

"Ilarion!"

I blink and Celine's image dissolves into Taylor's. The wind is still flapping around her body as though it's trying to wrap its arms around her in an embrace.

I can't believe I'm jealous of the fucking *wind.* Touching what I can't allow myself to touch.

"So that's why she moved out?" Her jaw works from side to side. "And then the first assassination attempt, the one that killed Vanessa," Taylor breathes. "Oh, God…oh, God." She lifts her gaze to me, her mouth turned down as though she's about to bawl her eyes out. "Is that why you eventually married her anyway? Out of *guilt*?"

My mouth falls open in disbelief. Do I need to wheel out a whiteboard to draw a diagram for her? "Taylor, have you been listening to a word I said?"

Taylor's bottom lip trembles. "Ilarion—"

"I'm going to be heading out of town for a couple of days," I tell her abruptly. It's for my sanity as much as it is for business. "I'll be back in time for Celine's charity event."

Her eyebrows pinch together, but she nods, almost in slow motion. There's a vacancy about her expression that breaks my goddamn heart.

So I decide to take advantage of it like the selfish bastard I am deep down. I step forward and run my fingers along her bare throat. She gasps at the unexpected contact. I watch her eyes go wide, but before she can stop me, I lean in.

My lips press hard against hers, easing them apart. I can feel her warmth, the blood coursing beneath her veins.

One thought trumps all the others.

She was fucking made for me.

When I release her, her eyes are still closed. They flutter open a second later, transfixed and wide with shock. Her lips are still parted, begging for another kiss.

But I've already taken too much.

So I turn and walk away from her, taking the memory of my stolen kiss with me.

46

TAYLOR

Every time I tell myself I'm not going to think about the kiss anymore, that's all I end up thinking about. Even now, a day later, while I'm riding in a town car with Celine right next to me, I can feel him, taste him, smell him.

Every time I reach up to touch my lips, I have to remind myself that I'm not alone in my room. I don't have the freedom to let my mind run wild.

It's been doing a little too much of that lately.

"Aw, come on!" Celine says, patting me on the arm and making me jerk out of my reverie. She laughs when she notices my expression. "Where were you?"

"Oh, uh…nowhere."

She crinkles her nose with amusement. "I was just trying to tell you to cheer up. It's criminal to look so down when we're going dress shopping!"

I've honestly never seen Celine look this animated. Her cheeks are flush with color and only half of it can be attributed to the blush she's got on. As usual, she looks amazing. She's wearing a skin-tight white dress with red stilettos and a matching clutch. She looks like she's going to a fancy cocktail party. But apparently, it's just a run-of-the-mill shopping excursion outfit.

That's new, too. The old Celine used to dread shopping.

"This is unnecessary," I say. "You have so many dresses in your closet. I could just borrow one of those."

"I'm smaller than you."

"Ouch."

Celine laughs. "Just being honest. And anyway, I want you to have something new and fabulous to wear for the ball."

"Ball now, is it?" I mutter. "That sounds intimidating."

"It'll be fun. And who knows? Maybe you'll catch the eye of some handsome young business tycoon and sparks will fly."

I choke. "I highly doubt that."

"For God's sake, you sound like —" I turn to her when she breaks off. But she waves away her own words. "Never mind. I'm in a good mood and that's the best time to shop. You're going to have a good time, too, whether you like it or not. The shopping will continue until morale improves."

I can't help but laugh. It does lighten my spirits to see her like this, but I'm still stuck thinking that this is just a temporary upswing in an otherwise lonely life. She's taken pains to avoid talking about Ashton. And recently, she's seemed determined to avoid talking about Ilarion, too.

Selfishly, I'm okay with that, given what happened between Ilarion and me yesterday. Before he left on his work trip.

"Did you get a chance to speak to Dad this morning?" I ask.

"I did, but just for a bit. He and Ilarion were pretty deep in conversation when I went to his room."

"Ilarion and Dad?" I blurt.

She shoots me a look framed by one raised eyebrow. "Yes. Why?"

"Nothing. I just wasn't expecting them to be so, um…chatty?"

"Is it actually that, or are you worried about something?" Celine asks shrewdly. "Ilarion promised me, Tay."

"I know he did. It's just—"

"So why aren't you giving him the benefit of the doubt? He's trying with Dad. He wants to bury their history. Purge all the bad blood."

"How can you be so sure?"

"Because—apart from the fact that I trust Ilarion—Dad told me."

My jaw drops. "He did?" I'm almost afraid to believe it.

Celine nods. "After Ilarion left, I asked Dad what they were talking about and he told me not to worry because Ilarion was just trying to make sure he was 'comfortable.' He doesn't want there to be any awkwardness between them."

"That sounds…positive," I venture. What I really mean is, *That sounds way too good to be true.* "When was this?"

Celine jaw twitches infinitesimally. "This morning, before Ilarion left."

"Oh. Okay."

"Don't be so skeptical. I can see that look on your face. You're not as good at hiding your emotions as you think you are."

It takes everything in me to keep my expression neutral. *If only she knew.* "Fine. I'm done talking about Dad and Ilarion; happy now?"

"Exceptionally," Celine teases with a triumphant smile. "Today is about trying on pretty things and buying whatever the fuck we want."

It's still weird to hear her swear. She used to be such a prude about stuff like that. My sister has found confidence aplenty in Zakharov House. But when I take a look at her personal life, I can feel the tethers coming loose.

We arrive in the heart of the upscale shopping district. The sidewalks are huge and clean, sprawling beneath ornate gas-powered streetlamps.

The first store makes me shiver with the feeling of being somewhere you don't belong at all. It's a black façade with one word printed in huge rose gold letters on the window: *TRIBE.* There aren't mannequins in the display box, just a shadowy waterfall of black curtains.

"Cee, are you sure we're in the right place?"

"I know it looks strange, but the magic is on the inside."

I have no idea how to respond to that. So I just follow Celine into the store quietly. I probably look like her mild-mannered assistant. I'm certainly dressed like it, in my high-rise jeans and mustard yellow crop top.

The store's interior is much less black and shady. The exact opposite, in fact—everything, from the walls to the carpets to the ceilings, are white. Mannequins in strange, contorted positions dance around the perimeter, draped with fabric so soft and ethereal that I'm still not one hundred percent convinced it's real.

"Tay, stop dawdling and keep up," Celine calls to me. I blink and realize she's halfway up a spiral staircase that leads to a mezzanine section of the store closed off from the rest of the space.

"This is insane," I mumble to myself as I follow her up.

The salespeople are obviously familiar with Celine. They coo over her like she's some high-class European princess with cash to burn and parties to attend. The moment I think it, I realize that's exactly accurate, except for the "European" part.

When I get to the top of the staircase, I find myself in a sitting room that's also entirely white. The sofas and the coffee table blend into the backdrop. I double-check to make sure the couch I'm about to sit in is in fact real before I let my weight settle down.

"Okay, so, Genesis here has picked out a handful of dresses that we can both try on," Celine explains, gesturing over to two racks dripping with gaudy gowns. "I told her you like simple and classic."

"And comfortable," I add.

Celine sighs. "You'll have to excuse my sister," she says, turning toward Genesis and her probably equally-ridiculously-named colleagues. "She's not used to places like this."

I feel a twinge of self-consciousness when the three stooges facing Celine swivel their heads in my direction as though I'm an elephant in the zoo.

I swallow my embarrassment. "If you don't mind, I'm just gonna hang out here for a minute."

"You don't want to try on a dress first?" Celine asks, obviously disappointed by my lack of enthusiasm.

"You first."

Shrugging, she grabs a dress and dips into one of the two dressing rooms that face us. Genesis grabs a tray from I don't know where and approaches me with her arms outstretched. "Champagne, ma'am?" she asks. "We have cocktails, too. Or wine, if you prefer."

"Um…anything non-alcoholic?"

She actually twists around to glance back at her colleagues. *Look at the loser asking for non-alcoholic beverages. How quaint.* "Of course, ma'am," she says with a smile that doesn't quite reach her eyes. "Let me go see if our in-house bartender can whip up a mocktail for you."

In-house bartender? At a clothing boutique? Goodness gracious.

Look out, Toto. We're not in Kansas anymore.

All the stooges have cleared away by the time Celine emerges from the dressing room. The dress she chose is a velvety red, with diagonal cutouts that display her midriff. It feels over the top to me. It doesn't really suit her skin tone, either.

"Well, what do you think?"

Way back when, I would have given her my unvarnished opinion. But this is a different Celine, and that makes me feel as though I have to be a different version of me when I'm with her.

"I think you look, uh, beautiful."

Celine frowns, her expression growing pointed. "Do you really think that?"

"Of course."

"Your leg is bouncing."

I look down and catch my knee jerking up and down like an engine piston. I stop abruptly. When I look back at Cee, she's got her accusing eyebrow aimed at me.

"Okay, I don't love the dress," I admit. "Pretty, but—"

"Too much?"

"Not right for your complexion."

She nods with a growing smile. "See? Was that so hard?"

"I didn't want to hurt your feelings."

"Shit, Tay. How fragile do you think I am?" she asks. "I can take the truth, even if it hurts."

That one feels like a gut punch, but I just sit there with a fake smile plastered across my face, trying to keep my thoughts from spilling into dangerous territory.

Instead of going for the next dress, Celine walks over and sits down next to me. "They went to get the champagne, huh?"

"Is this standard procedure in this place?"

"For what I spend here, yes." She laughs. "It's surprising how quickly you get used to it."

"Well, it suits you. That's a compliment," I rush to add when I see her starting to frown. I clear my throat, wondering how else I can insult my sister at our very first stop of the day. "So...will Ashton be at the ball?"

Her nose wrinkles up and she becomes inexplicably interested in the soles of her heels. "Of course," she mumbles without looking at me. "He's helping me coordinate, after all."

"Ah, right, of course. You two work well together."

Her eyes snap to mine and her jaw clenches. "Taylor. Seriously."

"What?" I ask innocently. "Just interested in your life."

"In my life?" she asks. "Or my relationship with Ashton?"

"A little of both, maybe."

She starts tapping her index finger against the buttery-white arm of the sofa. "I don't want to talk about it. I would have thought that was obvious by now."

"You've substituted happiness with diamonds and balls and fancy dresses. You realize that, don't you?" Her eyes tighten instantly. I'm terrified that I've already alienated her. But I'm even more terrified that I'll alienate her if I don't ask the questions that need to be asked. "I'm sorry. It's just that I need to understand what's going on with you."

My eyes land on her hands, on the thin scar that winds its way across her slim wrists. She turns them over immediately.

"Who told you?" she whispers.

"Ilarion."

She frowns. "That was not his story to tell."

"I made him. I can be very stubborn when I want to. Like now, for instance."

She sighs, her eyes betraying all the secrets she's been holding close to her chest. "Well—"

She stops short when she notices Genesis arrive at the landing with a tray of mocktails and macarons. "We'll take it from here, Genesis," she says without batting an eyelid. "It's time I have a talk with my sister."

47

TAYLOR

I squirm in place and offer up a silent prayer for no tears. I know I'm the one who asked, but now that she's willing to share, I'm wondering if it was the right move after all. The tears might end up being mine.

Because I don't know if I can answer "yes" to the only question that matters. *Am I willing to be as honest with her as she is with me?*

"You have to understand," Cee starts, her eyes scanning the room distractedly. "After the two of you disappeared, he was my only source of comfort. He never made me feel like a burden."

I put my hand on Celine's lap. "You know that if you'd come with us, Dad and I would have taken care of you, right?"

She nods. "I know that. Of course I do. But as good as your intentions might have been, the truth is that neither one of you had the resources to take care of me at that point. He did. He did everything under the sun, Tay. He helped me breathe and sit up and walk and run and read again. He held my hand through it all."

It's a strange feeling brewing in my gut. I'm proud that Ilarion stepped up the way he did. I'm grateful, too.

But the small, petty, shallow part of myself that I've always hated…that part is jealous.

Celine runs her perfectly manicured fingers through her hair. "But…it wasn't perfect. There were points during my recovery when I would lean in a little too close and he would lean away from me. If I moved to kiss him, he would make sure that I got his cheek, not his lips. He never initiated contact that was too intimate. He was so integral to my therapy that I didn't even notice he was keeping me at arm's length." She stops long enough to exhale slowly. "I guess I just assumed that he was giving me time to recover fully before we were…intimate…with one another."

I wasn't really sure I wanted to hear this part. But I asked for her story. It's not up to me to tell her how to tell it.

"And then one day, he walked into my room and told me that he couldn't marry me. That he wasn't in love with me, and he never would be."

"Well…shit."

She shrugs and I can tell from that one small gesture how heavy her load has been to carry. "Of course, I left; I moved out. I had to. I loved him, but I had my pride. He told me he wanted me to stay. He was confident that I wouldn't interfere with his life. But it seemed insane to me to continue to live in this house. So I moved back in with Vanessa and I tried to figure out how I had managed to lose my family and my fiancé in less than a year. And then our apartment was hit. Thanks, Benedict."

It feels wrong to have a conversation so heartbreaking in a space this blank and sterile. This is a messy talk. A teary talk. But we don't always get to choose where we end up when important things happen, I guess. I know that as well as anyone.

The most important moment of my life happened while I crossed the street.

"I identified Vanessa's body," she admits. It's the first time since she started talking that she's made eye contact with me. Hers are filled with tears. "It was one of the worst moments of my life. I went to pieces right there in the coroner's office. And the only person who was there to pick the pieces was—"

"Ilarion," I say before she can finish.

Celine nods. "He brought me back to his place and put me back in my room. And I realized that somehow, over the course of the last few months, his home had become mine. I guess it made me feel like I had nothing left. No family, no friends, no fiancé. I thought so hard that I thought myself into a hole." She looks down at her wrists for a moment, and for once, she doesn't try to hide the scars from me. "I wasn't thinking straight. I was on a bunch of pills for pain. I hadn't eaten in days. I was deep in my depression. It was a split-second decision. At the time, it made so much sense."

"Cee," I whisper, gripping her hand tightly.

"He saved me again," she tells me with the saddest smile I've ever seen. "Sometimes, it feels like I'm the great, unwelcome burden of his life. The dead weight he was saddled with."

"Don't say that."

She pulls her hand out from under mine. "It's true. But I suppose I've come to accept it."

"But you don't have to *keep* accepting it, Cee," I point out. "Not if it's not what you want anymore."

"'What I want'?" she repeats as though it's an alien concept. "What I want has changed so often over the years that I can barely keep track myself." She looks past me. "Can you hand me a cocktail? I need some liquid courage."

"Um…these are mocktails," I say apologetically as I pass her one. "Sorry."

She laughs humorlessly. "Figures. Still—I'm glad you made me talk. It's weirdly cathartic, I have to say." She takes a sip that turns into a long drag. By the time she puts the glass down, it's almost empty. "Ilarion was with me a lot in the days after my suicide attempt. But I could tell that it had changed nothing for him. He took care of me because he felt he had to. But he was never really *with* me. He always belonged to someone else. Probably even before I met him."

I wonder if she notices the way I stiffen, terrified that she's seconds away from unmasking me. But I hold my tongue and let her speak.

"It got to the point where I started to accept the distance. It became easier to be around him knowing that he had nothing to offer me other than friendship. I guess I started to feel like friendship was enough. And then—"

"Benedict again?"

Celine's face twists with anger. "Benedict fucking Bellasio. The man was relentless. I guess he assumed that killing me would be the perfect revenge. All he did was light a fuel under Ilarion. He went ballistic and weeded out all the men who so much as whispered Benedict's name. Then he spread the word: anyone who touched a hair on my head would be given the most painful death imaginable. Ilarion would see to it himself. A few weeks later, we announced our engagement."

"Shit."

"In some ways, it was almost romantic. Just without any of the romance."

"So when did you get married?" I ask, looking for some light at the end of this very long and dark tunnel. "Surely, something changed."

Celine frowns a bit at me, her mouth curved in a confused laugh. "What? We're not…we never got married."

I frown. "What does that mean?"

She tilts her head, peering at me with increasing confusion. "It means we never wed. I'm not…did you think we're married?"

My mouth drops open. I think I'm about to crap out my heart. "I…I don't understand."

"What's not to understand?" she asks. "We never had a wedding. Never exchanged vows. Hell, I don't think we ever ordered a marriage license."

"But your name…you're a Zakharov."

She nods. "Yeah, that was his idea. Smart, too. Legally changed my name to keep up appearances in case Benedict or anyone else started to suspect. Plus, it just made things easier when it came to establishing myself in high society." She winks at me like it's some fun little secret and not a nuclear bomb on my reality.

I keep opening my mouth and closing it, waiting for something to pop into my mind that will make sense. "I just… Sorry, I'm a little stunned," I admit at last.

Celine nods as though she understands where I'm coming from. "We weren't dating that long before he proposed, and then it seemed like it wouldn't be a big deal to wait. I actually thought it was romantic, to wait and see what happens."

"Right," I say even as I remember something she'd told me not long ago. "But, didn't you say you want a family?"

"Oh," Celine says as her eyebrows flatten out and her mouth curves down so low I wonder if she's going to start crying. "That."

I give her knee another squeeze. As much as I want to know, I refuse to put my curiosity above her mental well-being. "If you don't want to talk about it, then—"

"No," she says, cutting me off. "No, it's okay. I might as well tell you. I guess that was my way of saying that I was trying to convince him to give me a baby. Essentially, it's me pleading with him to sleep with me—if not for love, then for the purposes of reproduction."

She cringes as she finishes speaking. I tighten my grip on her leg. "Oh, Celine."

"It sounds pretty pathetic when I say it out loud."

"No, it doesn't."

She smiles sadly. "You're being kind."

"I'm really not. I'm not kind at all."

"Oh, Tay, I don't know where you've got this notion that I'm some wallflower who needs protecting. Lately, you've been looking at me like I'm seconds away from crumbling. I'm not as weak as all that."

Well, that was out of the blue. "I never said you were." *To your face.*

"Maybe not. But you look at me like I am."

I'm on the verge of denying it when I stop myself. She might be picking up on something subliminal. Who am I to tell her she's wrong when *I'm* not even sure?

"I'm sorry." I bite my tongue and try to gather my thoughts. "Can I ask you a question that you might not like?"

Celine raises her eyebrows. "We've gone down the rabbit hole now. So, shoot."

"Are you still in love with Ilarion?"

She doesn't answer at first. Her eyes flicker around the room as though she's searching for the answer elsewhere. Finally, she sighs deeply and her gaze veers back to me.

"You know, there are times when I wonder if I was ever in love with him," she says softly. Then she shudders. "I was young when I met him and he was this big, bold, confident personality. And so handsome that it hurt to look at him. He whisked me away to far-off places, showered me with presents and attention. He took me shopping, bought me jewelry, made me feel like I could have anything I wanted. It felt like a hurricane, where I was the eye of the storm. I feel like maybe I was so caught up in all that that I mistook infatuation for love. I mistook all the luxury and attention for adoration." Her laughter has an edge of despair.

"Oh, Cee…"

She chuckles. "Yeah, I'm hearing myself. Again, pretty pathetic."

"Stop saying that. You're not pathetic."

"I traded away my soul for a life of luxury."

"For safety," I correct her.

Celine winks at me. "And a little bit of luxury."

I return her smile with a shy one of my own. "You deserve so much better," I say. "You deserve to have a family with a man who wants you for *you*. Who wants to whisper sweet nothings and take you to bed every night. Not just for procreation; just for shits and giggles. Because you look hot to him and he wants you, endlessly."

This time, when she laughs, it actually feels real. For the first time, she sounds like she means it.

"At this rate, I've forgotten what it feels like to have a man inside me."

I wince a little, if only because I know *exactly* how it feels to have Ilarion inside me. If it never happens again, I'll still remember it to my dying day.

Celine notices the flinch and misinterprets. "Now, who's the prude?" she teases.

I elbow her sheepishly. "I'm no prude. I just think that you could easily have a man if you wanted. In fact, there's a man we both know who'd willingly volunteer for the honor."

Celine narrows her eyes at me. "Not this again, Tay."

"Here's another question you're not gonna like: do you have feelings for Ashton?"

If ever I'm going to get a straight answer out of her, this is the moment. Celine tilts her head to the side, and her hair falls across her profile, cloaking her expression from me.

"Celine?"

She looks at me through her long lashes. "What would it serve to admit that?" she asks. "Nothing can come of it."

"You're not married," I point out. It's a miracle I can even form the words; I'm still reeling from that revelation. "You're allowed to pursue your feelings for Ashton. It's what you want, Cee. It's what he wants, too."

"Ilarion?"

"Ashton!" And then I think it over. "Also, probably yes to Ilarion, too. If you'd just talk to him."

Celine's eyebrows stitch together. "Did he, um…did he tell you what happened between us?"

"Ashton? He mentioned there was a kiss."

"Yeah. That. He caught me by surprise."

"Does Ilarion know?"

"No! Of course not. I'm his…" She snorts out a laugh. "I'm his fake fiancée. Oh my god, I am dumb."

"Are you, though?" I ask. Although I feel no less dumb. "You've been playing charades to save your life. But how long does it have to last?"

"I didn't tell you all that to be judged, Taylor," Celine snaps. Just like that, I get a whiff of the lioness she's become over the years.

"I'm not judging you, Cee," I say quickly, holding my hands up in self-defense. "I'm just trying to make sure that you're happy."

She holds my gaze for a moment, and I see something there that reminds me of Dad. The words she says next only make the resemblance that much stronger. "Happiness is overrated, Taylor. Sometimes, it's more important to be safe. Ilarion offered me that. Safety, stability, comfort. It's probably not the choice you would have made, but it's the choice I did. Now, I have to live with it."

I stare at Celine, but all I can see is our father, staring back at me through my sister's eyes.

48

ILARION

"Fucking hell," Dima breathes. "It's a shithole."

Not a shithole, exactly, but seedy enough that you wouldn't think of finding anyone half-decent on the inside. The walls are made of a mottled concrete that gives the hotel the look of an old Cold War prison. The barbed wire coiled on top doesn't do much to dispel the notion.

Dima and I have been sitting outside the walls for hours now, on the back end of our second surveillance shift. Only one noteworthy vehicle has approached the hotel in the last twenty-four hours: a beat-up old Chevy with a busted grill, a broken taillight, and a license plate from out of town.

But the tinted windows gave it away.

"Can you seriously imagine Benedict Bellasio in a place like this?" Dima muses.

"It's not like I gave him much of a choice. I burned his empire to the ground. He had to be hiding in plain sight, somewhere we'd never suspect. Ratholes don't usually have room service."

"Then job well done. 'Cause this place is fucking *depressing*."

He isn't wrong. Even the earth seems sad and wilted. It doesn't want to be here anymore than we do.

"How long do we wait?" Dima asks, shifting impatiently in his seat.

"As long as it takes to be certain that it's him in there."

"You saying you don't trust the intel? Or do you just not trust the rat who gave it to us? I mean, I wouldn't blame you; Archie could be full of shit. For all we know, this dump has nothing to do with Benedict."

I shake my head. "You're wrong there. I can smell him all over this place."

Dima brightens up at once. "So does that mean—?"

"Yeah," I say, killing the engine. "Fuck waiting. Let's go kill this motherfucker."

We step out of the car and sneak around, dodging camera fields en route to our starting position. All around us, the shadows bristle and teem with snapping sticks, shifting rocks, the crunch of sand under boots.

The full might of the Zakharov Bratva is waiting in the darkness.

"Tell the men to wait for my signal," I say to Dima. "Then we strike."

Dima nods, practically foaming at the mouth, as he whispers into the walkie-talkie clipped to his chest.

When the orders are relayed, I go to the side door, pull it open, and slip in.

The interior of the motel is lined with decades-old carpet the color of blood, stained with cigarette ash and God only knows what else. It smells like perfumed rot. Potted plants dot the corners, pathetically dusty. Everything is eerily quiet.

A counter sits at the end of the foyer space. I walk toward it. At the sound of my footsteps, a woman pokes her head out of the back office.

"Oh!" she gasps, way too surprised for someone who in theory is supposed to be here to welcome guests. "Hi—uh, who are you?"

The question is pierced with panic. I see her hand moving towards something under the counter. "I wouldn't do that if I were you."

Her eyes go wide as she freezes in place. She knows why we're here; she doesn't even need to ask. "P-please, I just work here."

"It'll be okay," I say as I inch towards her. "If you stay quiet, then everything's going to be just fine."

From the furrow on her brow and the panic on her lips, I'm guessing she doesn't believe me. She starts backing away as I approach.

Just before she opens her mouth to scream, I vault over the counter and grab her, clamping my hand over her mouth to muffle the sound. I have no desire to kill her, but I need her to stay quiet. So, with one focused headbutt, her body goes limp in my arms. I fold her into a fetal position under the counter of her desk.

When I straighten up, Dima is standing by the mouth of the hallway. "I'm hearing footsteps," he whispers. "We've got to hurry."

The two of us head through the door that leads to an interior courtyard of sorts. There's a dead tree in the very center, surrounded by a dried-up pond and brown grass. We trek past it to a series of doors, most as dusty as the rest of this hellhole.

"Should we go one by one?" asks Dima.

I shake my head. "No. Deeper. Somewhere more fortified. He's gonna be nested up in the lowest rung of hell. As far away from danger as he can get."

Dima laughs darkly and the two of us venture down the staircase.

A lone fluorescent light flickers at the top landing. As we descend, though, we get swallowed up by musty darkness.

"Should we send the men in?" Dima asks.

I shake my head again. "No. Not yet. They'll only get in the way."

We approach a thick metal door. To my surprise, the *mudaks* didn't even bother to lock it. Idiots. They deserve everything that's coming to them.

I kick open the door hard and it careens open on its hinges, screeching wildly until it slams into the side wall. I stride into the room, which is clean and spacious and a hell of a lot nicer than the rest of this dump.

In the center of a huge bed lies a naked mafioso with his mouth hanging open and his eyes wide in shock. Three naked women are curled around his body. One has her hand wrapped around his cock. Another is hanging over him, her nipple inches from his mouth. The third is cowering at the foot of the bed with bruises blooming on her pale skin.

It's almost exactly the scene I expected to see.

Just the wrong mafioso.

"Gregor Bellasio," I say, hiding my disappointment behind a piqued eyebrow. "Fancy running into you here."

The younger Bellasio brother splutters unintelligibly, spittle flying out of his mouth. The women scatter, suddenly very interested in putting some distance between themselves and the target on the bed.

Dima cocks a gun and points it in Gregor's face. He freezes, halfway propped up on his elbows, his eyes darting back and forth between us. "H-how?" he stammers.

I shrug. "Research."

Gregor's eyes narrow. "Does this mean the old man came out of hiding?" he asks. "Benedict swore if he ever did, he'd come straight to us."

I laugh. "You're really that fucking dumb, aren't you?"

He gnashes his teeth, but the effect is undercut by the fear in his eyes. If that wasn't enough of a giveaway, his dick has shriveled down to the size of a mealworm.

"If Benedict really believed that Archie would come to him, he wouldn't have set you up here. He needed this place, but where is he?" I cock my head to the side. "Oh, Gregor. You dumb fuck. *You're the decoy.*"

"N-no. You're fucking wrong."

"Don't be naïve. He knew this safehouse was a risk because Archie knew about it. He wanted to know the minute Archie decided to resurface, to see which side the old man chose. You're going to help me clarify a few things for him."

His eyes are looking a little red and swollen around the edges. "You can't kill me!"

"You're the last person alive who gets to tell me what I can and can't do. Though the 'alive' part might not last much longer."

His prostitutes are in various stages of hysteria. One is sobbing, tears coating her red cheeks. Another looks like she's about to pass out. The third is shivering violently as though she's standing naked in a freezer.

"My issue isn't with you ladies," I tell them. "I hope he paid you well, but if not, I'm not going to kill you for bad taste. If you step outside and wait quietly, I'll let you leave without any trouble."

The brunette is the first one to jump at my offer. She nods, snatches up her clothes from the floor, and runs. After she's left the room without being shot in the back, the other two find the courage to race out behind her.

"Guess it's just us then," I say when they're gone, pulling out my own gun and dangling it in his direction.

"If you k-kill me, he will come for you," Gregor warns.

I sigh, already tired of this fool. "That's kind of the point."

"It won't just be you, either!" Gregor exclaims in a last-ditch attempt to buy himself more time. "He'll come for your fiancée, for your sister, for everyone you love. If you do this, even Celine's status won't protect her."

I smirk and aim. "I'm sure I'll manage just fine."

"*No—!*"

But the rest of his words are lost to the gunshot. His body twitches back, limp against the sheets, and bright red blood oozes onto the pillows.

One less Bellasio on the face of this planet.

Good fucking riddance.

I grab the paper and pen from the nightstand and scribble the words that I always suspected I'd have to write to Benedict. Then I walk out with Dima at my back. All three women are standing there, but now they're at least wearing clothes, more or less.

I march up to the brunette and hand her my note. "Give this to Benedict Bellasio. And tell him where he can find his brother's body."

49

TAYLOR

I barely recognize the woman in the mirror.

Blinking slowly, I finger the wispy material of my figure-hugging gown. The pink pearlescent fabric is complemented by the plethora of little Swarovski crystals woven into the neckline, bodice, and skirt. I've kept my hair down and my makeup minimal, but I still look like I'm trying to be someone else.

Someone like my sister.

The door opens and Adam runs in. The moment he sees me, he comes to a grinding halt. "Wow, Mama!" he gasps with wide eyes.

On his heels comes Edna, who's looking a little flushed herself. "I'm sorry, ma'am," she gasps, sucking in air. "He got away from me."

"Don't worry about it," I assure the nanny. Adam took to her more quickly than I did, but she's starting to grow on me. I turn to my son, who's still looking at me like he's just seen the sun. "What do you think, buddy?"

"You look like a princess!"

"Do you think so?" I laugh.

"Uh-huh. You look so pretty, Mama."

I lower myself down to a squat and raise my arms so that he can run into them. When he does, I hug him tight and place a kiss on his brow. "Be a good boy for Grandpa while Mama and Auntie Cee go out, okay?"

He ignores my question completely. "Where's Uncle Illy? He hasn't come to play with me in ages."

I stiffen up, painfully aware all the sudden of how the beads of the dress are digging into my ribcage. I'm vaguely aware of rasping, "I'm sure he'll be back soon, honey."

Ilarion said he'd be back for Celine's ball, but I haven't seen him nor heard from him since he left. Last I checked, Celine hasn't, either, and I don't want to pester her any more than I already have.

"Mama, did you find the present Grandpa left for you?"

"Present?"

"Yeah, he left you a present in your closet."

I frown, bewildered. "When?"

"This morning," Adam insists. "He said—"

"Ah good, you're dressed. Dad will meet us by the front door in ten minutes," Celine interrupts as she sweeps into my room in her own gorgeous gown. "Now, let me look at you. Oh, Adam, sweetheart, don't crush Mommy's dress."

I straighten up reluctantly and let her survey me.

NAOMI WEST

"Stunning," she proclaims. "Although, the hair… Shall I get my stylist in here? She can—"

"I'm good," I insist as I take in her nude lace ballgown. "You look fabulous, by the way."

"Thank you," she says, patting her chic updo. A few dainty wisps of hair are left deliberately loose to frame her heart-shaped face. She moves towards the floor-length mirror and I hurry to get out of her way.

Adam is already bored with all the dress talk. He's running around my room and using my bed as a trampoline. Meanwhile, my heart is throbbing painfully.

What did he say about the present Dad left me?

"Adam, honey, can you come here for a second?"

"Why, Mama?" he asks as he launches himself onto my bed.

"Tay, just let him play. Let me fix your makeup." Cee reaches for the makeup kit she'd forcibly bought for me on our shopping trip.

"There's nothing to fix," I insist quickly. "My makeup's done."

"That's it?" Cee asks in surprise. "It's so light."

"I like it that way. Can we just get this show on the road?"

She gives me a long-suffering sigh and waves me on. "As you wish. Spoilsport."

"Edna." I turn to the nanny. "Adam's been—"

I break off as my eyes land on my son. He's in the corner of the room, rooting through the old duffel bag I'd packed to come here.

And to my horror, he's tossing my snow globe back and forth between his hands.

"Adam!" I bark as the breath rushes out of me with irrational panic. "Put that away now! Before you break it!"

He's so startled that he drops it. It hits the ground with a sickening thump. I gasp and rush forward, snatching it up off the floor. I twist it in my hands, making sure there's no crack.

Thank God. It's okay. Everything is okay.

"I'm sorry, Mama," Adam says nervously. "I didn't mean to."

I take a deep breath, feeling like a monster for reacting the way I did. "It's okay, baby. I'm sorry. I overreacted; it's all good. Now, give me a kiss and go hang out with Edna, okay?"

He grabs my waist and gives me a quick hug before rushing for the door. Edna follows behind him and I turn to Celine. "Let's…"

I trail off when I see her face. She looks like she's seen a ghost. Even the makeup can't offset the sudden pallor. Her mouth is parted, and her eyes are fixed on the snow globe in my hand.

The moment I see her expression, my heart sinks.

She recognizes it.

Judgment day is here at last.

50

TAYLOR

"Cee—"

"Did he take you to the cabin?"

The question is direct and curt. There's no room for anything but the truth. "Yes, he did."

"When?"

"A long time ago."

"When?"

Her stony expression is hard for me to witness, but I deserve it. I deserve every last bit of the bloodthirsty accusation in her eyes. "Five years ago."

"When I was—*when I was in the coma?*"

I can feel my bottom lip trembling, but I bite down on my tongue and force myself to answer her. "Yes."

She lunges forward so suddenly, I almost take a step back. Is she going to slap me? Push me? Hurl curses at my face? I'd deserve them all, so the least I can do now is stand still and take it.

She doesn't so much as touch me. But she does snatch the snow globe from my hands. I give it to her, feeling my hands hang limply at my sides. I drop my head, but I hear her sharp hiss.

"Don't you dare. Look at me."

I bite down on my tongue again so hard I taste blood. I lift my eyes to hers. "I'm so, *so* sorry, Celine."

"I don't want apologies." Her eyes glow with a kind of simmering fire I've never seen before. "I want fucking *explanations*."

I nod mutely.

"All this time," she breathes. The heat of her breath feels like it's slapping me across the face. "All this fucking time. It was *you*."

"It wasn't an affair," I say quickly. "I swear, Celine—"

"Then what was it?"

"It happened…before you."

She scoffs. "Please."

"I swear. Remember the night that I had that massive fight with Dad? Right before you met Ilarion? I left the house for a run and when I came back, you and I talked for a bit? And I left that same night. That was the night I met him."

Her scowl morphs. "You didn't say a word to me about it."

"Because it was a one-night stand, Celine!" I practically shout. I never knew how much pressure I've been carrying around until now. Now that it's all deflating, I feel small and weak and sad. "And I didn't know his name and I didn't think I would ever see him again. But then I went to your engagement party and found out the guy you refused to introduce to me was *the same guy.*"

We both hear the accusation in my words. In my voice.

Have I really been blaming her this whole time?

She takes a few heavy breaths. "Why didn't you tell me then? Why didn't you just…just…stop me?"

My eyes feel like they're about to bug out of my head. "What, after the way you reacted to Alec? And you seemed happy. You were so in love with Ilarion, you wouldn't even leave his side once you knew what he was trying to do to Dad. What was I supposed to say? Or do?"

She sucks in a hurt inhale and turns away from me.

"Celine, please believe me. I never wanted to hurt you."

"Is that why you decided to go on a romantic cabin getaway with my fiancé while I was on my deathbed?" she demands.

As she should. It's a fair fucking question.

"Dr. Baranov, he…h-he told us that…" I trail off, realizing how horrible it sounds. "Oh, God, you're right. I'm awful. It was an awful thing for me to do, and I regret it every single fucking day."

"Do you love him?" she suddenly demands, looking me dead in the eye.

I can't bring myself to say it. I can't bring myself to lie, though. There's been too much of that already.

"It doesn't matter."

"'It doesn't matter'?" Celine stares at me like I've grown three new heads. "Holy shit, Taylor. *Of course* it matters. It matters to me, it probably matters to Ilarion, and it should matter to you, too."

"The only thing I care about is you. Everything I've done was for you."

She lifts a brow. All the shock and heartache is compounded into that one eyebrow. It's the only sign that her world is falling apart.

She nods once and then, without warning, flings the snow globe across the room. It hits the wall right next to the windows and shatters. I gasp, my body lurching towards the wall as though I can somehow stop it, reverse time, magically put the snow globe back together. I react as though the globe is a person I can save.

As if it's a future I almost had.

Then I catch myself. I stop short and look at my sister. She's Arctic fury in the flesh. The coldest wind I've ever felt, tearing me to frozen pieces.

"You're the reason he couldn't love me back," she whispers. "*You.*"

I blink and a fat tear runs down my cheek. "I tried not to love him at all," I croak, hoping that some part of my explanation will save us. "I tried so hard. I thought hating him was the answer."

Celine snorts. "There's a fuzzy line between love and hate. You should have tried indifference." She shakes her head. "Why didn't you tell me before you left?"

"You chose him." I'm surprised that my guilt is fading into anger. Bit by bit, word by word, I'm starting to finally understand what Ilarion has been trying to tell me this whole time. "Even after Dad told you everything. The spying, his betrayal, the fact that Ilarion only approached you and asked you to marry him as insurance, as revenge—and you still fucking chose him. *You,* Cee. You chose a man who didn't love you over your own fucking family."

Celine's bottom lip quivers almost imperceptibly. "I believed, even then, that he was a good man."

"And what do you believe now?"

She smolders. "I believe that he didn't tell me any of this because he was protecting you."

"No, Cee. He's not. He never has been. If he had his way, you would have known right then and there at the engagement party."

Conflict wars across her face. She's trying to justify everything with the reality that neither of us can deny. Not anymore. I know that expression because I've seen it in the mirror for literal years on end.

"I thought it would be better if I disappeared," I admit. "Especially since…"

Oh, shit. I said too much.

Fear pumps through my chest so hard that I can barely keep my focus on her. But she waits patiently. Then, seconds of silence later, realization clears the frown on her face.

"Oh my god," she breathes. "How did I not see it? Adam. *He's Ilarion's.*"

I swallow hard. "I found out I was pregnant the day you announced you were engaged. I didn't know a thing about your fiancé. And I didn't think announcing a surprise pregnancy at your engagement party was even remotely appropriate. So, I showed up with Mom and Dad, and you introduced us to your fiancé, and it was…him."

Celine nods in slow motion. "I saw the two of you talking at the party," she admits. "It looked as though you were familiar, but I just assumed you were getting to know each other for my sake. But then the Bellasios attacked…"

And just like that, all the fight leaves her body like a heavy sigh.

"Were you going to tell me? Ever?"

I hesitate, trying to figure out if there was ever any possibility of coming clean if the world hadn't caved in on itself. "I don't know, Cee. I'd like to think I would have. But…"

"But?"

I take a deep breath. Time for some actual fucking honesty. "But…after Alec, I didn't want to see you so hurt again. I wanted to be the one to sacrifice for you."

She shakes her head. "Why?"

"Because you were always there for everyone. You were the one taking care of me when I was sick. You were the one taking care of Mom when *she* was sick. You talked Dad through the worst of his depression and cooked for us all when everyone was too tired to move and you moved back home without being asked and you never, ever made any of it seem like a burden. You deserved to be happy, Cee. I wanted to give you a happy ending. I…I still do."

She stares at me for a moment, and I can see the remnants of her anger fade. "Don't you understand, Taylor?" she says. "It wasn't in your power to give me a happy ending. You don't get to control how other people feel. You don't have the right to tell Ilarion to love me, and you don't have the right to deny him his son. Or Adam his father." Her eyes veer to the broken pieces of glass on the floor. Then she takes a deep breath and that icy mask of hers settles back into place. "Come on now. We have a ball to attend."

51

ILARION

"She's not gonna be happy," Dima warns me as we make our way up to the grand ballroom on the twenty-seventh floor. "Not even a little bit."

Before I can sarcastically thank my second-in-command for stating the very-fucking-obvious, the elevator doors open to reveal…

My sister, decked out in a shimmering black dress that's far too tight for my liking.

On Taylor, I'd have been intrigued. On Mila, I feel like I need to avert my eyes.

"Whoa," Dima breathes. "Mila…you look amazing."

It takes everything I have in me not to react, to tell him to roll his lolling tongue back up in his mouth. Mila's face stays impassive but strained. I can practically see the pistons in her head surging as she tries not to blush.

"Yeah, thanks," she mumbles dismissively. She turns to look at me. "How did it go?"

"We found the safehouse. Exactly where Archie said it would be."

"But…?"

"Benedict anticipated it," I finish. "He set Gregor up there as a decoy."

Mila frowns. "Is he dead?"

"Long dead. But he's not the one I wanted gone."

She grins delightedly. "Still, I'll take the minor wins when we can get them. What's the next move?"

The door of the grand ballroom swings open. Noise, laughter, and music spill out into the foyer. "It's Benedict's move," I answer.

Mila blinks, confused. "What do you mean?"

"I offered him a truce—of sorts."

She looks like she's going to gag on my words. "A *truce*? With Benedict Bellasio? On what kind of terms?"

"He disbands what remains of his crumbling Bratva, writes off his remaining assets to me, surrenders himself to my custody, and he gets to live the rest of his life in decent comfort. Emphasis on 'gets to live.' It's the best offer he'll ever get."

Mila's frown deepens. "He's not going to accept that."

I shrug. "His choice to make. His life to gamble with."

"Are you sure about this?" she presses. "There's more at stake here. Not just Celine's life; there's Taylor and Adam to consider."

"Benedict has no clue about either one of them. As far as he's concerned, Celine's the only one he has to target."

"And you're willing to take that risk?"

"Better question: is he?"

"The man is desperate, Ilarion," Mila points out. "You've made your stance very clear: *touch Celine and he dies*. But what if his life no longer means that much to him? He's two moves away from losing everything. He might consider that reason enough to take her."

"Celine's no longer the shy kitten she was when I married her. She can hold her own."

"Is this about Taylor?" she asks with a weary exhale. "With Celine out of the picture—"

"Enough!" I snarl, far more angrily than the situation calls for. "That's enough. Put your party face on. We have a ball to attend."

Mila knows better than to question me, though she looks like she'd rather jump off a bridge than go dancing right now. Still, she knows her place. She sighs deeply and follows me toward the ballroom.

The space is decked out in true Celine fashion and everyone is dressed to the nines. It doesn't take me long to spot the eldest Theron daughter. She's standing in the center of the room, dead center beneath a grand chandelier that sparkles with the light of a thousand glass crystals.

She really is a beauty, but my eyes search for someone else. Someone who's probably lurking in the shadows, trying to hide her own beauty in the darkness.

It takes two scans around the room before I spot her near the balcony, her hands folded at her waist, her eyes heavy with disinterest, and…something else. Something I can't quite put my finger on.

Taylor is wearing a beautiful gown in a blush pink. She looks like the cherry blossom petals that drift past my bedroom window. Unlike Celine, though, she doesn't look remotely comfortable in her finery. Like Mila, she looks like she'd rather be anywhere else but here.

With anyone else but me.

And yet, being the cruel, selfish bastard that I am, I cut over to her. I've been deprived of her company for long enough. I've spent the last few days furiously trying not to think about the kiss I stole from her. But now that I'm back, not thinking about it is impossible. The closer I get to her, the more fiercely I can feel its memory sealed on my lips.

She doesn't sense me until I'm right behind her. Even then, her gaze is directly fixed on the balcony just beyond the twenty-foot doors that hug the left side of the ballroom.

"Taylor."

She turns with a start, but when she sees me, her eyes go wide with horror and she scrambles away. "No."

I wasn't exactly expecting her to jump into my arms after what I did in the garden before I left. But the fear in her eyes is alien and entirely unwarranted.

"What's wrong?" I ask.

"No," she says again, backing farther away from me. "Celine might see." Then she turns and strides in the opposite direction.

I let her go reluctantly, my mind churning. *Celine might see.* Normally, I'd say, *Who gives a fuck?*

But something has clearly changed. It isn't hard to guess what.

There's only one reason that Celine seeing might be a problem.

She knows.

I scan the crowd again, trying to spot her. When I finally find her, her gaze is firmly locked on me. Looks like it has been for a while.

She's standing next to Archie, who looks all sorts of miserable despite the charming smile plastered to his face. She turns to him and whispers something in his ear. Then she gestures for me to follow her. Biting down on my tongue, I trail her out into one of the private rooms adjoining the ballroom.

"Close the door behind you," Celine says in a tone I haven't heard from her before.

I latch it shut and walk over to her. I should be feeling guilt, but all I can feel is relief. It's finally out there. We've been waiting so long for this moment. I thought it would come with thunder and lightning, fire and brimstone. Instead, it's accompanied by the clink of champagne glasses and the muted laughter of the donor class.

I'm a step away when her hand comes flying towards my face.

I could easily sidestep the slap, but I choose not to. She deserves far more. Letting her hit me is the least I can do.

Her palm connects with the side of my face. Heat blooms. Pain follows. I take it all in stony silence.

She drops her hand to her side, flexing it open and closed. Her mouth is a vibrating mask of fury and sorrow.

"I suppose I deserve that."

The vein in her forehead twitches. Her mouth is a tight slash. "My sister," she rasps. "Of all the women in the world, you fucked my sister. You…you *chose* to fuck my sister." Celine trembles. Not just her jaw now, but her whole body. "*She's* the reason I never stood a chance."

Might as well be blunt while we're being honest. I'm done beating around the bush. "Yes."

She waits for me to say something else, but when I stay silent, her brow furrows. "That's it?" she asks. "That's all you're going to say to me?"

"What do you want me to say?"

"Did I ever stand a chance?" Her voice trembles over the words. It's easy to see what it's costing her. *How much* it's costing her.

"I met her before I knew you. And I didn't know who she was or who you were to her. It was a cruel coincidence, but it's what happened."

She lets out a dark laugh that's half-sob. "You could just lie to me, you know."

"I'm not that cruel."

Her lip quivers. "Right. But why not? You're used to being cruel to everyone else. Why not do it to me and just…lie?"

"Contrary to what you may be thinking right now, I actually do care for you." I scrub a hand over my face, my skin still tingling from Celine's slap. "I do love you. I'm just not...*in* love with you."

She closes her eyes. A single tear brims on the tips of her eyelash. "Are you in love with her?"

I sigh again. "Yes."

"So that's why you refused to sleep with me."

"Yes."

"Why we...we never actually married."

"Yes."

She nods and opens her eyes. "I spent so many nights jealous of your other woman. If only I knew it was my own sister keeping me awake."

"She doesn't deserve your hate. Or your anger. She tried her best to protect you." I let out a short laugh. "Fucking hell, she fought tooth and nail to protect you."

"Don't," Celine snarls. "You have no right to tell me how to feel about Taylor." Her eyes glisten with more tears she refuses to let fall. I take a step towards her, my hand reaching out, but she jerks away from me. "It's not fair. It's not fair that you get to have a family and I get nothing."

"You can have everything, Celine," I tell her. "You just need to make a decision."

"What the hell does that mean?"

I look her dead in the eye when I speak, only because I really want her to hear me. "Ashton won't wait around forever. It isn't fair to ask him to, either."

She starts to ask how I know, then thinks better of it and falls silent, swallowing back the question and instead just breathing slowly. We stand there for a while. Two ships passing in the night.

"Ilarion…" she says at last. "Thank you."

Then she walks out.

I watch her go, feeling freer than I have in years.

52

TAYLOR

Holy hell—was this dress always so tight? Or has it shrunk on me in the last few hours?

I've just settled on the second answer when I'm hit with a gust of warm air from the balcony doors. I turn in time to see Ilarion shut the door to a side room behind him and beeline straight toward me.

"You can't be here," I protest, pressing my back against the balcony railing. We're so high up. Too high up for this conversation, for this situation. I'm already dizzy as it is. "Please, I'm begging you—just leave me alone."

Of course, he ignores me. "You look beautiful, *tigrionok.*"

I don't allow myself to linger on the compliment. No matter how many butterflies it awakens in me. "Fine. If you won't leave, I will."

I try to move around him and retreat back inside, but he snags my arm before I can get far. He pulls me toward him, turning my buffer of safe space into firm body heat, the tidal wave of his cologne, and an ocean of nerves.

"I spoke to Celine."

"Doesn't matter. Let me go."

"She's leaving." He thinks it over and rephrases. "Leaving me, at least. For Ashton."

A shiver runs down my spine. "Still doesn't matter. I'm trying to do the right thing."

"By denying your feelings for me?"

"Yes!" I hiss. "My feelings for you are *wrong*!"

He seems to hesitate. "You don't mean that."

Deep down, I really don't. "I *have* to mean it, Ilarion."

"Because Celine still lives with me?"

"Because I…I…" *Fucking hell*, I can't think of anything. I'm still reeling from the idea that this nightmare I've spent five years dreading might finally be done with me. I squint at him. "Is she really leaving you for Ashton?"

Ilarion sighs. "More like she's letting go of pointless hope and going after something real. Something I could never give her."

"You didn't even try." I don't know why I'm such an emotional masochist, but the words keep flowing like verbal vomit. "You didn't even try to make it work with her."

"I couldn't make myself feel something that I didn't. And it's not fair to lie to her. To string her along over something she'll never have."

I wrench my arm out from under his and pivot away from him. I know he won't let me leave until he's had his say, so I don't bother trying. I walk to the balcony's edge instead, looking for a way out. Or maybe a way down. I wish I was Rapunzel in one of Adam's towers and I could just throw my hair over the edge like a rappelling rope.

"Cee seems to think you're a good man," I murmur out into the night.

"It usually depends on who you ask."

It's cold out here and my wispy dress isn't insulating me the way that I need right now. Of course, there's the heat of his presence; that's another beast entirely.

And I need to stay far away from it.

"How is she?" I ask.

"Still processing. But mostly…relieved."

My eyes feel like they're about to pop out of their sockets. "She said that?"

"She didn't have to. I saw it written all over her face."

"Ah. So you're just seeing what you want to see."

Now, he genuinely smiles and turns me to follow his gaze into the ballroom. Through the frame of the window, I see…

Holy shit.

Cee is wrapped up in Ashton's arms, and for the first time in…ever, actually…she looks truly happy.

The sinking feeling in my gut isn't because of what I'm seeing. It's from realizing: *I almost took that away from her.*

I shake my head and stamp my foot to ward off the cold, the fear, and worst of all, the hope. "It doesn't matter," I announce with a sigh. "She knows now. And that means that I need to figure out—"

"Stop it, goddammit," he snarls. "There's nothing to 'figure out.' She'll stay in her quarters until she and Ashton move things forward. Adam keeps his room. You'll move into mine."

I frown. "But she's a Zakharov. I don't understand how—"

"Legal name change." He says it so simply, like it's a totally normal thing for someone to do. "It helped keep up the ruse."

"The fake marriage."

He shrugs. "Worked on you, didn't it? And the Bellasios are not as nosy as you are."

"Ilarion."

"I told you, Taylor: she's family. By name, by friendship, and...well, by you, technically. And Adam."

He has me there. I fall silent and try to wrap my head around everything that's moving so, so fast.

So many lies. Noble ones, well-intentioned ones, hopeful ones. It doesn't matter in the end. A lie is still a lie, no matter how beautifully it's dressed up.

It's ironic—I felt some version of that over the years when I learned about Dad's double life. And somehow, despite how much I resented him for it, I allowed myself to fall into the same black hole.

I did to Celine what Dad did to his family.

What he did to me.

"Celine doesn't love me," Ilarion whispers. His hands come to rest gently on my waist, the heat of his palms burning through the fabric. "But you do."

I'm already at the edge of the balcony; there's nowhere else for me to go. I grip the edge of the rough stone and pray that I have the strength to withstand whatever hurricane he's going to rain down upon me with those eyes. Those hands.

I bite the inside of my cheek until I taste blood. "You can't say that."

"Of course I can. It's true."

"If she wasn't in love with you, she wouldn't have broken the snow globe," I blurt without thinking about my words.

Dammit, I scold myself the instant I see Ilarion's brows raise. "Ah. That explains the shattered glass."

"You took her to the cabin, too," I accuse. "That's how she knew."

"Yes, I did. Once, before I even knew the two of you were related. Before the garden party. Before any of this came to a head. If it makes you feel any better, we slept in separate rooms."

"That's not what I was asking."

"Wasn't it?"

Okay, so maybe it was. Who cares, though, right? What difference does it make? What hope is left?

"All these years," I whisper, allowing my gaze to lift to his. He's standing closer now. If I move even a fraction of an inch, I will touch him. "There was no one else?"

He nods once, slowly. His eyes bore into mine as if blinking will make me vanish. "There was never anyone else."

"Why stay faithful to me?" I ask. "You had no reason to."

His fingers brush along my arm. "I had *every* reason to," he corrects softly. "I know I've never told you that I love you. But why tell, when I could show?"

Those words...

Those words are the hurricane.

He grabs the side of my face and this time, I do nothing to stop him. I let go of the fight I've been clinging to. I let go of all the roadblocks I've created in my mind.

I gave him away because I thought it was the right thing to do.

But in the end, I could never truly give away what's rightfully mine.

"I'm sorry, Ilarion."

He shakes his head, his misty blue eyes swirling. "Don't tell me," he says, a teasing smile playing at his lips. "Show me."

They're almost on mine. I can feel the warmth of his breath. But a second before he makes contact, I hear a scream.

We jerk apart. Ilarion's body whips up straight with alertness.

"Stay here."

Of course, I don't listen. I follow him as he charges back into the ballroom. There's a crowd of people clustered in the center that we have to fight our way through.

"Celine!" Ilarion calls. "Dima! Mila!"

"Ilarion!" Dima's voice calls back from the center of the crowd.

The guests part and I see Celine on her knees. Mila is standing over her, face pale and furious.

"What happened?" Ilarion demands as he moves towards Celine.

I stand there, desperate to go to my sister, knowing that she probably doesn't want me anywhere near her. But then, she looks up and she makes eye contact with me.

"It's D-Dad," she stutters. "We were talking when two masked men busted in. They grabbed us both, but Dad fought back to try and protect me. They knocked him out cold and…and…"

She starts sobbing and Mila takes over. "We heard the commotion and busted into the room, but they were already leaving with Archie. They would have taken Celine, too, if we hadn't arrived when we did."

"*Blyat'*," Ilarion growls.

I drop to my knees in front of Celine. Her eyes are wild with terror as she grips my arms and squeezes. "They're going to kill him, Taylor," she gasps. "We're going to lose him."

"No," I say firmly. "No, we're not. Ilarion will get him back."

I glance up at Ilarion, but he's not meeting my gaze. He turns to Dima and Mila, both bristling with pent-up energy.

"What does this mean?" Mila asks her brother.

Ilarion smolders. "It means that Benedict has turned down my truce."

53

ILARION

The party disperses immediately. I end up in a car with Celine and Taylor as we race back to Zakharov House.

Celine sits on the far left, her gaze directed out the tinted window. Taylor is on the right, pulling at her nails until the manicure starts peeling away and piling up in her dress. The silence feels ridiculous, especially since there's so much to say.

"You can drop me off at the penthouse," Celine says abruptly. "I'll spend the night in the city."

"No, you won't. I've just smoked Benedict out of his hole. There's no telling what he might do."

"He has my *dad*," she hisses.

"And he wanted you as well. He would have succeeded, too, if you hadn't gotten very fucking lucky."

She flinches as though I've reprimanded her. "The penthouse," she repeats.

"It's not safe."

"I don't care. I need space."

Taylor flinches; there are lines on her forehead that I've never seen before. "Cee," she interjects softly, as though she's not sure she has the right to say her name. "Can we talk?"

Celine sighs. "I'm done talking for one night." She looks between the two of us. "In any case, this is not the time to be talking. Dad's missing, Tay."

"Maybe that's exactly why we should be talking about this."

I nod. "Your father would want the two of you to make peace. You're family."

"Family?" Celine repeats incredulously before she turns to Taylor. "Family doesn't lie to each other."

"That really depends on the family," I mutter.

She glares at me. "Now is not the time to develop a sense of humor, Ilarion." She clenches her jaw tight. "Though I'm sure the two of you must have had a good laugh at my expense."

I pinch the bridge of my nose. "Stop with the dramatics. Every decision made, good or bad, was for you. Just as every decision moving forward is to help you. I will make sure you have every comfort. You want houses, cars, money—have it all."

"I don't need you doing me any favors, Ilarion. I'm not a fucking charity case."

"For God's sake, woman," I snap, "just take the fucking gift. I'm trying to help you."

"Are you, though?" she questions. "Or is this your way of trying to buy my approval so that you're free to be with my sister?"

Taylor flinches like Celine just struck her. "Cee, I have no intention of making your life any harder than it already is. I don't need to stay. I'll just…go."

I bristle at that. Even now, even now that everything's out in the open…*godfuckingdammit.*

Celine's nostrils flare with anger. "Then what the hell would be the point, Taylor?" she scoffs. "What the hell is the end game of all this drama?"

"Celine, how can I—"

"Stop it," she snaps coldly. "I don't need your pity. I don't want it. Do you love him?"

I'm about to step in and shut this nonsense down when she asks the question. It makes me pause, and wait, because I really want to know the answer. More like, I need to hear her actually say it.

Taylor pales. "I…I don't…"

Celine turns her icy gaze to me. "Do you love my sister?"

I nod. "I do."

Celine nods and turns back to Taylor. "I'll ask again. Do you love him?"

"I love *you*, too," she protests softly.

"That's not what I'm asking."

"She never needed to choose, Celine," I say softly. "And she chose you anyway."

Celine closes her eyes and drops her face into her hands. A tear slips from Taylor's cheek as both sisters retreat into their silence.

Then, out of nowhere, Celine slams her hands down on the seat. "Then she chose wrong." She turns to Taylor. "Look at me. Stop glancing away, dammit—*look at me!* It's time to stop trying to save me. Stop treating me like a porcelain doll. Live your goddamn life. Love whoever the fuck you want."

The car stops. All three of us glance out to realize that we're back at Zakharov House. Celine takes a deep breath, gathers up her skirts, and leaps out of the car.

Taylor finally looks at me in the thudding silence of the vehicle. I have no idea what's lurking behind those petrified, teary eyes of hers. She shakes her head once, and then she gets out of the car. I follow close behind.

Celine has already disappeared into the house.

There's only Taylor, framed by moonlight.

54

TAYLOR

"I want Grandpa," Adam pouts.

My chest feels like someone sat on it all night. "I know, sweetheart, but I told you, Grandpa's gone away for a few days. He had some important work to do."

"What important work?" Adam asks, peering at me suspiciously. "I don't believe you." Scowling, he turns and scampers further into the garden.

"Adam!" I call after him. "Adam! Don't go too far, honey!"

He doesn't listen. He seems to want to put as much space between us as possible. He's not the only one in this house who feels that way.

Not that I can blame them.

Sighing, I trudge after my son all the way down to the fence along the southern boundary. But when I finally catch up to him, I realize that he's talking to someone.

I turn the corner and stop short. Celine is sitting on a blanket beneath the shade of a willow tree. She's wearing blue linen shorts and a cotton blouse, bare-footed and bare-faced. Gone are the jewels and the gowns I've gotten used to seeing her in. Even her hair is simple and free over her shoulders.

It's like turning the clock ten years into the past.

I know she sees me, but she doesn't acknowledge me. Instead, she picks up an apple from her basket and hands it to Adam. "There's more where that came from," she says, giving him a little wink.

"Thanks, Auntie Cee," Adam gushes, grabbing the apple and biting into it before he turns away.

"Stay where I can see you, okay?" Celine calls.

I probably should leave her to her solitude, but it feels as though the more room I give her, the more room I'm leaving for our relationship to fracture further.

"Celine." She jerks her head in my general direction, but she doesn't make eye contact. I figure that's as good as it's going to get. "I want you to know that I've started looking for places. I'm hoping to move by the end of the week."

That seems to grab her attention. She turns to me with a frown drawing her forehead into deep furrows. "Why?"

"Why? Why what?"

"Why would you leave this house? It's more yours than mine."

"No, it's not," I say adamantly. "This has been your home for years."

"It's been a sanctuary more than anything," she says with a sigh. Her defenses are gradually lowering, one brick at a time. Again, it's all I can and should hope for. "A place where I was safe from Benedict and his thugs. But now, I'd rather take my chances with him."

"Cee—"

She holds up one hand to shut me up. "I'm not looking for sympathy or apologies. I stayed longer than I should have. It took yesterday to make me see it. I'm serious about leaving, Tay. I'm serious about ending whatever relationship the world thought Ilarion and I had."

"I'm not asking you to reconsider. I'm just saying that I have to go, too."

"Why would you do that?" she asks with a skeptical scowl. "When you love him and he loves you?"

"Because you have feelings for him. And…and you had a claim to him first."

Her frown irons out for a moment. Then she exhales deeply. "Tay, don't do this. Don't do that thing you do—"

"What?"

"Your circular logic. Every time you're stuck facing a reality you don't want to face, you start sounding like a broken record. And you keep spinning and spinning no matter how bad it sounds."

"But he's your—"

"Have you not been paying attention?" Celine cuts in with a disbelieving laugh. "*We were never married.* He's more like a brother to me than anything else. We're friends and we're close, but he's been giving me the same kind of love he'd give me if *you* married him."

I feel my heart suddenly slam inside my ribcage just hearing those words. No matter what's happened, then or now, never once have I ever entertained the idea of being married to Ilarion. In my panic, I deflect with a nervous laugh. "There you go again. Being selfless."

She shrugs off the compliment. There isn't a trace of a smile on her face. "I'm not being anything. I'm just stating the obvious. I was stupid not to have seen it before. It seems so transparent to me now. And just so you know, I don't actually have feelings for Ilarion. What little emotion I felt for him died the moment I realized he was in love with you. Which, to be honest, is a huge red flag in and of itself. Real love doesn't snuff itself out that fast."

I can't breathe. I can't breathe and I'm pretty sure I'm losing my hearing, too. Her words are starting to muffle amidst the pounding in my ears.

"I don't want to lose you, Cee."

She meets my eyes for a second. "So that's it, is it?" she asks. "You're worried that if you run off into the sunset with Ilarion, you're risking our relationship?"

"Well…yes."

Cee smiles at me like I'm some adorable little kid caught doing something silly. "Tay. Really. You and Ilarion are *supposed* to be together. And Adam needs his father as much as you do. What kind of sister would I be if I made you choose between that and your family? No, I would never." Her walls are completely down now. she smiles sadly. "You're really blessed, Taylor. Don't fuck it up."

"But what about you?"

"That's my concern now," she says with an easy shrug of her shoulder. "Not yours. Actually, it was never your concern."

I push back my tears. "Can you ever forgive me?" I'm terrified of her answer, because honestly, I don't have anything left to lose.

She pulls an apple out of her picnic box and hands it to me before she gets to her feet. "Give that to Adam," she tells me. "I'll want to see him from time to time."

It's not exactly an answer, but it's something.

"I'm leaving for the penthouse soon. I'll probably be moving my things there in a few days." She turns to glance over her shoulder at me. "There's no reason for you to leave, too. Let Adam enjoy his new home. He deserves to be happy. All of us do."

55

ILARION

"Is it Dima?" Mila asks the moment she sees me pick up the call. "Put him on speaker."

I shoot her a glare and transfer the call to speaker. Then I gesture for her to follow me into the den. "Go on, Dima," I tell him as Mila shuts the door behind us.

"Benedict left us a little gift just outside the Southside warehouse. It was addressed to you and gift-wrapped. Fucker has a flare for the dramatics."

"Always did. Have you opened the box?"

"Just finished running checks on it. Looks like there's nothing poisonous or flammable. Want me to bring it over or should I do the honors?"

"Transfer to FaceTime," Mila barks. "And just open the damn thing."

"Ilarion?" Dima questions. Mila rolls her eyes.

"Do as Mila says."

The moment the video call pops up, I press the green button and Dima's face appears on the screen. He twists the camera around and I'm staring at a small white box with green trimming.

Dima pulls at the green bow and it falls open. He lifts the lid off the box and drops it almost immediately. It takes a moment before the camera focuses on what's inside.

"Fuck me… Is that a finger?" Mila whispers.

The camera twists back around on Dima's face. He looks pale but otherwise calm. "Pretty sure that's Archie's finger." I don't miss the sympathy in his voice.

"Bury it," I say without missing a beat. "And no one's to breathe a word of this to Celine or Taylor. *Especially* not in front of Adam. Am I clear?"

"He's going to carve the old man up, Ilarion," Dima presses urgently. "They might have to be prepared before that happens."

"That's not going to happen," I snap. "Because we're going to get to him before then. Finish up there quickly; I have a few leads I need you to follow for me."

"I'll join him," Mila says when I hang up. "Give me the locations and I'll meet up with Dima in the city and we can take it from there. I'll take Mikhail and Franz with me, too."

"Franz has other duties tonight," I say. "He's with Celine in the penthouse."

Mila's brows arch with surprise. "She moved out?"

"Not officially. But soon enough."

"I hope you don't mind me saying so, but…" She nudges me with her arm. "You seem relieved."

"I feel like I've been holding my breath for the last five years." I sigh. "I care about Celine, and I still want her to be safe. But now, maybe she can be happy, too. Maybe we both can."

"Is happiness in the cards for you, brother?" Mila asks with a raised eyebrow.

I narrow my eyes at her. "Shouldn't you be on your way to meet with Dima?"

"I'm going, I'm going," she mutters. "You better get some rest. You've been on the go for the last three days and, no offense or anything, but it's starting to show."

I scowl at her as she leaves with a parting smile. Once I've got the den to myself, I fall into my chair with an exhausted sigh. My whole body aches. When all this is said and done, I'll need a good chiropractor. I have knots in me that are starting to fucking calcify.

My eyes grow heavy and I allow them to close for a few moments.

Right up until I hear the creak of the door and they snap back open.

I'm met with a startled gasp that instantly feels like aloe on a sunburn. "S-sorry," Taylor whispers. "I didn't realize you were sleeping in here."

"I wasn't." But when I glance out the window, I realize it's pitch black. Maybe I was asleep after all. "Is everything alright?"

"Celine left a few hours ago."

"I know."

She looks like she's on the verge of crying. It doesn't take away from her beauty, though. Those soft green eyes of hers are conflicted, torn between what she wants and what she wishes she wanted instead.

Her silken blonde hair tumbles over her bare shoulders. I imagine kissing my way from those shoulders down to the valley between her breasts. But I keep my gaze firmly fixed on her face.

"Ilarion." There's a new cadence in the way she says my name. "Do you know anything more about Archie? Adam keeps asking for him and I have no idea what to say anymore."

She hiccups as she finishes speaking and a tear rolls down her cheek. She wipes it away quickly.

"I'm doing my best to find him," I assure her, rounding the table so that there's nothing between us but a foot of empty space. "I have Dima and Mila out there right now, chasing leads."

"Leads?" she repeats. "Is that all you have?"

I ignore the jab because I understand. *Shit*, having a family is making me soft. And I'm not exactly complaining. "It's been enough before. Trust that it will be enough again." She swallows, but it looks more like a gulp. "Taylor, listen to me: I will do everything in my power to get your father back safely."

"Will you really, though?"

"Why wouldn't I?"

"The obvious: he betrayed you to your worst enemy. If it was anyone else, you'd have killed him a long time ago."

"All true," I agree without mincing my words. "But he's not anyone else. He's Archie Theron. He's my son's grandfather. He's the father of the woman I love. That's you, in case you're wondering. It's always been you."

She trembles in the in-between space for one moment that lasts lifetimes.

Then she throws herself into my arms and presses her lips against mine, taking the kiss as though she's waited an eternity for it.

Fuck knows I have. Good *God,* I've waited so long for this. My mouth parts against hers and I slide my tongue between her sugary lips, needing to taste her more. More, more, *more.* I'm a starved man finally able to feast.

But despite that, I force myself to think about the aftermath. I force myself to think about how she'll feel tomorrow. So I summon up every last ounce of strength I possess and pull back just enough to let us both catch our breath.

"Are you sure?" I growl in her face, knowing that even if she says she's not, I might not be prepared to accept that answer.

She's mine and I'll burn the world down before I lose her again.

She nods. "I'm done fighting this. I love you, Ilarion. You are the only thing, the only man, I've ever wanted."

And just like that, our fates are sealed.

56

TAYLOR

His hands slide down my back and, a second later, I hear the fabric of my cotton blouse rip. Gasping, I pull away, but he's already thrown it to the floor beside our feet.

His eyes penetrate mine. It feels like a challenge. He's waiting for me to stop him. Daring me to. But I'm not about to back out this time. I've spent too much of my life avoiding the things that I crave the most.

Somehow, without realizing it, I turned into my father.

Without looking away, he unbuttons my shorts and pulls them down my legs. He doesn't break that intense eye contact, not even to look at my body. I'm relieved about that. If he looks down now, he'll see that I'm covered in goosebumps and stretch marks. Not that it matters; he can probably feel them anyway.

"I've waited a long time for this," he rasps.

"Me, too." I can barely form the words. I can barely breathe at all.

One brow slowly arches upward. "Have you?"

I nod.

"Prove it."

He lifts his hand and I realize that my bra is hanging off his index finger. *When did he take that off?* He releases it and it joins the growing pile of clothes on the ground. He bends to my hips and slides my panties down around my legs, baring me completely to him.

I place my hands on his chest. *My god,* he feels incredible. So strong, so solid, so *safe*. My fingers move without thought, undoing each button just to be able to touch another inch of his warm skin.

He watches my every movement as though I'm going to disappear. I can feel him holding his breath, as if exhaling will blow me away.

"I'm not going anywhere, Ilarion," I whisper. I manage a small, sheepish smile. "I've learned my lesson."

"And what lesson is that?" he asks as I slide his shirt down over his massive arms.

I drop to my knees in front of him to work the buckle of his pants open. I can see the desire rage across his face as he takes the sight of me in.

I can't help myself. I'm such a tease when I'm feeling as free as we are now.

"You like seeing me like this?" I breathe, fanning the words over his skin just above the top button. "On my knees in front of you?"

His breath hitches again. The corner of his mouth turns up. "It's definitely not something I thought I'd ever see again."

I unzip him and pull his pants down, hooking my thumbs inside the boxer briefs to take them off, too. His hardened cock nearly slaps me in the face. I'm discovering how much I love the heat of him against every inch of me no matter where it touches.

I'd forgotten how big he is. Just the sight of his cock has my own heat flowing between my legs. The ache in my core is filled with an anticipation that I've denied myself for years. The same as the ache I can feel thrumming through him.

Even after he's naked, I stay where I am, on my knees in front of him. It feels right, like I can show him how much I want him…and how much I've missed him…in the same way I'd beg for forgiveness for ever leaving him.

One hand gently takes the weight of his balls into my palm, while my other hand wraps around his thick shaft. I go slow; I want to savor this moment. I want to draw it out. I want to remember every detail as I experience it.

I've lived off memories and forbidden fantasies for years.

Now, it's time to bring them to life.

"Did you really not sleep with anyone for all this time?" I ask him as I massage his cock, rubbing his head with my thumb every time I reach the tip.

He shudders under my grip, his eyes rolling back for a moment before he answers. "I came into my hand more times than I can count," he answers. "But even then, I was loyal to you. You're the only woman I ever thought about."

Another swell of desire rolls inside me. "There was probably a moment, somewhere along the line," I muse, "when you were thinking of me and coming, and I was thinking of you and coming. At the exact same time."

The way his cock throbs in my hand tells me exactly how much he loves that thought.

"Maybe," he says in a low grumble thick with desire. "But it's not the same. It's never the same." His hands stroke through my hair, his fingers flexing against my scalp and sending shivers of delight down my spine. "Coming into my hand was never the same as coming inside you."

I bring his cock to my lips and run my tongue over his head. He shudders again. "Fuck," he breathes as his fingers tighten in my hair.

"You have no idea how many fantasies I've had of you over the years," I tell him. "I've lost count. I know we haven't actually been together much." I press a warm, languid kiss to that pulsing head. His knees actually tremble. "But in my head, we've fucked in every single position, in a million different locations."

"I hope you remember them all," he tells me. "Because we're going to live out every fantasy you've ever had."

Excitement pools in my gut. I could spasm in this very instant if he touches me. But I'm the one with some semblance of control and I'm not prepared to release him just yet.

"Starting with this one," I say before I run my tongue down the length of his cock…

And then plunge him into my warm, wet mouth with a deep suck.

"*Fuck*," he groans again.

I can't find it in me to be self-conscious anymore. I've wasted too much time already. So I don't care if it's perfect or pretty —I only care about the way he tastes, the way he throbs along my tongue.

Once I've worked us both into a rhythm, I pull him deeper toward my throat. Ilarion fists his hands in my hair and holds me in place. Now, it's his turn to grab control. He rocks his hips to fuck my mouth with his delicious cock. At one point, he pushes deeper than I anticipated, but the feel of his power makes me moan…makes my throat open…and he sinks in deeper. Holds there. Then slowly, panting, pulls back out.

He strokes his hands through my hair again, bundling it in his fingers and making me look up at him. I lick my swollen lips, hungry for more.

"Holy fuck," he gasps, "Where did you learn to do that?"

"Just trying to live up to my fantasies," I tell him. I give him a sultry little pout. "I'm not done."

He shakes his head. "You keep going and I'm going to come inside your mouth."

"Good." I flick my tongue along his shaft. "I'm hungry."

His eyes brighten with lust, but he continues shaking his head. "One day," he swears. "But not today." Then he pulls me up to my feet, grabs my hips, and hoists me onto his desk.

"Why not?"

"Because I'm not done with you yet."

His eyes leave my face and land on my breasts. I can feel my nipples tighten under his hungry gaze. He bends his face to my nipple and sucks it into his mouth. I gasp and arch into his mouth. Every warm tug, every swirl and flick of his tongue, sends a surge of pleasure straight to my clit.

"Fuck," I gasp. "Ilarion…"

He bites down on my nipple with his lips. The pain has me grabbing at his shoulders, but he soothes me instantly when his tongue laps over my breast. "My name is going to be the only one on your lips from now until the end of time."

He lifts his gaze to me and I nod in agreement. "Yes."

He smiles triumphantly. "Tell me, *tigrionok*," he says as he slips two fingers inside me. "Who do you belong to?"

I bite down on my bottom lip as his fingers explore my depths. I can hardly concentrate on his words, let alone speak.

He pushes deeper inside me. "Tell me."

"You," I gasp as my eyes flutter open, desperate for release.

"I can't hear you."

"You!" I cry. My hips writhe on the table, desperate to fuck myself on his fingers if I have to. "I belong to you."

"Will you run from me again?"

"Never. Never again."

"Good." He works his fingers faster inside me. Rubbing, spreading…*claiming.* "Because if you do—if you ever so much as think about leaving—I will drag you back into my bed and fuck you until you can't feel your limbs. I will fuck you and fill you so fucking deep inside every single hole of your body until my name is branded into your soul."

That alone is enough to make me gush on his fingers. But I manage to hold back, just long enough to meet his intensely dark gaze.

"Do you promise?"

The darkness in him softens with desire. He pulls his fingers from me and lifts them to his lips. I watch while he sucks me off his fingers. "Like fucking honey," he moans.

"Ilarion," I whisper.

"Yes, my queen?"

We'll talk about that implication later. Right now, I want —*need*—him to do something about that aching itch only he can scratch.

"Please, for the love of God…fuck me."

He pushes my legs open and moves between them. I couldn't close them if I wanted to; I know his fingers will leave faint bruises in the morning. *Good*. I want him to mark me, to brand me, to punish me for ever being so stupid as to run away from him. From this.

His cock rubs along my slit for a second before he shoves into me. There's no warning, but all I feel is a back-bending surge of pleasure dripping with relief. He doesn't stop until every inch of him is buried to the hilt.

He holds me there. Grinds into me as deep as he can go. My toes curl and I'm already crying out with wordless, sobbing gratitude.

Then he starts moving.

Hard.

Deep.

I hear the groan of the desk; I feel things fall off its surface. But Ilarion doesn't stop and I can't be bothered to care. I just watch his muscles flex as he fucks the fear and guilt right out of me.

Ilarion grabs the hair at the nape of my neck and forces me to look him in the eyes. He kisses me hungrily and his hips slow into deeper, more solid thrusts that make me feel him all the way up to my throat.

I know what he's going to do.

My whole body begs him to do it.

"Look at me," he snarls. "Look at me, *tigrionok*."

I bite my trembling lip as I do exactly that. He tugs my lip free with his thumb.

"You. Are. *Mine*." Each word is punctuated with a hard thrust. My lashes flutter; my eyes keep wanting to roll back in my head. But he won't accept that as an answer. He tightens his grip in my hair. "Say it back to me."

"Yes…" The moment the word touches my tongue, I feel that heated tension inside me snap. I'm falling, I'm shattering… I'm flying. "Yes…yes…yes!" It's all I can say. It's all my mind can conjure as I gush and spasm and buck on his cock.

He kisses me hard again, holding me to him so close it feels like every inch of me is wrapped around every inch of him. He breathes me in, tastes me, drinks me…and then he floods me with his own release.

I have no choice but to swallow his grunting moans, no choice but to feel the searing heat spread through my belly.

I want every fertile drop. I want every gasping breath.

I belong to him.

And he belongs to me.

We only pull apart to catch our breaths and only once he begins to soften inside me. But he doesn't pull out, doesn't pull away. He only tucks my legs around him, stroking the backsides of my thighs with his fingertips where he holds me.

Our brows rest together. And finally, I find my voice again.

"I couldn't admit it until now," I tell him softly. "But it was true from the very first night we met. Your name is already branded onto my soul, Ilarion Zakharov."

He nods and presses another kiss to my lips. "Right where it belongs."

57

ILARION

"How are we going to explain this to Adam?" she asks, wrapping herself up in my sheets.

It was inevitable that the sex would give way to conversation. I fucked her three different times last night, until both of us were wrung completely dry. But as sunlight filters into the open windows of my room, it's finally time to face the outside world with our new reality.

Her soft blonde hair cascading down her bare shoulders has my cock hard again. I can just about see the tops of her breasts, but her legs are in the way. She's got her arms wrapped around them and a crease in her forehead appears that I haven't seen since before yesterday.

"We tell him the truth."

"The truth? Ilarion, he's barely five!"

"We tell him that Auntie Cee is still his Auntie Cee. That I'm his father and you and I are together."

She sighs. "He won't understand."

"Yes, he will. Kids feel out the truth. He's probably already begun to suspect."

"We're going to need to get him therapy," she groans, falling back on the pillows and pulling the sheets up and over her head.

Smirking, I lean forward, grab the top of the sheet, and pull it down to reveal her face. "You're being dramatic."

"Yes, I am. Join me, won't you?"

"One of us has to keep their head on straight."

She glares at me, but the moment I place my hand on her inner thigh, the glare melts into a soft smile. "I don't want to leave this bed," she mumbles.

"Then don't."

"Ha, ha. If only." She glances at the alarm clock on the nightstand. "Adam will be awake soon. He's going to come looking for me. I need to go back to my room."

"We'll go together." I push off the covers and get to my feet.

She doesn't protest when I reach for my clothes. Instead, she beats me to them. She grabs my boxers and one of my t-shirts and tugs them on.

Fucking hell. I have more than half a mind to toss her right back into bed and pound the doubt and worry from her mind.

"You look good in my clothes."

She blushes. "I wouldn't need yours if you hadn't ripped mine."

"I'll have to make that a habit."

Rolling her eyes to cover a deeper blush, she heads for the door and peeps out of it, turning her head from side to side. "What the hell are you doing?" I laugh.

"I don't want anyone to see me leave your room."

"Taylor."

She throws me a glare that reminds me of Celine. "We have to be sensitive about this change, Ilarion," she insists. "For Adam's sake, as well as Celine's. Everyone has to get used to seeing us together and I don't want to shove it down their throats."

Her choice of words has me instantly remembering the night before. Her, too, apparently, because her cheeks go scarlet and she hides her face in the crook of her arm again.

"Okay, I think the coast is clear," Taylor whispers when she peeks back out. "Come on."

We've just stepped out into the hallway when Mila rounds the corner. She and Taylor stop short when they see each other. Taylor shuffles self-consciously from one foot to the other, her shoulders slumping with embarrassment, while Mila's face splits into a shit-eating grin.

"Well, well," she says cheerily. "Good morning to you two."

"Oh, God," Taylor groans.

"Great timing, huh?"

I roll my eyes. "I'm assuming you were coming to my room for a reason?" I ask, glossing over Taylor's awkwardness.

The smile drops off her face almost instantly. "Yeah. Unfortunately."

I get the measure of her news from her tone alone. All I want to do is make sure Taylor is out of earshot. "Taylor, why don't you go see Adam? I'll be with you soon."

She frowns, turning those tender emerald eyes on me, before sighing and nodding. Then she surprises me by pushing up on her tiptoes and placing a kiss on my cheek in full view of Mila. With that down, she disappears around the bend.

Mila gives me a smile. "Well, it's about time."

I roll my eyes. "You're one to talk. Now, tell me what's going on."

"Another package. Another one of his fingers," Mila tells me. "It was delivered to our doorstep only a few minutes ago."

"Fucking hell."

"There's more," she warns. "This time, it came with an address. It looks like he wants us to come to him. Some old factory downtown."

We go downstairs together, but nothing about this is sitting right with me. We've just reached the landing when Dima turns the corner. "Did Mila tell you?" he asks excitedly. "The fucker has just issued us a challenge."

"It's not just a challenge, Dima," I caution him. "It's a trap. Benedict Bellasio no longer has the manpower or the resources to launch a full-scale attack. Which means he has to gain the upper hand in other ways."

"He has Archie," Dima points out. "That's his upper hand. Literally, in this case. The upper fingers, at least."

"He's not going to risk his life on the assumption that Archie is important to Ilarion," Mila says. "Let's face it: the old man is expendable."

"No," I snap. "Not anymore." Dima and Mila both turn to me with wide eyes. "We have to get Archie back. *Alive*."

Dima and Mila exchange a glance. "And if we can't…?"

"We have to," I insist. "He's Taylor's father. Adam's grandfather. He may have been a traitor to me, but he was good to them. And for that, I can forgive his sins against the Bratva."

Dima's jaw sets with acceptance, but Mila's brow furrows. "I understand where you're coming from. I care about Taylor, too. I don't want to hurt her, but honestly, not every Zakharov man will be as forgiving as you. If he dies in the midst of this, it might not be the worst thing."

I stare Mila down until she lowers her gaze. "I've made my decision. Gather the men. We're going in and we're going in prepared. Whatever trap he's laid, we're going to destroy it head-on. Go."

Mila and Dima veer off to prepare the men. I go searching for Taylor and Adam. I find them in the breakfast nook with a stack of pancakes between them, maple syrup pooling around the edges of their plates.

"Ilarion…" Taylor begins, rising to her feet the moment she sees me.

"Uncle Illy!" Adam says excitedly. "Where have you been? You haven't come to play with me. And Grandpa's not here, either. Who's going to play with me today?"

I sit down and gather him onto my lap. "Your grandpa is off on important business," I explain. "And unfortunately, so am I. But when I get back, we're going to play so much, you'll be begging Mommy for a nap."

His face splits into a huge grin. "What are we gonna play?"

"Whatever you want."

"Promise?"

I cross my hands over my heart and his smile only gets bigger.

"So what's Grandpa doing?" he asks.

"I'm not sure. But I'm sure he'll tell you all about it when he gets back." I feel Taylor's gaze on me. Her left leg is bobbing up and down in a frenetic blur. I grab Adam by the stomach, tickling him a little as I plop him back down on his feet. He giggles hard and worms his way out of my hold. "Go on and eat those pancakes."

I walk to the door and Taylor follows me. "You have a lead?"

I nod. "I'm leaving now."

She takes a deep breath, tension pooling between her eyes. "Please bring him back safe, Ilarion."

"I will do my best."

I lean in and press a kiss on her forehead. Her hand cups my face for a moment and then I pull back. It feels strange to leave her now. To leave her at all.

But even though my life has changed, my responsibilities haven't.

"It's going to be okay," I assure her. I need to, even though I have no right to make such promises.

She nods, forcing a smile that doesn't touch her eyes. "Come back to me," she whispers.

I meet her gaze. "Always."

58

ILARION

Mila lowers her binoculars. "I can't see a thing. Meaning there's nothing in there to see. It's empty."

"Fuck it," I growl. "We're going in."

"What?" Dima and Mila both exclaim in unison.

"You don't want to send in a scout team to scope the place out first?" Dima adds.

"No. I'm not scared of Benedict Bellasio. Whatever he's got in there waiting, we can take." I raise my hand and signal for my men to take up positions along the flanks.

Dima and Mila join me on both sides as we surge in through the main entrance. It's been a while since this place has functioned as a soap factory, but it feels like the smell has clawed its way into the walls and fused itself with the building's foundation. Every breath is like scrubbing my skull clean from the inside out.

One of my soldiers places his hand on the first door we reach and pushes. It swings back easily, revealing empty darkness within.

No Bellasio guards. No booby traps. Nothing but shadow.

"This is too easy," Mila mumbles.

She might be right. But we've come too far to turn back now.

So, with a grimace, I cock my gun and venture into the black mouth of the doorway. At first, there's nothing but the putrid smell of neglect, cloying beneath the sting of the lingering soap. But there are signs of life if you know where to look. Nail holes where boards that used to cover up the broken windows have been pried free. Old footsteps in the dust.

I'm walking over to inspect one of the windows when I hear a sound in the corner. I whip around in alarm to see a single chair shoved into a corner.

In it sits Archie Theron.

He's bound to the arms and legs of the chair, with a gag preventing him from producing anything more than frantic gurgling noises in his throat.

My men do the same thing I did as they storm into the room at my back: they see him and freeze. In the blink of an eye, he's got a dozen guns trained on him, but nothing else changes. I'm waiting for an ambush, but it doesn't come.

"What the fuck is Benedict playing at?" Dima scowls when he joins. "There's no way he's just giving us the old man on a silver platter."

Archie's eyes are locked on me. He's making retching sounds with his throat. I walk forward, ignoring Mila and Dima's warnings to be careful, remove the gag from Archie's mouth, and fling it to the side.

"Where is he?"

Archie splutters over his own words. "G-g-gone," he rasps. "Long gone. I've been sitting here for hours. Th-there's a letter; he left you another letter."

"He left you *and* a letter?" I ask skeptically. "Something's not right about that."

"Ilarion…" Archie says desperately. "There's a bomb."

"We scanned the place with thermal cameras before we entered. There was no evidence of a—"

"It's not on the property!" he spits, choking over his own desperation. "I-It's…inside me."

Dima and Mila stiffen in my periphery. Archie doesn't bother letting his gaze wander. His eyes are huge and liquid with fear. "The bomb he implanted, he said it's not large enough to kill me. But it will maim me. It'll kill some part of me, and I can't—I won't live like that. I don't want my daughters to see me like that."

"Maybe there's a way we can—"

"There's no getting it out," Archie tells me with a shake of his head. "Go read the letter. It's over there, by the window."

One of my men races over to the window that Archie is gesturing toward with his chin. There's an envelope tucked under one of the boards that should have been up against the windows. He jogs it back to me and I rip it open.

The bomb detonates at noon. It will take one leg, maybe both, maybe more. It'll be fun to guess. Give my regards to Celine.

I glance at my watch.

"Well?" Mila asks. "How much time do we have?"

"Half an hour."

Tears pour down Archie's cheeks. His body shudders and whatever color remained in him is lost with the knowledge of how little time he has left.

"Ilarion, m-may I speak with you?"

I turn to my men and give them a nod of dismissal. Mila and Dima stay where they are, however. I glance toward both of them. "You can wait outside for me."

When Mila doesn't move, Dima takes her arm and drags her out of the factory. I wait until there's no one left but Archie and me.

For the first time, I allow myself to feel nothing but sympathy for the man. Until now, any sympathy I felt was tinged with remnants of my anger. With rage and dreams of vengeance. Now, though...well, fuck.

No one deserves to die like this.

Especially not for *his* sins. He may have betrayed me, but he did it to save his wife. For the first time, I understand what that kind of motivation means. I have Taylor to thank for that.

"*Pakhan*," he starts.

"It's Ilarion to you, Archie," I say. "We're family now."

Archie smiles through his tears. "I'm glad to hear you say that. It means I can ask you for one more favor."

I know what he's going to say before the words even pass his lips. "I'm not going to kill you, Archie."

"Please," he begs. His sunken eyes are suddenly clear. Certain. "Please, Ilarion. I can't live a broken man. I can't ask my daughters to take care of a broken shell of a person. They've done enough of that already."

"That's their choice to make."

"And what about *my* choices?" he protests, rocking back and forth in the chair with a subtle scraping of its legs on the concrete. "I deserve to decide how I live. And how I die. And since the day I chose to betray you, I always knew, deep down, that this was going to be my end. One bullet. A clean death. Painless. It's more than I deserve, especially from you. But I'm asking anyway."

I squeeze my fists so hard the knuckles groan. "I promised both your daughters I would bring you home safely. I promised Adam."

He keeps rocking. Back and forth, back and forth. "You shouldn't have promised them anything. Even if you bring me back alive, I will be destroyed. My body, my mind… I won't live as a burden to my daughters." He breaks off with a sob. "A-and, my boy, my little Adam—I can't bear for him to see me like that. Please, Ilarion. Please."

Fuck me.

I stare back at the old man and remember a time when I used to hate him. I wanted him to fucking *burn.* But now…

Things have changed.

"Let me try to get it out of you."

He smiles serenely. He still looks hopeless and resigned, but a flicker of realization still twitches his mouth up. "You really do love her, don't you?"

I don't bother asking which "her" he's referring to. "I do."

Archie nods. "Then I die knowing you will take care of my family."

"I give you my word." I can't forget that I made a promise to his wife before she died, too.

My hands are tied here. Maybe we were always going to end up in this position, him and I. Fate has been coming at us like a runaway fucking train for a long time now. I'm only now realizing that we've *both* been tied to the tracks.

The heaviness of what I must do settles over me. There is no backing out of this.

"They're my family now, too."

I take my gun out and cock it. Archie doesn't so much as flinch at the sound. "I was wrong about you, Ilarion. You are not your father's son."

I tighten my grip on the gun. "Don't get sentimental on me now, old man." The gravel in my voice surprises both of us. *Fuck*, when did he start meaning something to me, too?

Archie smiles. "Tell them…tell them I l-love them." A hitch in his voice drowns out the last part of his message, but it doesn't require repeating. They already know.

I wait for a moment when he looks down.

He doesn't see the bullet coming.

He doesn't see death at all.

It's the least I could give him.

59

TAYLOR

"I want Grandpa!" Adam cries, throwing his hands in the air. "He *never* leaves without saying goodbye!"

"I know, baby, but this time, um…there was something important he needed to do."

I'd brought him into the kitchen to try and distract him with a sweet snack. But one Biscoff cookie later, he started asking about Dad again. I'm running out of options.

Adam narrows his eyes at me. For a second, I don't see my sweet, innocent little boy; I see the man he will become. I see Ilarion.

"My love," I start, "I know you miss Grandpa, but—"

I'm on the verge of promising him that he will see his grandfather soon, but for some reason, I stop. I let myself play in the realms of different alternate realities and, in many of them, Dad doesn't come back at all. If there's even the slightest chance of that, I know I shouldn't be giving Adam false hope.

Nothing kills a person's spirit faster than that. I would know.

Instead, I try to gather him up in my arms, but he pushes away, aiming his anger at me because he doesn't know what else to do with it.

He's racing out of the kitchen when Celine appears in the doorframe. I spring upright, startled to see her. I'd expected her to steer clear of the house for days, weeks even, just to avoid me. The fact that she's here at all has to be a good sign, right?

Or maybe it's a bad one. I have no way of telling and recent history has proven that my instincts aren't good for a damn thing.

"Whoa," she says, squatting down in front of the bull-rushing Adam and opening her arms out so that he can't sneak past. "Where are you going in such a hurry, little man?"

"I'm gonna go look for Grandpa."

"One day, your mama and I are going to tell you all about Grandpa," she says cryptically. That grabs his attention immediately. I can't see his face, but his shoulders go still.

He's quiet for a moment before he takes the bait. "What about Grandpa?"

Celine arches an eyebrow in surprise. "He didn't tell you?"

Adam's little head shakes from side to side.

"He was probably waiting until you were old enough. But I think you're ready now."

"Tell me, tell me!" he insists.

I have no idea what Celine is about to tell him, but I realize that whatever it is, I trust her. Despite the tension between us right now, she still looks at Adam with nothing but affection in her eyes.

"Your grandpa is a *spy*," she whispers conspiratorially.

"Grandpa?" Adam sounds completely dumbfounded.

"Mhmm," Celine hums with a nod. "Why do you think you lived so far away from me for so long? Grandpa was trying to protect you and your mama. You guys were undercover."

"Whoa…"

She smiles. "Grandpa is a pretty cool guy."

"But…are you *sure?* Isn't he too old?"

"You're never too old to be anything," she advises him. "And if Grandpa is brave enough to go out there and be a spy, you need to be brave enough to let him do his job. Okay?"

Adam considers that for a moment. "I'm brave," he says at last.

"I know you are." She drops a kiss on his forehead before straightening up. "Now, why don't you go play in the garden?"

Adam turns to me, apparently forgetting that, just two seconds ago, I was persona non grata. "Mama, did you hear that? Grandpa's a spy! Isn't that cool? I'm gonna go practice being a spy in the garden, okay?"

"Okay, baby. Be careful."

"I don't have to be careful," he announces. "I'm a spy!"

He blazes off through the French doors that lead out into the patio. The moment he's out of earshot, I turn to Celine. "Thanks for that. Nothing I said did the trick."

Her face is carefully composed. "I find the truth can do wonders sometimes."

I nod. "*Touché.*"

She sighs and sits down at the table in the nook. When I continue to linger awkwardly off to the side, she glances at me impatiently. "Are you just going to stand there gawking at me or are you going to sit down?"

"Um…would you like me to?"

"I'd like for us to be able to have a conversation without risking a neck sprain. So, yes."

I pull the chair out and sit down next to her. There's still a fair amount of distance between us, both literal and metaphorical, but it's closer than I thought I would ever get.

"I've been doing a lot of thinking," she admits. "I had to stop, actually. My head was starting to hurt." She drums her fingers against the tabletop. "Where is the coffee?"

"Semyon just put on a fresh pot," I say. "I'll get you some." I leap to my feet to fill a mug and bring it back to her on a tray with a pot of cream and sugar.

She looks at the cream and the sugar. "You remembered."

"Of course. 'The sweeter, the better.'"

Just when I think she's on the cusp of a smile, she sighs. "I had this headache that I couldn't get rid of. So I decided to go for a walk. Of course, that's not exactly easy when you have four gigantic bodyguards trailing you."

"Four? Since when?"

She rolls her eyes. "Ilarion can be excessive sometimes."

"He wants you to be safe."

"Yeah, yeah, I know. Good intentions and all that. It makes it so much harder to hate him."

"If it's hard to hate him, maybe you just, um, don't want to hate him at all?"

She shoots me an annoyed glance. "That would make things easier for you, wouldn't it?"

"Celine—"

She sighs and shakes her head. "No, no. Please don't apologize again. I didn't come here to give you a hard time."

"You could. Maybe you should. I deserve it."

She pulls the mug of coffee toward her and adds the creamer and one teaspoon of sugar. It's the same way that Mom used to drink hers. *The sweeter, the better. Life is bitter enough as it is.*

"'Deserve,'" Celine echoes in a melancholy murmur. "Who's to say who deserves what anymore?" She sips her coffee and glances at me out of the corner of her eyes. "I asked Ashton to meet me at the park, you know."

My eyebrows leap up on my forehead. "Y-you did?"

She nods. "I didn't really think about it. I was lonely, I wanted to talk to someone, and he was the only one I could think of to call."

"I'm glad you did."

She abandons her mug and folds her hands over her chest. "We sat under the trees and talked for hours. Right up until the sun went down. Then we went for dinner."

"With all four bodyguards in tow?"

She laughs, the tiniest hint of a smile creeping onto her face. "Just a happy little six-some, yeah. He didn't so much as touch me, but still, I felt, it felt like… I'm not sure how to describe it."

I hazard an easy guess. "Like electricity all over your body. Like you're baking in a sun that only you can feel."

Celine's eyes go wide. "Yes, exactly like that." Then her face falls and she shakes her head slowly from side to side. "I wanted to stay away from love for a while," she admits. "But as it turns out, I don't think I have the power to fight this."

"No," I say in a small voice. "I understand completely."

"You're trying to say that this is how you feel with Ilarion?"

"No, I'm not saying anything at all," I tell her quickly. "I'm not justifying what I did or how I chose to deal with it. You have every right to be angry with me. You have every right to hate me."

"I'm not…angry with you, Taylor," Celine says bluntly. "I'm just…disappointed."

I don't want to let myself hope, but it's pathetic how quickly the emotion claws its way into my head. "Does that mean that there's hope for us?"

She reaches for her mug again but she doesn't drink. I wonder if she just needs a prop. Something to do with her hands. "We've already lost our mother. We stand the chance of losing our father." She lifts her gaze to mine. "I don't want to lose you, too."

I try hard to swallow the tears. "I don't want to lose you, either."

Celine sighs. And then she smiles. "We're going to be fine," she says with a subtle wave of her hand. "I'm just enjoying tormenting you a little bit. Allow me now; forgive me later?"

I feel myself returning her smile and then sharing a soft laugh as I nod.

I want to reach out to her, take her hand, maybe—but I'm too nervous. I don't want to cross her boundaries and risk getting thrown back a few paces.

This is progress.

"Excuse me, Ms. Zakharov?"

Both of us turn to the maid at the same time. Her name starts with an A, but I can't for the life of me recall what it is.

"This package just came for you. It's been scanned and checked, so security said I could give it to you."

"Thank you," Celine says, taking it from Millie.

It's a small blue box with a white ribbon. She pulls the ribbon apart and takes the lid off. It's not until my lungs start to complain that I realize I'm holding my breath. I want to tell Celine to be careful, but I also want her to hurry up.

"It's a flash drive," she mumbles, picking it out of the box. "And there's a letter."

I have a bad instinct stirring in my gut. It's telling me to call Ilarion, but I'm not about to be the first one to mention his name after our fragile, newfound truce.

Celine picks up the paper and unfolds it. Her eyes run back and forth across the paper—and then she pales.

"Cee, what is it?" I peer at the paper. "Is it Dad?"

She just hands me the note. The writing is unfamiliar, but I'm too focused on the words to pay that much attention.

You need to see what's on this flash drive. Once you've watched it, there will be a black Land Rover waiting at the corner of Pinehurst and Third. I can keep you safe.

I look over the note at Celine. "We need to tell—we need to show this to him, Celine."

Celine nods. "But first, we need to see what's on this drive."

60

TAYLOR

My hands are shaking as I follow Celine upstairs to her room.

Whatever is on that drive can't be a good thing. But she's right—we have to know what's on it. And it feels good to be at her side again.

Once we're inside her room, she locks the door and crosses over to where her laptop awaits. When she sits down, I remain standing just behind the sofa.

"Taylor."

I flinch when she says my name. "Yes?"

"Sit down."

"I'd rather stand."

"There's no point in stressing out before we know what's on here," she says, the very personification of reason. "Just sit and stop looking like the world is falling apart. You're freaking me out."

I swallow my unease and sit down beside her. She inserts the flash drive and a file instantly pops up on the screen.

It's labeled *CELINE*.

She doesn't even hesitate before she opens it. It's a video, opening zoomed in on a tall, broad-shouldered man standing in front of someone. It doesn't take me long to recognize who we're looking at.

"Ilarion," Celine whispers.

Almost as though he's heard her say his name, he shifts to the side to reveal the man he's facing.

"Dad!" I gasp.

The distance of the camera makes it a bit difficult to see details, but it's obvious that Dad is not okay. He's strapped in a rickety chair. His head keeps lolling to one side or the other and whatever he's saying to Ilarion takes great effort.

There's no one else in the dingy room but the two of them.

"Cee…what are we watching?"

"Shh!"

It's clear the two of them are talking, but their voices are absent. There's only a nauseating undercurrent of static. My heart is hammering so hard against my chest that it feels as though it's going to burst.

My first question is, if this is truly a rescue operation, why is Dad still bound to that chair? Why isn't Ilarion freeing him?

Dad lifts his eyes to Ilarion. There's pleading there. Thick depths of desperation. He says something. It looks like he's begging for his life.

I'm on the verge of collapsing. And then Dad looks down. It's a split-second moment. But Ilarion moves with the speed and agility of a man who came into this godforsaken room with a purpose.

He raises his hand. Aims. Fires.

I don't hear the gunshot, but I jump back as though it was aimed at me.

Dad falls back against the chair. His body doesn't so much as twitch.

Then the feed cuts to black.

I blink several times, but the image of Dad's pleading face is imprinted against the back of my eyelids. I feel like I'm losing my mind. If there was ever a time for my heart to quit, now would be it. I would actually welcome the relief of a fainting spell.

But it keeps beating, reminding me that even if my personal world is splitting apart, I'm still here.

I turn to the side and catch Celine's profile. Her eyes are still glued to the empty screen, but her mask of composure is starting to crumble. Her hands, flat on the desk, are trembling like leaves in a strong wind. Her spine is rigid, her jaw tight. Her eyes are filled with tears.

"Cee."

She blinks once and three fat tears roll down her cheek in quick succession. She sucks in a breath and jolts upright. "This isn't real. This isn't real," she repeats over and over again to herself. "This can't be real."

"Celine."

She leaps to her feet and starts pacing, knocking into the side table next to the sofa when she tries to clear the room. Her fingers are still shaking, and her face has lost all its color.

Seeing her come undone is what forces me to stop my own panic in its tracks.

Both of us can't fall to pieces. One of us needs to be the voice of reason and Celine has carried that load for far too long.

I step in front of her and force her to a standstill. "Celine," I say again. "The note. What did the note say?"

She frowns like what happened five minutes ago is now ancient history. "I-I can't remember."

"Let me see it again."

She pulls it out of her pocket and hands it to me.

You need to see what's on this flash drive. Once you've watched it, there will be a black Land-Rover waiting at the corner of Pinehurst and Third. I can keep you safe.

"We don't know who this is," I point out. "It may very well be Benedict."

"I was his prisoner once." Celine finally meets my gaze. "He wasn't cruel. In fact, there were moments when he was really kind to me. We actually kind of…got along."

"He was trying to manipulate you, Cee."

"Perhaps. But clearly, Ilarion is better at that than Benedict."

I flinch when she says his name. Despite what I've just seen, it's hard for me to believe. This is Ilarion. He may be a lot of things, but *this*? The kind of man who makes a promise, and then breaks it? Like that?

Some small desperate part of me clings to the possibility that what we saw was only one part of the puzzle. And in order to make sense of anything, we need to find the rest of it.

"We have to get out of this house," Celine insists.

"I agree, we do. But I don't think going to meet this car is the solution."

"What are you suggesting?"

"We go into the city, grab an Uber from there, and go somewhere no one knows where we are."

Celine scoffs violently. "Fuck, Taylor. Ilarion owns the entire city. It won't matter where we go; he'll find us."

"He didn't find me for five years. We'll be fine."

"That was because of Dad! And w-we don't have—*fuck*—we don't have him anymore. Neither one of us knows how to disappear like he did."

"Well, we have to try."

She fists her hands in the roots of her hair. "Don't be naïve, Taylor. We're going to need help to get out of the city. Whoever this person is, if they're willing to help us, then why the hell not?"

"Because it could be a trap."

"Not worse than the one we're already in!" Celine explodes, jabbing a quivering finger at the laptop.

"I saw it, too." I gulp, my throat painfully dry. "But there's… there has to be an explanation."

"The hell there is!"

I grab her hand out of the air. "Please, Celine. I just don't want us playing into Benedict's hands. We can't trust him."

"We have to trust someone. And right now, we don't have a lot of options. Go and grab Adam—we're leaving in ten minutes. Meet me at the entrance."

"Will they just let us leave?"

"You let me handle that part. Just get Adam. And make sure no one suspects that anything is wrong."

"The flash drive?"

"I have it." She wrenches it out of the laptop and stuffs it in her pocket. "Now, *go.*"

With a frantic nod, I rush out of her room. I plow through the house, slowing down only when I come across a maid. I find Adam in the gardens with Edna, tossing bread to the birds congregated at the fountain.

"Edna, would you mind running Adam a bubble bath?" I ask with a smile. "I'll bring him up in a bit."

She looks confused by my request, but she doesn't question it. The moment she goes inside, I rush around the water fountain and kneel at my son's side.

"Honey, guess what?" When he looks up at me, I say, "You, me, and Auntie Cee are going on an adventure."

"An adventure?" he repeats and then his eyes go wide. "Like a spying adventure?"

"*Exactly* like that."

He dusts his hands off and jumps to his feet. "Are we going to meet Grandpa?"

It takes all my strength and control not to burst into tears right then and there. But for Adam's sake, I rein in my emotions and put on a brave face. I can break down later. Right now, my son needs me to be strong.

"No, honey. We're going on a mission of our own. But—" I press a finger to my lips. "It's secret, okay? No one can know."

"Not even Uncle Illy?"

"Not even him."

"Aw, I was hoping he could come with us."

I grab his hand and pull him along the garden path. "Not this time, I'm afraid."

Not ever again.

When we get to the driveway, there's a silver Lexus parked just outside the front door. Celine is in the driver's seat and she's got the passenger side door thrown open. She glances at me and mouths, "Hurry."

I strap Adam into his booster seat in the back and then I jump into the passenger's seat. The second I'm in place, she guns the engine. The guards squint at us as we pass, but they make no move to stop us from zipping through the open gate.

"Auntie Cee, Mom said we're on a spy mission!" Adam declares excitedly from the back seat as we emerge onto the public road.

"We are, buddy," Celine agrees distractedly as she checks her rearview mirror every few seconds. "Hang in there, okay? We're gonna go a little faster."

"Cee, please," I beg. "Not Pinehurst and Third."

Her jaw sets firmly. "It's the only choice we have."

Three hard right turns, a mile of open road, and then a sharp left turn and I see the black Land Rover, parked exactly as promised.

"Shit," I breathe as my nerves pull tight with anxiety.

Celine doesn't even wait to see who might be waiting for us in the other vehicle. She gets out of the Lexus and walks over to the Rover.

"What's she doing, Mama?" Adam asks as he unbuckles his seatbelt.

"I'm not sure, baby."

Just then, Celine glances back at me and gestures for me to get out of the car. Nothing about this feels right, but she seems certain.

"Stay close to me, honey," I tell Adam before getting out of the car.

The man standing next to the Land Rover is tall and gaunt, with long, white-blonde hair and a silver scar over his right brow. His gaze passes over Adam and me with complete disinterest. "Get in," is all he says.

"Celine," I hiss, grabbing her hand. "Are you sure about this?"

"Get in the car, Taylor. We need to ditch the Lexus fast. They're going to be looking for the license plate number."

We're sitting in the back of the Land Rover when Adam's excitement starts to shrivel. He pushes his little body against mine and grips my hand tightly. "Mama, I don't want to be a spy anymore. I want to go home."

My heart sinks. "Hey, how about I tell you a story?" I suggest. "The elves and the shoemaker? You love that one, right?"

He shakes his head. "Grandpa tells it better."

I flinch. "I'll try to tell the story like he does, okay?"

Adam shakes his head again and burrows deeper into my arms. The gaunt man gets behind the wheel and, without a word, steers us away.

God only knows where we're going.

Half an hour later, we pull into the parking lot of a crumbling motel on the outskirts of the city. I can only imagine what is currently happening to the Lexus we left behind. It's probably swarming with Zakharov men and corrupt cops on the Bratva payroll, combing through the seats in search of clues like hunting dogs.

The gaunt man opens my door. He hoists Adam out before I can tell him to keep his hands to himself. He offers to help me down to my feet, but I ignore him and step out on my own.

My skin is crawling. Invisible ants crisscrossing over the back of my neck and knees. This place just feels wrong. Ugly and trash-strewn and anonymous. People die here and no one bats an eye.

We might die here and no one would bat an eye.

But Celine seems confident. Even as a man peels himself off a shadowy stretch of wall and saunters over to where we're standing in the blazing sun, she doesn't waver. Her chin is high and proud.

"My apologies about the unfortunate location, ladies," the new man croons. "It's the best I could do under short notice."

He steps out of the blind spot and I see him properly for the first time. It takes me a long time to recognize him because he's changed so much since we last met. He was thin and handsome then; now, he's got a taut beer belly, a salt-and-pepper beard, and a patchwork quilt of wrinkles marring his face.

"Hello, Benedict," Celine says. "It's been a long time."

61

ILARION

"We need to get our stories straight before we speak to Taylor and Celine," Mila warns.

The three of us are standing around the spot where Archie died. The chair has collapsed on the floor, its broken leg sticking out at an odd angle.

Archie's body has been moved into one of the vehicles. I want to prepare it before either Celine or Taylor happen to see it. He's going to look as content as it's possible to be in death before I let either one of his daughters near him.

"There will be no story," I growl. "I'll tell them the truth."

Dima's eyebrows hit the top of his forehead. "That sounds like a suicide mission."

"Give them more credit," I snap. "Both women are aware of the lengths that Benedict is capable of going to just to survive."

"Except, what was the point here?" Mila fires back, her brow wrinkling with skepticism. "I mean, all this just serves to piss you off. And really, for all he knows, he did you a favor. Why would he bother?"

That's been troubling me, too. From the moment the quiet settled in after Archie's heart stopped beating, I've been turning the question over and over again in my head.

Why?

"The point could have been Archie's death," Dima suggests. "The old man betrayed him by giving you his safehouse location. It's the reason he lost his brother."

"No. No, we're missing something."

Mila starts walking around the factory floor. Her footsteps echo against the walls. Rats and cockroaches skitter away from her in fear.

"Look around," I instruct Dima. "There was a trap here. We just haven't—"

I break off when I notice a thin wire at the far corner wall, arcing just over one of the windows. "Get me something to stand on," I order nobody in particular. "A chair, a box, anything."

My men procure a wooden crate and drag it over in front of the tall window. I climb up and follow the path of the wire. It winds along the mortar channels between bricks. Up, up, into a layer of shadows out of my reach. But where the rest of the wall is dusty, my fingertip comes away clean when I drag it down the wire.

It was put in here recently.

I keep searching with my eyes until I pick up the trail through the darkness. It goes along the upper rim of the ceiling…

And then I see it.

The glint of a camera lens, nestled in the corner.

I freeze. My blood runs cold. "It recorded the moment I shot Archie."

I jump off the crate and land in front of Dima. Mila jogs back to me, her eyes wide with alarm. They're both gawking up at the camera. I can't help but wonder who's on the other side of it.

I have a pretty good fucking guess.

I grab my phone and hit Taylor's number. It rings, but three chimes in, the line cuts off. Which means only one thing: she declined my call.

She heard her phone ring, she saw my number, and she chose to reject the call.

"He got to them already," I infer through gritted teeth. "Fuck."

"Still," Dima says, "they wouldn't put their trust in Benedict Bellasio, right? ...Right?"

Mila and I exchange glances. "If they saw me kill their father in cold blood, they just might. It's what Benedict counted on. Playing on their emotions. Their grief. Not only do they know Archie is dead, they had to watch him die. They watched me kill him."

"What do we do?"

"Call Zakharov House," I instruct. "Get a read on where Celine and Taylor might be. We work from there."

"On it." Dima whips his phone out.

I leave him to it and storm out of the factory with Mila tailing me. "Ilarion," she says gently, "if he has them—"

"I know he has them," I growl. "Benedict has no power anymore. He's desperate to buy time. The only way to ensure his safety is by taking something of mine. Something he can use as leverage."

Mila's shoulders drop. "He doesn't know about Taylor and Adam, though."

"It doesn't matter. If Celine knows, she'll have told Taylor. They'll be united against me now. Benedict has all the leverage he needs."

"Do you hear yourself?" Mila steps in front of me. "This is not some random *vor* you need to win to your side. This is *Taylor.*"

"I have done nothing to earn her trust, Mila," I point out. "She saw Archie and me talking in the garden. She saw me grab him. I could have told her then. I *should* have told her then. *Blyat'!*"

"You didn't tell her because Archie didn't want you to," she reminds me. "He wanted the girls to be oblivious. He thought that was the price for their safety."

"If I were to tell Taylor all this now, it would sound like an excuse. A way to justify murdering her father."

Mila frowns and puts her hand against the side of my face. "Look at me, brother," she says softly. For a moment, I don't see the hard, reserved woman she has become; I see the tender, maternal woman she could be if she just let her walls down long enough. "Ilarion, this is Taylor. You love her. She loves you. That has to mean something."

"We've been apart too long."

She sighs mournfully. "It's not like you to give up before the fight is over."

I take a deep breath. If there's a way forward here, I just don't see it. Taylor's not picking up, which means they've already left Zakharov House. They could be anywhere at this point.

They could be with any*one*.

"Ilarion!" Dima calls, jogging back over. "Celine, Taylor and Adam left Zakharov House about an hour ago. They took the Lexus down to Pinehurst and Third, where they jumped into a black Land Rover. I'm combing through security cameras on the street. I'm sure one of them will give us a plate number. Don't worry; we'll be on their tail before long."

I shake my head. "Forget that. There's a faster way to get to them."

Dima frowns. "How?"

"Archie gave us three other locations that Benedict might've used." *His last contributions to the Bratva,* I think bitterly. "Split the men. Send a contingent to each one. I'm not wasting any more time. We finish this today."

62

TAYLOR

"It's not the most luxurious of accommodations," Benedict says with a regretful little sigh. "But it's kept me hidden all these years. A little palace in the wilderness, so to speak. I had a room prepared for you. I hope it's big enough; I was only expecting one guest."

"I wasn't about to leave my sister behind," says Celine.

"Of course not," Benedict says with a simpering smile. "And the boy?"

I try not to stiffen, but his words have my spine terse with pain. "My son," I say. Adam clings tighter to my shoulders and buries his face in my neck. I'm happy about that; I don't want Benedict looking too closely at Adam and connecting the dots. It's bad enough that he thinks he has Ilarion's wife. If he knows he has Ilarion's son, too...

"Celine," I whisper to her as I sidle up to her side, "we shouldn't be here."

Benedict's eyes narrow. "I assure you, you're safe here. I simply wanted you to see who the real villain was. And if you didn't already believe that, you wouldn't be here."

"You're not innocent in any of this, Benedict," Celine says coldly.

"Maybe not. But I'm not the one who murdered your father," he tuts. "Now, come. Let me show you to your room."

Adam is slipping from my hip, so I hoist him up a little higher and follow Celine into the grungy motel. The inside is just as depressing as the outside, funky with the scent of rotting flowers. Everything is crumbling and either dying or already dead.

Benedict gestures ahead of us. "Take the second door on the left."

Celine hesitates for only a moment before she walks through the door, leaving me with no choice but to follow.

"Mama," Adam whispers, "what's going on?"

"Shh, baby. Keep your head down."

"I don't like him."

"I know," I whisper back to him. "I'll tell you when the coast is clear."

It's not as easy to carry Adam as it used to be. He's skinny but tall and the full force of his weight is nestled against my chest. But I'll be damned if I let him go while Benedict is anywhere near us.

The room on the other side of the door isn't as decrepit as the rest of the motel. The tile floors are clean, if nothing else, and the furniture doesn't look like it recently housed corpses. Beggars can't be choosers, I suppose.

"My brother loved this room," Benedict explains as he circles the space with pride. "Of course, it's free now. Your husband made sure of that."

He turns his gaze on Celine, but she doesn't so much as flinch. "What do you want from me, Benedict?"

"I offered you a different kind of life once, if you remember."

"I do remember," she retorts. "And then you tried to kill me. Twice."

He has the gall to smile at her. The gap of a missing tooth is eerily unsettling, though it fits with the yellowed, cracked tombstones of the rest of his leering grin. The years he's spent in exile haven't been kind to Benedict Bellasio. Like the rest of this place, he looks like he has one foot in the grave.

Strange, because the man I remembered was trim and fit, and above all, *vain.* To see him crumbling like this makes me wary.

Bad things happen when vain men let themselves fall to pieces.

"I was angry. I would go so far as to say I was desperate," he explains simply. "I wanted to hit him where it hurt and you were the only thing he seemed to care for. I must admit, I wasn't thinking straight at the time. I am happy you gave me the benefit of the doubt."

"I've done no such thing," Celine says. "As you said, anger and desperation can make us do stupid things."

Benedict's broken smile grows wider. "You are still as beautiful as ever, Celine." He glides towards her. If Adam weren't in my arms, I would jump between them. "It will be a blow to lose you."

"You're planning on killing me, then?" Celine asks.

He presses a hand to his chest in shock. "Of course not! Why on earth would I want you dead? Especially now that you've chosen to trust me."

I'm hoping Celine has the forethought to let him continue thinking that our presence here means that he is pulling the strings. That we're willingly cooperating. Celine might be, but I'm still holding out hope that there's another option. Not Ilarion, not Benedict, but a third way out that doesn't involve so much death and heartbreak.

My sister frowns. "How do you expect me to trust you?"

He reaches into his pants and pulls out something. I gasp, taking a step back, worried it's some sort of weapon. But then I notice the glint of silver.

"Here," he says, offering it to her. "A key to this room. You can lock yourselves in and no one will bother you." When she doesn't take it, he jangles it and smiles. "Trust starts with baby steps, *mi bella*. Small gestures."

She takes it reluctantly. My skin is still swarming with those invisible ants. Anxiety crackles through me in strange little pops and shivers.

Whistling, Benedict walks towards the door. "Ilarion might show up here," he warns. "If he does, I will try and hold him off. The key will get you out of this room. And *this* key will take you as far away from this place as you can go."

He pulls out a car key and sets in on the side table. "I tried to tell you at our first meeting, Celine: I'm on your side." Then he steps out and closes the door behind him.

Celine and I turn to each other at the same time. "Lock the door," we chorus in unison.

Rushing forward, she shoves the key into the lock and turns it. It clicks with a definitive *thunk*. "It's locked," she says, rattling the doorknob to be sure.

I breathe a sigh of relief and put Adam down on his feet.

"Mama! What's going on?" His little voice lifts with panic as he clings to me.

I drop down on the four-poster bed and take his hands in mine. "Spy work is not easy, my love. We just gotta be a little brave and a little patient, okay? You can do that for me, right?"

Adam bites his bottom lip uncertainly. "I just wanna go home."

"I know," I say as my heart swells with fear. "And we're going to go home very soon. We just need to take a little break here first."

"And then we'll go back?"

"We'll go somewhere safe."

He doesn't seem content with that answer, but he has no choice but to put his trust in me. I'm his lifeline now and I've never been more aware of that fact.

I push myself up onto the bed and open my arms out to him. "Come on," I coax. "I'm gonna tell you a story."

He crawls into my lap and rests his head on my chest. "Can you finish the elves and the shoemaker?"

"Of course."

I've told him the story so many times that I don't really need to think about the words as I say them. My thoughts run wild as I weave him images of midnight creatures and fancy shoes.

Celine paces by the door the whole time, her face scrunched with concentration. There's a thin line between focus and panic and she's tap-dancing on it.

Then again, so am I.

When I finish the story, I look down and see that Adam has fallen asleep in my arms. Moving carefully, I place him on the bed, cushioning both sides of him with a pillow. It was a habit I developed when he was a baby and he'd roll to the edges of my bed while I scrambled to quickly get dressed. He doesn't need either cushion anymore, but I still do it anyway whenever he climbs into my bed.

It must be nice to have someone who loves you who can make the world feel so safe. You can fall asleep in their arms and wake up to pillow forts to keep you from falling.

Who's setting up *my* pillows, though? Who's carrying me to bed?

Who's keeping me safe?

"Celine," I breathe as I pad over to her, "what are we going to do?"

She sighs, the breath hissing out through her teeth like a teakettle. "You were right. It was stupid to come here."

"I'm guessing the key was an empty gesture."

"He knows that we're trapped. That we don't have many options left," Celine says. "He's going to count on that. I think we might be able to slip past him. It's not like he has a ton of manpower."

I glance back over my shoulder at the little blob on the bed that's Adam. "Celine, shouldn't we...take a moment?"

She freezes and pivots on her heels to face me. "What are you saying?"

"I'm saying that I think we're missing something. I mean, Benedict had Dad. Then, somehow, we find this footage on a flash drive and Ilarion's with Dad and—"

"You think it was a setup?" she asks.

She doesn't seem angry, but I can't exactly read Celine as well as I used to be able to. "I don't know. My gut says that it might be."

"Your gut is also in love with *him*."

"But you're not. What does your gut tell you?"

Celine's brow furrows and she stares off at the window in search of answers in the sky. "Ilarion wouldn't hurt either one of us," she agrees slowly. "But...hurting Dad is a different story. I've never seen a traitor walk away without consequences, Taylor."

"Yes, but none of those traitors have been our father." I glance over at Adam. "And none of them were loved by Adam so much. Ilarion would never do anything to hurt him."

She runs a hand through her hair. "Fuck. Fuck. I don't know."

A sound like rolling thunder catches my ears, but it sounds too artificial to belong to the sky. "Did you hear that?"

"Trucks," Celine breathes. "Big ones."

Our eyes snap to each other. We both know what's happening, deep in our bones.

"Ilarion's here."

Celine's gaze brightens with focus. "This could be our chance. Benedict will be too distracted with Ilarion and his men to worry about us and vice versa. We could escape, slip away while everyone's fighting, and be long gone by the time anyone realizes we're not even on the premises."

I hesitate. The plan sounds good in theory. So why is it making my palms sweat and my heart race?

"Cee, I'm…I'm not sure that's the right decision for me. Or Adam."

Celine locks eyes with me. Then she grabs my hand and presses the key to my palm. "This is your call."

The blood drains from my face. "That's not much better. I can't trust myself. Not when it comes to him."

"What is love if not trust?" she asks. "Whatever you decide, no matter how you decide it, I'll support you. I've got your back."

I stare at my big sister. "I don't deserve you, Cee."

She smiles. "There'll be enough time to bathe me in compliments later, Tay. Right now, you have a decision to make and not a lot of time to make it."

63

ILARION

"Another shithole," Dima grumbles, looking up at the graying building in the distance. "Big surprise."

"I *am* surprised. Is this how he's lived all these years?" Mila asks.

We've been parked on the outskirts of the motel property for almost half an hour, a battalion of Zakharov soldiers stationed all around us. I've got two contingents of men waiting at the other two locations Archie had given me. This is the only one with any sign of life.

My gut tells me this is the place.

"It's better than he deserves," I growl.

I notice one of my lead scouts running towards us. "How many men?" I ask when he slows to a stop.

"It's hard to say, *pakhan*," the scout wheezes. "It's old and rundown, but it's built solidly. A concrete fortress. I spotted three men outside, but there could be dozens more on the inside."

"Dozens?" Dima balks. He turns to me. "Do you think that's likely? Maybe we should hang out for a bit longer, make sure—"

"Fuck that." I pull out my gun. "We're done waiting. Have the other men join us here. We go in guns blazing."

"Well, say no more." Licking his lips, Dima unholsters his own weapons and starts loading in fresh clips.

Mila is a little more reserved. Her eyes keep flitting toward Dima even as she prepares herself. "Do we launch a sneak attack?" she asks. "We can approach the building on foot. They won't hear us coming until we're right on top of them."

I shrug. "It doesn't matter. The Bellasios will be annihilated either way tonight. In any case, I want him to tremble with fear. We'll drive up to the building with full force and mow the motherfucker down."

A whoop rises up from the soldiers listening in on our conversation. We pile into the waiting caravan. Guns clack, tires groan, men puff and grunt as they jump into position. Everything roars to life, then we descend on Benedict's rathole like a fucking biblical plague.

The roar of engines takes us all the way up to the crumbling motel. I've just jumped out of the Rambler when the first enemy gunshot pierces the air.

"Get down!" I yell.

The windows of the hotel have been pushed open just enough for me to see the muzzle of a gun. I cock both my weapons and start firing. My men follow suit and before long, we've pushed right inside, throwing the Bellasio men back.

Bellasio men scramble through the narrow passageways in utter chaos. When they poke their heads out at the wrong time, they get blown away into the afterlife.

"Keep moving in!" I roar. "They'll be behind one of those doors."

We pass through a dark hallway and emerge into the ruins of a ballroom on the other side. I hear someone scream behind me and I turn to see one of my men collapse on his back against the broken tile. From the opposite side, more Bellasio men rush out of the doors like insects being forced out of their holes.

"There's more than we thought," Mila mutters from my right side.

I nod grimly and reload. "Stay close."

Of course, seeing as how she's pathologically allergic to following orders, she immediately takes off, throwing herself into the fray with reckless abandon.

"Goddammit, Mila," I snarl under her breath. Then I dive in after her.

My men and Bellasio's have woven in together now. I lose sight of Dima and Mila in the chaos and, until I clock them, I can't let myself look for Benedict.

I smell metal and blood. The air is thick with the cries of fury and pain. I use my fists just as much as I use my guns. And just as I'm about to shoot some fucker in the head, I spot Benedict in the far corner, cringing every time another gunshot sounds.

He's there. Right. Fucking. *There*. After five years of reaching for him and missing, I almost can't believe my eyes.

"*Benedict*!" I roar over the tumult.

He disappears from the doorway immediately without looking to see who yelled. I beeline toward him. I'm almost at the door when I hear a scream.

This one, I recognize above all the others.

"Mila!" I twist around and turn back into the fight.

It's thinned out a little. There are far more dead bodies than fighting men, but I have to give it to him—Benedict has managed to give us a fight despite his limited resources.

Dima is struggling with two Bellasio soldiers to get to Mila. She's on the ground, pressing her hands to a bullet wound in her stomach. Blood wells over her knuckles, thick and red.

I turn and sprint over to her, ignoring the heat searing through my knees. As I pass, I tackle one of the men assaulting Dima and put a quick bullet in his throat. Dima finishes the other one, then we both hurry to kneel by my sister's side.

"Mila! Mila, it's…fuck."

It's bad. Really bad.

"I'm fine," she says, but the blood seeping through her shirt says it's not fine. It isn't fine at all.

Dima falls to his knees on her other side. "Fucking hell, Mila! Why did you jump in front of that bullet?"

Her eyes find his. "Because if I didn't, you'd be the one bleeding like a stuck pig."

"I can take it."

"So can I," she snarls before turning to me. "What the fuck are you doing here? You should be chasing Benedict. I thought I saw him by that door."

"Mila—"

"Go. If he leaves with them, all this was for nothing," she insists. "Go!"

Dima grabs my shoulder. "I have her. I'm gonna make sure she's alright."

I can see the promise in his eyes. I nod once and take off, a handful of Zakharov men trailing at my back.

Benedict's door leads to a broader passageway that takes a sharp turn. At the end of it is another door, cracked open slightly.

"Come now, Ilarion," Benedict calls from out of sight. "Let's have a gentlemanly conversation, man to man. What do you say?"

I glance towards my men, giving them the silent signal to stay put. Then I enter the room with my gun dangling casually from my hand. He's standing in the center of the empty room and, for a moment, I wonder if I'm even hunting the right man.

"Fucking hell. Benedict?"

He grins, a sight made all the worse by his rotting teeth. "Have I changed so much?"

"You're fat," I say bluntly. "And old."

"Yeah, well, years of being hunted like a rat can do that to a man." His teeth make another horrible appearance as he pulls back his lips in a growl that looks more like a grimace. His beady eyes flicker over my shoulder. "I'm guessing my men are dead?"

"Most of them. Soon enough, the rest will be, too."

"Did they at least get a few of yours?"

I shrug. "Nothing that won't heal."

The room Benedict stands in is relatively well-kept. But I can smell the staleness in the air. As if the windows have been kept shut too long and mold is starting to creep into the crevices.

"This place smells like your death, Benedict."

He flinches, then sneers. "I think you'll find that I still have a card or two up my sleeve."

"Where are they?"

"The boy," Benedict murmurs. "Is it my imagination or does he look an awful lot like you?"

I regard him with a disinterested gaze, even though my insides are boiling. If I let my expression falter for even a moment, I will confirm his suspicions and he will have a stronger trump card than Celine.

"What boy?"

"The one clinging to your sister-in-law," Benedict says, his eyes never leaving my face. "She's a pretty one. Not as polished as Celine, but still, that kind of raw beauty doesn't go unnoticed. Did you fuck her?"

"She's been gone for years."

"With Archie, no doubt. I'd say that puts you as the chief candidate for the father." Benedict smirks knowingly. "The kid looks around the right age."

I arch a brow, feigning boredom. "You do have a habit of letting your imagination run wild, don't you? But I can see why you'd want to believe that. It'd give you another bargaining chip."

Benedict shrugs. "As far as I'm concerned, I have three chips. And I will play them all." Then his scowl darkens. "My brother was my only friend in this world, you know."

"I'd apologize, but it wouldn't be sincere. You did it to him, anyway. I was just the messenger."

"I have nothing anymore. No men, no money, no family, no hope of reviving the Bellasio mafia," he croaks. "I'll give you your women and the child. But I want something in return."

"Of course you do."

"Fifty million dollars and my freedom. That's all I ask. Fifty million is nothing to you."

"Maybe not. But your life means something to me. You forget, Benedict: you owe me, not the other way around. All I have to do is kill you. I'll find them eventually."

"No, you won't. They'll be long—"

He stops abruptly, his eyes going wide as they land on someone just behind me. I steal a glance and, in that split-second I let my guard down, Benedict has a gun aimed at my head.

Taylor freezes at the door, her eyes flicking between me and Benedict.

"What are you still doing here?" Benedict growls at her. "You dumb bitch."

"I did think about leaving," Taylor says, turning her gaze on me. "But I needed to look you in the eye first." Her voice hitches with sorrow. "How could you?"

"Because he's a fucking monster!" Benedict yells, jerking his gun upwards. "Now's your chance to escape! I—"

"I saw…" Taylor says in a voice so small I almost miss it.

That's when I realize that Benedict is not the one I should be facing. So I go against the grain and turn my back on Benedict and his gun. I take the risk of his bullet in my back and face Taylor.

Who seems very prepared to put a bullet in my front.

Her eyes are wide with disbelief, her shoulders tight with tension. "You killed my father," she accuses. "After you promised to protect him."

"That's right," Benedict chimes in. "He can't be trusted."

"*Shut up!*" Taylor yells. "I'm talking to Ilarion. I want to hear from *him*."

"I did kill Archie," I say, meeting her betrayed eyes. "I did it because he asked me to."

She recoils. "Liar!"

I take a fraction of a step toward her, but she lunges backward, so I pause in my tracks. I engage the safety on my gun and slide it across the floor to her. Then I cock my second gun and hold it out to her, butt-first.

"What are you doing?" she gasps as I stride forward and press it into her hand.

I keep a firm grip on her wrist as I bring it up to my face, pressing the nose of the gun to my forehead. "Let me tell you what happened. If you still don't believe me when I'm done, then shoot."

There's sweat edging in from the corners of her brow. The color drains from her face and she shakes her head. "No…"

"Yes," I snarl. "The choice is in your hands, Taylor. As is my life. It's your call now."

64

TAYLOR

It's your call now.

That's what Celine said to me, too, right before I'd locked her in the room with Adam. I can feel the weight of this decision trying to bury me whole. The only thing that keeps me surfaced is the knowledge that my son's survival depends on my choices.

I glance past Ilarion to Benedict. His eyes are fixed on me, his arm still raised, aimed at Ilarion's back. I don't ask him to lower the gun.

Slowly, I turn my gaze to Ilarion. Even after what I saw on that flash drive, he's still the man I love. My feelings for him are still as potent as ever. They're just fighting against a tide of betrayal and hurt.

If I don't believe his explanation, then I will shoot. For Celine's sake, as well as Adam's.

It's the only way I'll be free of Ilarion and men like him.

"Okay," I say. "Go on. Tell me."

"Benedict had an explosive planted inside Archie," Ilarion says. Over his shoulder, I notice Benedict roll his eyes.

"Then why kill him yourself?" I rasp. "Why not just let the bomb do it?"

"Exactly!" Benedict exclaims.

I look past Ilarion at the sad former don. "I thought I told you to shut the fuck up." He flushes bright red, but holds up his hands to indicate that he's done interrupting. I turn my attention back to Ilarion, still pointing the gun at his head. "Well?"

"Archie told me that the bomb wasn't large enough to kill him, but it was big enough to maim him. He didn't want to live like that."

I can feel my nostrils flare. "So he could have lived—but you chose to kill him instead?"

"*He* chose, Taylor," Ilarion intones. "He chose to die whole, rather than live a half-life. He didn't want to be a burden to you or Celine. He didn't want either one of you seeing him that way." He pauses and his eyes suddenly grow sad. "He didn't want Adam to see him like that."

"He wouldn't have chosen to die."

"Is it so hard to believe?" he asks me. "Your mother made the same choice."

I suck in my breath. "This…this was different. He had a chance to live, to be okay. To watch Adam grow up."

"He knew the consequences when he joined the underworld, when he first took the mark of the Bratva. He got to choose his own death. Not very many have that privilege."

"Privilege?" I cry out. "How dare you!"

"Look at me," he orders. "Look me in the eye, Taylor." It's not until he says that that I realize I have been avoiding it. How can I, and then shoot? "You wanted an explanation. Be brave enough to take it."

I swallow hard. "I saw the two of you in the garden."

He nods. "I was trying to get him to tell me Benedict's location. I knew he had inside information on what safehouses he might be hiding out in. At first, he refused to tell me."

"So, you were threatening him?"

"I walked away from him, didn't I?" he points out. "I allowed him to stay in my home, breathe my air, eat my food. He had sanctuary under my roof and he knew he was safe from me. He also knew that the moment he gave me Benedict's location, the Bellasios would come for him. And still, he came to me. He decided to end it by ending Benedict."

I close my eyes for a moment, ashamed of the tear that falls down my cheek. "You could have turned him down," I whisper. "You didn't have to kill him."

Ilarion's eyes are dark, the blue in them eaten away by pupils blown wide. "I made a decision. I chose to do what Archie wanted, instead of what you would have wanted."

I swallow a sob, but my thoughts are drowned out by Benedict's words.

"Don't believe a word he says, Taylor! There was no bomb! He was looking for a reason to kill Archie from the beginning. A traitor never goes free in the Bratva. Don't let him get inside your head!"

I glance at Ilarion, waiting for him to say something, defend himself, try to convince me. But he says nothing to that end. "I told you everything," he says softly. "It's your decision now."

"Kill him, Taylor! I can get us out of here," Benedict's voice is grating on my nerves. "Just kill him!"

I stare at Ilarion for a moment, taking in his sculpted features, the sad, downward tilt of his eyes, the strength of his jaw. He's such a beautiful man. A *good* man. That's what Celine believed. That's what I chose to believe all these years, too.

But sometimes, choosing to believe something doesn't make it true.

I think about my sister.

I think about my son.

But most of all, I think about my father.

I love you, Dad.

Then I take a deep breath. I pull the trigger hard and the bullet feels like it's fired from my own soul.

I scream. Or at least, someone does. I jerk backwards, my shoulder in pain, but I don't fall. Ilarion's arms are around me, holding me up.

But Benedict Bellasio is on the floor, writhing in pain.

"Oh God, oh God, oh God…I shot him." My eyes widen more. "And I *missed*!" My breaths are coming in hard and heavy now. The adrenaline giving way to something this side of panic.

"It's okay, *tigrionok*," Ilarion says calmly. "It's gonna be okay."

"I can't believe I missed!"

"You made your choice," he whispers in my ear. "I'm proud of you."

He guides me down to my knees and then he walks over to Benedict's spasming body. I'm not sure where the bullet has pierced him, but it wasn't in the head like I intended.

Ammonia and fear stenches the air. I'm pretty sure that Benedict Bellasio has pissed himself.

I glance up and take in Ilarion's tall form. He's standing over Benedict, looking down at him as though he's a scrap of toilet paper on the sole of his shoe.

"Goodbye, Benny."

He raises his hand. I see the sheen of black metal. I close my eyes. A second later, there's another gunshot. A definitive one.

I know without looking that Benedict Bellasio is finally gone.

I don't open my eyes until I feel Ilarion's arms around me, until his breath is at my ear and his heart is beating alongside mine.

"How did you know I was telling the truth?" he asks me.

"I didn't," I say honestly. "I just chose to believe you."

He presses a kiss to my temple. "I'm sorry. I had to do it, Taylor. I had to give him the death he wanted. But for what it's worth, I am sorry he's gone."

I nod, dropping my head against his chest and letting the sobs rip through me. I accept that my father is gone. I accept that the love of my life killed him. And I choose to believe that those facts won't destroy us.

I can only hope it will make us stronger. That is the choice I make in this moment. That is the choice I will continue to make.

Over and over again, if I have to.

I choose *him*.

65

TAYLOR

The clock says noon, but I can hardly believe it after the day I've just had. It feels like this morning has stretched out into years.

We buried Dad three hours ago, under a huge cedar tree with feathery leaves that will shed over his grave. Adam clung to Ilarion most of the morning, a subconscious attempt to seek comfort in the last paternal figure he has left.

Celine and I stood together, side by side, trying to come to terms with the fact that we were now orphans.

I can't remember what filled the hours between putting Dad in the ground and sitting here at my dressing table, staring at my reflection in the mirror. All I can really recall are fleeting moments that will forever be frozen in time.

Celine taking my hand and promising we would always be there for each other.

Mila, bandaged and bruised, forcing herself out of a car to attend the funeral of a man she hated, just because she knew what it meant to me.

Adam crying hysterically and Ilarion scooping him up and carrying him around until he calmed down.

There was a lot of sadness today, but I was not so far gone that I couldn't see the hope there, too. Somewhere amidst the tears and the grief, I looked around and saw the fledgling foundation of a family. A little broken, a little dysfunctional, a little mismatched.

But a family, nonetheless.

I blink and focus on my reflection. I didn't apply a lot of foundation; that's why I look so pale. My lipstick has all but faded, too, but my bun remains fixed in place. Not a hair out of place. That was Celine's handiwork. Even in grief, her finish is flawless.

I remove the pearls from around my neck, then I pull at the pins that are holding my hair together. I put them away and comb out my hair until I look a little more like myself. Once that's done, I duck into the walk-in closet and swap my mourning clothes for a soft cotton dress. Yellow, because I'm sick of seeing black and also because it's what Mom would have chosen.

Once I'm comfortable, I pad over to the window of my new bedroom. Technically, it's Ilarion's room, but he keeps assuring me that it's ours now.

It offers the best view of the gardens. I can see the whole expanse of the lawn sprawled out like a green carpet. Mila and Dima are sitting on white garden chairs, taking in the sun.

Dima stayed by Mila's side through most of the ceremony. He helped her to sit and stand, brought her water and food, asked her if she needed anything again and again, even after she snapped at him to stop hovering.

There is hope there, too. Another thing I choose to cling to.

I turn from the window when I hear my door open. Adam skitters in, dressed in khaki shorts and a white t-shirt.

"Hey, baby. Where've you been?"

"With Daddy," he says. "He told me that he's going to take me to the zoo tomorrow. Will you come with us?"

"I'd love to."

He nods and climbs into my lap. He adjusted surprisingly well when we sat down with him and explained that things were changing in our home. Grandpa was gone to be with Grandma and Uncle Illy…well, that was a bit more difficult to explain. It was Celine who swooped in and explained how Uncle Illy was *also* a spy, which is why he had to keep things secret until now.

Things like how he's really Adam's father.

I kiss the top of his head and hold him tight. "You okay, sweetheart?"

"Daddy says that Grandpa died a hero. Daddy says that being a hero means putting other people before yourself," he recites, looking at me with those big, beautiful eyes of his.

I stroke his hair. "He's right."

"Grandpa is a spy *and* a hero." He pauses and bites his lip. "I wish Grandpa weren't a hero or a spy, though. I wish he was here."

I feel my lip trembling, but I bite down hard and stop myself from losing it. "I know, honey. Me, too. But we don't always have control over things. You'll understand when you're older."

"I don't want to be older."

I press him to my chest. "Grandpa will always be with us. In pictures and memories. We'll keep him alive that way. We'll love each other for him."

Adam frowns. I'm pretty sure he's understanding only half of what I'm saying. I talk anyway in the hopes that one day, what I'm saying will make sense to him.

"Did you get the present he left for you?" Adam asks abruptly.

I stop. "What?"

"The present he left for you," Adam repeats. "Did you get it? He left it with your clothes."

I forgot all about that. He mentioned it to me the night of Celine's ball, the night that she found out about Ilarion and me. I put him down and get to my feet.

"Come on," I say, taking his hand. "Let's go look for it."

I head down the hall to what used to be my room. It still feels like my room, considering most of my things are still here. I've yet to move all my stuff into Ilarion's—*our*—room. I'm shuffling clothes aside and seeing nothing, nothing—and then...

There.

An envelope, tucked between a pair of running sneakers. The same ones I wore the night I met Ilarion, actually. The synchronicity sends a chill rippling through me.

I rip the seal and pull out the letter nestled inside. I'm so greedy for Dad's words that I swallow the entire letter in seconds. By the time I get to the end, I'm shaking.

"Mama, are you okay?"

I smile through my tears. "I'm okay, baby. Grandpa wrote me a beautiful letter."

"What does it say?"

"It says that he loves us," I say simply. "Can you do me a favor and go get Auntie Cee?"

I left her in her room half an hour ago. She wanted to sort her things into boxes. Moving Day was three days away and she is nothing if not compulsively organized.

While Adam is gone, I take a deep breath and read the letter again.

Hello, Little Bird—

I'm not sure under what circumstances you're reading this letter. I hope that I'm the one who's just handed it to you and you're reading it and laughing and telling me I'm silly. But I have a feeling that's unlikely.

I think it's more likely that I'm no longer there and you're sad because you think you could have saved me. The truth is, I knew my fate from the moment I decided to enter the Bratva. I made certain decisions and, even then, I knew they were the wrong ones, but I did it anyway. Because I thought I had no choice.

Remember, there are always *choices.*

Which is why I went to Ilarion and told him what he needed to find Benedict Bellasio. I know that, in doing so, Benedict will come after me. I know that I might not survive whatever comes next. Most importantly, I want you and Celine to know: I'm more than ready to die. I've wanted to leave ever since the day I discovered your mother was no longer part of this world.

I've lived all these years without her only because I felt that you and Adam still needed me. But I know now that the three of you will be fine without me. Celine is a force to be reckoned with. You are stronger than you know. And Adam is made up of Ilarion's strength and your kind heart. All three of you will be fine, I'm sure of that.

I can die at ease, knowing that Ilarion will take care of you. And that you girls will take care of each other. Tell Adam that I'm sorry I couldn't be there to watch him grow. But I stole a few years with him and, for that, I'm grateful. I love you all, my little birds. My little flock.

I'm looking forward to spending the rest of eternity with your mother. She's waited for me long enough. I know there are sunflowers wherever she is.

Love always,

Dad

"Taylor!" Celine bursts into the room with Adam at her heels. Her cheeks are flushed and her eyes are wide. "Is everything alright?"

I offer her the letter. "He left this for me the night of your ball."

She takes it and I watch as her eyes whiz through the letter like mine did. By the time she gets to the end, they're glistening with tears.

She folds the letter and looks up at me. "So you were right to trust Ilarion."

"Did you have doubts?"

She smiles. "For a moment. But I meant what I said when I said I would support you no matter what."

I hug Celine tightly, breathing in her scent. She's the last remnant of our parents for me. I'm probably the same for her. So holding her feels like holding all of us. The last of the Therons.

When we pull apart, both our cheeks are wet. We laugh together. "I have to go talk with Ilarion."

She nods. "Go on. Get."

I squeeze her hand and turn to go. "How about we do dinner tonight, just the two of us?" I suggest at the door before I leave.

She gives me a self-conscious smile. "That's a great idea. But do you think we could do it tomorrow?"

"Of course, if you have plans."

"I do have plans, actually." She blushes again. "With Ashton."

"Oh, is that so?" I can't help or hide my impish grin.

She laughs and swats me. "Get outta here," she reprimands before turning to Adam. "Adam, let's do something, just you and me."

"Puzzle?" he suggests.

"Perfect."

I leave the two of them to it and go downstairs towards Ilarion's den. I pass by the gardens where Mila and Dima are still sitting out in chairs on the grass, basking in the cool weather. I find Ilarion at his desk. But he's not deep in work like I expect. He's just sitting there, leaning back, with his face aimed at the ceiling.

He straightens when I enter, a worried frown etched across his brow. "Taylor. Is everything okay?"

I walk right up to him and climb onto his lap. "I found something. From my dad."

He raises his eyebrows. "Oh?"

"He wrote me a letter. He hid it in my closet the day of Celine's ball."

"Son of a bitch," he breathes with a chuckle. "What was in it?"

"Things that a dying man says to his children. Things he hopes they'll pass down to their children. He knew he was going to die, Ilarion. At least, he knew there was a good possibility of it. He was prepared. I'd say a good part of him was even hoping for it."

He brushes his hand across my cheek. "You look…happier."

I nod. "I did believe you," I whisper. "But it's still nice to have proof." I curl into his chest and breathe in his earthy masculine scent. "I'm gonna miss him. But he was ready to go, just like Mom was."

"Very few people get to say they're ready."

I nod. "I hope I can meet my death the same way."

"Hopefully. But not for a very, very, *very* long time."

I smile and cup his face with my hands. "You'd miss me—is that what you're trying to say?"

He shrugs. "I'm never going to know what it's like to miss you again, *tigrionok*," he says confidently. "I don't plan on being without you."

I press a finger to his lips. "You might not always have that kind of control. What if, after decades together, dozens of kids and grandkids later, I die first?"

I'm only teasing, but his brow irons out with seriousness. "Then I'll raise you from the dead until I'm ready to go, too."

"You know, I honestly believe you could."

He presses his lips to my neck. "Watch me."

EPILOGUE: ILARION
THREE MONTHS LATER

"Where is Taylor?" Mila asks. "The two of you are usually joined at the hip."

I roll my eyes. "We are not."

We're sitting in the garden, sharing a pitcher of margaritas. It's a bit early in the day for alcohol, but Mila has been in an unusually good mood lately, so when she suggested it, I couldn't turn her down.

"No? When was the last time you spent a day apart?"

"We spent five years apart. Anyway, you're one to talk. You and Dima take turns guarding the door when one of you has to go to the bathroom."

"Kiss my ass, Ilarion. He's just grateful that I saved his life."

"And he's repaying you by following you around like a lovesick puppy?"

She gives me the middle finger. Her nails are manicured—that's strange. She's wearing a dress today. Also strange. But you don't have to look far to find the reason.

Then she drops her hand back into her lap and sighs. "Not that it's any of your business, but…I told Dima."

My eyes feel like they're about to pop out of their sockets. "You told him. As in, you told him everything?"

She nods. "A couple of weeks ago. Nearly had a nervous breakdown halfway through, but I threw back some vodka and that gave me the push I needed. I told him that I would need to take things slow. Like, glacially slow. He seemed open to it."

"He's nuts about you. He'll wait for as long as it takes."

A faint flush blooms over her skin. It makes me grin—I haven't seen my sister blush in a very long time. I'll take it, as long as she keeps smiling the way she's been doing, too.

She smiles fondly and props her feet up onto the table. "Where's my little nephew, by the way? I haven't seen him all day."

"That's because he's over at Celine and Ashton's new place with Taylor. He's helping her settle in."

"Good. I'm happy for her. Next steps are hard."

Just then, we hear the sound of running footsteps. "Daddy!" Adam yells from the doorframe. "Auntie Cee has a room in her house just for me!"

"Guess he's here after all," I mutter with a cheesy grin as I try to pretend like the sound of his voice calling me "Daddy" doesn't make my heart explode with joy every time.

I turn and swoop him up. "A whole room all for you? Sounds cool, buddy."

"I took some pictures for you," he yells. "I'll go get Mom! They're on her phone." Then he wiggles out of my arms and runs right back into the house.

The moment he's gone, Mila looks at me and sighs. "He seems like he's adjusting well."

"More or less," I agree. "He knows that his mom is with me and his auntie is with 'Uncle' Ashton. Everything else will come in time."

"Okay," Mila says. "That's that, then, huh?"

I smirk. "That's that."

Taylor appears at the porch with Adam in tow. "Mama, show Daddy and Auntie Mila the pictures!" Adam says excitedly. "I want them to see the swing and everything."

"Swing?" Mila says with her nose scrunched up. "Geez, someone's really working for the title of Favorite Aunt. I'm gonna have to up my game."

"You two are both his favorite aunts," Taylor insists diplomatically.

"But today, Auntie Cee is my favorite," Adam adds with a cheeky grin.

"You little punk!" Mila cries as she launches herself at Adam and starts tickling him. He starts screaming with laughter as he tries to wriggle out of her grip. When he breaks free, he streaks off across the lawn. Mila goes racing after him.

When they're gone, I reach for Taylor. "You were gone a long time," I complain as she slips onto my lap.

She laughs. "Celine has a lot of crap. It's tasteful crap, though. The house is coming along."

"I have no doubt." I kiss her hard on the lips and when we finally pull apart, she's breathless.

"Whoa, you *have* missed me."

I push her off my lap and jump to my feet. "Come on, I have something for you."

"Like a gift?"

"Exactly like that. Come on."

Laughing, I lead her up to our bedroom and close the door. Then I retrieve my little present from the table in front of the window.

"Here you go," I say, presenting it to her.

Her eyes land on the snow globe and go wide with shock. "Oh my god…"

"It's an exact replica," I explain. "I tracked down the original maker and had him redo it. Turns out, it's a surprisingly complex design. I commissioned it over a month ago and he only just finished it."

She approaches me at snail speed, her eyes never veering from the globe in my hands. "It's perfect," she says. "It's—You —I—It's wonderful, Ilarion. *You* are wonderful."

"I have my moments."

Taylor examines the snow globe with awe and, when she's had her fill, she places it on her dresser, pride of place in front of the mirror.

Then she turns back and loops her arms around my neck, her smile growing mischievous. "I have to find a way to thank you."

I raise my eyebrows. "I agree. It's only polite."

"I've got some ideas."

She pulls off my shirt, then my pants. Then she walks me back to the bed and pushes me down onto my back. She strips down while I watch and then she slides onto her knees in front of me.

She hesitates for a moment, right in front of my erect cock. It doesn't take much for her to make me this hard; usually, just blinking in my direction will do it. Today feels different though.

Her eyes meet mine, and I feel a fierce sense of pride.

This woman is *mine*.

After all we've been through, she's finally mine.

She leans over and takes me into her mouth. "Fuck," I moan.

Her head bobs as I tense and groan up to the ceiling. Like always, we don't last long before I need more. I pull her up and she straddles me. When she slides me into her, I feel like I can finally breathe again.

I grab her ass to hold on while she starts to grind up and down on my dick. I watch her breasts bounce and sway, watch her hair fly wildly around her face.

She's fucking *mesmerizing*.

I slap her ass, and she only rides me harder. Her breaths come faster. Soft whimpers escape her throat and I feel her start to tighten around me.

"Come for me, baby," I murmur.

There's nothing like watching this woman orgasm. One day, I'm going to paint a picture of her face in the exact moment when her body releases itself on my cock. I want to be staring at that face when I die.

As her body shivers with her first orgasm, I push forward and sit up, pulling her onto me more. I thrust myself into her and press my lips against her neck.

I fuck her just by holding her, pulling and pushing her up and down as she trembles and wriggles and moans.

Her nails dig into my back as I fuck her harder still. I roll us onto my feet and bounce her on my cock, in my arms, suspended in the air with only my embrace to anchor her. She trusts me to do it. It doesn't cross her mind to do anything but that.

And when she comes, she comes screaming my name on her lips. I pull her as hard and deep as I can go and I empty every ounce of love and passion I have for her exactly where it belongs.

She'd told me once that my name was branded onto her soul. Every day since then, I try to make sure I carve my name in a little deeper.

EXTENDED EPILOGUE: TAYLOR
ONE YEAR LATER

Download the Extended Epilogue for a peek at Ashton and Celine's wedding, Mila and Dima's future, and a surprise proposal!

CLICK HERE TO DOWNLOAD
https://dl.bookfunnel.com/gz9z32d5w4

Printed in Great Britain
by Amazon

30882544R10264